CALL FOR BLOOD

Steve Doherty

Call For Blood

Steve Doherty

ISBN-10: 1517115779
ISBN-13: 9781517115777
Library of Congress Control Number: 2015914481
CreateSpace Independent Publishing Platform
North Charleston, South Carolina

To my daughter, Stephanie, my greatest supporter and fan.

CHAPTER 1

Calcutta, India

C amille Dupont watched as Jon Preston's gaze moved from her to the entrance of the ballroom of the Ambassador Hotel. She turned her head and saw a party of six entering the room: three men and three women. She tensed when she recognized the face of one of the women, suspected of being a Japanese agent, entering with the French Indochina delegation. The agent was more beautiful in person. Her hair was short and matched her oval face. Either she was a mix of Japanese and European, or her eyes had been altered surgically. She guessed the latter.

Camille and Jon were both Allied intelligence agents. She was a member of the Office of Strategic Services, or OSS, the US version of the British Special Operations Executive or SOE. Jon was a member of the US Army's Counterintelligence Corps, or CIC. Both were skilled agents, but Jon had trained as an agent for four years while attending Ohio State University, and he was a walking killing machine.

Camille turned her head back toward Jon and watched his eyes drink in every detail of the three men and three women of the delegation.

"She's beautiful," Camille commented.

Jon nodded his head and continued to watch as the delegation was seated four tables away from the guest-of-honor table, where the supreme Allied commander of the Southeast Asia theater, Admiral Louis Mountbatten, was talking to several people. Seated next to Mountbatten was Ralph Block, the special assistant to the US commissioner in India. Despite this title, Jon knew that Block's real job was the head of overseas operations for the US Office of War Information. In this capacity Block supervised as many as 150 men who were conducting psychological warfare and disseminating disinformation in China, Burma, and India. This fit with Block's background, as before the war he was the director of publicity for Samuel Goldwyn in Hollywood.

So, Mr. Block, you're in counterintelligence, too, Jon thought.

During the meal, Camille noticed Jon smile and nod his head in the direction of the female assassin sitting with the Indochinese delegation.

"Did she just smile at you?" Camille asked.

"Actually, I think she's flirting with me," Jon said.

"Well, if she does it again, I may kill the bitch myself."

"Then again, she could be taunting me. After all, they have our photographs too."

Two of Jon's fellow agents and members of his covert King Cobra Team, Miles Murphy and Henri Morreau, were posing as ballroom staff; both men were highly skilled members of the British SOE and just as deadly as Jon. Henri was working as a wine steward, serving wine to the head table and the tables nearest the guest of honor. Miles was mixing drinks at the bar in the back of the room, near the entrance to the kitchen. Each man was assigned a quadrant of the ballroom to monitor.

After one of the native servers finished serving a table near the guest of honor, she passed Henri on the way back to the kitchen. Henri recognized her as another of the suspected assassins from the photographs he had memorized. Henri turned and followed the server, walking through the two swinging doors into the kitchen, ten steps behind the woman.

Sitting next to Camille was Kathleen Lauren, who, like her, was an agent with the OSS. Kathleen recognized the second female assassin at nearly the same time as Henri did. She hurriedly excused herself and moved toward the kitchen. Camille, meanwhile, was facing the opposite direction and didn't notice the second assassin or Henri's actions.

Jon also noticed the second assassin passing by their table on her way to the kitchen. A minute after Kathleen left, he got up and walked toward the back of the hall, where servers, carrying large trays of food, were still moving in and out of the two swinging doors.

"Stay put. I need to check on something," Jon said.

Camille turned and followed Jon with her eyes until he disappeared behind the two kitchen doors. A short time later, Kathleen came out of the kitchen and returned to her table; she was visibly shaken.

She noticed tears streaming down Kathleen's cheeks and the smell of cordite from the discharge of a weapon lingering on her clothing. Camille's attention was so focused on Kathleen that she didn't see Jon exit the kitchen looking extremely concerned. His eyes moved left and right with the precision of a leopard searching for its prey.

"What happened?" Camille asked.

"One of the assassins; she nearly killed Henri. I...I shot her."

"Did any of our agents get hurt?"

"Yes, one was stabbed."

"Who?" Camille questioned. "Oh God. Not Jon?"

"No, one of the agents working in the kitchen."

Relieved that Jon and Henri were OK, Camille returned her gaze to the Indochinese delegation. It was at that moment she realized the female assassin was missing from the delegation's table. She looked back toward the kitchen area and saw Jon standing near the restrooms. She was startled to see the suspected assassin pointing a gun at Jon. Camille tensed and, holding her breath, reached inside her purse and withdrew her automatic.

Akemi Nakada, an assassin for the Japanese intelligence service, had been walking past the entrance to the kitchen, heading toward the women's restroom, when the kitchen door opened far enough for her to see her sister, Akiko, lying on the floor in a pool of blood. With anger in her eyes and tears streaming down her face, she continued walking toward the ladies' room. Several paces before entering, she turned around just in time to see the American agent she had made eye contact with earlier walk out of the kitchen and stop. She moved to within ten feet of him before speaking.

"You killed my sister, didn't you?" Akemi asked.

Jon turned his head to the left. He was not startled to see the assassin, but he was concerned when he noticed the small-caliber automatic weapon in her left hand, tucked close to her evening gown.

"Death is an occupational hazard in our business," Jon replied.

"I tracked you from Chittagong to Fort Fredrick and then to Calcutta. I figured you and your team would be here tonight. You are very clever, Agent...?"

"Preston," Jon answered. "And you are?"

"Akemi Nakada."

Akemi raised the small-caliber automatic and pointed it at Jon's heart. "Well, Agent Preston, I'm going to kill you now."

Before she could pull the trigger, Jon activated the derringer attached to a spring mechanism on his forearm and fired twice. The first shot hit her in the left lung, while the second hit close to her heart. As Akemi fell to the floor, she raised her gun and fired, just missing Jon's head.

Camille sighed in relief when Jon fired his weapon first. After the shots, chaos erupted in the ballroom, and men and women were ducking under tables or fleeing the room. During the confusion that followed, Kathleen let out a soft moan and slumped toward the table. The woman sitting on the other side of her screamed. Camille turned to her left to see Kathleen trying to grab at her back. She scanned left and right as she saw a native server moving toward the head table with a thin stiletto in her hand, blood dripping off its point.

Camille jumped up from her chair, raised the .32-caliber Beretta in her hand, and fired twice before the server reached Admiral Mountbatten, six feet away. The assassin fell to the floor facedown, still clutching the stiletto. Camille walked over and stood over the assailant with her gun poised to shoot. She kicked the knife from her hand.

Three down, she thought. *God, I hope there are no more.*

Jon sprinted across the room to where Camille stood, knelt down next to the assassin, and felt for a pulse in her carotid artery. When he found none, he rolled her over.

"I'll be damned," Camille said.

"Jon! Jon!" Camille cried out, her own voice waking her from a deep sleep.

"It's OK, darling," Jon said. He held her tightly. "You're having a bad dream. Everything is OK."

"Jon, they were triplets. They were sisters. What if they have a brother or another sister that's an assassin? What if they come after us?" Her voice quivered with fear.

"I'll protect you, Camille. I'll protect you." Jon held her tightly, stroking her hair and kissing her cheek. "I'll protect you, darling. I promise."

CHAPTER 2

USS *Saratoga*, Pacific Ocean

The aircraft carrier USS *Saratoga* steamed at ten knots on a south-easterly heading. It detached itself from a larger carrier task force carrying out diversionary strikes on the Japanese home island. It was reassigned to provide night-fighter coverage for the US Navy task force, which had landed seventy thousand marines and support personnel on the beaches of Iwo Jima. The *Saratoga* departed the South China Sea with only three destroyers as its escorts; it normally had six.

Below the flight deck of the *Saratoga*, Lieutenant Neil Doten sat on his bunk talking to his copilot and best friend, Ensign Jack Fruend. Jack lounged on a bed four feet away. Neil and Jack, the sole surviving members of their eight-man Consolidated PBY Catalina amphibious aircraft crew, continued their discussion from the previous day about their captivity at the Kao-Lan Island prisoner-of-war camp.

"You're still having nightmares about our captivity, aren't you?" Doten asked.

"I've been waking up several times during the night. What about you?" Fruend asked.

"Same. I can't get Charlie's and Don's screams out of my head. I feel as if I let them down." A tear streamed down his face.

He had known crew members Charlie Ruscher and Don O'Rilley since their Catalina flying-boat upgrade training at Pensacola Naval Air Station.

"You can't think like that. You didn't let them down. The Japs picked them at random; it just wasn't our time."

"Then God let them down!"

"No, Neil. The Japanese murdered them."

"Did you tell Agent Preston about your dreams?"

"No. Did you?"

"No, he didn't ask. Plus, I didn't think it was of intelligence value."

"He'll be back to interview us again in a couple of weeks. If we think of anything important, we should write it down and discuss it. It may trigger some other memories of intelligence value."

"I doubt if Agent Preston will return. From the rumors I've heard, he's one of the best US agents in Asia. He'll be off on another mission, maybe to rescue more American prisoners. They'll send a different agent to follow up."

Four weeks ago, Doten, Fruend, and eleven other American prisoners had been rescued from a Japanese prisoner-of-war camp by a small group of Allied intelligence agents; Preston was the team leader. While imprisoned on Kao-Lan Island, ten miles off the coast of French Indochina, Doten and his crew experienced firsthand the cruelty and atrocities that their Japanese captors were capable of committing.

Lieutenant Doten shook his head, trying to forget that six of his crew members had been subjected to gas-gangrene experimentation during their captivity. Doten was forced to watch as the Japs tied his crewmen to trees thirty feet from a small shrapnel bomb loaded with the biological agent. The Japanese had carefully protected each airman's back, sides, neck, and head with metal shields. The backs of their legs and buttocks, however, had remained unprotected. The purpose of the experiment was to wound the airmen and study the effects of the biological agent on the human body. Doten was forced to witness the event and had cringed when a Japanese physician ordered the explosive to be detonated.

The Japanese allowed the injured men to return to their dank hut, where the lieutenant and the other prisoners treated their wounds as best they could. After five nights, the Japanese pulled one of the wounded men from the hut and took him to the medical building. They placed the airman on a table and secured his arms and legs with leather straps. Heavier leather straps were placed around his hips, thighs, head, neck, and chest.

After the senior physician was satisfied the prisoner was secured properly, two junior physicians performed a vivisection, or a live dissection, to determine what damage the gas-gangrene infection had done to the internal organs. Screaming in agony until he passed out, the airman bled out and died in fifteen minutes.

The vivisections continued with one airman a day over the next five evenings. The dissections were performed without euthanizing the airmen or providing them with anesthesia.

Over a period of five years of working on human subjects in northern China, vivisections had become the standard operating procedure at all of the secret Japanese biological- and chemical-research facilities under the command of Unit 731.

Physicians who were new to Unit 731 were carefully indoctrinated. Senior Japanese physicians would have a prisoner shot, sometimes in the leg, but most often in the abdomen. They would then instruct the new physician in cutting open the test subject, each time without the aid of anesthesia, to remove the bullet and repair the damage. After the new physician sutured and closed the wounds, he was ordered to kill the subject.

The main purpose of the surgical exercises was to teach the new physicians how to treat wounded soldiers at the front lines; avoiding the needless death of the test subjects was not required. The secondary reason for the exercises was to desensitize the new surgeons to death.

How could medical doctors, responsible for relieving human suffering and saving lives, possibly do such things to other human beings? Lieutenant Doten asked himself. Neil wanted to believe the Japanese were cruel and incapable of being humane, but he knew differently. Nevertheless, he hated them for what they had done to his men.

Each of the last five nights before their rescuers arrived, Lieutenant Doten was awakened to the screams of one of his men as the Japanese physicians began their incisions, which started under the rib cage and extended through the length of the abdomen to the pubis. The screams and pleas continued for what seemed like an eternity to Doten, before the pain and shock finally rendered each man unconscious.

Doten became so upset he vomited every time they cut open one of his men. He believed the Japanese did their vivisections at night to deliberately drive fear into the prisoners. Neil's navy flight instructors had taught him that the Japanese firmly believed in their superiority to all races, and especially Americans. To add to the humiliation, the Japanese scientists referred to their test subjects as wooden *logs*, which further degraded the prisoners' status to less than human.

Lieutenant Doten and Ensign Fruend were so enraged by the treatment of the prisoners at the Japanese POW camp that they chose not to return to Honolulu and then back to the States after their rescue. Instead, they opted to stay with the carrier and continue their combat duty, flying the Grumman J2F-5 amphibious biplane. After thirty days of medical treatment and recovery time, they began flying combat missions. Little did they know that the Japanese were planning an attack against the *Saratoga*.

The previous day, Lieutenant Toshio Tanaka received a report from a Mitsubishi F1M reconnaissance aircraft that an Allied aircraft carrier and three destroyers had been spotted southwest of their island. Taking advantage of the low cloud cover over Chichi Jima Island, Lieutenant Tanaka and five other Imperial Japanese Navy pilots lifted off from Susaki Airfield, 150 miles north of Iwo Jima.

The 888-foot-long and 106-foot-wide Lexington-class carrier was built in the 1920s and held eight General Electric turboelectric-drive engines, which produced 180,000 horsepower for its four propeller shafts. It could cruise at a speed of ten knots for over ten thousand miles with its complement of three thousand three hundred officers and enlisted seamen. The *Saratoga* was a prime target.

Lieutenant Tanaka had been very fortunate as a youngster. After taking an intelligence test and scoring very high in the last year of lower-secondary school, he was chosen to be an Imperial Navy officer candidate. In upper-secondary school, grade ten through grade twelve, he received the education required of all Japanese officer candidates. At the end of his schooling, he was third in his class and was selected for higher officer candidate schooling. After serving as an ensign in the Japanese Navy for a year, he achieved the rank of sublieutenant or lieutenant junior grade. Since his interest lay in flying, he entered flight school as a flight probationary officer at the Imperial Air Corps Academy. After completing school in late 1944, he completed advanced training in the Mitsubishi A6M Zero and deployed to Susaki Airfield in the Bonin Islands, six hundred miles southeast of Japan.

As Lieutenant Tanaka flew toward the *Saratoga*, he reflected on the last week. Susaki Airfield had been the target of a half-dozen Allied bombing attacks. During one attack, Tanaka and two other pilots had responded to their aircraft. Tanaka had successfully launched his aircraft and engaged the American bombers, shooting one down. The other two officers did not make it off the runway. Now, his squadron had only eight aircraft.

Tanaka led his formation south, flying one hundred feet above the waves. He caught sight of the American aircraft carrier and its escort destroyers at 1648 hours. He radioed to his group, "Attack only the aircraft carrier."

The Mitsubishi A6M Zero had the distinction of being one of the most successful fighter aircraft in the Japanese arsenal. Usually based on an aircraft carrier, Lieutenant Tanaka's squadron had deployed to Susaki Airfield in January 1945 because most of the Japanese carriers had been sunk or damaged. Their mission on Chichi Jima Island was to stop the American bombers on their way to bomb Japan. Three days after American marines landed on Iwo Jima, he and his men had been asked to fly one last mission for the empire. This mission would be against an American aircraft carrier. It would be a one-way trip.

The night before their suicide attack, Lieutenant Tanaka and his five wingmen wrote farewell letters and poems to their loved ones. Tanaka's brief poem read, *I love my parents and sister. I love my emperor and my country. It is to them I give my life.*

The morning of their mission, their commander presented each of them with a *senninbari-hachimaki*, or headband, a strip of cloth approximately one meter in length decorated with a thousand stitches. Each senninbari, made by a different Japanese woman on the mainland, was embroidered with the slogan *Bu-un cho-kyu*, meaning "Eternal good luck in war." Before takeoff, Lieutenant Tanaka and his five wingmen performed a final task by taking a ceremonial drink of sake to give them a spiritual lifting. They toasted their emperor by yelling, "*Tennoheika Banzai!* [Long live the emperor!]"

Lieutenant Tanaka and his men were expected to carry out their *tokubetsu kōgeki tai* mission by flying their Zeros, each loaded with fuel and one 320-pound bomb, at their maximum speed of 332 miles per hour into the midsection of the *Saratoga*, slightly above the waterline.

Lieutenant Doten and Ensign Fruend sat on their bunks talking and drinking coffee. They were interrupted by a broadcast over the ship's speaker system at 1700 hours: "General quarters! General quarters! All hands, man your battle stations." The ship's Klaxon, with its *bong, bong, bong,* followed the announcement. In less than a minute, the two eight-inch and six four-inch antiaircraft guns on the *Saratoga*'s port side began firing at the incoming Japanese aircraft.

At one hundred feet above the waves, Lieutenant Tanaka and his men jinked their aircraft left and right to avoid the tracer bullets coming at them from the guns of the USS *Saratoga* and its escorts. Out of the corner of his right eye, Tanaka caught a bright flash; one of the aircraft had exploded. Despite the murderous fire from the *Saratoga*'s antiaircraft batteries, Tanaka and the four remaining aircraft continued in their task. Tanaka's aircraft hit the *Saratoga* first; the remaining four aircraft impacted seconds after his.

Wracked by five horrendous explosions as the bomb-laden Japanese planes penetrated the seven-inch armor plating, the *Saratoga* shuddered. Two of Tanaka's wingmen had popped up and dived into deck of the carrier, rendering it useless for flight operations.

Forty feet below the deck, Lieutenant Doten lay unconscious next to a bulkhead ten feet away. The kamikaze, which had struck the side of the *Saratoga* ninety feet from where Lieutenant Doten sat, had blown hot metal throughout the crew quarters. When Doten came to, he was pinned under several steel lockers torn from the opposite wall, blood was streaming down the side of his head, and a thin, ten-inch-long piece of steel shrapnel had pierced his right thigh. The steel lockers had protected him from being burned by the fuel from the Zero. Despite the excruciating pain in his leg, Neil struggled for ten minutes and finally untangled himself from the lockers.

"Jack? Jack!" Doten called out. He searched frantically through the thick smoke. "Jack, are you OK?"

Doten crawled across the deck of the smoke-filled quarters, looking for his copilot. He found Jack's body lying twisted and lifeless in a pool of blood. Lieutenant Doten rolled his friend onto his back and saw that shrapnel had severed the carotid artery on the left side of his neck; in a matter of seconds, his friend had bled out.

When a squad of firefighters entered the quarters and began putting out the flames, they found Lieutenant Doten sitting on the deck holding his friend in his arms. It took two navy corpsmen to pull Ensign Fruend from his arms before they could check for a pulse.

"He's dead, Lieutenant. We need to get you to sick bay. You're losing a lot of blood," the corpsman said. He tied a tourniquet around the stunned lieutenant's leg. Neil looked at the corpsman and nodded his head in silent recognition as tears continued to stream down his face. Then he looked down at his wounded leg and passed out.

CHAPTER 3

Singapore, Malaya

A gent Jon Preston was permanently assigned as a special-mission operative to the British Special Operations Executive (SOE) in Calcutta in January 1944. The SOE, a clandestine organization formed by Winston Churchill in July 1940, was commissioned to conduct guerilla warfare against United Kingdom enemies and to recruit, instruct, and aid local resistance movements. The SOE's mission also included reconnaissance behind enemy lines and espionage, sabotage, and assassination.

Jon, highly intelligent with a photographic memory, could grasp a situation quickly and make split-second decisions that were always correct. He and two SOE agents, Miles Murphy and Henri Morreau, of similar intellect and disposition, made up the original King Cobra Team. Miles and Henri trained originally as British Commandos, but because they excelled during their commando training, they were chosen for placement with the SOE. George Linka, a US Army lieutenant colonel and liaison to the SOE at their training facility in Ceylon, joined the team in late 1944. Prior to the war, George was an American Baptist missionary in Japan, and he spoke fluent Japanese.

The King Cobra Team was the brainchild of the US Army chief of staff, General George C. Marshall. Marshall wanted a fifth element of Allied agents wreaking havoc behind Japanese lines in the China, Burma, and India (CBI) theater of operations. Agent Preston was the brightest of the forty-four special-mission agents deployed to the different US theaters of war in January 1944. Because American manpower was limited, Preston was General Marshall's answer for Asia. All special-mission assignments came directly from the general and were sanctioned personally by President Roosevelt, who eagerly approved the King Cobra Team concept.

Preston and his team were debriefing their last mission with Colonel Jim Sage, the commander of the G-2 unit in Manila, when they learned about the attack on the USS *Saratoga*.

After getting the rescued POWs to the *Saratoga* and resting for a day, Jon and his team had departed the ship because the *Saratoga* had received new orders assigning it to night-patrol coverage of the American assault force on the Japanese-held island of Iwo Jima. On February 21, the USS *Saratoga* had suffered extensive damage from a kamikaze attack that killed over 120 sailors.

"Lieutenant Doten is alive—wounded by shrapnel, but still alive," Colonel Sage said. "However, his copilot, Ensign Fruend, was killed in the attack. The *Saratoga* is steaming to the Marshall Islands for repairs before heading back to the States. Lieutenant Doten was evacuated to Kwajalein Atoll; from there he was put on a C-47 and flown to Pearl Harbor."

"Colonel, can you have someone from the CIC unit in Pearl look in on him?"

"I'll send the request and make sure he knows it was initiated by you."

"Thanks, Colonel. He's been through a lot."

The four agents sat quietly while Colonel Jim Sage briefed them on the ongoing battle at Iwo Jima. There was a brief knock on the door before it partially opened and Colonel Richard Arvin stuck his head in. Arvin was one of six colonels who, for security purposes, carried verbal orders from the Pentagon to the King Cobra Team.

"I heard you boys are bored and getting into trouble," Colonel Arvin said. "Do y'all think you're ready for another mission?"

"Yes, sir," the four agents said in unison.

"Great, but first let's take care of some administrative stuff. Agent Preston, you've been promoted to lieutenant colonel. You are now the youngest lieutenant colonel in the US Army. Agents Murphy and Morreau, Her Majesty's Royal Marines have seen fit to promote y'all to the rank of major," Arvin said. He pronounced the title as *majuh* in his naturally slow southern drawl. "Plus, the four of y'all are awarded a Silver Star for your mission to Kao-Lan Island and a Bronze Star for each of your missions to Hong Kong and Canton. These awards will add more color to your growing rows of ribbons. Since the missions are classified top secret, the citations will be placed in your classified personnel files and will remain there for at least fifty years. I'll be hosting a party for y'all at the officers' club later this evening, so congratulations, gentlemen."

Colonel Jim Sage had been a professor at Ohio State University when the war started. Jon had developed a strong friendship and bond with the then professor Sage while taking one of his classes. Toward the end of his last year at OSU, Jon had introduced the tall, lanky professor of towering intellect, and integrity of a saint, to his army-intelligence instructors at Fort Hayes. Army intelligence recruited Sage in June 1943 and gave him a commission with the rank of colonel. Six months later, he was transferred to the Pacific theater.

Colonel Arvin shut the door to the briefing room, opened his briefcase, and laid several folders and a map on the table.

"Your next mission will be against another Unit 731 facility. This one's in Singapore."

Unit 731 was the designation the Japanese had given to their secret biological- and chemical-warfare research unit headquartered in northeast China. At least two dozen smaller sister units had been discovered by the OSS during their covert activities in China, Thailand, and French Indochina. Since their invasion of China in 1927, the Japanese had totally disregarded the Geneva Convention rules on the fair treatment of civilians and prisoners of war. Unit 731 conducted illegal biological and chemical experiments on both Chinese military and civilian prisoners. Only in the last six months had the OSS discovered that the Japanese were also conducting their horrendous experiments on Allied prisoners of war.

"Correct me if I'm wrong, Colonel, but isn't Singapore still a Japanese stronghold?" Agent Murphy asked.

Miles Parker Murphy, a native of London, had a doctorate degree from the University of Edinburgh. He worked as botany professor at Bangkok University from 1937 through 1941. When war was declared against Japan, he joined the Royal Marines. After completing commando training in 1943, he was recruited by the British SOE and became a member of Jon's special-mission team from its inception. Miles was the intellectual of the team, but his always smiling and happy disposition fooled everyone.

"You're correct. Singapore is one of the largest Japanese strongholds in southern Asia, along with Malaya, Sumatra, and Borneo."

"What's so damn important that we have to go into Singapore, Colonel?" Jon asked.

"We've recently discovered that the Japanese are manufacturing some of their biological and chemical weapons in Singapore. One of our British SOE agents in the area got the information from a Singapore resident who works in the bubonic-plague laboratory at Raffles Medical University. His job is to remove fleas from uninfected rats and transfer them to rats infected with bubonic plague. Once the fleas feed on the infected rat's blood, they become carriers and can infect anyone or anything they bite. He then removes the fleas from the infected rats and—very carefully, I might add—and ships them to their experimental laboratories in the field. He told the SOE agent the next shipment would be going to a prisoner-of-war camp in Thailand. The fleas will probably be used on Allied prisoners and, because of the size of the shipment, possibly against Allied divisions moving through Cambodia, Thailand, and Indochina into southern China."

"Where exactly in Thailand?" Henri Morreau asked.

Henri Isaac Morreau had been born in Paris but grew up in Saigon after his father became the vice president of Asian operations for a large French lumber company in French Indochina. After college in Paris, Henri returned to Asia and worked his way up to a general manager's position in the company's Rangoon, Burma, operation. After the Japanese invaded Burma, Henri joined the Royal Marines. He was recruited by the SOE in 1943 after completing his commando training. He joined Jon's team at the same time as Miles Murphy. As a soldier, he preferred straight talk and honesty. He was also somewhat of a practical joker and used humor when he was tense—his was of relieving stress.

"A village called Phetchaburi. It's about one hundred fifty miles southeast of Bangkok. The village is located seven miles inland from the eastern coast. The camp is three miles east of the village."

"I've been there. I worked the area for the lumber industry. There's good lumber to the west of the village. To the east, the forest is less dense, and there's a lot of land cleared for farming," Henri said.

"How will we be getting to Singapore, Colonel?" Linka asked.

"You will be flown by a Royal Navy PBY to the submarine USS *Coho*, which is on patrol in the South China Sea. The *Coho* will rendezvous with a fishing boat commanded by one of our British SOE agents in Malaya, Major Andy Larned. Larned grew up on fishing boats before he became a Royal Marine. His father was a former Royal Marine officer and a fisherman for years before he became a harbor pilot in Singapore back in the thirties. Larned will get y'all to an abandoned dock half a mile south of the university. Your main target is the bubonic-plague laboratory in the Tan Teck Guan Building."

"Won't it be twice as dangerous with four of us going?" Jon asked.

"We're splitting the team into two units. You and George will attack the Tan Teck Guan Building while Miles and Henri take on the Old Administration Building, four blocks to the east of the plague laboratory. The Japanese took over the building and converted it into a laboratory dedicated to mustard-gas research."

"If we go in at night, won't all of the physicians be gone?" Miles asked.

"We're not out to capture any physicians or microbiologists this time. We want the labs and the buildings destroyed."

"Wouldn't bombing be just as effective?" Linka questioned.

"Possibly, but bombing does not guarantee that the facilities will be totally destroyed, and it would also result in dispersing the plague bacteria and the mustard gas across the city. Thousands of innocent people would die. We need y'all to go in and rig the buildings with incendiary explosives. The incendiary explosives are made with white phosphorus and will burn hot enough to destroy the bacteria and the gas. We'll stop their production for at least four months."

"Will the *Coho* be picking us up and bringing us back to the Philippines?" Miles asked.

"No, Miles, y'all will be heading west into the Malacca Strait. Major Larned will rendezvous with the British submarine HMS *Storm*. The *Storm* will get you past the tip of Sumatra into the Andaman Sea, where a PBY will pick you up and get you to Rangoon. From Rangoon, a B-25 will fly you to Calcutta; there y'all will be briefed on your next mission."

"Phetchaburi?" Henri asked.

"Yes, Henri, Phetchaburi."

"When do we leave for Singapore?" Jon asked.

"In two days. Until then, I suggest y'all study the material in the folders and memorize the map of the university area. I have an explosives expert dropping by in two hours to go over the incendiary devices and the timer fuses. I'll check in on y'all later and take you to the club for dinner and then a promotion party at the bar."

CHAPTER 4

USS *Coho*, South China Sea

The flight to the USS *Coho* took just over four hours. Once on board the 2,200-ton submarine, they were greeted by the boat's captain, Commander Royce Janca, and his executive officer (XO), Chad Spivey. The chief of the boat (COB) escorted them to their temporary berths, where they stored their gear. The incendiary devices were stored in a special munitions compartment of the *Coho*. Once under way, the *Coho* ran on the surface for six hours before submerging just before daybreak.

The USS *Coho*, a 312-foot *Gato*-class submarine, was launched in June 1941. Like all standard US Navy submarines built during this time, it had a double-hulled construction. Its inner hull, or pressure hull, consisted of eight watertight compartments. The outer hull housed water ballast and fuel tanks that held enough diesel fuel to give the *Coho* a cruising range of eleven thousand nautical miles. It could stay submerged for up to forty-eight hours.

Major Andy Larned stood at the helm of his sixty-foot fishing boat and guided it on a northeasterly heading, plowing through the five-foot swells of the South China Sea to his rendezvous point with the American submarine. Larned's father was British and his mother Malayan, which made him Eurasian. His father had been a Royal Marine stationed in Singapore when he met Andy's mother. After they married, the marine captain decided to leave the service and start his own fishing business. Larned grew up working on his father's boat, and by the time he graduated from high school, he knew how to operate and repair every part of the sixty-foot vessel, including the diesel engines. Larned graduated as the valedictorian of his secondary-school class in Singapore and with help from his father was offered a scholarship to the Royal Military Academy in Woolwich, England. He received a commission in the Royal Marines in 1935, and as the top graduate at Woolwich, he was given his preferred assignment. He chose Singapore.

The Japanese attacked the British stronghold of Singapore in February 1942. After eight days of fighting, Singapore fell, resulting in the largest surrender of troops in British history: eighty thousand soldiers. Before the British forces surrendered, Major Larned and the marine intelligence detachment he commanded were ordered into the jungles of the Malay Peninsula to organize a guerilla resistance. The resistance group was attached to Force 136, the cover name for the British SOE in the Southeast Asian area.

At 1300 hours, Major Larned slowed his boat, put the transmission in neutral, and began cycling its engine: two-thirds power for thirty seconds and power down for thirty seconds. He did this for thirty minutes straight before transmitting Morse code with his powerful spotlight in the designated southeasterly direction.

The captain of the USS *Coho* had been on the conning tower, or conn, for two hours. He was about to be relieved by his XO when he received a call on the boat's interphone.

"Skipper, we have a radar contact at four miles, bearing 210 degrees," the radar operator told him.

"Does sonar have anything yet?" Captain Royce Janca asked.

"Aye, Skipper, he's picked up engine and small screw noise. The engine is cycling at thirty-second intervals."

"Battle stations surface," Captain Janca ordered. Immediately following the order, the *bong, bong, bong* sound of the battle alarm rang throughout the boat, and submariners began hurrying to their battle stations.

Jon, Miles, and Henri were already awake and in the galley having coffee when the battle alarm sounded. George was sleeping.

"I'd better go tell George what's going on," Jon said.

The sound of the ship's Klaxon alarmed George, and he sprang out of bed, hitting his head on the upper bunk. Jon entered the XO's quarters to find George sitting on the floor, rubbing his head. There was a large red welt on George's forehead.

"Gotta watch out for that top bunk when you get out of bed," Jon said. He extended his hand and helped George stand up. "We're at our rendez-vous point. We'll probably be getting in the life raft in twenty minutes or less."

When the boat broke through the surface of the ocean, the XO opened the outer hatch and rushed onto the bridge. He immediately be-gan searching with his binoculars in the direction of the radar contact.

"Morse code, Skipper, off the port bow," Lieutenant Commander Spivey called. "It reads 'Outhouse,' sir."

"That's the correct code. Reply with 'Halter.'"

"Aye, aye, Captain. I'm sending it now."

"Have they acknowledged?"

"Acknowledgement received, Skipper."

In the Conn, Captain Janca turned to his chief of the boat and said, "COB, inform our guests that we're preparing the life raft."

The COB was a noncommissioned officer aboard a submarine who served as the senior enlisted advisor to the commander and his executive officer.

"Aye, aye, Captain," the COB responded. He turned and climbed down the ladder to the lower level of the submarine.

Fifteen minutes later, the captain ordered all engines stopped. The four agents exited the boat at one of the deck hatches and moved toward the raft floating on the port side of the submarine. Within minutes, the agents began rowing toward the fishing boat twenty yards away.

One of Major Larned's crew helped the agents into the fishing boat and stowed their gear, the explosives, and the life raft. Once everything was se-cure, Major Larned pushed the throttles to full power and turned the boat south-southwest toward Singapore. Below deck, Jon pulled two war-paint kits from his duffel bag and handed one to Henri and one to Miles.

The war-paint kit was an invention of the OSS. It allowed white-skinned agents to color their skin and hair in order to match the skin and hair color of the natives of the areas they were infiltrating. After thoroughly wash-ing his hands, arms, face, and neck to remove any oils from his skin, each agent applied iron-oxide powder to his skin while it was still wet and a darker agent to his hair. Within an hour, all four agents had completed their skin and hair coloring. They now looked like ethnic Eurasians, at least for the next twelve hours.

CHAPTER 5

Singapore, Malaya

Otto Wok, a technician in the Raffles Medical University plague lab, had been visited several weeks ago at home by his long-time friend and high-school classmate Andy Larned. He knew the information he provided to his friend was valuable; the bubonic plague was capable of killing hundreds of thousands. He also knew Larned was a British Royal Marine, and he suspected Andy of being a member of the notorious guerilla force known as Force 136. Larned gave him explicit instructions not to stay at the lab after dark, and he knew this probably meant that Force 136 planned to raid and destroy the lab. They would kill anyone in the lab during the raid. He decided to heed Andy's warning and thereafter was careful not to stay at the lab past eight in the evening.

Jon went to the boat's wheelhouse while the others prepared their weapons and incendiary devices and went over their assignments once more.

"Major Larned," Jon said, "I'm Agent Jon Preston."

"Is everyone settled in, Agent Preston?"

"Yes, but please, call me Jon. How long before we arrive at our destination?"

"About six hours."

Jon moved back to lean against the bulkhead and bumped against something hard. A loud "Aaawk, sweet Jesus!" was followed by a rustling sound.

"Scarlet macaw," Major Larned explained. "Swears like a sailor when he's awake, but otherwise he's pretty good company. My father bought him off a Brazilian merchant captain before the war; the bird was only eight months old. My father took him on all his fishing trips. He speaks nearly five hundred words and over sixty phrases. His name is Marteen."

"Isn't he a liability to a covert operative?"

"Not at all. He adds to my cover. Who the hell would suspect an operative of having a noisy macaw on board?"

"I see your point. Does he talk a lot?"

"Sometimes he talks too much—most of it totally inappropriate. His favorite line is 'Brenda, show me your panties.' I think my dad taught him to say it just to irritate my mom."

Jon chuckled and shook his head. "Well, good luck with Marteen."

At 2000 hours, the boat entered the Singapore Straits. Two hours later, Captain Larned brought it alongside a dilapidated dock a half mile south of the university medical center. He saw no sentries or roaming guards at the dock or onshore.

Miles and Henri exited the boat first and moved a hundred yards east before turning north toward the Administration Building. Jon and George left five minutes later. Neither pair of agents encountered any patrols on the way to their targets.

At the Administration Building, Miles and Henri found an entrance on a side of the building where an outside light was missing its bulb. Miles checked the door.

"It's locked."

Miles pulled his lock-picking kit out and selected a tension wrench and a pick with a ninety-degree hook on its end. Miles placed the tension wrench in the lower portion of the keyhole and applied clockwise tension. He inserted the pick in the top of the keyhole and ran it in and out several times, raking the pins to loosen them. Next he used the pick to lift up the farthest pin and turned the tension wrench to lock the pin behind the cylinder drum. He did the same for each of the five remaining pins, turned the tension wrench a final time, and unlocked the door.

They entered the building and locked the door behind them. Only then did both agents turn on their red-filtered flashlights. Miles searched the lower level for people while Henri stood guard. No one was on the ground floor, so they moved upstairs. They found the mustard-gas laboratory on the second floor; the door was painted yellow. Miles picked the lock to the lab and entered a long darkened hallway. When they closed the door behind them, a Japanese lab technician stuck his head out of one of the offices. He stared at the agents for a second and finally walked toward them. Henri raised his silenced .22-caliber pistol and placed a shot in the technician's forehead. The .22-caliber bullet rattled around inside the technician's skull, scrambling his brain. He died before he hit the floor. They checked the other rooms together but found no one else.

Henri stood watch at the lab door while Miles placed his backpack, containing a seventy-five-pound incendiary charge, in a recess between two large cylinders labeled Oxygen. On either side of the cylinders was a thick windowed room with heavy sealed doors.

The oxygen in the tanks should enhance the explosion, Miles thought.

Miles pulled out a pouch containing five pencil fuses engineered for a sixty-minute delay before they detonated. The fuse could be activated only by crimping a small copper tube containing a glass vial of acid. The crimping would break the glass and release acid into the tubing, where it would corrode a small wire. The corroded wire would eventually break and release a striker, which would hit a percussion cap and trigger the detonation. Miles selected a fuse, inserted it into the puttylike explosive compound, and crimped the copper tube with a pair of needle-nose pliers.

"Time to leave," Miles stated.

Several blocks to the west, Jon and George picked the lock on the front door of the Tan Teck Guan Building. After they went inside, they heard footsteps coming down the hallway. They hid in the shadows until a Japanese guard entered the foyer. As the guard turned left and away from them, Jon eased out of the shadows, put the barrel of his silenced pistol against the back of the guard's head, and fired.

"Find the lab. I'll take care of the body," Jon said.

George searched the rooms down the hallway. Since he spoke and read Japanese, he easily found the door marked Bubonic Plague Laboratory. George called Jon and then listened at the lab door as Jon unpacked and prepared the seventy-five-pound incendiary device he had carried. After activating the sixty-minute pencil fuse, they exited the building, locked the door behind them, and headed cautiously back toward the dock and the boat.

Halfway to the boat, Jon raised his right arm and stopped. He and George crouched behind two large palm trees and waited.

Jon whispered to George, "Japanese sentry taking a leak behind those bushes."

By the time George located the Japanese soldier, the soldier had finished peeing and was aiming his rifle at Miles and Henri, who were walking about ten yards east of the guard. The soldier shouted something in Japanese. Miles and Henri froze. As the guard walked toward them with his rifle extended from his shoulder, Jon rose from his position and silently came up behind him. Jon kicked with his left foot and collapsed the guard's right knee; then he grabbed the guard's rifle and hit him in the side of the head twice, rendering him bloody and unconscious. Jon and his team members then hurried the last two hundred yards to the boat.

"You should have killed him," Henri stated.

"I wanted him to live and tell the authorities he saw men dressed in black. I want them to know they are vulnerable and we can strike anywhere and anytime," Jon said.

"Putting the fear of God in them?" Miles asked.

"Something like that. They won't fear us until they know what we are capable of. In an hour they will know we can strike even in their strongholds."

"They will put more resources into protection instead of putting them in the field," Miles said.

"Let's hope so. The more soldiers we can remove from combat, the sooner we can defeat them."

As the last agent boarded the boat, Major Larned went to full power and headed into the Strait of Singapore. He turned the boat southwest toward the Malacca Strait. *Five more hours before we find the sub*, he thought.

Thirty minutes later, the cupric chloride had eaten through the lead wire in the pencil fuse and released the striker onto the percussion cap. A broad smile crossed Miles's face when the first explosion went off in the Administration Building and a five-hundred-foot fireball lit up the night sky. *The oxygen worked great*, Miles thought. Ten minutes later, the Tan Teck Guan Building exploded, creating another fireball and more chaos on the university campus.

"Mission accomplished," Miles stated.

"Not yet," Jon said. "We still have to make it through Jap-controlled waters to the sub."

Major Larned continued powering the boat west, passing Buckhorn Island and moving closer to the Malacca Strait. When the boat came abeam Sudong Island, however, a searchlight beam from a Japanese patrol boat flooded the deck with light. It was followed by a voice on a bullhorn ordering the boat to stop. A worried look crossed Larned's face as he throttled back and stopped the boat. Jon and the others grabbed their Thompson submachine guns and a handful of grenades. Miles also grabbed a satchel charge.

Shaped much like the US Navy's seventy-foot PT boat, only twenty feet shorter, the Japanese patrol boat pulled to within five feet of the fishing boat. Larned saw seven Japanese sailors standing on the forward and aft decks and two sailors manning the forward and aft .32-caliber machine guns. Six sailors carried carbines. A Japanese officer spoke in Malaysian over a bullhorn, telling the fishing-boat captain to prepare to be boarded. He held an automatic pistol in his right hand.

"Aye, aye, sir, you have permission to come aboard," Major Larned shouted.

"Aaawk, hoist the Jolly Roger, hoist the Jolly Roger," Marteen squawked.

George overheard several Japanese sailors laughing and commenting on the parrot, which served to lower their defenses. Before the first Japanese sailor stepped onto Larned's boat, all four agents tossed their grenades and opened fire. After the grenades exploded, most of the firing stopped. A bullet from one of the sailors, still returning fire, hit Major Larned in the arm before Jon shot the sailor. Jon and George continued firing as Miles activated the pull igniter on the satchel charge and tossed it onto the Japanese patrol boat. "Hit it!" he shouted.

Major Larned pushed the throttles to full power and began moving away from the patrol boat. Less than a minute later, the Japanese boat exploded, sinking almost immediately.

A loud "Aaawk!" erupted from the Marteen's cage, followed by "Sweet Jesus, save us."

"Amen to that, Marteen," Jon stated.

George pulled the first-aid kit from the wall of the wheelhouse while Jon cut away Larned's bloodied sleeve. Major Larned's first mate took control of the boat while Jon and George tended to the major's wound.

"You're lucky, Andy. The bullet struck you at a downward angle, entering your bicep from the rear. It passed through the muscle and exited at the front of the arm," Jon said.

"We are all lucky," Larned stated. "The Japs were unprepared for any resistance. They didn't even get off a shot from their machine gun."

Jon pulled two sterilized Carlisle dressings from the first-aid kit, sprinkled the enclosed packet of sulfanilamide on the entry and exit wounds, and covered each with a dressing.

"Do you want a shot of morphine?" Jon asked.

Immediately, Marteen squawked, "Gimme a drink, you sod!"

"Negative," Larned said. "I need to stay alert for the trip back."

Jon put the morphine syrette, which looked like a small tube of toothpaste with a needle on the end, back in the first-aid kit and placed the kit in its storage container on the bulkhead. He handed Larned four aspirin.

By 0500 hours, they had traveled eighteen miles up the Malacca Strait. Major Larned disengaged the engine and began cycling the motor at thirty-second intervals. Thirty minutes later he started signaling in Morse code, pointing his flashlight due north.

On the bridge of the HMS *Storm*, Lieutenant Commander Larry Mercer observed a light in the distance signaling Morse code.

"Captain, I have a Morse-code signal from a boat two hundred meters off our port bow. Signal reads 'Cotton Tail.'"

"All stop," Captain Don Cowan ordered over the intercom. "Send our reply."

"I'm sending our reply, sir: 'Tumbleweed.'"

By the time the submarine came to a full stop, the four agents were in the water and rowing their six-man life raft toward the HMS *Storm*; fifteen minutes later they were aboard. When they climbed to the bridge, they were greeted by the sub's captain.

"I'm Captain Don Cowan. The chief of the boat will take you below and show you where to stow your gear and where you'll bunk."

After the agents descended into the conning tower, Captain Cowan ordered, "All ahead two-thirds; come left to heading 350 degrees."

The HMS *Storm* turned north and remained on the surface for another thirty minutes, but before the sun rose, Captain Cowan ordered the helmsman to dive the boat.

"Dive! Dive! Dive!" the chief of the boat repeated over the ship's intercom, an announcement that was followed by two loud blasts from the sub's Klaxon: *ahoooga, ahoooga.* The men on the bridge hurried down the ladder into the conn. The last man down was the XO, who closed the hatch and yelled, "Hatch secured."

"Green board," the COB reported seconds later over the intercom, followed by "Pressure in the boat," as the interior lights switched from red to white. The "Green board" notification informed the crew that the boat was sealed, watertight, and ready to dive.

"Take her down to four-zero meters," Captain Cowan ordered.

Before the 218-foot HMS *Storm* began its dive, the main air-induction valves slammed shut, and the irregular gurgle of water entering into the ballast tanks could be heard throughout the boat. The two eight-cylinder, 950-horsepower diesel engines stopped, and the boat switched over to the battery-powered Metropolitan-Vickers electric motors for its underwater propulsion.

Twelve minutes later, the diving planesman called out, "Level at four-zero meters, Captain."

"XO, you have the helm," Captain Cowan said. "I'm going to say hello to our visitors."

CHAPTER 6

Calcutta, India

After their return to Calcutta, Jon and his team completed their after-action report and sat in the briefing room at the SOE detachment. Jon introduced his commander, Colonel Michael MacKenzie, to the newest member of the team, Lieutenant Colonel George Linka. George had been assigned to Jon's team by General Marshall while Colonel Mackenzie was on emergency leave and while Jon and his team were in the Philippines. Once the introduction was complete, Jon updated Colonel MacKenzie on their last four missions.

Late that afternoon, Colonel Richard "Rick" Dixon flew in on a C-47 and came immediately to the SOE detachment. After formal introductions, the team sat down to listen to the Pentagon colonel brief their new mission.

Colonel Dixon, assigned to the Army Intelligence Directorate (G-2), Asian Division, at the Pentagon in Washington, DC, was one of six army colonels in G-2 responsible for traveling to the special-mission agents located in the various theaters of operations and verbally communicating their assignments directly to them. In the past, written orders and orders transmitted by wireless had been intercepted, and many agents had died. Therefore, the army chief of staff, General George Marshall, had changed the method of communicating with his special-mission agents in the field. Now, nothing was written down, and the orders were always communicated verbally.

"Gentlemen," Colonel Dixon told them, "the village of Phetchaburi, on the southeast peninsula of Thailand, will be your next target. Phetchaburi is a small farming community one hundred fifty miles southeast of Bangkok. The village has approximately two thousand inhabitants and is located seven miles inland from the Gulf of Thailand. The POW camp is three miles east of the village. It's not confirmed by our OSS assets in the area, but we believe the camp is a holding point for the fleas infected with bubonic plague, the ones sent from the laboratory you all destroyed in Singapore. Our OSS agents in Burma, Thailand, and French Indochina have not reported any outbreaks of plague yet, but if we don't act soon, we believe it's just a matter of time before an outbreak will occur. Your job is to intercept and destroy the plague-infected fleas before they can be used. Any questions?"

"Colonel, do we know how many Allied prisoners are at the Phetchaburi camp?" Jon asked.

"The last report we received, over a week ago, stated at least one hundred twenty American, Australian, and British soldiers were interred there."

"What about the camp? How big is it?" Henri asked.

"The camp is around five acres in size. It's surrounded by a ten-foot-high barbed-wire fence, and there are four guard towers that are at least ten feet off the ground. Twenty-five guards, three cooks, and a camp commandant make up the Japanese presence."

"What kind of OSS or SOE assets will we have to help us, Colonel?" Miles asked.

"You'll have over a hundred Thai guerillas under the command of Captain Lloyd Craig; he's OSS. Captain Craig grew up in Thailand. His parents were Baptist missionaries in this area from 1920 to 1935. He speaks multiple languages, including several Thai dialects. He is one tough agent, and the Thai people are loyal to him."

"How are we to deal with the Japanese physicians, sir? Do you want us to take them prisoner?" George asked.

"We'll need you to interrogate enough Japs to determine when, where, and how they are shipping the infected fleas. Otherwise, no Japanese prisoners this time, George."

"What do we do with the POWs once we take the camp?" Miles asked.

"Captain Craig has located a landing area large enough for a C-47 transport to land and take off. Once we receive your shortwave message stating 'Greenfield,' plus the number of POWs, we'll send the required number of transports to pick everyone up."

"What if something goes wrong and we can't take the camp?" Jon asked.

"We'll have a sampan and HMS *Storm* on standby off the east coast. If you need to abort, transmit 'Black Diamond' on your designated frequency, and the sampan will pick you up and transport you to the HMS *Storm*. The pickup point is a small cove two miles north of your insertion point. You'll need to be on the north side of the cove the night after the planned raid. At the cove, use your flashlight to transmit the code words 'Red One' at fifteen and forty-five minutes after the hour."

"Do you have any more questions?" Colonel Mackenzie asked. "If not, get out of here and get a good night's rest. We'll go over more details and the maps of the camp tomorrow morning."

Three days later, the agents took off in a dull black B-25H that was on loan to the British SOE from the American government. The North American B-25H was a medium bomber powered by two Wright R-2600 Cyclone fourteen-cylinder air-cooled radial engines, each producing 1,700 horsepower. The aircraft had a cruise speed of 230 miles per hour and a range of 1,174 miles. On this particular H model, the bomb racks had been removed and extra fuel tanks added because this aircraft was used solely for carrying agents, commandos, and supplies. A second and smaller bomb-bay door was added for agents to jump from.

The B-25 flew five hours from Calcutta to Rangoon. After landing and refueling, the bomber flew another 350 miles to its drop zone. During the flight, Jon and the other three agents were too restless to sleep; the cramped space and the constant noise and cold also didn't help. By the time the pilot called over the interphone, "Thirty minutes to your jump," they were tired, stiff, and banged around from the constant turbulence. They stood up when the bomb doors opened. When the green light turned on, they jumped through the open bomb bay into the pitch-black night.

Henri was the first to jump. The fall from five hundred feet came quickly, but there was a sliver of a waxing moon, and he saw the ground before he landed and rolled as soon as he touched the ground to break his fall.

He heard a loud "Oof!" from one of the other agents, who hit the ground heavily and knocked the air out of his lungs.

They were greeted by Captain Craig and half a dozen Thai guerillas. It took only minutes to collect their chutes and gear and move into the dense jungle, where the guerillas had a camp set up approximately six miles from the POW camp.

At the camp, Jon took a moment to evaluate Captain Craig. He estimated the captain to be a little over six feet tall, but he had broad shoulders and more muscle than Jon did. His angular face and assertive voice revealed him to be a hardened veteran, and his Thai guerillas appeared to be just as hard. Jon and the others agents listened carefully as Captain Craig turned on his red-filtered flashlight and showed them a hand-drawn map of the prisoner compound. He pointed out the locations of the guard towers, the single entrance to the compound, the guard and cook quarters, the commander's quarters and office, the mess building, and the prisoner huts. A mile and a half outside the camp was a weapons-test area.

All the buildings were constructed from bamboo, with roofs made from thatched elephant grass, except one large structure at the far edge of the camp that was made from rough, locally milled lumber. Craig told them that the Japanese used this structure for their medical experiments. He also told them there were now thirty-five guards, five cooks, six medical personnel, and a new camp commandant staffing the camp. The last commandant had died from a snakebite.

Although Captain Craig had drawn his map accurately, Jon still needed his team to scout the facility. He hoped they could find a work detail outside the compound, because he wanted a chance to talk to one of the prisoners. He needed to obtain as much inside information and detail as possible.

Three hours before sunrise, Captain Craig woke the four agents. His men prepared a breakfast of cooked rice and strong dark tea. Jon and the others added the beef jerky they had brought along. Craig then led the four agents and ten of his guerillas to an area of the jungle and a hill that overlooked the camp. The small hill was a hundred feet above the camp and overgrown with bamboo trees and ten-foot-tall elephant grass. They crawled through the tall grass to a treeless area that gave his team a good view of the compound.

On the northwest side of the camp, Jon noticed that the elephant grass had encroached close to the barbed-wire fence. Captain Craig told the agents that the prisoners were clearing the perimeter of the compound in this area.

"That will be an ideal location to talk to a prisoner," Jon said. "Let's get closer in."

"I heard an interesting rumor about you. Is it true that you killed a king cobra with just your foot?" Captain Craig asked.

"Unfortunately, yes."

"Why unfortunately?"

"Because it gave me notoriety and gave the Japanese a nickname and a description of a European to look for. The Japs have been hunting me and my team ever since."

"Yeah, I guess word of someone killing a cobra with a twist of his foot would get around quickly. How close have they come to finding you?"

"Too close. We lost one British agent, and one American agent was wounded in their last attempt, and we damn near lost Admiral Mountbatten."

At 0800 hours, a group of ten prisoners marched out of the camp and around to the northeast quadrant; they were watched by four guards. When they reached the partially cleared area, the guards gave them machetes. The prisoners began chopping at the tough bamboo-like clumps of elephant grass, some of which rose as high as twelve feet. Some of the stalks looked to be five inches in diameter.

Long before the prisoners began their work, Jon and Henri had crawled their way into the elephant grass and hidden among several thick bunches close to where the prisoners had stopped clearing the grass the day before. After a while, one of the prisoners finally worked his way to a clump four feet from the agents. Jon spoke to him in a soft whisper.

"Keep chopping and don't turn around. What's your name, soldier?"

"Charlie Mulligan," he replied.

"Charlie, I need some information about your camp. Dammit, I said keep cutting and don't look in my direction."

Mulligan kept cutting and answered all of Jon's questions. Some of the answers made Jon's blood run cold. So much so that he wanted to spill Japanese blood. The Japs were conducting experiments with weapons:

grenades, bayonets, and flamethrowers. Charlie didn't know about any biological or germ weapons, but he told him that the large Japanese truck that the Japs maintained at the camp had been driven to the coast earlier in the week. Two prisoners went along and unloaded six wooden boxes from a small freighter. Charlie told him this seemed a bit unusual because they usually got food supplies from the freighter. Not that day.

"Where are the boxes now?"

"Stored in the large wooden building."

Bingo, Jon thought. *We may have found the plague fleas.*

"Charlie, don't say anything to anyone. Understand?"

"Yes, sir."

After Jon and Henri returned to the small hill, Jon told Captain Craig he wanted to see the camp's weapons-testing area.

"I wouldn't recommend it. It's pretty gruesome. There are burned bodies out there. According to two of my men who were observing the Japs, they tested a flamethrower on them and left them to die."

"I understand, but I need to document the atrocity with photographs."

Within an hour, the group reached the edge of the jungle twenty-five yards from the weapons-testing site. Five large trees with the tops sawed off eight feet above the ground stood in the middle of a clearing. Secured to the trees by steel cables were the charred bodies of five Allied prisoners killed in the name of testing a new type of Japanese flamethrower. Jon was filled with rage and determined to exact his revenge in Japanese blood.

"We'll take the camp tomorrow, before dawn," Jon told the group. "Let's head back and finalize the plan."

CHAPTER 7

Phetchaburi, Thailand

Jon decided the night before that the team would penetrate the barbed-wire fence near the area where the prisoners had been chopping elephant grass. They now hid in the tall grass outside the camp's fence. One of the Thai guerillas sent out to reconnoiter the compound came back and informed him that the guard towers were not manned. *The Japanese will lose this war, if for no other reason than that they are too damned cocky and confident,* Jon thought.

Captain Craig watched with interest as Henri crawled on his belly and hid in a clump of elephant grass, waiting for one of the roving guards to pass his position. After the guard passed, Henri crawled up to the fence, removed the wire cutters from his canvas bag, and clipped a five-foot hole in the rusting barbed wire. *This guy is fearless,* thought Craig. Five Thai guerillas entered through the opening and dispersed to find the roving guards.

Twenty minutes later, one of the guerillas returned and reported to Jon and Captain Craig, "All the guards have been neutralized, sir."

"How many?" Jon asked.

"Six."

Miles and Henri entered through the opening and carried their satchel explosives to the guards' quarters. Jon and George followed and made their way to the commandant's hut. Captain Craig and twenty more guerillas entered last and covered the five POW huts and the medical building. Twenty guerillas stationed themselves a half mile down the dirt road toward Phetchaburi; they would engage any unaccounted-for Japanese coming to the camp and turn back any villagers curious about the explosions. The remaining sixty guerillas hid in the jungle outside of the compound.

As the first light of dawn began to show itself, three cooks left one of the barracks, went to the mess area, and started their cooking fires. After the fires were going, three of Captain Craig's guerillas surprised the cooks, knocked them unconscious, and bound and gagged them. They would be needed later to prepare meals for the prisoners.

On Jon's signal, Henri and Miles dropped satchel charges into the guard huts and scrambled behind a large double-axle truck parked ten yards away. After the first explosion, Jon and George rushed into the commandant's quarters. As the commandant bent down to pull up his trousers, Jon knocked him unconscious and secured his hands and feet.

At the five prisoner huts, Captain Craig and a group of Thai guerillas stopped the POWs from leaving. The few Japanese soldiers who survived the explosions were shot by the Thai guerillas as they stumbled out of the remains of their demolished huts. By the time the sun peeked over the horizon, the camp was secure. Much of the compound was strewn with bamboo and body parts. At the other end of the compound, Thai guerillas guarded six Japanese in white lab coats lying prone on the ground with their hands on their heads.

As George walked up to the Japanese prisoners, he looked at Captain Craig and said, "We'll interrogate the physicians. Otherwise, no prisoners." Craig nodded his head and pulled his .45-caliber automatic from its holster. After identifying two physicians, Craig clubbed the other four on the head, rendering them unconscious.

"I'll let the guerillas handle them."

George nodded his acknowledgment and thought, *I guess Craig doesn't want the death of Japs on his conscience, no matter how sadistic they are.*

Miles and Henri found the senior-ranking Allied POW and asked him to gather his men together. Lieutenant Colonel Charlie Mulligan gave the order to form up. The POWs, malnourished and in rags for uniforms, eagerly mustered into five separate lines of twenty-five each. Six prisoners were too sick to get out of bed and listened to their liberator's instructions from their bunks.

As Miles and Henri briefed the prisoners, Jon set up his small, low-powered Paraset wireless radio and transmitted the code word "Greenfield One-Three-One," denoting that the mission was complete and giving the number of POWs needing to be airlifted out. Twenty-five minutes later, Jon received an encrypted reply.

Jon turned to Captain Craig. "Six C-47 transports will land tomorrow at dawn. Do you see any problems with holding this position until then?"

"There are no other Japs within fifty miles of here. Don't worry. We'll hold it."

Once again Jon was amazed at how easily the compound fell. He had expected more than ten guards to be on night patrol and at least two towers to be manned. They had caught the Japanese flat-footed once more. He never questioned good luck, though; he'd take it any time. Jon raised his head toward heaven and said a silent prayer: *Thank you, Father, for protecting us once again.*

As the three cooks came to, they were put to work fixing the morning meal. Rice and smoked fish would have to do until they reached Calcutta. George spoke to the cooks and ordered them to brew twenty gallons of tea. Afterward, Jon and George interrogated the commandant in his hut. George explained to Major Takumi Sato his precarious situation. The major was obviously nervous because his eyes were darting, sending short, intense glances across the room. He readily answered the questions that Jon recited and that George then translated into Japanese.

"Are there any Japanese troops stationed at the village of Phetchaburi?" Jon asked.

"No," Major Sato answered.

"How often do you check in with your headquarters?"

"Every two weeks."

"When did you last check in?"

"Four days ago."

"Did you report in after the shipment of boxes arrived on the transport ship?"

Major Sato remained silent until George reminded him they could always turn him over to the Thai guerillas, instead of taking him prisoner.

"Yes."

"Do you know what is in the shipment?"

"No."

"Why don't you know?"

"I was told not to ask. They only gave me instructions that a small plane would land to pick up the boxes."

"Do you know the plane's destination after the pickup?"

"I was told not to be concerned, but I overheard one of the officers on the boat mention Hanoi."

"Crap," George said aloud. "They intend to fly the fleas to Hanoi. From Hanoi they can send the supply of fleas anywhere in Asia."

"Then we need to intercept the aircraft and interrogate the pilots. Ask the major if he knows when the aircraft is due to land," Jon said.

"When will the aircraft land to pick up the boxes?"

"Tomorrow afternoon, at 1400 hours."

"That means we'll have to stick around after the prisoners are flown out. Those aircraft are going to attract some attention. Tell the major he earned a ride to an American POW camp. I'll check with Captain Craig to see how long he can remain with us."

The following morning, Captain Craig and five of his Thai guerillas set up their portable AN/UPN-1 Pathfinder marker beacon at the grass landing strip one mile from the camp. When Craig connected the battery and flipped the on switch, the beacon started transmitting range and azimuth to aircraft on a frequency known by the inbound C-47s. At 0700 hours, the first of six C-47s could be seen on final approach to the grass strip, and at 0705, the first C-47 flared, touched down, and rolled to where Captain Craig was waving a smoking bamboo torch.

Miles and Henri took turns delivering prisoners to the airfield in the Japanese Type 94 heavy-duty truck. It took ten trips to get them to the transports. By 0930, the last C-47 lifted off and headed toward Rangoon. Jon waited until the last of the prisoners were loaded on the aircraft before he allowed Captain Craig to put Major Sato on the plane and secure his hands and feet. Five minutes after takeoff, each C-47 was joined by two US Navy Hellcat fighters, which would escort them all the way to their destination.

After the last aircraft took off, Jon sent a coded message to the SOE detachment in Alipore, a suburb of Calcutta, informing them that he was going to wait for a Japanese transport to land and interrogate the crew.

The SOE transmitted back that a C-47 would be on standby to pick them up once they got the information they wanted.

After taking off from Hanoi, the Japanese pilot leveled off at eight thousand feet and pulled the throttles back to maintain a cruise speed of 250 knots. He had been flying the Kawasaki-Lockheed Super Electra for three years. Normally he enjoyed flying and was a talkative man. Today, however, he was quiet, disappointed because his request for a transfer to fighters had been denied once again by the Imperial Japanese Army (IJA) Headquarters.

His copilot read his after-takeoff checklist, checked the engine temperature and oil pressure, and reset the radar altimeter to 29.92 in the altimeter's Kollsman window because they would be landing within a mile of the Gulf of Thailand, which was at sea level.

The Kawasaki-Lockheed Super Electra, called a Thelma by the Allied air forces, was licensed to Kawasaki and initially built as a civil freight and mail carrier. After the war started, it was used as a small military transport for both cargo and passengers. The Thelma was powered by two Mitsubishi Ha-26-I, fourteen-cylinder radial engines. Each engine produced 875 horsepower, and the aircraft could reach a top speed of 260 miles per hour, faster than an American B-24 bomber.

At half past twelve in the afternoon, Captain Craig and four of his guerillas, now dressed in Japanese uniforms, drove the heavy-duty truck to the airstrip and waited. Two hours later, the Japanese Super Electra flew over the grass airfield once to observe the wind sock and determine the direction of the wind. It then completed a 180-degree turn into the wind and landed.

The pilot taxied to within ten yards of the heavy-duty truck. After he shut the engines down, two Thai guerillas, dressed as Japanese soldiers, approached the aircraft, each carrying a wooden box. When the copilot opened the door, he was welcomed by two .45-caliber Colt semiautomatic pistols pointing at him. Two additional guerillas climbed aboard the aircraft, relieved the pilot of his pistol, and escorted him off the aircraft.

They then returned to the camp, where the pilots were taken into the commandant's office and George began his interrogation.

"If you want to live, you will answer my questions," George told them. "Otherwise, we will turn you over to the Thai guerillas and let them deal with you. After they torture and kill you, they will cut your ears off and place your severed heads on bamboo spikes."

George knew that most Japanese soldiers were either Buddhists or Shintoists, who believed that the human body must go to heaven undefiled. They also believed that after they died, their soul was pulled to heaven by their ears. He knew that it was likely that both pilots were familiar with the horror stories from Burma about Kachin warriors defiling the bodies of ambushed Japanese soldiers and thus denying their entry into heaven.

After hearing this threat, the Japanese pilots, more nervous than ever, began to plead for their lives. *Well, I guess they're ready to talk*, George thought.

"Where are you flying after you take off from here, Lieutenant?" George asked the pilot.

"South of Nanning," the lieutenant replied.

"Why are you flying there?"

"We are to drop one of the crates, from altitude, into the countryside."

"Where are you going next?"

"Liuzhou."

"Are you going to drop another crate from altitude?"

"Yes."

"Where else are you dropping crates?"

"Yulin is our last drop."

"There are a total of six crates. What are you planning to do with the three remaining crates?"

"We are to deliver two crates to the medical facility at Wenchang. The last crate we are supposed to deliver to the camp at Swatow, on the Chinese coast northeast of Canton."

"It looks like the Japs are trying to start a plague outbreak in southern Asia," George stated. "And it looks like we have discovered another facility where they are performing medical experiments. What do you want to do about it?"

"Once we get back to Calcutta, we'll transmit the information to G-2 at the Pentagon and let them figure it out."

"What do we do with these guys?"

"Well, they have cooperated, and they're only transport pilots. How about taking them back with us and turning them over to the military police?"

"Why not leave them for the guerillas?"

"I've seen enough death on this mission. Plus, they may have additional intel that counterintelligence can get from them on flights they've completed recently."

Jon moved to a table where he had set up his wireless radio and transmitted a message to his SOE detachment. An hour later he received a reply that a British C-47 would pick them up at daybreak.

After informing the others, Jon went back into the commandant's hut, lay down on the single cot, and fell asleep. He didn't wake up until George shook him. It was 0400 hours the next morning.

CHAPTER 8

Calcutta, India

Captain Richard Dubois, US Navy, was sitting in a large mahogany captain's chair in the all-teak wheelhouse of the luxury yacht *Anne Marie*, docked in a Hooghly River yacht basin on the southwest side of Calcutta, when OSS agent Camille Dupont entered from the starboard outside door. She was escorting a US Army corporal, a courier sent by the commander of the Army Counterintelligence Corps detachment in Calcutta.

"Courier with a package for you, Captain," Agent Dupont said.

The corporal handed Captain Dubois a sealed envelope and had him sign for it. After he secured the signed voucher, the corporal thanked Captain Dubois and left the boat.

Dubois, a detail oriented intellectual and graduate of the United States Naval Academy, had been a member of President Franklin D. Roosevelt's Secret Service detail until late 1943. After President Roosevelt's close friend and confidant, General William Donovan, the director of the OSS, discovered Dubois carried a sea captain's certification, he convinced the president to reinstate him in the navy at the rank of captain and release him to the OSS. Donovan then sent him to India and placed him in charge of the *Anne Marie*.

General Donovan set Dubois up with an ideal wartime covert operative's cover. Dubois was to be an opium trader in Southeast Asia. He was given all the documents and credentials he needed to begin his covert mission: assignment of rights as an opium dealer with the governments of India, French Indochina, Burma, Thailand, China, and Malaysia. All were valid opium rights and were on file in government offices in New Delhi, Hanoi, Rangoon, Beijing, Saigon, and Singapore. Dubois's credentials could get him into any port in Asia, including those held by the Japanese. Along with the trading rights were French passports and the French registry for the *Anne Marie* and the names of two dozen customers for Dubois's business. In addition, Dubois was put in command of four beautiful but highly trained female OSS agents to masquerade as a rich playboy's entourage.

Over the last year, Captain Dubois and his team, along with Agent Preston's team, had successfully shut down two Japanese spy rings.

The *Anne Marie* was the fastest 126-foot diesel yacht built in Asia in 1926. It cruised at nine knots and had a top speed of fourteen. With its twenty-one-foot beam and eight-and-a-half-foot draft, it displaced 191 tons of water. Its crew complement numbered twelve: eleven seamen and a captain.

The *Anne Marie's* quarter-inch steel hull was constructed with lapped plating, secured with speed rivets countersunk into the outside hull to create a smoother surface. Its decks were constructed of two-inch-thick teak decking, and its teak wheelhouse was large and extravagant. The single driving force behind the original design of the boat, owned by an ultrarich banker in Calcutta, was passenger comfort. General Donovan leased the yacht from the banker, who put the yacht in dry-dock storage soon after the Japanese invaded Burma.

After the incident with the three Nakada sisters, Captain Dubois had sent a coded wireless message to the Directorate of Intelligence at the Pentagon requesting funds to refit the *Anne Marie*. Within three days he received approval to proceed with the refit.

The first thing Captain Dubois did was to call his crew and agents together to discuss a name change for the boat. Once everyone was present, he told them what their orders were and that the boat was being moved to an undisclosed location to make the changes.

"You already know the Japanese have photos of the boat from our mission in Chittagong last year. So, in addition to changing the looks of the *Anne Marie*, we will need to change its name. I want all of you to put your heads together and agree on a new name."

Within an hour, the crew and agents decided on a new name for the yacht. They recommended to the captain that the name be changed from

Anne Marie to *Jacqueline*, after one of the captain's fallen female agents and the twin sister of Agent Kathleen Lauren.

After two months, the yacht's looks were finally complete: its super-structure was altered by removing one of the two radio masts, and the smokestack was made longer to look sleeker. On the fantail and foredeck, green canvas sun covers were installed, green canvas was added to the lower and upper side railings, and a green-and-red strip was painted the length of its hull.

Captain Dubois opened the envelope and retrieved a folder containing several photographs of a Eurasian man of medium height and build with a small woman sitting across from him at a restaurant. Clipped to the photographs was a typed page, signed by both the OSS and CIC commanders, explaining that Aamod and Harita Arora were Japanese spies. They would be arriving that evening at 1700 hours at the Howrah Train Station on the train from Nagpur. Captain Dubois and his agents were the only assets available to intercept the couple.

"Camille, we've got orders to capture this couple and bring them to the OSS detachment. They're Japanese spies," Dubois said. He handed her the photos and folder. "If we can't arrest them, we're to terminate them. Do you have a problem with that?"

"Not at all, sir. They're Japanese spies."

The last two weeks in Calcutta, the temperature had ranged between 98 degrees at night and 112 degrees in the afternoon. This afternoon was no different, and the two were uncomfortably hot in their taxi as it crossed the cantilevered bridge to Howrah Station. Captain Dubois gave Camille a brief history of the bridge and station.

"The old bridge, built in 1871, was torn down in 1938. Its engineers expected it to last only twenty-five years."

Camille did a quick calculation. "It was used for sixty-seven years."

"Yep. This new bridge was completed in 1941."

"What did the old bridge look like?"

"It was a four-hundred-foot pontoon bridge built in four separate one-hundred-foot sections. To make room for boats too large to pass under the pontoon bridge, the two central sections had to be moved aside. The old pontoon bridge carried more traffic than the London Bridge back in England."

"This bridge looks to be just as crowded with people, taxis, and trucks as the London Bridge," Camille said.

"Ah, you've been there."

"Yes, when I was sixteen."

Their conversation ended abruptly as a young Indian boy darted in front of the taxi and the driver braked hard. After the taxi moved on, Captain Dubois continued.

"Howrah Station is located on the west bank of the Hooghly River. The station is one of the divisional headquarters of East India Railways. It is four stories tall and one thousand feet in length, and with fifteen tracks, it is the largest train station in India."

Their taxi approached the station on Guiersen Road, stopping in front of one of the twenty-eight station doors. "Watch where you step. It can get pretty nasty in there," Captain Dubois said.

Upon entering the building, they had to walk carefully through the hundreds of people making their home on the marble floors of the station. Sanitation was nonexistent, and disgusting brown water was pooling throughout the station. Camille saw several children defecating in a dark corner.

Carrying luggage so as to look like ordinary travelers, they slowly made their way to the platform receiving the train from Nagpur. It was early. They eased through the crowd and stood near the first-class cars, waiting fifteen minutes before they recognized the Aroras exiting a car forty feet away. Due to the vast number of people, Captain Dubois had decided not to approach the couple or try to capture them in the station. He therefore let the Aroras pass, and then he and Camille turned and followed them out of the station, observing as they entered a car with a Great Eastern Hotel logo painted on its trunk and doors.

Captain Dubois hailed a taxi and followed the Aroras to the hotel on Old Court House Street, across the river and less than a mile from Howrah Station. After the couple entered the hotel, Captain Dubois and Camille exited their taxi and entered through the hotel door behind several couples from other taxis.

Dubois and Camille stood in line two couples behind the Aroras and listened carefully as the desk clerk called a porter over, told him their room number, and handed him the room key. Five minutes later, Dubois reached the desk and asked for a second-floor room near the Aroras. The desk clerk assumed that they were traveling with the Aroras and gave them a room two doors away.

After entering the room, Camille asked, "What's the plan?"

"I'm going to go downstairs and bribe one of the front-desk people to call the Aroras and tell them a complementary basket of fruit and a bottle of champagne will be delivered to their room. Then I'm coming back up here and changing into the waiter's uniform in my suitcase. While I'm gone, you need to change into the housekeeping uniform I put in your suitcase."

"Do you want me to enter behind you when you go in?"

"No, you'll act as my backup and stand in the doorway. Wear the hijab; it will hide some of your face. Otherwise, they might recognize you from the station."

"What about your face?"

"I'll add a mustache and spectacles. Plus, I won't be wearing my hat."

With that, Captain Dubois went back downstairs, returning a few minutes later with a basket of fruit, a bottle of champagne, and two tall stemmed glasses.

Fifteen minutes later, Captain Dubois, disguised as a British waiter, walked the two doors down from their room and knocked on the door of room 214. As soon as Aamod opened the door, Captain Dubois threw the basket of fruit and the bottle of champagne at him. Aamod tried to duck, but the oranges, grapes, and tangerines hit him in the face while the bottle dropped straight down and landed on his foot. The distraction lasted only a second, but it was long enough for Captain Dubois to grab the nine-millimeter pistol from the small of his back and aim it straight at Aamod's head.

"Hands in the air, Aamod," Dubois commanded. He quickly scanned the room for Harita.

Harita Arora was sitting on the far side of the bed when Captain Dubois pulled the pistol on her husband. She reacted quickly and grabbed her revolver from the nightstand, but Camille entered with her silenced nine millimeter and put a bullet in Harita's right shoulder before she had a chance to fire. Harita's gun dropped from her hand, and she collapsed on the bed.

After securing Aamod's and Harita's wrists and ankles, Camille put gags in their mouths. She then applied a makeshift bandage to Harita's shoulder to stop the bleeding and propped her up against the pillows she stacked at the headboard. Captain Dubois picked up the hotel phone and asked for a local number.

Colonel Ronnie Ray, the CIC detachment commander, picked up the phone on his desk.

"Colonel Ray."

"Ronnie, this is Richard. I have our friends secured. The lady is wounded," Captain Dubois said.

"I'll send an ambulance and four of my men to take them into custody."

After he put the phone down, Captain Dubois pulled a syringe and vial of the barbiturate sodium pentothal from his coat pocket and injected Aamod and Harita with a low dose of the serum. Within minutes, both spies were in a deep sleep.

The army ambulance arrived within thirty minutes, and four men with two stretchers entered the Great Eastern Hotel and rode the elevator to the second floor. The ambulance driver told the two clerks at the front desk that a man and his wife had committed suicide. He gave them the room number, 214, and told the clerks that the police had been notified. Thirty minutes later, two stretchers and four men exited the elevator and made their way to the ambulance. Behind them, Captain Dubois and Camille, both crying and holding handkerchiefs to their faces, walked through the lobby and out of the hotel, playing their part as the grieving friends.

The army ambulance drove the Aroras to one of the OSS detachment's holding facilities on the American base. Their individual cells were small and hot, barely ten by ten feet. There was an army cot in one corner and an enameled pot to relieve oneself in the other corner. It served as a grim reminder of their hopelessness.

For two days, the Aroras underwent interrogation. Harita broke first and gave the American agents everything they wanted to know. It took another day before Aamod talked, and it was only after the Americans cut him a deal not to execute him and his wife. After the OSS agents had extracted all the information they could from the Aroras, they were moved to the army stockade, where they would await trial and sentencing by an army tribunal.

Later in the evening, Colonel Ray sent a courier to the *Jacqueline* and delivered a message to Captain Dubois. He wanted to meet with the captain and his team in the OSS office the following afternoon at 1300 hours.

Colonel Ray was sitting at his desk going over the interrogation reports on the Aroras when Captain Dubois, Kathleen, and Camille were escorted into the room by a sergeant. The sergeant left and closed the door behind him.

"Thank you all for coming," Colonel Ray said. "We've extracted some interesting information from the Aroras about a Japanese submarine that will be rendezvousing with a fishing boat off the coast of India. The submarine is supposed to transfer two Japanese agents. The fishing boat will bring them up the Ganges River and then up the Hooghly River to Calcutta. The Aroras are supposed to meet up with the two agents and hunt down our team who took out the Nakada sisters. The Aroras had in their possession photographs of you, Jon, Miles, Henri, and your four female agents."

"That's not good," Dubois said.

"We also learned from intelligence sources in Japan that the Nakada sisters' father was a Japanese Navy admiral," Colonel Ray stated. "Their father's status in the military allowed the girls to attend the best schools and universities in Japan, despite the Japanese tradition of not educating women. They were superior students. Shortly after Pearl Harbor, the triplets entered the Japanese intelligence service, following in the footsteps of their older sister, Asami, an instructor at the intelligence academy in Hiroshima."

Colonel Ray handed Captain Dubois the comprehensive report on the Nakada sisters. He read the OSS report with keen interest as Camille looked over his shoulder and read.

In July 1944, the triplets deployed to India to take down the three Allied intelligence agents who were creating havoc behind Japanese lines. One of the agents, an American, had been given the name "Cobra" by a Kachin headman after stepping on and then killing a king-cobra snake with just his boot. The three sisters, Akemi, Akiko, and Akira, found the Allied team by tracking their suspected transportation, the luxury yacht *Anne Marie*, and photographing the suspected Allied agents in Ceylon.

During an attempt to assassinate Admiral Lord Louis Mountbatten, the supreme Allied commander of Southeast Asia, the triplets underestimated the cunning of the Allied team guarding Lord Mountbatten. All three sisters were killed in the attempt. The older sister had gone missing from Hiroshima and was assumed to be in or heading for Calcutta.

"So the Japs have sent their older sister after Jon," Camille said.

"It gets worse," Colonel Ray said. "They also have teams of intelligence agents searching for them in southern China, Malaya, and French Indochina. They believe Jon's team is responsible for the raids on the Japanese medical facilities in Canton and Singapore, as well as the death of one of their agents in Hong Kong."

"Sounds like they want our guys real bad-like," Kathleen said.

"What do you want us to do, Colonel?" Captain Dubois asked.

"We want you all to find the two spies coming to Calcutta and capture them. Colonel MacKenzie and I will have ten teams of Indian agents watching where the Ganges River empties into the Indian Ocean. We have twenty small fishing boats scattered in the ocean, watching for a submarine, and another ten pair of watchers along the Hooghly River and at the Port of Calcutta," Colonel Ray said.

"Not taking any chances, are you?"

"No. We want these people caught and dealt with."

"Can you tell us where our boys are now?" Camille asked.

Colonel Ray hesitated before saying, "Clark Field in the Philippines. They just got back from capturing another Japanese POW camp that was conducting medical experiments on Allied prisoners. They rescued and repatriated one hundred thirty-one prisoners. The Japs will be plenty pissed at them now because they destroyed a large supply of fleas infected with the bubonic plague that the Japs intended to disperse among our troops in Thailand."

"Good for them."

"I understand you made some modification to the *Anne Marie* over the last two months, Captain," Colonel Ray continued.

"Yes. After we took out the Nakada sisters, we changed the appearance of the *Anne Marie* so the Japs couldn't easily identify it. We went from two masts to a single one, constructed a facade around the smokestack and made it look bigger and sleeker, changed the color of the canvas sun cover on the fantail, added colored canvas to the side railings, and added a four-inch green-and-red stripe the length of the hull."

"Do you think it will fool the Japanese?"

"I sure as hell hope so!"

"Did you use a builder in Calcutta?"

"No. I had the repairs done at a boatbuilder's dock forty miles down-river. I wanted an isolated location to avoid scrutiny."

"I can't wait to see it. Did you change its name?"

"Yes, we did. It's now called the *Jacqueline*, after Kathleen's twin sister."

"Is it ready to put to sea?"

"It's ready when you need us, Colonel."

"Actually, I'd like you all to cruise down the river into the Indian Ocean for a few days and keep a sharp eye out for that fishing boat and Jap submarine. I would like you to take aboard two of my top agents; they need a break, and a cruise might relieve some of their stress. If you agree, I'll send them to the boat tomorrow morning. I would like for you all to stay out there until you hear from me."

"You don't think this cruise will put us in jeopardy? The Jap submarine captain might have a description of the *Jacqueline* and try to sink us."

"I'm sure this is a secret mission for the submarine. I don't think that they would risk sinking your boat. They want to remain hidden and not draw attention to themselves. We'll also have a navy destroyer and a frigate cruising in the area. I don't think they will be interested in doing anything but getting their spies to the rendezvous point and then skedaddling."

"I'll trust you on this one, but if we get sunk and die, I'm coming back to haunt your ass for the rest of your life."

"Ditto, for me," Kathleen said.

"Good luck. I'll see you when you get back."

CHAPTER 9

Clark Field, Luzon Island, Philippines

With their mission to Phetchaburi completed successfully, Jon and his team were ordered back to Clark Field in the Philippines. The 1,550-mile trip in the C-47 took close to twelve hours because they had to veer south over the South China Sea to avoid enemy fighters close to the French Indochina and Chinese coasts.

After they landed, they were met at the aircraft by a staff car driven by Colonel Jim Sage. The colonel gave them three days to rest before their next mission briefing. The time off was earned and sorely needed, but Jon and the others would never admit that they were exhausted. Though the clandestine work was extremely stressful, Jon didn't want the time off. He was eager to get back to work. He wanted to go after more Japanese biological- and chemical-experimentation facilities and wanted retribution against the Japanese physicians responsible for perpetrating atrocities on Allied prisoners. Colonel Sage, however, wouldn't budge on this; they needed time off, and he insisted they take it.

"When you come back, a colonel from the Pentagon should be here with your next mission," Colonel Sage said.

On his first day off, Jon found a Catholic church a little over a mile from the Clark Field main gate. He went to confession in the afternoon and attended the evening worship service, where he received Communion. The next day he returned and found a priest to talk to. Father Lupe Alvarado was in his sixties and had a warmth and kindness about him that Jon liked. Jon felt that he could speak openly with the priest.

"Father, during my last mission, I discovered the bodies of five American prisoners hanging from the trees where they had been burned to death by a flamethrower. Something inside me has changed...It's as if a switch has been flipped inside me. I'm consumed with revenge. I can hear a call for blood in my head from the dead Americans. They were so young. Young men who will never return home, who will never hug their mothers, wives, or children. I don't think I will ever forget that scene."

The priest listened to Jon and finally said, "Jon, your anger is a natural reaction to such atrocities. I have personally witnessed atrocities that the Japanese committed against my people after they invaded the Philippines. I had the same feelings as you. I wanted all Japanese dead, too; revenge is a natural human reaction, even for a priest."

Father Alvarado explained he had to pray for months before he felt the pain, anger, rage, and hatred lift from his heart. He counseled Jon about the evil and heinous crimes and atrocities that had been inflicted upon captives since time began. Only time and prayer, Father Lupe told him, would heal him of these feelings. Until the war was over, he should use those emotions for good.

"Rescue more POWs and bring them home, Jon," Father Alvarado said. "Continue doing what you do best and help shorten this war. God will forgive you for what you do to accomplish your missions. Yours is a holy cause."

The three days went by fast, and when the four agents walked into the G-2 offices, Colonel Norm Hayward, one of the Pentagon colonels that delivered their mission tasking, was having coffee and talking to Colonel Sage.

"Gentlemen," Colonel Hayward said, "it's good to see you again."

Colonel Hayward had arrived that morning, and after flying for nearly ninety hours in six different aircraft, he looked tired, and his uniform was disheveled.

"Norm, you look like hell," Jon stated.

"I'm sure you wouldn't fare much better if you'd flown four days from Washington to get here."

"Frankly, I'd probably look a lot worse. They don't give ordinary GIs like me the VIP treatment."

"Are you kidding? I got bumped by a wounded army private in San Francisco. He was heading home to Honolulu."

"Colonel Hayward is going to his quarters to rest and get cleaned up," Colonel Sage said. "He'll give you your mission briefing tomorrow morning at 0900 hours. In the meantime, I need you all to complete your mission reports from your last mission and then go over them with me."

Twenty-four hours went by fast, and Colonel Heyward was still tired the next day. He entered the briefing room just as Jon, George, Miles, and Henri concluded the briefing on their last mission.

"Don't let me interrupt you," Colonel Heyward said.

Colonel Sage stated, "Just finished."

"Good. Let's get started before I fall asleep standing up."

Colonel Hayward pulled a map out of his briefcase and pinned it to the wall to the left of their table. He explained that army intelligence had suspected for some time that there was a Japanese POW camp in Swatow, China, conducting either biological or chemical experiments on the Allied prisoners. The information Jon and his team had sent G-2 by coded message from Phetchaburi had confirmed their worst fears.

"Over three hundred Allied prisoners are interred in Swatow. Most of them are American sailors and airmen who survived their ships being sunk or their aircraft being shot down. The facility encompasses nearly fifteen acres. At least sixty Japanese guards, along with medical personnel, are at the camp. And according to our Chinese informants, the camp commandant and his men are brutal as hell."

"That is a lot of Japanese firepower and a lot of space to cover, Colonel," Jon stated. "We'll need three days for observing the camp and planning our best infiltration areas. To take a camp of that size, we'll need at least three hundred resistance fighters, and that's if there are no other Japanese infantry regiments close by."

"We've come to the same conclusion. Our Chinese agents are telling us there are three Japanese divisions, or about sixty thousand soldiers, stationed in and around the city of Swatow. Two divisions of infantry and armor form an arc around the city that extends three miles out from the edge of the city. The third division is guarding the Swatow Bomber Base, which is four miles northeast of the city and six miles north of the river where a sampan will drop you off. The POW camp is located five miles east of the airdrome."

"What's the goal of this mission?" George asked.

"Our goal is to take the camp and get our POWs into the hands of one of the Chinese armies on the north fork of the Hanjiang River, northwest of Swatow. You'll be supported by a regiment of two thousand Chinese soldiers. Approximately seventeen hundred soldiers will attack the airfield with mortars and light armor. This should provide enough diversion for you and the three hundred Chinese soldiers at your disposal to take the camp."

"How will we be inserted?" Miles asked.

"The USS *Coho* is patrolling off Luzon. She'll take you to a rendezvous point five miles off the Chinese coast. The *Coho* will meet up with a sampan, which will take you up the north fork of the Hanjiang River. From there you will be met by one of our Chinese American OSS agents, Captain Daniel Wang. Wang has been in China since 1942. He will have three hundred Chinese soldiers under his command for this operation. In the folders on the table are the details on the POW camp and the Japanese troop positions around the city and the airfield."

"Colonel, with sixty thousand Japanese soldiers in the area, don't you think this is an awful risk we will be taking?" Jon asked.

"Yes, it is, but it will be totally unexpected. Do you want me to give the mission to another team of agents?"

Jon looked at Miles, Henri, and George. All shook their heads; they wanted to go. "Looks like we're the ones for the job, sir."

Jon and his team studied the information for two days before they boarded the navy PBY taking them to the USS *Coho*.

Once again they were greeted on the *Coho* by Captain Royce Janca and his XO, Lieutenant Commander Chad Spivey. They were given the same berths that they had slept in their last time on board. After they stored their gear, they met Captain Janca in the dining room next to the ship's galley.

"Well, I see you all are at it again," Captain Janca stated. "From what I know about China and Japanese troop strengths, it will be a tough mission."

"Hopefully we'll get a lot of help from our Chinese brothers," Jon said.

"I hope to hell there's at least a division or two. The Japs are really entrenched along the coast. We'll be dropping you near Swatow, which has the third-largest port in China. The Japanese invaded Swatow in 1939 and secured the harbor. Since early this year, only half of the ships leaving Japan have been able to make it through the East China Sea to supply the Japanese position in southern China. Some of those ships are *Sunosaki*- and *Ashizuri*-class tankers that carry aviation gasoline to Japanese airfields on the coast. In fact, we'll probably run across several coming out of the Strait of Formosa heading north."

"We should be OK, Captain," George said. "The Japanese are getting their butts kicked all over the South Pacific. They're probably short on food and ammunition and pretty well demoralized. They won't be at their peak in preparedness, and except for the higher-ranking officers, they probably don't give a rat's ass by now and just want to get home safe. This can give us the edge we need."

"Will you torpedo the ships you come across on our way to Swatow?" Miles asked.

"No, we're under strict orders not to engage. The crew is pissed, of course. They want to sink everything that comes by, but that's the nature of these covert missions. Secrecy is paramount."

"Yes, engaging the enemy could compromise our mission. Maybe you'll get a chance to sink some enemy ships after you drop us off," Jon remarked.

"I've heard a lot of rumors about you and your team. Some people say you guys have captured several POW camps and freed over a thousand Allied prisoners. Others say you've kidnapped important Japanese officers. Whatever you're doing, I'm sure a lot of GIs are grateful."

"That's those hotshot OSS guys. They're always bragging about their missions," Jon said.

"OK, I get it; everything is top secret. Thanks anyway for helping our boys."

After Captain Janca left, Henri turned to Jon. "So, who's been talking?"

"Probably some of the POWs we rescued. It's hard to stop the scuttlebutt, regardless of how many times you tell them it's top secret."

"Let's pray it hasn't compromised us."

"Hell, after all the camps we've taken and what we did to shut down their spy rings, I'm surprised they don't have the whole damn Japanese Army after us!"

Everyone in the group laughed.

CHAPTER 10

Swatow, China

After the USS *Coho* rendezvoused with the thirty-foot sampan, it took the team another twelve hours to reach their destination. The weather was foul, and rain was coming down steadily when they arrived at the large bend in the river, just north of the village of Hantou. Shortly after the sampan touched the sandy shore, Jon brought out his flashlight and flashed four dots and two dashes; he repeated the process every fifteen minutes for over two hours before receiving a reply of three dashes and three dots.

"Time to go," Jon said. He then jumped over the side of the sampan and headed inland.

Captain Daniel Wang emerged out of the heavy downpour and introduced himself to the four agents. As he walked them off the sandy beach, the sampan was pushed back into the river and paddled away, lost instantly in the continuous downpour.

The group followed quietly behind Captain Wang. They weaved in and out of bamboo-forested areas and across a myriad of dikes holding back the water of several hundred acres of rice fields. It took the team close to three hours to walk to a small cottage four miles northeast of the river. Once inside, Captain Wang explained that the house had been abandoned by Baptist missionaries after the Japanese invaded. The Baptist faith was popular in this region, and once a month the Baptist minister would slip back into the area and hold services and serve Communion to his parishioners.

To Jon, the house smelled of cardamom, possibly used as a medicinal by the absent missionary, and the dampness accentuated the smell. Despite being bereft of furnishings and color, the house did not leak, and Jon was glad to be out of the downpour.

"How far are we from the POW camp?" Jon asked.

"Three miles," Wang answered.

"What's the terrain like?" Miles asked.

"We are on the edge of a heavily forested range of hills. The southernmost part of the range begins fifty yards behind the house. We can make our way east through the forest and reconnoiter the camp from as close as twenty yards from the outer fence."

"What about Japanese patrols?" Henri asked.

"You won't find any Japanese patrols in the woods, because of a local superstition that the woods are haunted. The Japanese are superstitious and will not go near the forest."

"What about the Chinese soldiers? Will they go into the woods?" Jon asked.

"Yes, that's where the three hundred Chinese soldiers I command are camped. Shortly after I arrived here in 1942, I created the superstition. I saw the forest as a potential resource for what we do. After I scared half a dozen or so locals, the story of the haunted forest took hold. The Chinese love to tell stories and played it up big to the Japanese, who are rather gullible when it comes to spirits."

"Rather ingenious, mate," Miles stated.

"Certainly is," Jon agreed. "Where are your troops bivouacked?"

"On the north side of the hill. The Chinese have ten divisions to the northwest, so the Japanese like to stay close to Swatow; they don't want to start an engagement that might bring those divisions into play and endanger their bomber base. The base had been flying bombing missions every other day until last week. I suspect they're low on fuel and munition because we haven't seen any convoys come in from the harbor.

"The Japanese bombers' primary targets have been the sixty thousand troops of the US Tenth Army, which established an eight-mile beachhead on Okinawa, and the fourteen hundred ships supporting them. They've also been bombing the fighter base the Allies established at Iwo Jima."

"When can we scout the camp?" George asked.

"I assume you want to scout the camp during the day and also at night. Why don't you rest now and we'll go out later this afternoon? The rain should lighten up by then. I've got agents posted throughout the area and around the house. My men will let us know if any patrols are headed this way."

By the time the group left the house later that afternoon, the rain had slowed to a drizzle, and visibility had improved to a quarter of a mile. When they entered the forest, Jon discovered the hill was steeper than it looked and was covered with a wide variety of conifers and a few deciduous trees, mostly maple.

They climbed four hundred feet at a steep incline before Captain Wang turned them west. Two hours later, they came to a flat outcropping of rocks approximately twenty-five yards in length. At the center of the outcropping, they climbed another fifty feet upward to a well-hidden cave. The entrance was narrow and only large enough for one man to walk through. Once inside, however, the team found that the cave opened up into a large cavern that ran sixty feet back into the mountain before hooking right for another thirty feet. At the back of the cave, a spring provided fresh water, which pooled in a small depression in the floor before running off into a crack in the rock.

"We'll hole up here until you're ready to scout the camp. You can view any part of the camp from the entrance of the cave without being seen. I'll start a fire to give us some warmth."

"Won't the smoke give our position away?" Miles asked.

"There's a natural flue that runs straight up through the rock and out on the north side of the hill, most likely created by earthquakes. The smoke escapes there."

"Do the Japs know about the cave?" Jon asked.

"No, they won't step foot onto the mountain."

"I'm glad you started the superstition."

"To make it realistic, I rigged bedsheets to a thin wire cable that I set up between two large maple trees. When I discovered a local wandering into the woods, I had one of my men pull the sheets across a hundred-foot stretch of the forest while another man hid up the hill, made noises, and threw stones down the hill. On more than one occasion, I scared the hell out of the men and women who frequented the area to pick mushrooms; after that they did not return. We usually ran the scam early in the morning, when the fog was still heavy, or late in the evening, when heavy shadows blanketed the forest. From twenty-five yards away, the sheets look like a ghost flying through the trees."

"I bet you had a hell of a good time back home at Halloween," George stated.

"Yeah, I like a good practical joke."

Another hour passed before the rain ceased and the visibility cleared, allowing them to see for nearly a mile from their hidden vantage point. Jon looked through his binoculars and was amazed the Japs would build a POW camp this close to a range of hills. He surmised they thought the hills would act as a natural barrier that would keep the Chinese away, especially after hearing the stories of the haunted forest.

"Are there any creeks running from the hill to the camp?" Jon asked.

"Yes. Two running creeks lie at the base of the hill, a half mile on each side of our position. They run south on either side of the camp. You can get as close as twenty yards to the camp on either creek. The Japanese use them as a source for their water."

"Have you checked them for booby traps or mines?" Henri questioned.

"I've been through both. As of two days ago, neither are mined or booby-trapped. The creeks are rather deep in places. The Japs use these areas for bathing when the weather is warm. They are both easily traversed."

"What about patrols?" Jon questioned.

"The only patrols I've seen are on the inside of the fence; six guards make the rounds day and night. During cold weather, three soldiers drive the perimeter in a truck, with two in the cab and one on the machine gun mounted on a bar above the truck's cab."

"You've done your homework," George said.

"Henri, Miles," Jon said, "I want you all to take the creek on the west side. Scout and sketch the camp and determine which huts belong to the Japanese guards and which ones belong to the prisoners. Identify the headquarters, the chow hall, and the medical facilities. Daniel will escort us down the hill. George and I will take the creek to the east. We'll also scout the southern perimeter."

Jon turned to Captain Wong. "I want you to wait in the forest at the bottom of the hill. If we're discovered, use your suppressed rifle to help us out. If you decide you can't help us, bug out and keep watch for us at the house."

Jon finished, folded the sketch of the POW camp in his hand, and said, "Let's get ready to move out."

The men moved to gather their gear. Before the agents left the missionary's house, they used their war kits to apply coloring to their faces, necks, and hands to make them look more Chinese. They also streaked their faces with brown and green makeup so that their facial features would blend in with the vegetation around the creek.

Before leaving the Philippines, Colonel Hayward told Jon that he would also have B-25 bomber support on the mission and gave him the details. Heyward instructed Jon not to tell the other members of his team. Jon's only thoughts were, *Good God, does he suspect a security leak in my team! No way, but I'd better follow his orders. If I don't and the colonel hears about it, he will tear me a new asshole.* Jon didn't like keeping the others in the dark, but for security reasons he did as the colonel instructed.

Only Jon and Captain Wang knew about the twenty American B-25s that would be attacking the bomber base in support of the 1,700 Chinese troops. The bombers would be in contact with Captain Wang and would let him know when they were twenty minutes out. Wang would signal the Chinese, and they would attack with mortars and machine guns to draw the Japanese into their defensive positions on the base perimeter. When the B-25s arrived, they would drop incendiary and napalm bombs to destroy the bombers on the ground as well as the Japanese defenders.

The creek on the east side of the camp was narrow and curved southeast for a quarter mile before edging back toward the prisoner camp; in several places, the banks were over twenty feet high.

Jon and George made their way through the creek, stopping several times to hide from Chinese farmers working in one of the fields to the east. After forty minutes, they reached the midsection of the camp.

"Not much activity on a rainy day," George whispered.

"I imagine activity will pick up soon; it's getting close to mealtime. Then we'll have a chance to count the number of Japs in the compound."

Jon and George moved another hundred yards south before they made their way up the creek's bank and nestled into a thicket of brush beneath a large evergreen that was leaning at a forty-five-degree angle over the creek, its roots exposed by decades of erosion caused by the runoff from the hills above.

After thirty minutes, guards began to herd prisoners from their quarters into a line where the cooks had pots of rice, vegetables, and hot tea set on several tables. Jon saw two lines forming, one for the Japanese guards and another, twenty yards away, for the prisoners. Once served, the prisoners quietly returned to their huts to eat. Several prisoners caught talking were ruthlessly beaten by the guards.

Two Japanese trucks had passed the southern section of fence twice since Jon and George had taken up their position. Jon counted six guard towers around the complex, which was surrounded by a ten-foot-high barbed-wire fence. In the middle of the compound, there was a smaller fence with a gate, separating the far northern portion of the camp from the rest. Jon surveyed this area, noticing several acres of last summer's garden and half a dozen goats grazing in another fenced-off area.

Someone is getting fresh vegetables in the summer and goat milk, and I bet it isn't the prisoners, Jon thought.

Jon tapped George on the shoulder and motioned for him to follow. The duo slid back to the creek bottom and continued south for another half mile, to where the majority of the camp buildings were located. They ducked behind another fallen tree just before two Japanese soldiers carrying large buckets walked to a part of the creek twenty-five yards south of them. After making their way down a man-made entrance to the creek, they dipped their buckets into the water and then carried their burdens back to the camp.

"I bet you they're getting water for the commandant's bath tonight," George said, chuckling.

"You practicing to take Bob Hope's job?"

"No, just trying to get rid of the butterflies in my stomach. This is scary stuff."

Jon only nodded. With the afternoon drawing to a close, they saw a squad of men march in front of a building with a flagpole flying the Japanese flag. At a nod from an officer, one of the men lifted his bugle to his lips and played the Japanese version of retreat while another two men lowered the flag. Out of the corner of his eye, Jon saw a single soldier on the covered porch of the building next to the flagpole. He stood at attention, saluting the Japanese flag.

Obviously the camp commandant, and probably a lieutenant colonel, based on the size of the compound, Jon thought.

Jon and George made their way back up the creek to where Captain Wang was hiding in the forest just before the sun went below the horizon. By the time they got back to the cave, Miles and Henri were already there. Jon briefed them, and Henri added the details they provided to the sketch he had drawn of the camp.

"After we eat, I want you two to scout the east side of the camp, where most of the quarters are located," Jon told them. "A mile down the creek, the wire fence is only sixty feet from the creek bed. After dark, crawl up to the wire, test it to see how rusted it is, and find a location where we can enter unobserved."

"Captain, how close is the nearest bridge to the camp?" Jon asked.

"About half a mile south of the camp. You can get there by going down the west creek. What have you got in mind?"

"Since it's the only access to the camp from across the river, we need to mine the road at the approach to the bridge and place charges under the bridge. Once we blow up the bridge, it will stop any reinforcements from getting to the camp."

CHAPTER 11

Swatow POW Camp, China

When they returned to the cave the next day, they met a dozen of Captain Wang's Chinese officers and enlisted platoon leaders. Captain Wang spent two hours with the soldiers, going over the attack plan. Miles and Henri went back to the east creek to monitor the daytime activities at the camp. Jon and George went out to reconnoiter from the west creek. After two hours, Jon and George moved farther south and checked out the bridge. They spent all day gathering information, returning to the cave as night fell.

When they returned to the house, Jon made minor changes to the entry point into the camp, moving it twenty yards farther south to a natural blind spot for two of the guard towers. Captain Wang briefed the Chinese soldiers on the change and told them to have everyone in position on the mountain by midnight. After the soldiers left, Jon and Henri grabbed their backpacks, which were filled with explosives, and made their way back to the bridge. Only a small sliver of a waning moon provided light, but Jon and Henri had practiced the routine in the dark before deploying. They could complete the task blindfolded.

Two hours before the raid, Jon and Henri planted two mines on the road ten yards to the south of the bridge. Two more were placed just one yard from the bridge. Jon hoped that the first vehicle down the road would contain the officer or ranking noncommissioned officer of the responding troops. Confusion and lack of coordinated action would result once the Japanese leadership was out of the way.

Henri set six C-3 charges along the underside of the forty-foot bridge, while Jon ran the detonator cord. Across the bridge entrance, Jon placed a strip of contact fuses that would activate the detonators and blow the bridge once a vehicle crossed the strip. After their work was completed, Jon and Henri made their way to the small creek and returned to the cave where Miles and George waited.

Twenty minutes later, and much to Jon's surprise, the three hundred Chinese soldiers made their way down the hill and positioned themselves on either side of the rock outcropping. From Jon's experience, the Chinese never arrived on time. He deliberately chose not to mention this to Captain Wang.

At 0100 hours, Jon and George made their way to the southern end of the east creek, while Miles and Henri journeyed to the southern end of the creek to the west. A half hour later, Captain Wang had his soldiers in position on either side of the camp. Captain Wang notified Jon's team that his men were in place by making the call of a whiskered screech owl, an old Navajo warrior trick. The haunting call sounded like a soft, smooth tone of Morse code floating on the wind. Wang had learned the owl call from the grandfather of a Navajo friend as a teen at summer camp in Arizona.

Lieutenant Yoshihiro Hayashi stood outside the commander's office after performing his night-duty rounds of the camp. Swatow was his first assignment as an officer in the Imperial Japanese Army, and he performed his nightly duties with the vigor of a young officer.

He stood in the light from the office window and reread the letter from his mother describing the Allied firebombing of Tokyo. Hayashi's mother and father had watched in awe and horror as two-hundred and eighty B-29 bombers dropped 1,700 tons of incendiary bombs on the urban areas of Tokyo. Their house, situated in the hills to the northeast, had not been hit, and the fires had not reached them. However, many sections of the city had been engulfed by the fire, killing over one hundred thousand residents.

Lieutenant Hayashi finished brewing his second pot of tea and thought about the girl that his father had arranged for him to marry. His bride-to-be, Chiyoko, was a gorgeous, petite young woman; she had just turned seventeen. He had met her before he embarked on his assignment to China. They were to be married on his return to Tokyo in August.

Several small thumps in the distance, which sounded like antiaircraft fire, disturbed the lieutenant's thoughts. Seconds later, a series of loud booms broke his concentration as Chinese mortar shells landed inside the air base to the south. An even larger boom followed as a shell ignited one of the bombers that was loaded with bombs for its morning mission. Lieutenant Hayashi hurried outside the building and stared southward; the sky was lit with a red hue. More explosions were seen as a second wave of mortar shells hit the base.

The perimeter guards of the POW camp were distracted by the explosions. As the explosions continued to the south, Captain Wang's scouts cut the barbed wire and entered the compound. The first two scouts took out their guards easily, but as the third scout crept up behind the remaining guard, he stepped on a rotted stick, and it snapped loudly. The guard turned to see the Chinese scout rushing him. The Japanese soldier fired his rifle a millisecond before the scout could strike with his knife. Henri was ten yards behind and watched as the scout went down. He quickly fired his nine-millimeter Beretta, taking out the Japanese guard. The sound of the mortars in the distance drowned out the cry from the sentry's lips and the report of the pistol.

Several officers, including the commandant, stirred from their quarters and joined Lieutenant Hayashi outside the commandant's office. The commandant spoke first.

"An American bombing raid on the base. Nothing for us to worry about."

He was about to say something else when another series of louder explosions erupted from the bomber base. The first group of five B-25 Mitchell bombers had released their bombs, guided by the fires caused from the mortar attack. Five minutes later, another series of explosions occurred as the second wave of B-25s roared over the base. The third and fourth waves of B-25s were also spaced at five-minute intervals.

As the commandant turned to look back toward the prisoner huts, he noticed Lieutenant Hayashi fall to the ground, followed by another officer. The commandant crouched down, thinking that shrapnel was falling and hitting his men. As he moved to tend to Lieutenant Hayashi, he heard several aircraft in the darkness overhead, followed by a series of explosions that rocked the camp.

The commandant turned to his right to see the three enlisted quarters erupt in flames from a large explosion. He first thought one of the American aircraft had dropped a couple of bombs on the camp until he noticed two large groups of Chinese soldiers rushing across the compound. The commandant drew his pistol, but before he could fire, he heard the sound of a pistol cocking behind him. He spun around and saw a man with a camouflaged face pointing an automatic weapon at his head.

"Not a good night for you, Colonel," George said in Japanese before squeezing the trigger.

George turned toward the Japanese quarters as several soldiers came running out of the burning building screaming, their clothes burned off their bodies. They were quickly dispatched by the Chinese soldiers. In his peripheral vison, George caught a glimpse of Jon throwing a grenade; an instant later, a Japanese patrol vehicle erupted in flames.

Miles, Henri, Captain Wang, and a group of Chinese soldiers made their way to the prisoner barracks and told the POWs to stay inside until the camp was secure.

A loud explosion erupted at the bridge a quarter mile south of the compound. Jon looked in the distance and saw a Japanese troop carrier engulfed in flames. He saw a second vehicle swerve past the truck and make it onto the bridge. It blew apart when the C-3 detonated and destroyed the bridge.

Thirty minutes after the raid began, the Chinese soldiers had eliminated all of the remaining Japanese resistance and captured three Japanese physicians. Jon walked over to where George stood. He was reading from a ledger near a blazing guard barracks.

"What did you find?" Jon asked.

"From what I'm reading in these logbooks, they are experimenting with smallpox and skin burns," George stated. "The last of the smallpox victims were cremated three days ago along with the burn victims. It looks as if they were getting ready to shut down their operation."

"How were the prisoners burned?"

"The log explains that they would tie the prisoners to a pole and hit them with flamethrowers."

Captain Wang walked to where Jon was standing and asked, "What do you want to do with the Japanese physicians?"

"Turn them over to the Chinese and tell them that they tortured and killed Chinese prisoners with flamethrowers," Jon stated.

"They'll be killed for certain," Captain Wang said.

"After what they did to our troops, do you think I give a damn?"

"I'll take care of it, sir," Captain Wang replied. "Do you want all of the documents we found in the medical facilities?"

"Yes, get those to the nearest OSS detachment and have them flown to Clark Field. After you finish your search, destroy the medical facility."

George knew what the Chinese soldiers would do to the prisoners. He had seen it in western China close to the border with Burma. They would place a dozen razor-sharp punji sticks upright in the ground and break an arm or a leg on each of the Japanese physicians. The physicians would then be tied to stakes in the ground and spread-eagled over the punji sticks. The physicians would have to hold themselves above the razor-sharp sticks. Eventually, they would tire and not be able to hold themselves up any longer. When they gave up, they would impale themselves on the punji sticks. The Chinese would then laugh and say that they committed hara-kiri.

George did not have any compassion for these men and would not regret their deaths after what they had done to the Allied prisoners. However, he was concerned about Jon. It wasn't like him to be so casual about death. *Something has changed him*, George thought.

Jon walked over to where Miles was kneeling. Henri was sitting on the ground and leaning against the camp's flagpole, his right pant leg soaked with blood. Miles had cut away the material of Henri's pant leg and tied a tourniquet around the leg, and he was now applying a sterile bandage to his wound.

"I think it's a through and through," Miles said, "but I can't really tell in this light. It doesn't appear that the bullet severed a major artery or broke any bones,"

As Miles was about to inject Henri with morphine, Henri held up his hand.

"Not now. Wait until we get on the boat. I want to be coherent in case we run into trouble," Henri stated.

"All right, mate, but it's going to hurt like hell. Try not to move around too much. I don't want you to start leaking blood all over that beautiful dressing."

"Let's rig a stretcher and round up our guys. We need to get everyone out of here," Jon stated.

"The senior Allied prisoner, Colonel Ben Helton, is coordinating with his men. There are twelve that will need to be carried out," George said. "Thirteen, with Henri."

"Jon, an additional two hundred Chinese soldiers have arrived to help us evacuate the men," Captain Wang said. "It's time for me to get the four of you back to the river and onto the sampan. I have assigned four soldiers to carry Henri."

As they were about to pick up Henri and begin moving out, a British officer walked up to the group.

"Major Ballangy, how the hell are you? We haven't seen you in over a year," Jon said.

"I've got a change of orders for you, Agent Preston."

"What kind of change?"

"I have orders to get you and your team to Nan-hsiung Airfield. You and your group are needed in Calcutta, and apparently so am I."

"Did they mention if it was urgent or just a change in plans?"

"Nothing in the message."

Jon nodded at Henri and smiled. "Looks like we're going to fly home. However, I think the war might be over for you."

"In your dreams. I'll be back in no time. I'll take that morphine now. It's probably going to be a rough trip to the airfield."

CHAPTER 12

Calcutta, India

The trek to Nan-hsiung and the flight to Calcutta took eleven days. Jon, Miles, Henri, George, and Major Ballangy arrived intact but exhausted from the trip. Army doctors at Nan-hsing wanted to hospitalize Henri and keep him there, but Jon wouldn't allow it. There were too many enemy agents in China, and Jon didn't want to place Henri in jeopardy. Henri was patched up and given heavy doses of antibiotics because an infection had set in by the time they reached Nan-hsiung.

When they landed in Calcutta, the newly promoted SOE commander, Colonel Michael MacKenzie, met the group as they came off the aircraft.

"Good God, you guys are filthy," Colonel MacKenzie said.

The colonel then walked over to where Henri lay on a stretcher, bent down on one knee, and clasped his hand firmly. "It's good to have you back, Henri. You all right?"

"I'm doing fine, Colonel. My wound got infected on the trek from the POW camp, but the army doctors dosed me heavily with antibiotics at Nan-hsiung, and the nurses kept the wound clean during the flight. I'll be dancing in no time."

Colonel MacKenzie then stood and told Henri he would visit him in the hospital later that afternoon. He told Jon and Miles they could take the next seven days off.

MacKenzie then turned to George Linka, "I'm meeting with you and Colonel Kenneth Taylor next Tuesday at 1500 hours at the OSS detachment. I'll catch you then." Colonel MacKenzie said.

Jon walked toward the Base Operations Building, where the familiar faces of Corporal Tommy Ray and Sergeant Ed Slater greeted him with two large grins.

"Wow, you guys got promoted; congratulations are in order," Jon said.

"Your wife called and told me when you all were landing," Corporal Ray said. "I've kept everyone's tents clean, and there are fresh sheets on all the bunks, sir."

Jon, Miles, Henri, and George used their quarters in the American tent city when they had to work and sleep at odd hours or when they were on standby to deploy on another mission. This happened with almost all of the missions they planned.

"Thank you," Jon said. "I'll catch up with you all in a couple of days and bring you a care package. You still want American whiskey, or would you like some scotch and gin this time?"

Corporal Ray conferred with his friend and turned back to Jon. "We'll stick with the American stuff, sir."

"All right. Now, if you'll excuse me, Camille is rather eager to say hello."

Camille ran to Jon and hugged him for nearly a minute before releasing him. "God, you're dirty, but I'll take you regardless."

Camille released Jon and walked over to Miles and Henri. She hugged Miles and welcomed him back. She knelt down and kissed Henri, who was now sitting upright on his stretcher. "Thanks for taking care of Jon."

Camille rose and faced Jon and George. "Captain Dubois is taking us downriver on a cruise. Henri, once you are cleared from the hospital later this evening, we expect you and your family to join us. Colonel MacKenzie has already made arrangements for an army nurse to join us on the cruise. George, I expect you to join us on the *Jacqueline*; there are three single ladies who would like the presence of your company."

"The *Jacqueline*?" Jon asked.

"We changed the name of the boat. I'll tell you all about it on the way there."

During lunch, Camille briefed Jon and the others on why Captain Dubois had changed the name and looks of the boat while they were gone.

"Good grief, I thought the Japs would have given up by now," Jon said.

"Apparently not. The OSS discovered the triplets were the daughters of a high-ranking Japanese admiral. The Japs have sent another team to Calcutta to look for you, as well as teams to China, Malaya, and Thailand. They're looking mostly in the vicinity of POW camps, according to the intercepts that were decoded in Honolulu," Camille said.

"I guess we're lucky we hit them where they didn't expect us on our last two missions, but I don't suppose they can cover all the camps. Their resources are already spread pretty thin."

"It gets more complicated. The triplets have an older sister in the intelligence service, and according to the OSS, she's gone missing from the intelligence school where she was teaching."

Jon thought carefully for a minute. "I wouldn't be too concerned, Camille. She probably looks like her sisters and will be easy to spot."

Not buying Jon's attempt to keep her from worrying, she shrugged her shoulders and changed the subject.

"Can you tell me where you all went on your last mission?"

"A location in China that was not heavily fortified. A place we would be least likely to be seen or heard from and where the Japs would never expect us to hit."

"Did you rescue more POWs?"

"Yes."

"How many?"

"Over three hundred."

"Good Lord, the Japanese must really be angry at you now. How could you possibly rescue three hundred POWs?"

"We had a lot of help from our Chinese friends and the Army Air Corps," Jon replied.

The *Jacqueline* returned to Calcutta the following Tuesday. After they docked, George and Kathleen Lauren left to run some errands, one of which was to meet with Colonel MacKenzie and Colonel Taylor at the OSS detachment. Once they had departed, Captain Dubois sat down next to Miles and Henri in the dining area.

"Later this evening we'll meet back here to discuss our next mission," Captain Dubois said. "Henri, you'll be working planning and logistics until you're cleared for combat duty. A staff car is available to take your wives home before our meeting; it will return to take you home after we're through. Now, everyone, enjoy the rest of the day on the boat."

At 1700 hours, an army staff car picked up Henri's wife and drove her to their cottage on a hill overlooking the Hooghly River. For security purposes, a separate vehicle picked up Miles's wife and drove her to another cottage two houses away. Unknown to either family, Colonel MacKenzie had assigned Kachin rangers to guard their houses around the clock. The cottages were located in a heavily wooded area, and the rangers watched from well-hidden posts.

After all the civilians left, Captain Dubois started the meeting. "Our next assignment is here in Calcutta. Colonel MacKenzie and Colonel Taylor, the new OSS detachment commander, put me in charge of the planning and command and control of this mission. Our job is to find and take down the two Japanese agents smuggled into Calcutta over a week ago. They're here to find and kill the agent they know only as Cobra, which is the name given to Jon by the Kachin tribesmen after the raid on the Hintok Bridge nearly a year ago. My guess is that the older sister of the Nakada triplets is looking to avenge the death of her sisters.

"The OSS has interrogated the two Japanese agents they apprehended two months ago. The agents revealed they were to meet a second couple being inserted into India. The captured couple didn't know the other couple's arrival date, but navy intelligence in Honolulu intercepted a message sent to the Japanese consulate in Calcutta. The message arrived only two days before a Japanese submarine was scheduled to insert the second couple off the coast of India. Our navy never had a chance to intercept the submarine."

"Did the message give their names?" Jon asked.

"No, but the message referred to the team as the Futago Fèng Huáng, which means 'twin male and female phoenixes.' Since the Japanese are highly superstitious, they probably gave the team this name because they thought it would empower their agents with supernatural abilities."

"Who captured the agents?"

"The OSS passed the information to me. Camille and I captured the Malayan couple after they entered Calcutta and checked into a hotel."

"So this is why you changed the looks and name of the boat?" Miles asked.

"Just one of the reasons, but it's also why we moved the boat to this hidden location. We may want to use the *Jacqueline* on other clandestine missions, and we don't want the Japanese to be able to identify it."

"Good luck with that, Captain," Miles said.

"It's not the only luxury yacht in India."

"I know, Captain, but it's the only one sailing the Indian Ocean. We didn't see a single yacht while we were out this week."

"I've noticed this too. I've already talked to the new OSS unit commander, Colonel Taylor, and asked him to see what he can do to remedy the situation."

"Was the OSS able to track down the second couple?" Jon asked.

"They tracked them up the Ganges River but lost them in the dark before they reached Calcutta. We have a photo of them taken from long range, but it's too grainy to identify them. We believe they are both Eurasian."

"That's not a lot of help, Captain. Ten percent of the population is Eurasian."

"Henri is going to help the ladies develop a plan of attack to track down the new Japanese agents. The three of you are being sent on a different mission."

"Do you think sending us out while assassins are in town is wise?"

"Frankly, I do not. I would prefer the three of you working with the ladies, but General Marshall thinks otherwise. There's a colonel inbound from Washington. He'll be here tomorrow."

"I've never refused a mission, but I guess there is always a first time."

"Jon, you can't refuse a special mission. It's probably a mission to free more POWs, saving more lives," Camille said.

"Camille, you ladies have only limited experience in catching spies. I'll talk to whomever the Pentagon is sending with our mission tasking and see if he can do anything. The least they can do is to provide you all with more OSS or CIC agents to work with," Jon said.

CHAPTER 13

Calcutta, India

A day later, Jon and Miles were invited to meet in Colonel Ronnie Ray's office at the CIC detachment. His office looked sterile; there were no photos on the walls, and his desk was bare. Colonel Ray guided them into the briefing room, where they were greeted by Colonel Ronnie Masek, who had just flown in from Washington. Colonel Masek was a tall, lean, and always-smiling Texan who had graduated from West Point in 1928. Jon looked around the room when he arrived and noticed Colonel MacKenzie and Lieutenant Colonel Linka were already there.

"You all are the last to arrive, so we can shut the door and get started," Colonel Ray remarked.

Colonel Masek walked to the front of the room and pulled down a large map of Asia. He picked up a long wooden pointer and pointed at northern China.

"Gentlemen, the latest intelligence, provided by the Chinese Communists and our OSS assets in northern China, gives us an even more comprehensive picture of the secret Japanese biological- and chemical-weapons development program the Japs call Unit 731. The unit is headquartered in the city of Pingfang, sixty miles from Harbin, which is the largest city in northeast China. The unit is commanded by an IJA medical officer, Lieutenant General Shiro Ito. The Unit 731 compound covers nearly six square miles and over one hundred fifty buildings and is composed of ten thousand personnel, which includes most of the best and brightest medical and scientific minds from Japan. The Communists believe Lieutenant General Ito has personally directed the mass murder of somewhere between two hundred thousand and six hundred thousand Chinese with their biological experiments and another two hundred thousand with their chemical experiments. In addition to captured Chinese soldiers, their victims include civilian men, women, and children. Even whole villages are being wiped out. We sent a team of OSS agents into the Harbin area four months ago, and they came back with some horrifying information.

"The OSS agents discovered that the Japanese are conducting medical experiments with some of the worst diseases known to humankind: plague, cholera, typhoid, anthrax, gas gangrene, botulism, smallpox, and a host of others. They have conducted experiments in replacing the blood in the human body with antifreeze, injecting human kidneys with horse urine, exposing prisoners to freezing temperatures, subjecting prisoners to lethal doses of x-ray radiation, and even burying their subjects alive to analyze the length of time it takes for them to suffocate. Their chemical-weapons tests include mustard gas and other similar nerve-affecting chemicals. They've done testing with bombs and grenades that release both biological and chemical agents on the Chinese population."

Colonel Masek picked up a glass of water, took a drink, and let the information he had just given them sink in for a minute before he continued.

"You are already aware of what we found at Kao-Lan Island, Canton, Singapore, Phetchaburi, and Swatow: flea-borne bubonic plague and weapons testing with gas-gangrene grenades and flamethrowers. Now we need to figure out where we want to strike next. G-2 analysts have a few suggestions, but the decision where to strike next will be up to this group. We know for certain that large experimentation units are located at Changchun, Beijing, Nanjing, Guangzhou, Qiqihar, and Hailar; these are major Japanese strongholds. We've also identified at least five other smaller Unit 731 field testing units located at POW camps in Saigon, Hanoi, Beiyinhe, Hsinking, Haikou, and Wenchang."

"I think we need to look at the 731 units closer to the coast. Colonel, do you have any information on the camps at Haikou and Wenchang?" Linka asked. "They're both on Hainan Island."

"Yes, we sent reconnaissance flights over both those locations several weeks ago. Our SOE analysts are telling us there are least a hundred POWs at each camp. The camps are over five acres in size, and each has anywhere from twenty to thirty guards, plus support personnel. We have not been able to determine if they are testing any biological or chemical weapons on Allied prisoners," Colonel MacKenzie stated.

"I think we can assume they are experimenting with plague," Jon said. "The aircrew we captured at Phetchaburi was supposed to drop off three crates of plague-infected fleas at Wenchang."

"What about the camp at Saigon?" Miles asked.

"The Army Air Corps has flown three reconnaissance missions over the facility in the last two months. The camp is close to thirty acres in size and holds at least five hundred POWs. Our native agents in the area took photos of Japanese soldiers using prisoners for bayonet practice as well as flamethrower testing. There is also a bombing site ten miles from the camp where aircraft drop chemical bombs and other ordnance on the POWs," Colonel Ray said.

"I know that look on your face, Jon. What are you thinking?" Colonel MacKenzie asked.

"Sir, I've studied the maps of Hainan Island. I'm thinking that we could hit Haikou and Wenchang at the same time. The Haikou camp is located on a river six miles east of the city, close to Puqian Bay. The Wenchang camp is located only a mile inland from Gaolong Bay. We could insert Miles and a team of Royal Marine commandos to take the camp at Wenchang. George and I could take another team of commandos and take the camp at Haikou. Of course, this all depends on getting Royal Marine commandos and support from the navy."

"To hit both camps would require a least one carrier group to provide air support. Most of our carriers are a thousand miles from Hainan Island, busy with the invasion of Okinawa," Colonel Ray said.

"On the other hand," Colonel Masek said, "the last major Japanese battle group was destroyed two weeks ago. The battleship *Yamato*, destroyers *Hamakaze* and *Asashimo*, and light cruiser *Yahagi* were sunk in the East China Sea three hundred miles north of Okinawa. We just might be able to get a carrier tasked for this mission. I'll send a message to General Marshall and ask for his help."

Twenty-four hours later, Colonel Masek was briefing them on the response from the army chief of staff.

"The British carrier HMS *Illustrious* is in the Philippines and has just completed repairs. It was scheduled to return to Sydney for more extensive repairs because it has only one propeller that is usable. However, General MacArthur's headquarters is making it available along with one destroyer, two destroyer escorts, and two landing ship docks, or LSDs, capable of carrying up to sixty fully equipped marines. Four companies of Royal Marine commandos will be accompanying the LSDs. The *Illustrious* and its escorts will be on station, fifty miles southeast of Hainan Island, in eleven days."

Colonel MacKenzie sent a message to the Royal Marine commandos unit in Ceylon, asking for an experienced commando to be temporarily assigned for a mission of high importance. A day later, Sergeant Major Bobby "Fatman" Walsh arrived to be the fourth member of Jon's team. The sergeant major, a veteran of the North Africa and Burma campaigns, had acquired his nickname as a child, when he was quite chubby. At six foot three and 210 pounds, Walsh was now lean, hard, and all muscle, but his nickname hadn't changed. He kept the name as a reminder of his youth and vowed that he would never be chubby again.

Within three days, Jon's team and Sergeant Major Walsh had devised a plan to take the two POW camps on Hainan Island. They presented their detailed plans to both Colonel MacKenzie and Colonel Ray.

"The way we see it, sir, the four companies of commandos mean that at least two hundred men will be available for taking each POW camp," Jon said. "We'll need the LSDs to approach the southeast side of the island and off-load ten LCM boats. The LCMs will carry the commandos to their respective insertion points. Six additional LCMs will be standing by offshore to carry prisoners out. Walsh, Miles, George, and I will need to be inserted onto the island thirty-six hours in advance of the commandos, to collect information on each camp. We won't be able to return to the LSD to brief the remaining commandos, so we'll brief them after they land. We'll need two fishing boats to get our two teams to the beaches near our respective targets. George and I will take Haikou, and Miles and Sergeant Major Walsh will take Wenchang. Sergeant Major Walsh will now explain the proposed commando positioning."

"Sir, the photos of each camp show four guard towers with thirty-caliber machine guns and at least four soldiers patrolling the perimeter fences," Walsh stated. "We'll use four commandos to take out the roving guards. After the guards are down, four teams of two commandos each will be inserted into the compound to take out the guard towers. After the towers are secured, two SOE agents and twenty-five commandos will enter the compound, blow the troop barracks, and capture the camp commandant and radio shack. We'll use the remaining commandos to secure the outside perimeter and set ambushes on the roads to the villages. After we recon the camps, we'll brief the commando team leaders on their responsibilities. Any deviations from the plans will be ad hoc as we go."

Jon stood up and asked, "Does anyone have questions?"

"My only worries are the three Japanese explosive-motorboat (EMB) squadrons on Hainan Island," Colonel MacKenzie stated. "These are manned, eighteen-foot suicide boats that each carry seven hundred pounds of explosives. There are two squadrons on the south side of the island, six miles west of Wenchang, and one squadron at Haikou. If our task force is discovered, the LSDs, LCMs, and commandos will be in jeopardy."

"Sir, the LCMs will only be on their own for a short time. At daybreak, a squadron of Royal Navy Corsairs will attack the Japanese airfield at Haikou," Sergeant Major Walsh stated. "The Corsairs will be carrying a combination of high-velocity aircraft rockets (HVAR) and napalm bombs. A squadron of Royal Navy Avengers will attack the EMB squadron at Haikou Bay. Another squadron of Avengers and Corsairs will attack the EMB squadrons at Shinchiku Bay and Xincun Bay on the southern end of the island. After the Corsairs complete their strike missions, four Corsairs will stay and provide air cover over each camp while the other aircraft head back to the *Illustrious* to be refueled. Once we radio that the camps are secure, a PBY will be dispatched to pick up the four of us and fly us back to the LSD. Each group of LCMs will be met by a destroyer escort and a flight of Corsairs that will escort them to their LSDs for pickup."

After making certain none of the team members had any other questions, Colonel MacKenzie rose to leave. "Thank you for such a thorough briefing, gentlemen. I'll see you when you get back."

CHAPTER 14

Hainan Island, China

A t 0130 hours, a fishing boat rendezvoused with the destroyer escort USS *Thomason* fifteen miles southeast of Hainan Island. After Jon and George climbed aboard, the boat headed northwest toward the POW camp at Haikou. Thirty minutes later, a second fishing boat rendezvoused with the destroyer escort USS *Finnegan* fifteen miles south of Wenchang and took Miles and Sergeant Major Walsh to their insertion point near Wenchang.

Jon and George got off the boat at an isolated beach in Hainan Bay on the far northeast side of Hainan Island, five miles northeast of the Haikou POW camp. After they crossed the beach and entered a largely unpopulated area, they encountered a large forest of Hainan white pines. The needlelike leaves measured anywhere from two to five inches in length and were arrayed in fascicles of five. The tree's cones measured a full five inches in length and had thick, woody scales and large seeds that made a loud pop when stepped on. Avoiding the cones was a laborious undertaking. It took Jon and George over two hours to make it across the hilly slopes to a location overlooking Puqian Bay, where they observed the prisoner camp. By 0630 hours, the camp was awake, with Japanese soldiers lined up in five rows completing their morning ritual of calisthenics and judo practice.

The camp's layout was a perfect square with buildings aligned north to south. Jon counted thirty-two guards exercising, eight guards in the towers, four guards patrolling the perimeter, and eight cooks in an open lean-to preparing breakfast.

The camp was built between two hills running east to west, and a freshwater creek ran from the base of the larger hill to the north all the way to the ocean. At 0730 hours, the POWs formed up outside the eight bamboo huts that were built four abreast; from the looks of it, each hut slept twenty-five to thirty men. Four groups of prisoners formed up into a single line and came to attention when one of the men shouted, "Atten-hut!" Toward the southern end of the compound stood two wooden buildings. Jon and George got a glimpse of three men in white lab coats, two entering and one exiting one of the buildings. Thirty yards across the compound from the prisoner quarters were three guard huts. A smaller building to the north had cables running to it from a forty-foot radio tower set up outside the barbed-wire fence.

Commandant's office and quarters, Jon thought.

George drew a map of the compound and annotated the best possible entry points for the commandos, one near the guard quarters and the other near the commandant's hut. No light poles or lights were visible.

At Wenchang, Miles and Walsh made their way through a large grove of fruit trees, close to the edge of a forest of pines that separated the POW camp from the sand dunes near the beach. The ground around the camp was flat with the exception of a small hill a quarter mile to the west, and the camp itself appeared considerably smaller than what Miles had expected. There was a three-acre garden on the south side of the camp that extended all the way to the fence. Miles and Walsh identified the commandant's office, which had a radio antenna next to it. Thirty yards from the office lay the cooking facilities and two guard quarters. On the other side of the compound were four raised bamboo huts with thatched roofs that the prisoners occupied.

By 0930 hours, the heat and humidity were almost unbearable. Walsh discovered a small creek running from the northwest to the southeast. The creek passed within ten yards of the southwest side of the compound and then hooked southwest and ran into a small cove at the edge of the ocean. Although shallow, the creek maintained a steady flow of water. Miles prayed that there weren't any saltwater crocodiles in the area.

During an afternoon rain shower, Miles and Walsh crawled through eight-foot-tall elephant grass and got to within twenty-five yards of the

Wenchang camp. They couldn't chance going any closer because of the ten-foot-high guard towers, but at least they found a way of getting close to the camp.

After making minor changes to the sketch they had drawn from the aerial photos, they crawled out of the creek and made their way back into the thick pine forest. They reviewed their insertion plan and decided that they didn't need to make any changes to it.

At 0100 hours the next morning, two hundred Royal Marine commandos exited the LCM-3 boats on the beaches, where the two pairs of agents flashed their Morse-code signals and waited. When the commandos exited the boats near the Haikou camp, Jon led them off the beach into the pine forest. George briefed the four squad leaders and released them back to their squads to brief the rest of the men. With the half-moon still high at 0300 hours, the agents and commandos began moving toward the camp. A similar scenario was playing out at Wenchang.

By 0400 hours, the teams at both camps had moved into position. A single lantern at the commandant's hut was the only light in each camp. Four commandos left their positions with only a knife. Twenty minutes later they had cut through the fence and were moving inside the compound. After the ground patrols were eliminated, they signaled the main group with a red-filtered flashlight. Eight other commandos then left their positions and moved into position beneath the four guard towers.

The guard towers proved to be unchallenging, and finally four red-filtered flashlights acknowledged that the task was complete. Twenty-five commandos penetrated the wire fence near the four guard barracks. At exactly 0500 hours, the commandos quietly lowered their C-3 satchel charges inside each of the guard quarters and then took cover a safe distance from the huts. Five minutes later, the exploding charges destroyed the barracks.

The camp commandant came running out of his quarters at Haikou, and a bullet in the head from Jon's .45-caliber pistol greeted him. The two medical personnel on night duty at the camp were captured as soon as they rushed outside the medical building. At Wenchang, the penetration of the camp went just as quickly.

At Haikou, George interrogated the two physicians they had captured. He discovered that the physicians had been experimenting with cholera and typhoid. Inside the medical building, the commandos discovered eight patients who had been injected with the pathogens.

"How long ago did you inject them?" George asked the younger of the two physicians.

"Forty-eight hours ago," Dr. Atsushi Endo replied.

"What's the incubation period?"

"Five days for both diseases."

While the Japanese physician was answering George's questions, Major Larry Peterson, the Royal Marine physician assigned to the Haikou commando unit, was listening as George repeated the answers in English. After he finished questioning the Japanese physician, George looked at Dr. Peterson.

"I can treat the cholera with prontosil and the typhoid with penicillin, but we'll need to isolate them on one of the boats and get them back to the LSD. If the carrier can come to where the LSD is, we can get them aboard and into an isolation ward," Dr. Peterson said.

George turned back to Dr. Endo and asked, "Why did you do it?"

"Not because I wanted to," Dr. Endo replied. "I am appalled by the experiments on humans. I graduated at the top of my medical school's class. I was drafted into the army and ordered to conduct the experiments. If I had not, they would have killed me and my family."

George looked at the commando guarding the two physicians. "Take the physicians with us and grab all of the notebooks you can find. Use the satchel charges on the medical buildings. Let's start moving everyone to the beach."

By the time everyone had made it to the beach on Puqian Bay, twelve LCM-3 boats sat beached in a neat row with their ramps down. With the beach being fifteen miles from the city of Haikou, they knew they would go unnoticed, except by a few fishermen in sampans, and none of them, hopefully, carried radios.

Dr. Peterson took the eight infected prisoners into one of the boats and departed first.

The HMS *Illustrious* cruised toward the island at ten knots along with its destroyer protection. The USS *Finnegan* and USS *Thomason* loitered one mile offshore, waiting to escort the LCM-3 boats back to their mother ship.

On the southeast side of the island, Miles's team infiltrated the Wenchang camp and completed its mission. One of the Japanese-speaking commandos interrogated the two Japanese physicians they had captured and discovered they were conducting experiments with small-pox and botulism. When asked how many patients were in the facility, the Japanese physician told them none. They had just finished the autopsies on the last four prisoners two days before. All the bodies had been cremated a half mile away from the camp.

Miles instructed the commandos to go through the medical building and collect all the medical notes and logs. By daybreak, the Allied prisoners and marine commandos were making their way to the boats.

An hour after the sun rose, the Japanese facilities at Haikou Airfield and the EMB facilities in Haikou Bay were burning infernos. At Haikou Airfield, the Corsairs had caught sixteen Japanese fighters on the ground; after two passes, all had been destroyed. The Corsairs also sent rockets into the aviation gasoline storage farm. After expending their ordnance, the Corsairs headed back to the carrier, leaving a black cloud covering the airfield and the buildings and troop quarters ablaze.

Hitting Haikou at the same time as the Corsairs, a squadron of Avenger torpedo planes had caught the EMBs in their berths at Haikou Bay. On their first run, each of the seven Avenger aircraft dropped a single Bliss-Leavitt Mark 13 torpedo. On the second bombing run, they each dispensed their two 250-pound bombs on the Japanese Navy diesel farm at Haikou harbor.

At almost the same time, two squadrons of Avengers attacked the EMB squadrons at Shinchiku Bay and Xincun Bay on the southern side of the island. On the first bombing run at Shinchiku Bay, the Avengers dropped their torpedoes. The Corsairs followed, firing their rockets at the remaining EMBs and the fuel-storage tanks. After the bombing run was completed, the Corsairs formed up and headed east to provide cover for the POW camp at Wenchang. On the Avengers' second run at the base, an antiaircraft shell blew up the bomb on one of the Avenger's wings, vaporizing the aircraft and its crew of three. The remaining six Avengers dropped their bombs on the docks and base facilities and headed back to the HMS *Illustrious*.

At Xincun Bay, seven Avengers, flying in a half-mile separation formation, dropped their torpedoes. The torpedoes from the last Avenger hit a refueling barge, which blasted fuel and fire over the entire dock. Within minutes, the dock erupted in flames, and the boats that had been untouched by the torpedoes caught fire. When the Corsairs made their run on the fuel facility, two antiaircraft batteries located on a hillside north of the base opened fire. Two Corsairs were hit after they released their rockets. One crashed into the hillside, and the other ditched five miles out at sea, where the pilot was picked up by a circling PBY. All of the rockets from the Corsairs found their mark in the Japanese fuel tanks and base buildings, and two rockets hit the headquarters building. Once they finished their run, the five remaining Corsairs took turns concentrating machine-gun fire on the antiaircraft positions, knocking both out before the Avengers began their bombing run. After the Avengers released their bombs, the small Japanese base was completely destroyed.

Once the twelve LCM-3 boats departed the Haikou camp and headed west along the northern coast, they could see the black clouds of smoke rising from Haikou Bay. The four Corsairs that had been orbiting above the POW camp had been relieved by four Corsairs with full fuel tanks. After an hour of sailing, the boats from both raids rendezvoused with their respective LSDs.

After all the boats and men were secured aboard the LSDs, Jon left the deck and made his way to the officers' mess.

As he walked up to the sergeant major, Walsh commented, "You look pale. Are you OK?"

"Not sure. This is our sixth mission in four months, but to tell the truth, I picked up malaria on my last visit to Luzon. After we returned to Alipore, I got an appointment with a doctor there. He said, if anything, it was a mild case. He issued me quinine, but I ran out of pills right before this mission. I need to ask the navy doc for some more when we get to the carrier."

"I think you need to go to sick bay right now," Walsh said. He watched closely as Jon stumbled slightly and struggled to control his balance.

Jon opened his mouth to answer, but his eyes rolled into his head and he fell forward into Walsh's arms. The sergeant major eased Jon to the floor, knelt beside him, and yelled, "Medic!"

CHAPTER 15

Calcutta, India

Colonel Michael MacKenzie hung up the phone and resumed his conversation with Colonel Lew Miller, who had just flown in from Washington. Colonel MacKenzie was worried about his number-one agent, Jonathan Preston, and his King Cobra team. In their first year of operation, Jon's team had become one of the most successful clandestine teams in Asia, and possibly in the history of the British Secret Intelligence Service.

"How is Jon?" Colonel Miller asked.

"Doing much better. After collapsing on the LSD, the medics rushed him to sick bay and then transferred him to the *Illustrious*. He remained unconscious and delirious for three days. By the time he was well enough to eat solid foods, the *Illustrious* arrived in Australia. He and his team spent two days in Sydney before boarding a C-46 that flew them to Rangoon. They landed in Rangoon four hours ago and should be boarding a B-24 in two hours for the journey to Calcutta," Colonel MacKenzie said.

In 1944, Colonel MacKenzie had initially rejected the idea of having an American agent as part of his SOE contingent. In the beginning, he had been very rude to Jon and wanted no "Yank" on his team. He had changed his opinion after the first five missions Jon's team planned and successfully executed, and he'd had to eat his own words and apologize to Jon.

The missions that MacKenzie thought unthinkable and undoable, Jon's team executed brilliantly. He would never underestimate anyone ever again, whether Brit or Yank; even the Frenchman's skills were outstanding.

Colonel MacKenzie had quickly discovered Jon did not think like most people did and he brought a new perspective to tactical planning and mission execution. His thinking was all out-of-the box ideas. What MacKenzie thought impossible, Jonathan Preston made possible.

The American was adroit at what he did, but when he arrived at the SOE offices later that day, he looked extremely tired, and the intensity in his eyes was gone.

"Lew, I don't think we should send Jon or his team on any more missions for a while," Colonel MacKenzie stated. "In the last sixteen months, Jon's team has worked nearly nonstop and completed over twenty-five missions. I think the stress is getting to him, and the malaria has certainly weakened him."

"Michael, after seeing the boys yesterday, I certainly agree with you, but where would we be without Jon?" Colonel Miller asked. "His skill, adaptability, and brilliance are immeasurable in this business. I'm certain a hell of a lot of agents would have been lost if Jon had not been assigned to your unit. Without his brain functioning clearly, I'm not sure we will catch these spies that have been sent to kill him. These new Jap spies are certainly cleverer than the previous teams."

"All right," Colonel MacKenzie said, "let's let him rest up for ten days away from Calcutta. I'll send Jon and Camille downriver for another recuperation cruise, but I want George and Kathleen to accompany them. I'll keep Miles and Henri here; they'll be invaluable teachers for my two new agents. I want the new agents to pick their brains and learn how they think and strategize. In fact, just being around Henri the past two weeks is already improving the girls' thought processes."

"What happened to the leads the girls had on the Japanese spies?"

"Those didn't pan out. I've assigned five SOE teams to the task, and we've got six of Colonel Ray's OSS teams working with us. I'm hoping we can flush them out and discover where they are staying this week. Henri's been doing well in the office, planning the logistics and keeping track of all of the team's efforts. He's been bugging the hell out of me to let him do something in the field, so I'm putting him in charge of monitoring the teams on the ground. I'll send him out in a car and let him monitor the real-time activity; maybe he'll discover something the others have overlooked. Once Jon returns from the cruise, we'll ease him back into the hunt. In the meantime, let's pray we catch these bastards."

"I'll order Jon to stand down and notify G-2. Make sure that Captain Dubois knows this cruise will be recuperation as well as a working vacation for Jon. Can you send duplicate copies of everything collected on these spies to the *Jacqueline*? Otherwise, Jon will go crazy sitting around in the sun drinking martinis."

Early the next morning, the *Jacqueline* left the yacht basin and cruised south. By the afternoon of the second day, it entered the Indian Ocean. When Captain Dubois entered the lounge, Jon, George, and Kathleen were hard at work.

"My rule on speaking only French on this boat still applies, people," Captain Dubois reminded everyone.

"Sorry, Captain," Jon said. "George is having a little trouble with his French, so we have to tutor him."

"That's understandable. Don't forget that dinner tonight will be formal. Brunelle is laying out clothing in your rooms as we speak."

Jon and George arrived to the dining room early and were served a delicious cocktail made from a mixture of dark rum, Thai orange liqueur, lime juice, and guava juice.

Camille and Kathleen arrived fashionably late. George turned to greet the ladies and was speechless. George knew the girls were all lookers, but he had never seen them in formal attire. *Absolutely gorgeous*, he thought. Jon was quick to notice George's mesmerized gaze at Kathleen.

Jon was just as struck by Camille's attire. She wore an emerald-green taffeta strapless gown, arm-length emerald-green gloves with a diamond bracelet on her left wrist, a diamond necklace, diamond earrings, and emerald-green heels. Jon loved Camille's Irish setter red hair, and the emerald-green gown made her look even lovelier than usual.

George had lost his wife in an auto accident before the war, and he hadn't even looked at another woman until now. Kathleen Lauren was wearing a black faille sleeveless gown. It had a plunging neckline laced with small gold braided chains that accentuated her ample bosom, a narrow gold sequined belt, and black arm-length gloves with a diamond and gold bracelet on her left wrist, a diamond necklace, diamond earrings, and black heels. With her long silky black hair falling elegantly down her back and across her shoulders, she was a crown jewel; George was smitten. Although he was polite to Captain Dubois, Jon, and Camille, he hardly paid any attention to them, focusing most of his attention on Kathleen. The others thought it was humorous and wonderful.

Trying to keep up a conversation about sailboats, yachts, horses, and automobiles, Captain Dubois became frustrated because the conversation always seemed to move back to the war and their mission. The Japanese spies who had entered Calcutta two months before became the main topic. The SOE and CIC teams had had no luck in finding the spies. Another Japanese message, intercepted a week earlier by Colonel Matt Whitely's team in Honolulu, revealed that the Japanese were dispatching another two spies to Calcutta.

Matt Whitely had been one of thirty-eight Allied prisoners that Jon's team had rescued from a railroad prison camp in Thailand in 1944. Matt Whitely was the only reason for taking the camp, because he was one of General Douglas MacArthur's key planners for the ultimate invasion of Japan.

Colonel Miller had told Jon that catching the Japanese spies would be his number-one priority once they returned from their cruise, if the spies were still not found and captured by that time. After three days on the boat, Jon had to admit he was feeling less tired and more refreshed; there was certainly a lot less stress. Jon did not like being on a cruise while British and American agents were putting their lives on the line to track down the spies in Calcutta. He was uneasy about the second set of spies. Camille tried to keep Jon's mind off the matter. Despite her efforts, Jon still could not take his mind off the spies who wanted him and his team dead.

Although Miles Murphy was given five days of vacation after returning from the Hainan Island mission, he showed up at the SOE detachment the morning of the fourth day. For the first half of the day, he reviewed reports and studied the photographs the Allied agents had taken of suspected Japanese spies and discussed them with the team working the case.

"What if they are no longer a couple? What if they are now acting independently?" Miles asked.

"I hadn't considered it. Do you think we should?" Henri asked.

Without realizing it, Miles was thinking outside of the box, as Jon had taught him. He reviewed the agent reports again, looking for individuals taking photographs of army personnel and army facilities. After sorting the photos into male and female piles, he found several photos of the same man and woman taking photographs of the Calcutta wharves, ships, and fuel-storage facilities. Miles also discovered two previously unidentified Eurasian men photographing American and British soldiers, both in and out of uniform.

"Bingo," Miles said.

"What did you find?"

"I've come across something I think is important. An Asian man and woman photographing our facilities and two Eurasian men photographing only Allied soldiers. Which leads me to believe they are looking for someone specific."

Henri summoned Colonel MacKenzie, who entered the room to look at what Miles had found. Miles told them how he had found the pattern. The colonel wanted to view the photos. He instructed Miles to get copies to all the SOE agents in the field and to take several copies of the photos over to Colonel Ray's CIC detachment.

Before leaving the room, Colonel MacKenzie told them, "About time you two started thinking like the Yank."

Colonel Michael MacKenzie had recently recalled one of his best SOE agents from China, Major Jim Ballangy. Ballangy had been in the field too long: over three years. After a week in Calcutta, the major complained of being bored. Colonel MacKenzie loaned him to the CIC commander, Colonel Ronnie Ray, to head up his inexperienced team of agents looking for the Japanese spies who had recently infiltrated Calcutta. Major Ballangy and Miles met the next day, Miles explaining the logic and the pattern he had discovered. Jim picked up on it immediately. After he sorted through all the photographs taken by Colonel Ray's CIC agents, he noticed the same pattern emerged in a group of photographs no one had reviewed yet: a couple photographing facilities and two men photographing Allied soldiers.

"I believe you've found our two sets of spies," Major Ballangy said. "I think the two men photographing soldiers may be the ones after Jon. I'm going to suggest you let the CIC agents concentrate on these two men.

I'd like you to tell your agents to photograph anyone they talk to. We just may find there are additional Japanese agents in town. The Japanese spies are very disciplined and methodical; they'll probably continue their routine of photographing soldiers until they find the women. Let's hope they don't accidently find out you all are still alive."

Another intelligence agent who thinks like Jon, Miles thought. *What is the probability they would both be in Calcutta at the same time?*

Unable to recognize his change in thinking, despite what the colonel had said, Miles began to wonder if he and Henri were the only agents who didn't think this way.

By the time Jon returned from his brief vacation, Miles, Henri, and Major Ballangy had accumulated enough evidence to pinpoint the Eurasian male and female as the second set of spies that had entered Calcutta two months back. After Jon reviewed what Miles, Henri, and the major had compiled, he was convinced too. Finding the other two spies wasn't blind luck, and he congratulated Miles on doing such thorough detective work.

"Excellent work. Do we know where they are staying?"

"As far as the couple is concerned, the gentleman is registered at a small hotel on Armenian Street called the Bimla Guesthouse. His French passport is under the name of Allan Jarnot. The address on the passport is in Hanoi. The female is staying at a more upscale hotel on Tiretta Bazar Lane, the Hotel Ananda Bhawan. She is registered under the name of Marlene Pinault, her passport is also French, and her address is also in Hanoi," Henri said.

"What about the two men?"

"We photographed them talking to Jarnot and Pinault at three different locations. We have photos of each man talking to the couple and another two photos with all four together. One of the men is staying at the Middleton Chambers Hotel on Middleton Street. The other is at the Victoria Guest House on Park Street, a few blocks away. We have not gotten their names yet, but both are tough-looking customers."

"How do you plan to take them down?"

"Well, we thought of having the girls take down the female spy. The four of them should be able to pull it off without too much trouble, plus Camille's experience is an asset. This woman may be expecting something similar to what we did to the Auroras. We followed her to the Great Eastern Hotel, where she made inquiries about them."

"This is extraordinary work, guys. Why don't you all work with the ladies and put together a plan of action? Henri, I know you're itching for some action, so you can go along with the ladies and sit in the hotel lobby while the girls execute the capture. George and I will take Jarnot."

"I've a similar plan for the CIC to take down the other two spies," Major Ballangy said, "but I'd like to do it after they're asleep."

"All right, Jim, your CIC team takes the two men while the SOE takes down the man and woman. Colonel Ray and Colonel MacKenzie want me to take the briefings on the plans and approve them. That is, if it's OK with you all?"

"Absolutely," Henri stated. Miles only nodded.

"No problem," Major Ballangy said.

"Work out the details with your team members this afternoon and tomorrow morning. You can brief me separately tomorrow afternoon."

CHAPTER 16

Calcutta, India

Camille, Kathleen, Brigitte, and Monique completed their mission planning and briefed Jon. It was an excellent plan, and with the exception of a few minor changes, Jon gave them the green light to proceed. As the ladies took two days to get everything in place, Jon watched the women closely. Brigitte and Monique were overly chatty. Jon had seen the same tendency in Camille and Kathleen during their mission to Chittagong the previous year. The tension was natural and would keep them alert. Jon had felt the same tension in his first game with the Red Sox farm club six years earlier. *That game wasn't as deadly as this one, Jon. The worst you did was strike out and commit an error. In this game someone can get killed. I'll have a long talk with Brigitte and Monique and point out their vulnerability*, Jon thought.

Henri seated himself in the Hotel Ananda Bhawan's reading room, located between the dining room and the front desk. The room was small, open to the lobby, and smelled of stale smoke. Five different newspapers were stacked neatly on the table next to his chair. Henri sat in the chair closest to the lobby pretending to read a copy of the *Calcutta Statesman*.

Marlene Pinault stood in the shadows of a stairwell and watched the two suspicious women she had noticed earlier; they were off to her left, close to the lobby. Pinault saw them enter the hotel from the street. They were dressed far too formally for the hotel, each wearing a suit coat. A new restaurant hostess and a new waitress added to her suspicions. After seeing everything she wanted, she walked back up the stairs to the second floor and took the elevator to the lobby. She felt confident of being able to handle anything involving these women if they turned out to be Allied agents.

Henri had an unobstructed view when Pinault got off the elevator. She was dressed nicely, wearing a flowery, loose-fitting dress. She walked directly to the crowded dining room, as she did every evening at 1900 hours, and waited to be seated. Within a minute, Camille walked Pinault to a table and seated her facing away from Henri. Camille informed her that Kathleen, her waitress, would be with her as soon as possible.

A few minutes later, as Kathleen was writing down the spy's order, she couldn't help noticing that Pinault was crying. Kathleen wondered if this woman had been coerced into spying for the Japanese, like the woman Captain Dubois and Camille had captured a month ago.

"Is something wrong, Miss?" Kathleen asked.

"I really don't want to be here in Calcutta. My...My husband forced me to come here," Pinault said. She held a handkerchief to her nose and blew into it.

Kathleen's defenses dropped, and she felt sorry for the woman—her first mistake and deviation from their plan. "If you would like to come with me, Miss, I can introduce you to someone who can help you."

After the spy nodded her head, Kathleen made her second mistake when she told Pinault to follow her and then turned her back on the spy. Kathleen walked two steps before realizing her mistake. When she turned around and faced the woman, Pinault had a small-caliber pistol in her hand, hanging at her side. Before Pinault could raise her arm to fire, two subsonic bullets struck her between her shoulder blades. Stunned, Pinault stared at her abdomen. She tried to speak, but blood began streaming from her mouth and garbled her words. Pinault collapsed to the floor and discharged her pistol, the bullet barely missing Kathleen and embedding itself in the back of a chair where a young girl sat eating.

Immediately after the spy went down, Henri rose from his seat, held up a badge, and yelled, "Police, ladies and gentlemen. It's all over now. Please remain calm."

Brigitte Prefontaine had reacted quickly as the spy removed the pistol from her purse, firing her weapon at the same instant Henri did. Now she moved to the fallen Japanese agent. Searching for a pulse, she found none and shook her head at Henri. Camille walked through the maze of stunned customers and draped a linen tablecloth over the dead woman. Henri hobbled with his cane over to where Kathleen stood, staring at the dead spy. After realizing how foolish she had been and how close she had come to being killed, Kathleen lowered her head and began crying. Henri reached over to Kathleen, lifted her chin, stared into her eyes, and whispered in her ear.

"This is your first mission on your own, Kathleen. Learn from your mistake, or the next time you might be the one lying dead on the floor. Now go to the reading room and sit down or go over and wait with Monique while we take care of this."

After Henri fired, he had picked up the walkie-talkie, concealed in a soft leather valise on the floor beside him, and radioed for the ambulance they had on standby. Idling on a side street only a few blocks away, the ambulance arrived in minutes and removed the body. Thirty minutes later, no trace of the incident was noticeable in the hotel. Henri hoped that Pinault's partner wouldn't learn of the incident until it was too late.

At 0300 hours, Jon's team entered the Bimla Guesthouse. Jon had been updated by Henri on the fiasco at the Hotel Ananda, but he still held on to the hope that they could take Allan Jarnot alive. Jon needed information from Jarnot regarding who they were getting their orders from. While Jon waited on the ground floor, George made his way along with two SOE agents and two Kachin rangers to the third floor and room 313. When they arrived, George let the six-foot-three and 220-pound SOE agent kick the door in. George entered first, followed by the two agents; the two Kachin rangers remained in the hallway. The room was empty.

"What the hell? We've been covering all the exits since this afternoon," George said aloud.

Four rapid shots came from the bathroom. Both SOE agents fell to the floor. One of the Kachin rangers rushed past George, leaped across the bed, and threw his double-edged fighting knife through the half-open bathroom door into the heart of Allen Jarnot.

As the ranger searched the dead spy for information, the second ranger attended to the wounded SOE agent that had kicked down the door. He was having trouble breathing, and blood was bubbling through his lips from a bullet in his right lung. Jon knelt next to the other downed agent and placed two fingers on his neck. He turned to George. "He's dead. One of the bullets went through his heart.

After calling for an ambulance from the phone in the room, George turned to Jon. "This is my fault," George said. "I didn't anticipated Jarnot would be sleeping in the bathtub. I was caught by surprise."

"No, it isn't. It's my fault. I reviewed and approved your plan. I didn't think of it either."

An hour later, the cleanup at the Bimla Guesthouse was under way, and Jon and George were at the SOE detachment briefing Colonel MacKenzie and Henri on the situation.

"OK, guys, let's end the blame game," Colonel MacKenzie stated. "This is war, and crap happens. Just make sure that Major Ballangy is aware of this tactic so his team is fully prepared when they go after the two men tonight."

"I'm on my way to see him now. How is Kathleen holding up?"

"She and the others are back at the boat. She's furious with herself. I think she's on the verge of quitting and asking for a desk job. I told Camille to give her a sedative," Henri stated.

"How did the others girls handle themselves?"

"They did their jobs professionally. Brigitte Prefontaine reacted fast; she fired her pistol at the same time I did. Put a bullet in Pinault's heart."

"Has Brigitte shown any signs of remorse?"

"I've kept an eye on her, but no, she hasn't. She did her job of protecting Kathleen."

"All right, Jon, you head out to see Ballangy. Henri, go get some rest and come back this afternoon. I'll meet with your team at 1500 hours," Colonel MacKenzie stated.

CHAPTER 17

Calcutta, India

"George and his men got caught completely off guard, Ronnie," Colonel Mackenzie exclaimed over the phone. "Who would have thought the son of a bitch would be sleeping in the bathroom? He shot two of my agents. One's dead, and the other's in critical condition."

"I'm terribly sorry about your men, Michael. Could Jon come over and review our plans this morning?" Colonel Ray asked. "Major Ballangy's teams are going after the two Japanese operatives tonight."

"Jon and George left for your detachment five minutes ago. Who does Major Ballangy have running the teams?"

"Captain Red Handy and Captain Bud Helms; they're both top-notch officers but have no experience in this type of fieldwork."

"I'm concerned that the two men might find out what has happened to Pinault and Jarnot. Do you still have agents watching them?"

"Yes, but they have done nothing that would suggest they know anything."

"Well, we've done our part to keep the incidents quiet. Let's hope it stays that way."

At 1300 hours, Jon and George arrived at the CIC detachment and entered the building. They walked immediately to the large briefing room where Colonel Ray and Major Ballangy were talking to the two CIC team leaders.

"Hey, guys, glad you could make it," Major Ballangy said. "Captain Handy and Captain Helms are our team leaders. Let's get started, shall we?"

Over the next two hours, the two captains briefed their missions. Jon and George asked a lot of questions. Mostly "What would you do if…" questions, some of which the two captains didn't have an answer for. Jon and George's job was to help them plan for the unexpected and fill in the gaps in their plans. They offered multiple ideas to add to their scenarios, and by the end of the meeting, both agents were confident that they had covered every possible thing that could go wrong. Jon was worried that he had missed something.

"Gentlemen, in this business, traditional thinking will get you killed," Jon told them. "You need to be constantly thinking outside of the box. Only then can you outsmart these bastards. You need to remember these guys are the best of the best, or the Japs wouldn't have sent them. They are betting their lives they can outthink us. You need to constantly out-think them, because it's your life and the lives of your men that are on the line tonight. Anything else you can think of, George?"

"Just one thing. When you do make a mistake, you must accept the fact that you're not infallible. You can't always think of everything that can go wrong. Yesterday an agent was killed, and one was seriously wounded; they were my responsibility. It's hard on you when you make crucial mistakes, but you need to learn from them and move on quickly in this business."

"From what you've been briefed on and what we've helped you with, you are fully prepared to execute this mission and be successful. Just make sure you go over everything with your team members several times. You want everyone on the same page. Cover the 'What would you do if…' questions we went through and make certain they know what to do in a contingency. If you don't have any other questions, I think we're through here."

Captain Bud Helms led his team to the Middleton Chambers Hotel at 10 Middleton Street at midnight. Bud and three CIC agents entered the hotel and made their way to room 206.

Shortly thereafter, Jon, Miles, and George arrived in a taxi at a position three blocks from the Middleton. Jon had thought of another scenario, and he didn't want anyone to suffer from one of his mistakes. All three agents had darkened their lower legs and feet, arms, necks, and faces.

They were all dressed in a traditional Hindu *shalwar kameez* of loose-fitting white trousers and a long black coat-like garment. They also wore white khadi side caps that had a wide band and were pointed in the front and back, much like the US Army garrison caps. At night nobody would recognize them as European.

Jon sat on a bench at a trolley stop twenty-five feet to the left of the hotel's front door. Miles positioned himself in the rear of the hotel, and George was in an alley on the opposite side of the hotel from Jon.

Ten minutes after Captain Helms's team entered the building, a Thai woman exited the front door and turned right. Jon immediately got to his feet and followed the woman. When she was ten steps from the alley, George exited from the shadows with his pistol drawn and faced the woman. She stopped and turned in the opposite direction, only to see Jon coming toward her. She opened her purse and fumbled to extract her .25-caliber pistol.

"I wouldn't, especially if you want to stay alive," George said, now standing three feet behind her.

The woman continued her efforts to withdraw her gun until she felt Jon's silenced 9mm Beretta resting against her forehead.

"A bullet in the brain will be quick. Live or die, your choice," Jon said.

She hesitated for a second, then dropped her gun to the sidewalk and raised her hands. "You are really good. I thought I had you fooled."

"The team in the hotel was fooled. I always expect the unexpected."

"You're Cobra, aren't you?"

"You must have me confused with someone else."

George cuffed the woman while Jon kept his gun leveled at her. Once she was secured, Jon frisked her for additional weapons, finding a .32-caliber pistol in a thigh holster. After he removed the pistol, Jon walked down the alley and retrieved Miles.

Captain Helms was greeted by Jon, George, and Miles as he and his team members exited the hotel.

"What's with the getup?" Captain Helms asked.

"I thought of another scenario we hadn't discussed," Jon said. The spy's a woman, not a man. She walked right past you and out the front door."

Jon handed the cuffed women and her guns over to Captain Helms. "Sorry to rush off, but we need to get over to Park Street to see how the other team is doing."

Jon, Miles, and George arrived at the Victoria Guest House at the same moment the OSS agents exited the hotel.

"No one home," Captain Handy told them.

"We've been outsmarted," Jon stated. "Let's head back to base. I'll tell you all about it there."

CHAPTER 18

Calcutta, India

Anna D'Arras had been spying for the Japanese for two years. Her husband had held the job of Malayan minister of defense before Singapore fell to the Japanese. After Singapore fell in February of 1942, the Japanese imprisoned him. Three months later, he stood trial and received a death sentence from a Japanese military tribunal.

Anna was given the choice by the occupying Japanese of becoming a Japanese intelligence agent with a specific mission to hunt down and kill Allied spies or watching her two young boys and her husband hang.

For nearly a year, Anna D'Arras had been tracking down the whereabouts of an Allied agent called Cobra. The first three Japanese agents sent to take down the Allied team had been killed. Over the last year, the Japanese military had suspected the Cobra Team of destroying five Japanese medical research facilities and repatriating over six hundred Allied POWs. The Japanese intelligence establishment had been consumed with anger over the death of their triplet female agents, and they wanted the Allied agent removed before he could do any more damage. The Japanese had sent two additional teams to India, a husband and wife along with two female agents disguised as men. Until now, Anna had worked only as an analyst for the Japanese intelligence organization. The mission to Calcutta was Anna's first mission as an assassin.

Two weeks in an American Army jail cell felt like hell to Anna. The oppressive heat and humidity caused her to drop eight pounds of weight she couldn't afford to lose. She constantly worried about how long it would take the Japanese to find out she had failed her mission and execute her family. She also wondered when the Americans would execute her. Most of the hours in her cell were now spent praying. Upon her request, an American Army chaplain came to visit her. She openly confessed her sins and accepted Communion from the Catholic priest. She was now prepared for her trial and execution.

Jon and Major Ballangy sat in one of the briefing rooms at the SOE detachment, reviewing the information extracted from Anna D'Arras. She had not resisted their interrogation. In fact, she had given them more than expected, including the name of the female assassin with her, the names and locations of her superiors and how she contacted them, how message drops were handled, how the spies were to leave India, and the reason she had turned assassin and spy.

A week after Anna had given her captors the information they wanted, a CIC team arrested Marie Ancelet at a family restaurant in Chittagong. Marie gave up without a fight and now sat in an isolation cell in the same building where Anna was held.

"What would you think of turning these two women into double agents?" Jon asked.

"It's an excellent idea," Major Bellamy replied. "They could get a message to the Japs that your team has been terminated, then retreat back to Singapore and spy for us. Simple as a-b-c."

"I've never done this before, but I can tell you nothing is that simple. I'll send a message to G-2 at the Pentagon to see what they think."

It didn't take long for G-2 to respond. The message Jon received from G-2 stated that a colonel plus one officer would be arriving in four days. Jon hoped this meant they were sending someone experienced with handling double agents. In the meantime, he needed to take a quick trip to Chittagong to follow up on the information Marie Ancelet had given them during her interrogation.

Upon completing his review of Marie Ancelet's interrogation, Jon called on his friend Tex Marin at the Second Fighter Squadron, four miles west of Calcutta. Jon had run across Tex during a mission into Burma to collect intelligence behind enemy lines during the battle to retake Myitkyina. Marin acted like the stereotypical, larger-than-life Texan. He was credited with shooting down a dozen Japanese aircraft and was one of the most decorated pilots in Asia. As a half American and half Mexican from a small town in southwest Texas called Uvalde, close to the Mexican border, Marin was out to prove he was the best. Jon first met Tex at a party he hosted for the USO troops on the Fourth of July, 1944. Flying with the 118th Tactical Reconnaissance Squadron, Tex had just come off a mission where he downed two Japanese fighters while flying air cover in his P-38 Thunderbolt. He arrived at the party in his khaki uniform, with cowboy boots and a white Stetson hat. Jon instantly took a liking to the tall, smiling, broad-shouldered Texan, and over the course of the next two months, they became close friends.

On several occasions in the past, Tex had taken Jon up in a Stinson L-5 Sentinel observation aircraft. The Stinson, designed to operate on short, unimproved airstrips, was powered by a six-cylinder, 190-horsepower Lycoming O-435 engine. Its fuselage, constructed of chrome-moly tubing, an alloy made from chromium and molybdenum, was covered with doped cotton fabric. The wings were fashioned from spruce spars with plywood ribs and skin.

Jon asked Tex to fly him to Chittagong and then back to Calcutta the following day. Shortly after Jon arrived at the airfield, Tex received approval from his squadron commander to fly the mission. Thirty minutes later they were airborne, cruising a thousand feet above the jungle canopy.

At the airfield in Chittagong, Jon called the Circuit House and asked for the manager, Alain Chandra. After a brief discussion, Jon was given a reservation at the exclusive luxury hotel, and Alain sent the hotel limo to pick them up.

"You like to travel in style," Tex said.

"Wait until we get to the hotel."

When the limo turned into the half-mile-long driveway and approached the monolithic structure, Tex produced a low whistle. "You aren't lying. God, just how big is this place?"

Jon gave Tex some of the details. "It's two hundred twenty-five feet in length and one hundred twenty feet wide on the end wings; those are where the huge royal suites are located. You'll love the bar, too: mahogany and beautiful carvings of animals. When you use the bar or room service, charge it to the room; I'm paying. I have to change clothes and head into town, so make a reservation at the hotel restaurant for 2000 hours."

Alain arranged for a taxi to take Jon to a small leather-goods shop downtown. As Jon walked through the shop door, a small Burmese man raised his head and greeted him.

"Jon, how wonderful to see you again. Are you back in town on the yacht? Is my son Brunelle here too?" he asked.

"Not this time, Ed. I'm here alone, but I could use your help."

After they discussed his needs and had lunch together at the shop, Ed had one of his employees take Jon to the restaurant he sought. He also gave Jon the name of the restaurant's owner and told him the owner was a good friend of his.

Before Jon entered the small, family-owned restaurant, he was greeted by the smell of fish and the heavy, sweet pungency of pork liver. When he entered the open door, an elderly but friendly Asian woman smiled and greeted him.

Jon asked for the owner and told the woman Ed had sent him. She then walked him into a back room, where her husband was sitting and writing in a ledger.

"I'm a friend of Ed and his son Brunelle," Jon said. "I just need to ask a few questions, and then I will leave."

The man didn't say anything but nodded his OK.

"Do you remember seeing this woman several weeks ago in your restaurant?" Jon asked. He handed the man a black-and-white photograph.

The man stared at the woman's photo and nodded.

"Did you notice if she was accompanied by anyone when she came in here?"

The owner spoke to his wife in their native language. She gazed at the photograph and replied to her husband.

"No, but she talked to a gentleman at the table next to her for a long time. Then four men came into the restaurant and took her away," the owner stated.

Jon handed the man several photographs the OSS agents had taken of patrons before they entered the restaurant and whisked the woman away.

"This is the man," the owner said. He handed Jon the photograph of a rough-looking man in an ill-fitting suit. "He left, looking quite upset, soon after the woman was taken."

"Do you have any idea who he is?"

The owner nodded. "He owns several fishing boats down at the docks. His name is Captain Aung. I occasionally buy fish from him, but if you go to visit him, be extremely cautious. He's a very dangerous man."

"Thank you. You've been a great help."

Jon returned to the hotel and went to the manager's office. In addition to being the hotel manager, Alain Chandra headed up of one of the two CIC detachments in Chittagong and held the rank of first lieutenant in the US Army. He gave Alain the photograph of the fisherman and his name. He asked Alain to observe Captain Aung's activities. Jon wanted to know if Captain Aung was taking anyone to sea with him, besides his crew members, when he went out to fish. He also wanted to know if anyone, besides his crew members, got off the boats when they returned. He asked Alain to have his men take photographs and dispatch them to the SOE detachment in Calcutta.

CHAPTER 19

Somewhere over Burma

Second Lieutenant Toshihiro Nagano had been airborne for nearly two hours in his Nakajima Ki-27 fighter. He had taken off from one of the last Japanese airfields in northern Thailand, Chiang Rai, with a wingman. Both pilots had recently graduated from fighter training school and had arrived at their combat squadron three weeks before. Most of the pilots at Chiang Rai had less than one hundred hours of flying experience, as the more experienced fighter pilots had been reassigned to forward combat theaters or to carriers. Today's mission was meant to increase their flying proficiency and keep them out of trouble. Their squadron commander had ordered them to patrol west into Burma and find targets of opportunity, which he knew they would not find.

Shortly after takeoff, Lieutenant Nagano's wingman had engine trouble and returned to the Chiang Rai airfield. Nagano needed the flying time, so the tower ordered him to continue with the patrol on his own. His Ki-27 aircraft carried external wing tanks and could stay airborne for nearly four hours before having to land. Lieutenant Nagano had been flying for nearly an hour when he spotted a small, single-engine aircraft flying five thousand feet below him.

After consulting his drawings of Allied aircraft, Lieutenant Nagano determined he had identified a Stinson L-5, an American reconnaissance aircraft. He slipped his goggles over his eyes, eased his yoke left, and flew his aircraft in a slow arcing curve toward the enemy aircraft.

Unarmed; easy kill, thought Lieutenant Nagano.

After breakfast, Jon and Tex checked out of the Circuit House Hotel, and the hotel limo then drove them to the Chittagong airfield. Before entering the base operations building, Tex asked, "What do you say we take a detour before heading back to Calcutta?"

"Exactly what kind of mischief do you have in mind, Tex?" Jon asked.

"Two hours east of here is a region called the Pagan Plains and the location of the ruins of the ancient Kingdom of Pagan, the first kingdom that unified all of the fractioned regions we now call Burma. There are over two thousand Buddhist temples, pagodas, and monasteries located on the plain. I thought we could fly over the area and do a little sightseeing. Maybe even land and go through some of the temples."

"Don't you think that will be a little dangerous? There are still some surviving Japanese units in the area."

"Hell, knowing you, they would probably lay down their arms and surrender."

"Well, as long as we get back to Calcutta before dark, I don't see why we can't."

"We have to fly south first, so we don't have to fly over Mount Victoria. It's ten thousand feet high, and this crate can't fly over it. I'll fly thirty miles south of the mountain, turn east, and fly through a mountain pass. We'll come out of the mountains about fifty miles southwest of Pagan."

After handing the sergeant in base operation their flight plan, Tex and Jon walked to their aircraft. Thirty minutes later they lifted off from the airfield and headed south, flying at 105 miles per hour.

Two hours into their flight, as they exited the three-thousand-foot-high pass, Tex began his turn to the northeast. As Tex rolled out on their new heading and leveled the wings, he noticed a reflection from the sun northeast of their position.

"I don't think we're going to get to go sightseeing through those temples today. We have a visitor at our one o'clock position, forty-five degrees above the horizon," Tex said. He quickly put the L-5 into a steep dive.

Struggling to keep the contents of his stomach down, Jon asked, "American or Japanese?"

"The air wing didn't schedule any fighter sorties this far southeast today, so it's most likely a Jap fighter. Probably a Nakajima Ki-27; most fliers call it a Nate. It's an older fighter. A lot of them were sent to Asia after the Zero came out. The Japs still have several squadrons flying out of Thailand."

"What are our chances against the Nate?"

"Head-to-head, nil, but if we can get into that valley five miles off to our left, we have a chance. He can fly as low, but not as slow, as we can. If he doesn't shoot us down on his first pass, I can outmaneuver him until he runs low on fuel and has to head home."

"That's encouraging."

Within minutes, the Nate was firing at the Stinson. Tex saw the tracers, inverted the L-5, executed a descending half loop to the left, and rolled out as the Nate swept past them heading south. Despite the evasive split-S maneuver, several rounds from the Nate struck the left wing of the L-5, but they caused little damage. Tex dropped the nose of the L-5 and leveled off five hundred feet above the treetops, between two hills.

The camouflage paint on the L-5 gave them a reprieve until the Nate's pilot found their shadow on the top of the mountain canopy. The Nate did a 270-degree turn, climbed, located the L-5, and dove at them from the rear. Tex banked the L-5 left just in time to avoid the Nate's fire. On the Nate's third pass, Tex banked the aircraft hard left and did a 360-degree turn back to his original heading. The Nate pilot missed them again.

"Do you see that ridge ahead of us? I'm going to fly toward it and hope the Nate follows me."

"I hope you are not planning on flying us into the ridge."

"Not exactly, but we might get a little close to it."

Tex looked back in time to see the Nate coming around to line up on them again. He began banking, turning the L-5 hard right and then hard left to move out of the way of the incoming 12.7-millimeter rounds. Jon's head hit the window, nearly knocking him unconscious. When Tex turned toward the 4,500-foot ridge, he was only a hundred feet above the treetops. The ridge he was aiming for was the northern boundary of a narrow river running west to east. Tex approached within fifty yards of the ridge before banking hard right to follow the river through a narrow rock-walled gorge.

"If this doesn't work, we're both dead. Lord, I sure could use your help," Tex said.

Tex put the L-5 between the rock gorge walls. Jon gasped; there were barely thirty yards of clearance on either side of the L-5. Tex glanced back and caught a glimpse of the Nate following him into the canyon. He slipped the aircraft lower until Jon thought the wheels would touch the water. Jon looked out the small back window, calling out the Nate's position relative to the L-5, as Tex continued jinking the aircraft hard left and then hard right to throw off the aim of the Japanese pilot bent on killing them. Jon was convinced they were going to hit the wall of the canyon, but Tex yanked the aircraft in the opposite direction at the last moment every time, missing the ridge by no more than five feet. Tex saw the Nate drawing closer and slowed the L-5 to sixty knots. He banked hard left into the 4,500-foot cliff and gave the Stinson full power.

Certain he had his kill, Lieutenant Nagano slowed his aircraft to just above its stall speed so he wouldn't overshoot the L-5. He thought the American had made a mistake in turning down the narrow gorge, which limited the L-5's maneuverability. Lieutenant Nagano was so fixated on his target that he turned to follow as the L-5 banked hard to the left. A moment later, Lieutenant Nagano realized his error; he pulled back on his stick and went to full power to try to climb above the ridge. The last thing he saw was the rock ridge filling his windshield. When the Nate impacted, it erupted in a ball of flames.

After Tex rolled the L-5 out on a westerly heading, Jon heard him sigh with relief.

"Thought he had us for sure," Jon said.

"He must have been a new pilot with very little experience; otherwise he would have had us on the first pass. He did what a lot of young aviators do. He focused too much on the kill and too little on flying his aircraft. He totally lost his awareness of the terrain."

"Does that count as a kill?"

"Yep."

"Since I'm in the aircraft with you, do I get credit for half a kill?"

Climbing the L-5 and forgetting about the sightseeing tour, Tex turned his head toward Jon. "Why the hell not, hotshot?"

CHAPTER 20

Calcutta, India

Colonel John Renick looked and felt exhausted. This was his sixth trip in four months, and the strain of carrying verbal orders to special-mission agents in two theaters of war had taken a toll. The physical stress of flying sixty hours from Washington, DC, to Calcutta had caused him to drop over thirty pounds. As soon as he finished this mission, General George C. Marshall, the US Army chief of staff, had promised him he would be moved into the G-2 Plans Directorate. Lieutenant Colonel Steve Schaefer, the son of his longtime friend and classmate at the military academy, would be taking his place. Schaefer had distinguished himself in India, Burma, and Thailand, becoming a rising star in army intelligence.

After they landed in Algiers, an American OSS agent greeted Colonel Renick and introduced him to the female army captain with him, Kelly Popper. Popper, a thin, attractive brunette, did not go unnoticed by the ground crew surrounding the aircraft. Despite her good looks, Popper was a seasoned OSS agent. In 1942, she parachuted into France, stole a bicycle, and rode it to Paris. For two years she ran two Nazi double agents for the covert American agency. After the French Second Armored Division and the US Fourth Infantry Division liberated Paris in August 1944, she moved to an OSS liaison position with British intelligence in Paris. Upon receiving orders from General Donovan, the director of the OSS, she packed her bags and flew to Algiers. She had to wait only one day in Algiers before joining up with Colonel Renick.

Unlike most of West Point graduates of 1916, eager to go into combat and command men, John Renick desired research. With off-the-scale intelligence, he had graduated at the top of his class, and the Pentagon had chosen him to fill a staff position at US Army headquarters, an assignment that was intended to groom him for a command position later in his career.

After Congress declared war on Germany in April 1917, the army reassigned him to the newly created signals intelligence organization. For the duration of the war, he immersed himself in decoding German military communications and developing codes for use by the army signal corps. After the war ended, he resigned his commission and went to work for the American Telephone and Telegraph Company. When the United States was attacked by Japan in 1941, he volunteered for service. Happy to be back in an army uniform with a commission as a lieutenant colonel and an assignment to military intelligence, Renick attacked his new job with the same energy he had when deciphering German codes. Within two years he was promoted to full colonel and given a new job working directly for the chief of staff. Thus he found himself here, tired as a dog and in the midst of yet another mission to Asia, albeit his last.

Twenty-four hours after flying out of Algiers, Colonel Renick and Agent Popper landed in Calcutta. The thermometer at base operations read 110 degrees Fahrenheit. To Kelly it felt like they were walking into a furnace. She thought she would be soaking in sweat after two minutes, but the arid air quickly evaporated the moisture from her skin. She mentioned that she had experienced the same type of heat in California. Colonel Renick was quick with his answer.

"This is highly unusual weather for Calcutta. Today, the wind is out of the northwest. Tomorrow the wind will be from the south, bringing ninety-eight percent humidity, and your clothes will be soaking with sweat."

"In that case, I guess I had better buy some lightweight uniforms more appropriate to the climate."

Colonel Renick exited the staff car and put his wheel hat on, covering what remained of his graying red hair.

"You won't be wearing your uniform around here. Some lightweight and loose-fitting civilian attire will be your best option."

As they entered the SOE detachment, Colonel MacKenzie's shouts resonated throughout the offices.

"Sightseeing! You went sightseeing? You're not a bloody damn tourist. For crying out loud, what the hell were you thinking? You're too damn valuable to be gallivanting around ancient Burmese ruins. The Jap fighter...You could have been killed. You all should have flown straight to Calcutta. Now promise me you won't do anything this stupid ever again."

"I promise, sir," Jon said. He slowly backed out of the colonel's office and bumped into Colonel Renick.

"Sounds as though you're in a bit of trouble. What happened?" Colonel Renick asked.

"It's nothing, Colonel. Is this the plus one referenced in the message sent last week?"

"Agent Jon Preston, meet Agent Kelly Popper. Kelly has been reassigned to Calcutta from the OSS detachment in Paris. Who's in the office with you today?"

"Miles and George are in the briefing room, going over the transcript of the interview with the two captured Japanese agents. Henri's hobbling around on crutches somewhere in the building. He probably walked into the officers' club to grab a bite to eat."

"Go get him, please. I'd like to introduce Agent Popper and discuss what she will be trying to accomplish with the captured spies."

"Sir, shouldn't we include Colonel Ray and Lieutenant Colonel Taylor?"

"We'll be meeting with them later today."

After Jon left to find Henri, Colonel Renick walked into Colonel MacKenzie's office. "Are you having problems with the hired help, Michael?" Colonel Renick asked.

With everyone present, Colonel Renick introduced Kelly Popper to the group. He explained how successfully Kelly had run double agents in Paris and expressed his confidence that she also would be successful in running their two female spies. First, however, she had to determine if the two women were suitable to be double agents and if they would fully cooperate.

"Whether I can use them depends on their level of cooperation and motivation," Kelly said. "Without significant motivation, they won't take risks and won't be effective. I'll need a day to study the transcripts of their interrogations, and then I'll need a day to talk to each woman. I need

to determine why they will work for us, because it needs to be something we can leverage. I'd like to begin interviewing the women in two
days. Tomorrow, I need to do some shopping for clothing suitable to this
climate."

"I know the right people to hook you up with, and I'm certain I can get
you better accommodations than an officer's tent," Jon stated. "Colonel
Renick, if you'll drop her off here when you're through at Colonel Ray's and
Colonel Taylor's offices, I'll take her out to the *Jacqueline*."

At a little after 1800 hours, Jon and Kelly arrived at the *Jacqueline*.
She sat in awe of the 126-foot luxury yacht. Being quite familiar with sailboats, she liked the red-and-green stripes running the length of the hull.
Prior to the *Jacqueline*, she had only seen stripes on racing sailboats. As
they approached the movable walkway, Captain Dubois walked out onto
the deck.

After walking aboard, Jon approached Captain Dubois. "Captain, I
want you to meet OSS agent Kelly Popper. She arrived from Paris today
and is assigned to Detachment 101."

"Welcome aboard the *Jacqueline*, Agent Popper. Can I assume Kelly
needs some accommodations during her stay in Calcutta?"

"I was thinking she could berth with Monique, Captain."

"I'm sure Monique will welcome the company. Why don't you two
step into the lounge? I'll summon the other ladies. Dinner will be served
in an hour. Casual attire."

Once introduced, Camille, Kathleen, Brigitte, and Monique chatted
with Kelly for the entire hour before dinner, totally ignoring Jon, George,
and Captain Dubois. All four girls said they would take Kelly shopping in
the morning. They assured her the clothing would be of excellent quality
and would be inexpensive. Eager for news about the war with Germany,
they prodded Kelly for information about when the Germans might
surrender.

"The day I left Paris," Kelly said, "the German Army in Italy surrendered. So, it shouldn't be much longer, but you can never tell with Hitler."

"What's Paris like now? Are things getting back to normal yet?"
Camille asked.

"Supplies are starting to come in from the United States and South
America: grain, canned foods, cigarettes, and booze."

"What about shopping? Are the clothiers working yet?" Brigitte asked.

"For crying out loud," Jon stated, "I don't think I can listen to any more of this."

Camille elbowed Jon in the ribs and told him to be quiet. Jon turned to the bartender.

"Juan, give me a double scotch, neat." A second later Camille elbowed him again.

During dinner, Jon updated everyone on Agent Popper's mission to Calcutta, but before he could finish, Brunelle rushed into the dining room and handed Captain Dubois a message.

Captain Dubois rose from his chair, tapped his spoon on his flute of champagne, and asked for everyone's attention.

"Ladies and gentlemen, it pleases me to announce the unconditional surrender of all German forces to the Allies. Let me remind you, however, we are still at war with Japan."

Captain Dubois turned to his bartender and steward. "Juan, I think this news calls for the good stuff. Would you bring out the 1928 Dom Pérignon? Make sure the crew gets champagne as well."

CHAPTER 21

Malacca Strait, Malaya

Colonel Renick laid a map of Sumatra on the table in front of Jon, Miles, and George. He pointed at a POW camp called Trandjoeng Balai.

"The camp is located four hundred miles inside the Strait of Malacca. We've learned from a recent intercept that a leading Japanese scientist, Dr. Takeo Tsuchinya, will be there in ten days. He's involved in research at the Unit 731 camp in Pingfang, where he heads the Chemical Warfare Department. We want you to kidnap him from the Trandjoeng Balai camp and bring him back here," Colonel Renick stated.

"What about the prisoners?" Jon asked.

"They are not our mission this time. But we need to grab Dr. Tsuchinya before the Russians or the Chinese Communists get him."

"Is he that important?" Miles asked.

"According to our analysts in Washington, he's the leading expert in the world on chemical warfare. He consulted with the German Army's chemical research program before the war in Europe started. We cannot afford to let the Communists get him. Until this war is over, a majority of our resources will be dedicated to capturing and bringing out as many Unit 731 scientists as possible; you all will play a big part in it."

"What about their war crimes? Aren't they going to stand trial and be hanged?" George asked.

"Many scientists will hang, but not until we get as much information out of them as possible."

The following morning, the three agents boarded an American PBY and flew six and a half hours across the Bay of Bengal to their rendezvous with the American submarine USS *Coho*. After the agents were aboard, Captain Janca piloted his boat on the surface for another four hundred miles, passing the Nicobar Islands before turning southeast. The *Coho* submerged before they reached Sanbang Island and then entered the Malacca Strait. The boat resurfaced after sundown and remained on the surface for the remainder of the night, submerging only when their radar spotted a ship or an aircraft.

Two nights later, the *Coho's* sonar picked up the sounds of a small fishing vessel with its engines idling. The captain submerged the boat and approached the vessel.

"Slow to five knots," ordered Captain Janca. "Bring it to periscope depth."

From his position at the periscope, the executive officer, Lieutenant Commander Chad Spivey, identified a motorized fishing boat in the bright moonlight.

"Twenty degrees off the port bow, Skipper," Spivey said.

At 2100 hours, the fishing boat began signaling "Flashlight" in Morse code.

"Morse code, Skipper. It's the correct code word," Lieutenant Commander Spivey said.

"Battle stations surface," Captain Janca ordered. The *bong, bong, bong* of the battle alarm rang out throughout the boat. Once the boat surfaced, submariners scrambled to open the hatch and rushed out onto the bridge to their battle-station positions, installing and manning the three machine guns and loading a shell in the five-inch deck gun.

When Captain Janca crawled through the hatch and stepped onto the bridge, black seawater could be heard boiling around the *Coho* from compressed air pushing water out of the ballast tanks. He ordered his communications officer, standing next to him, to signal the fishing boat with the submarine's code word: "Cotton Tail."

The fishing boat acknowledged receipt and began moving toward the submarine. It stopped fifty feet abeam the submarine's port side.

Inside the submarine, Jon, Miles, and George gathered their equipment. They wore jungle fatigues and green knit watch caps. By the time they reached the aft deck, their six-man life raft floated beside the boat. Within minutes they began rowing toward the small fishing boat.

As they boarded the boat, the first mate greeted the trio and told them to store their gear below deck. As Jon entered the wheelhouse, where Major Larned began throttling up the engines, he was greeted by Andy's scarlet macaw.

"Welcome aboard, you sorry sod," Marteen squawked.

"Hello, Marteen. Andy, it is great to see you again. How's the shoulder?" Jon asked.

"Healed, but still tender."

"Any trouble with the Japs this trip?"

"Japs! Japs! Kill the slant-eyed bastards," Marteen squawked.

"Not this time. I moved my boat to a new location twenty miles south of Penang. The only Japs around are associated with a small Jap outpost in Penang."

"I see Marteen's learned some new phrases."

"You can blame that on my first mate."

"Do you have any new information on the Trandjoeng Balai camp?"

"Three of my men scouted it out this morning; looks like there are close to sixty POWs. There's an airfield a mile north of the camp. A Kawasaki-Lockheed Super Electra is parked there, guarded by two Jap soldiers. Sergeant Ryan Grist will be leading you to a camp set up in a heavy bamboo forest, and he's sketched a map of the POW camp for you. After I drop you off, I'll be moving the boat into a hidden cove four miles north of here."

Onshore, Sergeant Grist guided them into his camp. Several marines sat around, using red-filtered flashlights for lighting.

"I don't allow fires. If you're hungry, I brought along some cooked rice. Water is in the canteens over by the tent," Sergeant Grist said.

"Thanks," Jon said. "I brought some dried pork. It should go good with the rice."

"We'll leave for the camp before daybreak."

"Sergeant, are there any tigers in these woods?" Miles asked.

"There are no tigers on this island. Why?

"The last time I camped in a bamboo forest like this one, one of our Kachin guides was dragged off by a tiger. We found him the next day, his body half-eaten and draped across a tree limb twenty feet off the ground."

Everyone but Miles slept well. Before daybreak, the three agents and Sergeant Grist worked their way toward the POW camp, two miles away. When the sun rose, they stopped at the edge of a small clearing, where the sergeant pointed out the airfield and the Kawasaki-Lockheed Super Electra sitting under camouflaged netting.

As they trekked closer to the POW camp, they heard a Japanese bugle sounding reveille. When they reached the edge of the jungle and looked out at the camp, they saw a Japanese flag being raised and the guards and prisoners standing at attention and saluting. After the guards secured the halyard to the pole cleats, the commandant gave a brief speech and dismissed most of the guards and prisoners. Three guards separated five prisoners from the group and marched them to a bamboo structure on the far north side of the compound.

"That's the medical unit. I've seen four different men in white coats go in and out of the building. When the prisoners are brought out, they are dead. Their bodies are taken to a pit, over there in the northeast corner, and burned," Sergeant Grist said.

The three agents looked toward the pit and saw a guard pouring liquid from a can onto the ground. The guard then struck a match and threw it to the ground. A trail of fire walked its way for thirty feet before a huge ball of fire erupted in the pit, cremating the prisoners killed during the night.

"I can't wait to kill these buggers," Sergeant Grist stated.

"We're not here to take the camp and rescue the prisoners. We're here to kidnap the medical officer that flew in on that aircraft back there," George said.

"So that's why you requested a pilot."

"What do you mean?" Jon asked.

"The message from the OSS detachment stated that your team needed a pilot who could fly that Electra. That's why I'm here."

"I wonder why no one told us." Miles stated.

"I assume because the OSS didn't know if they could get me here in time. I was patrolling on the eastern coast of the Malay Peninsula when the SOE located me. The OSS gave me their L-5 to fly across the peninsula and meet Major Larned."

"Then I guess we go to Plan B," George said.

"Let's figure out a way to kidnap this scientist first. Then we can focus on flying the Electra out of here," Jon said.

CHAPTER 22

Trandjoeng Balai POW Camp, Sumatra

Before returning to their base camp, Jon, Miles, and George and Sergeant Grist scouted the compound from two different quadrants while two of Sergeant Grist's men kept an eye on the airstrip. If anything unusual happened, they were to report it to Grist without hesitation.

For the next four hours, the three agents planned how they would infiltrate the camp. The elephant grass encroached within ten feet of the fence, so getting close without being discovered and penetrating the fence would not be a problem. Sergeant Grist and his men would capture the airfield while Jon and George got the chemist out of the camp.

"What do we do if we can't determine which Jap we are looking for?" Sergeant Grist asked.

"That's why we brought George along. He lived in Japan before the war and speaks fluent Japanese. However, if the Japs won't talk, we'll employ some stick therapy," Jon said.

"What's stick therapy?" Sergeant Grist asked.

"It's simple. You pull your dagger and stick it in a knee or an elbow until they point out the right person. The therapy is quite effective," Miles told him.

Jon stood when one of the men watching the airfield came running into the camp.

"What's up, Corporal?" Sergeant Grist asked.

"They're warming up the airplane, sir."

"Quick, let's move to the airfield. This guy might be leaving," Jon stated. He grabbed his gear and moved toward the airstrip. Miles and George did the same and hurried to catch up with their team leader.

It took twenty minutes for them to reach the airfield. The aircraft's wheels were still chocked, and its starboard engine was running at idle. The door to the plane was open on the port side, and the small airstairs lowered to the ground. A single Japanese guard stood watch, moving clockwise around the plane.

"Miles, you and I will take out the guards. Sergeant, after the outside guards are down, you and George get in the aircraft and take out the pilots and anyone else in the aircraft," Jon said.

Jon and Miles moved through the tall grass and picked a blind spot to the guards' view at the rear of the aircraft. They rushed up behind the small bamboo hut and crouched. Both withdrew their daggers and their silenced pistols. George and Sergeant Grist stayed right behind them.

"George, say something in Japanese and get the guards to come our way," Jon stated.

George yelled to the guards in a panicked but authoritative voice. The two guards who rushed around the corner of the building were startled by Jon and Miles. They raised their rifles to fire, but two silenced shots killed them. Jon moved the bodies away from the hut and into the tall grass while Miles stood guard.

"What did you say to get them to come so fast?" Jon asked.

"I told them I had been bitten by a snake while taking a crap and to come quickly."

"George, since the aircraft is facing away from the building, can you approach it and call out for help from behind the stairs? Maybe one of the pilots or crew will come to your aid," Jon suggested.

"It worked once; might as well try it again." He and Sergeant Grist crept toward the aircraft.

George approached the aircraft from the left-rear quarter, knelt beside the airstairs, and yelled in his panicked voice, loud enough to be heard over the engine noise. He then ducked under the aircraft and waited until one of the Japanese pilots came rushing off the aircraft. When he reached the bottom of the stairs and turned around, George put a bullet in his heart.

Sergeant Grist and George rushed into the aircraft. Grist bumped into the flight engineer and knocked him down. George shot him in the eye and followed the sergeant to the cockpit. The startled pilot pulled his pistol and turned to fire, but Sergeant Grist fired first and placed a single shot into the side of his head.

"You get in the pilot's seat and get this thing ready to go. I'll get the dead Japs off the aircraft," George said.

Jon saw George dragging the flight engineer out of the aircraft and rushed up to help.

"Any more?"

"One more, in the cockpit."

"Dump him with the others. I'll grab the other one."

After Jon moved the pilot's body, a Type 95 scout car, the Japanese version of the Willys jeep, drove out of the jungle a hundred yards away. The scout car rolled to a stop ten yards from the Electra. A small Japanese man in the front passenger's seat got out, grabbed his briefcase from the front floorboard, and motioned for the guard in the rear seat to bring his suitcase.

"You take the guy with the suitcase. I'll get the driver," Jon said.

A pistol shot from thirty feet was nothing for Jon, and he placed a shot in the driver's left temple. When George fired, the Japanese soldier carrying the suitcase fell to the ground dead. Thinking that the soldier had stumbled and fallen in his rush to get the bag to the plane, the scientist admonished him. The Japanese doctor turned and looked back at the scout car, noticing the driver slumped forward in the seat and the blood splattered on the windshield. Before he could react, George yelled over the engine noise as he rushed up behind the doctor.

"Hands in the air," George said.

Jon picked up the suitcase and the briefcase that fell from the terrified chemist's hands. On the aircraft, Miles bound the doctor's hands and feet with leather straps and tied him to the seat. Miles sat down in a seat across from the doctor, aiming a pistol at his midsection. George walked up to the doctor and squatted next to him.

"What is your name, Colonel?"

"Dr. Takeo Tsuchinya."

"Are you Dr. Takeo Tsuchinya, the world-famous chemist?"

"I am," Colonel Tsuchinya said. Pride and arrogance exuded in his voice.

"Well, Colonel, we're taking you back to India to be tried and hanged for war crimes."

Dr. Tsuchinya turned pale, closed his eyes for a second, and looked at George with both fear and anger in his eyes.

Sergeant Grist started the number-two engine and rechecked the instrument panel. "Engine pressure, oil temperature, no red lights. Good to go," he said out loud. Before taxiing he dialed in the radio frequency to contact Major Larned on the fishing boat. Once airborne, Sergeant Grist put the aircraft on a heading of three-zero-zero degrees and made his first radio call.

"Sandpiper calling Marteen."

"This is Marteen; go ahead, Sandpiper," Major Larned replied.

"Marteen, call home and pass our estimated time of arrival to Alpha Ninety-Six Echo. I don't want any of the good guys in white hats taking a shot at us."

"I'll pass your ETA along, Sandpiper."

The SOE provided Major Larned with the aircraft's call sign and the location of their refueling stops. *Alpha* designated their first stop, and *Ninety-Six Echo* represented the longitude for Rangoon, ninety-six degrees east. They would stop there, taxi into a hangar, and change to a different aircraft. No one would walk outside the hangar because they did not want any Japanese spies taking photographs of the agents or of the Japanese scientist.

Jon sat quietly, lost in deep thought. Despite the last-minute changes, this mission had seemed too easy. Either his team was getting really good or the Japanese were getting very lax. *A little of both, with a lot of luck from above*, Jon thought.

Jon was a faithful Catholic, but a week had passed since he had last prayed and a month since his last confession. He bowed his head and gave thanks to the Lord for protecting him and his team once more. *Father Doherty would scold me for not praying daily*, he thought.

CHAPTER 23

Calcutta, India

Captain Dubois and the five female OSS agents had been busy over the last three weeks. Kelly Popper interviewed the two captured Japanese agents and determined they would be suitable candidates for double agents. By the end of the third week, they were ready to be sent back to Singapore with a mission to obtain the names and locations of agents spying for the Japanese in southern Asia and India.

Kelly's goal was to send Anna D'Arras and Marie Ancelet back to Singapore, where they would report the success of their mission to their Japanese masters and begin collecting information for the OSS. Along the way, CIC, OSS, and SOE intelligence agents would track the women, photograph their contacts, and document their extraction route. Ten days after their return to Singapore, an SOE agent, who would be their communications lifeline to Calcutta, would contact them.

Jon and Camille lay in matching adjustable wooden chaise lounges on the aft deck of the *Jacqueline*, away from the green-canopied section of the deck. They discussed what they would do after the war. Camille wanted to know more about America. What is Ohio like? How cold are the winters? Can a woman get a good job? Camille held a degree in elementary education from the University of Southern California, Los Angeles; she had originally wanted to be a teacher. Now she wasn't so sure. After serving as an OSS agent, she didn't know if the life of a schoolteacher would be exciting enough.

Jon answered all of her questions except the one about a good job.

"Camille, after the war is over, nearly a million American soldiers will be returning to the United States and looking for jobs. Women will be laid off from many of the jobs that men held before the war. However, if you start a business, you could control your own destiny."

Camille was overjoyed to hear this. She knew Jon was actually encouraging her.

"Then I will start a business."

"What kind?"

"Well, my parents owned a bakery and a jewelry store. I worked in both until I graduated from high school. I can grade a diamond, and I can make great cinnamon rolls."

"After the war, a lot of GIs will be getting married and having families. There will be a huge demand for both skills. I'll write my father and ask him to find us a location. After we get home, you can choose what you want to start."

"What will you do?"

"I've saved every cent of my GI pay, and we both have our percentage of the diamonds Captain Dubois gave us after we captured the Japanese spy in Chittagong last year. Those diamonds would be a great start to a jewelry store."

"Excellent idea. I used to design rings and necklaces for my father. I would make the wax designs, cast them in gold, polish the settings, and set the jewels in them. I know the jewelry business very well."

"Then it's settled. We'll start with a jewelry store. We can always open a bakery later and set it up close to the college campus."

"I am so excited. I hope this war ends soon."

Jon heard the tension in her voice and assured her they would get through the war.

As Jon sat there, his thoughts turned to the Unit-731 medical-experimentation camps he and his team still needed to raid. He read the latest report from the OSS about the additional medical camps discovered in Saigon, French Indochina; Mytho, Indonesia; Victory Point, Malaya; and Woosung, China. He wished he could send out extra teams and raid them all in the next thirty days, but their resources were limited. They would take them one at a time.

In the morning they received a message stating that a G-2 colonel was inbound from Washington. Jon felt somewhat relieved. He didn't like idle time, even though most of it was used to complete his after-action report on the extraction of Colonel Takeo Tsuchinya.

A day later, Colonel Steve Schaefer entered their briefing room and said hello to everyone. As they all stood to greet Schaefer, Jon noticed the eagles on his uniform.

"When did you get promoted to full Colonel?" Jon asked.

"A month ago when I was reassigned to the Pentagon."

"Don't tell me you are Colonel Renick's replacement, mate," Miles said.

"That's me."

Over the next two hours, Colonel Schaefer briefed the agents on all the information the OSS had collected on the POW camp near Saigon.

"The camp is located fifteen miles south of Saigon on the Mekong River and only five miles from the South China Sea. It's approximately five hundred yards east of the Mekong River. It's supplied by a small, ten-ton steel boat that docks on the river every other week; supplies and new POWs are off-loaded there. There is no airfield associated with this camp because the area is heavily forested."

"Do we know what kind of medical experiments are being performed on our boys?" Henri asked.

"From what we've learned from the POWs on work details outside the camp, we believe it to be cholera, diphtheria, or yellow fever. The POWs said they heard the victims coughing, throwing up, and asking for water, which are just a few of the symptoms of these diseases. However, none of the prisoners ever returned to their huts. Apparently, the Japanese perform vivisection on every test subject to determine the damage to the internal organs. After they're finished, they burn the bodies."

"How many prisoners are we talking about, Colonel?" George asked.

"Around sixty."

"What's our mission, Colonel?" Jon asked.

"We want you to capture the physicians and bring our boys home."

"How will we get there?" George asked.

"You'll fly from here to Chittagong. At Chittagong, you'll board a Royal Navy PBY. It will fly to a point east of Andaman Island, where it will rendezvous with a fishing boat you're familiar with."

"Captain Ahab?" Jon asked.

"Yes, Captain Ahab's boat will refuel the PBY with aviation fuel. From there you will fly across the southernmost peninsula of Thailand into the South China Sea. The PBY will make a second rendezvous with another fishing boat, which will get you up the Mekong River to your destination. You leave in two days."

"Won't we be at risk of being shot down by Japanese fighters?" George asked.

"Our OSS contacts are telling us the closest Japanese fighter base is over three hundred miles north of your destination."

"Well, that's reassuring. How will we get the prisoners home?" Jon asked.

"We've lined up eleven sampans owned by relatives of our local OSS agents. They regularly fish in the South China Sea. They will pick up the prisoners and get them into the South China Sea, where they'll be met by a British destroyer escort. The destroyer will get them to Manila in the Philippine Islands."

"Where will we be heading afterward?" Jon asked.

"You all will rendezvous with a PBY, which will bring you back to Calcutta. Essentially, the same route you came in on."

CHAPTER 24

Saigon POW Camp, Thailand

The British PBY, guided by an AN/UPN-1 radar beacon set up on the forty-foot Vietnamese junk, landed thirty minutes before sunset. After paddling the six-man life raft to the junk, Lieutenant Dahn Nguyen, an OSS agent from Saigon, greeted the three agents.

The junk looked unusual for a sailboat with its two irregular and blunt-shaped sails. The bow appeared to be too low, the stern too high, and the transom, at the rear of the boat, unusually wide. Unlike a traditional sailboat, the flat-bottomed junk lacked a keel. In order to avoid slipping and being blown leeward, the boat was equipped with a daggerboard, a retractable centerboard.

As they sailed toward the entrance of the Mekong River, Jon asked about the junk's seaworthiness. "The junk's hull is constructed with six watertight compartments, which enables the boat to stay afloat even if one compartment is damaged and flooded," Lieutenant Dahn stated.

Lieutenant Dahn further explained that the sails were made from sturdy bamboo battens and spaced at three-foot intervals, and around each batten the sailcloth was sewn to separate the sail sections into individual sheets. If a sailcloth panel was damaged and torn, the tear in the sailcloth material would stop at the individual batten. Lieutenant Dahn concluded by telling Jon that the junk was the most seaworthy boat ever built.

Once under way, the agents sat under a sun cover made of bamboo and thatch. A small Vietnamese man named Dinh offered the agents a piece of fruit. The smell of the fruit almost overpowered Jon.

"What kind of fruit is this?" Jon asked.

"It called durian," Miles responded.

"Smells like a combination of almonds and turpentine, but it tastes good."

"It's one of those things that you either love or hate. Some people find the smell pleasant, while others find it overpowering and repugnant."

Before the war, Miles had held a position as a professor of biology at the University of Bangkok and was well versed in most of the edible fruit throughout southern Asia.

"Well, the jury is still out for me," George stated. He continued to eat the questionably tasteful fruit.

As they approached the Mekong River, Lieutenant Nguyen gave the agents native clothing to put on over their jungle fatigues and conical straw hats to put on their heads. Before the PBY landed, each agent darkened his face, neck, arms, and hands with the coloring agents provided in the OSS war kit they carried.

By 2300 hours, the boat had passed abeam the dock used by the POW camp. The boat stopped three miles farther upriver, beside a large tree that lay in the Mekong River next to the shore. After the agents and the lieutenant exited the boat, it departed. Lieutenant Dahn guided them along a narrow jungle path for over a mile before being greeted by three Vietnamese soldiers with British Lee-Enfield, .303-caliber, bolt-action rifles. They guided the agents to a base camp a mile closer to their objective.

At the base camp, the agents huddled around one of several small fires. The dense jungle assured that no one would see the fires from a distance, and the prevailing wind from the west kept the smoke away from the POW camp.

Lieutenant Dahn showed the trio a sketch of the camp, which was sixty yards wide and a hundred yards long.

"The commandant's office and quarters are located in a building on the north side, next to the radio tower. There are six rectangular huts in the compound. Four are for prisoners, and two are for the guards and support personnel. Two additional huts are located forty yards from the others," Lieutenant Dahn said.

Jon assumed the huts were where the medical team conducted its biological and chemical experiments.

"How much of the jungle is cleared around the camp?" Jon asked.

"Around ten meters."

"How many guards are they using on the inside perimeter?"

"Six during the day and four at night."

"Do any guards patrol outside the camp?" George asked.

"None that I am aware of."

"We need to take a look at the camp later tonight," Jon said.

At 0100 hours, Jon, Miles, George, and Lieutenant Dahn left the camp for the POW compound. They came in from the north and moved around the compound in a clockwise direction. Midway on the south-to-north section, Miles crept up to the fence and tested the wire.

When Miles returned to the group, he told them, "The wire is rusted and crumbles when you cut it. It won't be a problem to breach."

"OK, let's head back. We'll do more reconnaissance tomorrow morning," Jon said.

The next day, Jon, Miles, and George broke into two teams. Jon and Lieutenant Dahn took the south end of the compound where the POW work details had been working the last three days. Jon wanted to talk to one of the prisoners. Miles and George would explore the north end.

When Jon and Lieutenant Dahn reached their area, the prisoners had already begun work clearing the perimeter brush with machetes. Two prisoners stood among the ones doing the work. One oversaw the work while the other sharpened machetes dulled by the tough bamboo. Only four guards kept an eye on the twenty prisoners. Jon assumed that the prisoner overseeing the work detail was an officer, and that was whom he wanted to talk to. When the officer moved to within two feet of a large bamboo clump to take a leak, Jon spoke.

"Are you the senior officer in the camp?" Jon whispered.

"No, that would be Commander John McKinney. I'm Lieutenant Jerry Jones."

"How many POWs are there in the camp, Lieutenant?"

"One hundred and two, but that number may be less tomorrow. The Japs are doing some kind of medical experiments on the men; tomorrow is the day that they start a new round of experiments."

"I assume you know to keep your head down when the shooting starts?"

Jones nodded.

"Don't mention a word of this to anyone. Is that clear, Lieutenant?"

That afternoon, Jon, Miles, and George walked through their plan to take the camp. Lieutenant Dahn, using his wireless radio, arranged for the fishing boats to be ready to take on the prisoners and get them to sea. They would hit the camp at 0300 hours, when most of the Japanese soldiers would be in a deep sleep and slow to react to an attack. Most of the Japanese, however, would not get the chance to wake up.

With their flashlights pointing ahead of them, the camp guards performed their nightly circle of the camp. Four of Lieutenant Dahn's best fighters entered the compound after the guards passed their hidden locations. Each took out his target quietly and efficiently and dragged the body through a section of cut fence into the jungle.

Miles and George cut through the wire fence and penetrated the compound close to the Japanese guard quarters. They placed four explosive charges under each hut and waited behind a large mound of dirt next to the cooking hut. Each satchel charge contained ten pounds of plastic explosive with three pounds of ball bearings embedded in the puttylike compound. When the charges exploded, most of the inhabitants of the huts would be killed by the red-hot ball bearings.

Jon and Lieutenant Dahn cut through the fence and entered the compound next to the commander's quarters. Jon, surprised to see a guard in front of the commander's hut, admonished himself for not noticing the guard on their previous visit. He directed Lieutenant Dahn to enter the quarters and take out the commander after he eliminated the guard. Jon then pulled out his silenced .22-caliber pistol and crept to within eight feet of the guard, raised his pistol, and fired. The rather-loud pop didn't appear to wake anyone.

After Jon took out the guard, Lieutenant Dahn rushed the door of the commandant's hut. As he passed through the door, a sword entered his abdomen. The look on Dahn's face was one of utter surprise. When the commandant pulled his sword out, the lieutenant crumpled to the floor, gasping for air. The commandant was about to swing his sword and take the lieutenant's head off when he heard the click of a pistol cocking. He looked up and saw Jon's weapon leveled at his head. A split second later, a .22 round entered the commandant's head, bounced off the walls of his skull several times, and scrambled his brains. He died before his body hit the floor.

After the explosions, several Japanese stumbled out of the remains of their huts. The Vietnamese fighters were ruthless. They cut off the heads of the Japanese soldiers and placed them on bamboo poles within minutes.

Sprinting toward the medical huts, Miles and George saw six men exit the huts, each rubbing the sleep from his eyes. Four Vietnamese fighters greeted them.

"Lie down on the ground," George shouted in Japanese.

They quickly complied.

"Which of you are the physicians?" George asked. No one spoke. "Point your hands at the physicians now, or I'll start shooting you one at a time."

The physicians didn't move, but four hands pointed to the two men lying down in front of the others. George grabbed one of the men by his hair and yanked his head up.

"Are you the head physician?" George asked.

"No, the major is. I am his assistant," the frightened physician said.

Miles ordered the Vietnamese fighters to tie the hands of the two physicians and move them to the commander's quarters. After Miles and George walked away, the remaining Vietnamese fighters hacked off the heads of the four Japanese lab assistants and stuck their heads on the six-foot-tall bamboo stakes that one of the fighters secured in the soft ground.

"How's everything on your end?" Miles asked.

"The lieutenant is dead. If I had gone through that door first, it would be me lying dead on the floor of that hut," Jon stated.

"But you didn't, and you're the one that's alive."

Lieutenant Dahn's second in command walked up to Jon and told him that the first three boats were ready to take POWs aboard. Jon motioned the young fighter to come with him. He then walked over to where Lieutenant Jones and Commander McKinney stood and told them to follow the Vietnamese officer to the boats.

"Two men died during the night," Commander McKinney said. "Can we bury them before we leave?"

Jon nodded his head. "You and the burial detail will be the last ones to the boats, so make it quick," Jon said.

Jon stayed until they buried the two men. He bowed his head as Commander McKinney said a short prayer over the two graves.

You can't save them all, Jon thought.

He said amen after the prayer and headed toward the last boat.

CHAPTER 25

Calcutta, India

Jon lay awake in bed with Camille tucked snugly into his left side. A bad dream had awakened him, and he couldn't go back to sleep. It was the same dream as the night before and a dozen other times: Five American prisoners were screaming as the flamethrower spewed its propane over their bodies. Jon did not arrive in time to stop the Japanese. All he could do was watch in horror as the Allied soldiers, tied to trees with wire cable, screamed and burned and twisted in agony.

Enraged by the Japanese treatment of the prisoners, Jon wanted to hose every damn one of them with a flamethrower and inflict the same pain and agony the Allied soldiers went through.

Not a healthy attitude for a Christian, Jon thought. *We're supposed to offer mercy and grace.*

Killing had become too easy for Jon the last year and a half. Now he hardly thought about it. He wondered if he was becoming more like the Japanese physicians: methodical, insensitive, cruel, and unremorseful.

Light was starting to filter through the small port-side window, and Jon decided to get up. He showered, put on a fresh change of clothes, and went topside. Captain Dubois was standing on the fantail watching the sunrise.

"You always up this early?" Jon asked.

"Almost every morning. I love to watch the sun come up. What about you? You usually sleep in when you come back from a mission."

"Bad dream."

"Same one?"

"Yeah, same one. Can I borrow your car?"

"You know where the key is; just fill it up before you come back."

An hour later, Jon entered a small white adobe Catholic mission and sought out his friend and confessor, Father Ed Doherty. The elderly priest stood in the main courtyard to the left of the chapel, talking to several children. When he looked up and saw Jon walking toward him, he grinned from ear to ear, happy to see that Jon was well and unharmed. Father Doherty invited him to sit down at one of the large picnic tables while he went to get them each a cup of coffee.

"So, what brings you here at this early hour?" Father Doherty asked.

"I'm having bad dreams again."

"Is it the same dream you've been having, or is it a new one?"

"It's the same one. I'm to the point now where I'm only getting a couple of hours of sleep a night. I can't go back to sleep once I wake up."

"Have you thought about seeing a specialist for this problem?"

"A psychiatrist? Are you kidding? The army would classify me as a nutcase and send me home."

"Maybe it would be the best thing. You've been on two missions every month since we met. Maybe it's time to let someone else do the job."

"I can't, Father. Too many lives depend on what I do. Besides, I'm very good at it. It's just that I'm really angry at the way the Japanese treat their prisoners. They treat them like they're animals instead of human beings."

"Jon, war is ugly to begin with, but the Japanese culture makes it even worse. Their warrior code disregards human life for the sake of pride and arrogance, which they mistake for honor and duty. And from what I understand about their culture, this is driven into them during their schooling and even in college."

"Yes, I know. And it goes back centuries in their culture. But my anger makes me feel like I'm no better than they are. On every mission I can't wait to take these bastards out. And that's what bothers me."

"Jon, you're not the only one. I take confession from dozens of GIs who feel the same way. Pray to the Lord; ask him to remove these feelings. Now, get back out there and do what you do best, helping end this awful war."

"Yes, sir," Jon said as he rose to leave.

An hour later, Jon sat at the breakfast table with Camille and Kelly. Kelly explained how she ran two double agents in Paris during the German occupation. Jon noticed that Camille was eating up every word Kelly said. He was glad Kelly had taken Camille under her wing and was teaching her how to run double agents. He thought it would broaden Camille's experience base, which he knew would prove to be beneficial once Kelly moved on.

Later, George picked Jon up at the yacht and drove to the SOE detachment; Camille and the others had left earlier, complaining they had a lot of work to do. Jon noticed a parked British staff car when they arrived. Mounted on the front bumper was a flag with four stars.

Jon and George entered the detachment and noticed the staff was in a tizzy, hurrying to get coffee and tea for their VIP visitors. The desk sergeant told them to go to the briefing room immediately. Colonel MacKenzie was there, talking with Lord Admiral Louis Mountbatten, the supreme Allied commander of the Southeast Asia theater, and his deputy commander, Lieutenant General Raymond Wheeler.

"Jon, George, welcome. Let me introduce Lord Mountbatten and General Wheeler," Colonel MacKenzie said excitedly.

Jon noticed that Miles and Henri were also in their dress uniforms. Jon had had to wear his dress uniform today because Camille had taken all of his other clothes to the laundry. "They're moldy," she told him as she left the yacht. If he had discovered what was happening, he would have stayed on the yacht.

When Camille and the other female agents entered the room with Captain Dubois, Colonel Ray, and Lieutenant Colonel Taylor, all in dress uniforms, Jon knew something was up. It was no accident that his clothes were sent to the cleaners.

"Ladies and gentlemen, please take your seats. Agents Preston, Murphy, Morreau, Lauren, and Dupont, would you please come forward," Colonel MacKenzie commanded.

Before the award ceremony began, Colonel MacKenzie reminded everyone present to remain standing until the citations were read and the awards presented. Over the next ten minutes, Colonel MacKenzie read the citation to accompany the award of the Military Cross to Jon Preston, Miles Murphy, Henri Morreau, Kathleen Lauren, and Camille Dupont. He spoke of the valor of confronting three enemy assassins and saving the life of Lord Mountbatten when enemy agents had attempted to assassinate him in 1944. After a few minutes of talking about each recipient, Lord Mountbatten pinned the Military Cross on the pocket of each agent's uniform. Lord Mountbatten and Lieutenant General Wheeler came to attention and saluted the agents. After thanking them, they left the room and headed to their staff car.

After congratulating Miles, Henri, Kathleen, and Camille, Colonel Ray shook Jon's hand.

"It's not every day you see an entire team being awarded for heroism. This is only the second time of this war," Colonel Ray said.

"I wasn't aware of that," Jon replied.

"Well, I'm glad they awarded the entire team. You all have earned it twice over as far as I'm concerned."

"I could have done without all the ceremony. It's a waste of time."

"Yeah, but it gives the brass something to feel important about, while you guys do all the work."

Later that afternoon, Colonel MacKenzie called his three agents into his office.

"As recipients of the Military Cross, you all have the option of being transferred to noncombat positions," Colonel MacKenzie said.

"What if we don't want a noncombat position?" Jon asked.

"Well, in that case you can continue doing what you do with this unit. Is this the choice of each of you?" Colonel MacKenzie asked.

"Yes, sir," the agents replied in unison.

"Great; then here's a message you all should read," Colonel MacKenzie said. He handed it to Jon.

The message was from General George C. Marshall. It congratulated each of the Military Cross recipients and thanked them for their dedicated service. It also stated that a G-2 colonel was inbound to Calcutta and nothing more. *General Marshall was never too wordy*, Jon thought.

"What if we didn't choose to stay?" Jon asked.

"I have another message for you," Colonel MacKenzie stated. "But in a personal message to me, the general stated I wouldn't need it. He anticipated what the three of you would say."

"I hate being a foregone conclusion," Jon said. "When will the colonel arrive?"

"Tomorrow."

CHAPTER 26

Calcutta, India

Jon, Miles, and George were sitting at a table in the SOE detachment when Colonel Richard Arvin walked into the planning room. Jon jumped up from his seat and shook the colonel's hand vigorously.

"How are you doing, Colonel?" Jon said.

"Doing great. Where's Henri?"

"He's at the base clinic getting a physical exam so he can be put back on combat duty."

"Great. I'll wait until he gets back to start the briefing. Although he and Miles won't be going on this mission, he's still part of the team. Let's go into the officers' club and get some lunch. I'm starving."

Several hours later, Henri returned from the doctor's office with his new bill of health and his combat status reactivated. Colonel Arvin opened up his briefcase and laid several folders on the table. He explained that the folders came from Colonel Ray's CIC detachment and contained all of the information that the SOE, OSS, and CIC had collected on Unit 731, the Japanese biological- and chemical-experimentation unit, headquartered in northeast China.

"Guys, we're sending Jon and George to Harbin to bring out the head of the Japanese biological- and chemical-research unit, Dr. Shiro Ito. He is the commanding general of Unit 731 and its sister units. I am sorry we have to leave Miles and Henri home, but putting four Caucasian agents into Harbin would be too risky. I would normally send only one agent on this type of mission, but I need a Japanese-speaking agent to go with Jon," Colonel Arvin said.

"Why not just kill the bastard?" Henri questioned.

"Because the US Army's determined that he is more valuable alive than dead. The army wants him for their biological and chemical research, and we need to get him before the Russians or the Chinese Communists do."

"Sounds like a tall order. Isn't Manchuria still under Japanese control? I've read they still have ten divisions around Harbin," Jon said.

"Yes, the Kwantung Army and Thirtieth Army control the region, but they are occupied with a major Soviet buildup to the west. They've moved most of their troops out of Harbin into western Manchuria. We think this is the only chance we'll get to grab the doctor. It will be your most dangerous mission to date. However, on the bright side, there are a lot of Caucasians already in the Harbin area, mostly Russians, so you won't stick out like a sore thumb."

"That's almost three thousand miles away. How do you intend to get us in and out of there?"

"Thirty-one hundred and twenty miles, to be exact. A B-25 or Lancaster will fly you out of Chungking into Mongolia and from there into Manchuria. We need to act fast on this because the Japanese Army may be crushed by the Soviets in a matter of weeks. We're going to fly you all to Chungking tomorrow and position you for the next leg of the journey. We're still trying to find a refueling location in northwest Russia, but the Soviets aren't cooperating. We may have to change the route at the last minute."

"I guess we'd better study up and be prepared."

"Y'all have never gone on a mission without all the information, but this extraction is critical. This will almost be a plan-as-you-go mission. However, you'll have the help of OSS assets in the area, and they've set up several places for you to stay—safe houses. We're timing it so there's a full moon, to help the flight crew get the aircraft safely in and out of the drop zone. Y'all will be parachuting from five hundred feet in the dark."

Two days later, with a new route planned, Jon and George took off in a British Lancaster bomber for Yenan, China, and then on to Harbin. The Lancaster was one of the most successful long-range night bombers employed in the war. The crew was experienced, having flown over a hundred nighttime insertion missions in the last twelve months.

Four Rolls-Royce Merlin liquid-cooled V12 engines powered the Lancaster. It could cruise at a speed of 250 knots or 287 miles per hour and had a range of over twenty-five hundred miles. This particular Lancaster was modified for the clandestine service. The upper gun turret had been removed and the side gunports sealed to provide less drag. The original bomb-bay doors also had been removed and two separate bomb-bay doors installed. The forward bomb bay carried extra fuel tanks with enough fuel for the Lancaster to travel an extra seven hundred miles. The aft and smaller bomb bay was the exit from which agents would parachute.

The Lancaster's service ceiling of nineteen thousand feet would easily carry it over the portion of the Himalayas they were flying over. On the route through eastern Mongolia and then to a point thirty miles southeast of Harbin, it would fly at a much lower altitude to avoid making vapor trails. Vapor trails formed when the exhaust gases from the aircraft's engines met the cold higher-altitude air, and vapor trails could be seen in the bright moonlight from both the ground and the air.

Jon and George tried to sleep during the eleven-hour flight, but it was impossible due to the heavy turbulence. When they did manage to fall asleep, they soon would be awakened by another updraft or downdraft. The Lancaster crew members fared better because they were used to the rough passage. After passing over the 6,700-foot-tall Greater Khingan Range in eastern Mongolia, the Lancaster gradually dropped to an altitude of five hundred feet above the ground and approached Harbin from the southwest. Their insertion point lay thirty miles southeast of Harbin.

Once the aircraft descended below five thousand feet, the radio operator informed the agents that they could get out of their cold-weather gear. Fifteen minutes from their drop point, the pilot turned on a small red light located on the bulkhead that separated the bomb bay from the aft section. Jon and George got to their feet, checked and rechecked each other's parachutes, and tightened the harness straps between their legs even further. Five minutes from the drop point, the aft bomb-bay doors opened, and the men hooked their static lines to a three-foot stretch of wire cable on the side of the bulkhead.

When the green light came on, the agents exited through the bomb-bay opening a second apart. When their chutes opened, their velocity went from 120 miles per hour to 12 miles per hour within a second. Fourteen seconds later, they landed in an open field and were immediately helped out of their gear by a Captain Guy Wong and a small group of Chinese freedom fighters. The freedom fighters quickly gathered up the chutes and harnesses to dispose of later.

Captain Wong then took Jon and George to a house four miles from the drop zone. Jon and George put on native Chinese clothing over their khaki clothes. They slept most of the morning and afternoon, and just before sunset, a wagon loaded with wheat straw drawn by two oxen pulled up to the house. Captain Wong jumped off the wagon, hurried the agents into the forward section of the wagon, and covered them with the straw. For this mission, Jon and George carried the lighter, British-made, fully automatic Sten Mark III submachine gun. In addition, each carried a Colt .45 automatic and a silenced .22-caliber pistol.

"We probably won't be stopped by the Japanese, but if we are, we will probably need to use force to get out of the situation," Captain Wong told them. "I'll say the word *cōng* [pronounced *chonk*] if something goes wrong. *Cōng* means *chimney* in Chinese. Otherwise, stay hidden and quiet until we get to our next destination."

CHAPTER 27

Harbin, China

It took three hours for them to reach the next safe house. The dirt road was filled with holes washed out by rain, and halfway there it started raining. When they arrived, they were bruised and soaking wet.

When Jon exited the cart, he spat straw from his lips and asked the captain where he could pee. As he ran around the side of the house, George followed close behind. Four minutes later they returned, relieved and thirsty.

Inside the small wood and mud-brick house, an elderly Chinese woman greeted them. The house was tiny but warm. She offered them hot tea by pointing to the only piece of furniture in the house, a small table on the straw floor. She motioned with both hands, cajoling each to help himself.

"This is my great-aunt," Captain Wong said. "She is close to ninety-six years old, or so she thinks. Her entire family is prepared to help us. Tomorrow you will stay in her great-grandson's house in Harbin."

"Were your parents from this region of China?" Jon asked.

"My great-grandparents were brought to America in the eighteen fifties to work on the railroads. I am a third-generation American. I grew up in San Francisco, where my grandparents owned and operated a restaurant and a laundry. Now my father owns them."

"So, your family stayed in touch?" George asked.

"Yes, up until the Japanese invasion in 1937; then nothing got through. In 1942, with the help of the Soviets, I was smuggled into the region, where I made contact with them. My family has been helping me ever since. They even helped me recruit agents for the OSS. Two of them work at the Unit 731 facility, which is only ten miles from here."

"What's our next stop?" Jon asked.

"Tomorrow morning, we'll take another wagon to my cousin's house on the outskirts of Harbin. He's a very successful farmer and merchant and has a large, two-story brick home. Tomorrow night we will get you into the city to my aunt's great-grandson's home. He lives three blocks from the mansion your Japanese doctor lives in. It was confiscated by the Japanese when they entered Harbin. It belonged to a wealthy Russian exporter who fled to Russia before the Japanese captured the city. The doctor has his family there, although with the Russians preparing to invade, I assume they will be leaving soon."

The following night, Jon, George, and Captain Wong entered Harbin. Despite a curfew, there were quite a few local people moving about the city; most appeared to be merchants. All of the Japanese Kwantung Army troops that had been patrolling the city were now at the front, preparing to fight the Russian army. The only organized presence was the local police. They were forced to cooperate with the Japanese, but they carried no weapons.

In the morning they had a breakfast of rice and dried diced apples. Jon knew the eating habits of the Chinese wouldn't provide enough protein for him and George, so each had packed ten pounds of smoked beef. The three agents munched on jerky while Captain Wong laid out a sketch of the house and grounds where Dr. Ito lived.

"Since the army moved to the western front, Dr. Ito has only two full-time guards. His chauffeur serves as a third. The drive to the Unit 731 facility takes about forty minutes. He gets home around 2100 hours, but he sometimes works all night at the facility. Lately, he has been spending more time at home. I assume this is because he believes he will be separated from his family for a long time when he sends them back to Japan," Captain Wong said.

"The best time to take the doctor is while he's at home and most vulnerable," Jon said.

"I agree."

"And he is likely to be more cooperative if we can get his wife and children out with him."

"Was this your original plan?"

"Yes, we were hoping his family would still be here when we arrived," George replied.

"What do you say to you and I doing a little sightseeing this evening and checking out the house?" Jon asked.

"Sounds good to me," Captain Wong said. "It would be best if we leave after 2100 hours, while most of the people are indoors eating supper. If the doctor is home, we can check out his full security detail."

By 2200, Jon and Captain Wong were within a block of Dr. Ito's residence. After they made their way to an alley at the rear of the house, they saw a lighted kerosene lamp in an upstairs bedroom. They saw the outline of a man against the shades, bending over as if to kiss one of his children good night. He picked up the lamp and exited the room. The light moved into another upstairs room of the two-story mansion.

They waited a minute for their eyes to readjust to the darkness before moving to the west side of the house. Before they moved, they saw a match light up on the north side of the house; a single guard was walking toward the rear of the house with a cigarette between his lips. They saw no other guards outside.

They got to the west side of the house in time to see the lamp extinguish in what they believed to be the doctor's bedroom. Before they moved again, Jon noticed movement inside the house; he assumed at least one guard was on duty inside during the night. The third guard, the chauffeur, would be sleeping on the bottom floor of the residence; the Japanese doctor wouldn't want him anywhere near his children at night.

After they returned from their reconnaissance mission, they woke George. Jon had formulated a plan on the way back to the safe house. Jon laid out his plan so that he could get everyone's feedback.

"This will work only if the doctor returns home. What if he stays at the facility all night?" George asked.

"We'll try again the next night or the next," Jon exclaimed.

"We need to put a time limit on this. We won't go unnoticed forever."

"You should be good for at least ten days," Captain Wong said. "After ten days, people will start talking, no matter what their loyalties."

The next evening, Jon and Captain Wong left the safe house after sunset. George and one of the Chinese freedom fighters left fifteen minutes later. By 2000 hours, everyone was in position in the alley behind the house.

"The doctor's not home yet," said a freedom fighter.

A few minutes later, a second freedom fighter made his way to Captain Wong and whispered something in his ear.

"One of our radio operators, who lives next to the road the doctor takes to the 731 facility, just radioed and told us the doctor's staff car has passed his house. We have about twenty minutes to put things in place," Captain Wong stated.

Jon and Captain Wong crept to the back of the house, near a head-high window. Captain Wong reached down and grabbed a handful of mud from a puddle. He smeared the mud on his face and clothing and knocked on the back door. When the one guard who stayed with the family during the day opened the door, he saw a ragged-looking beggar holding his hand out for food. Before the guard could say anything, a loud pop from Jon's silenced .22-caliber pistol sounded from the darkness. The bullet struck the guard in the forehead. Before the guard could fall backward into the house, Captain Wong reached up and grabbed him by the collar. He lifted the dead guard onto his right shoulder and carried him to the alley, where he dumped the body behind a large pile of rotting firewood.

Jon, followed by George, entered the house and turned down the kerosene lamp in the kitchen. A few seconds later, Captain Wong entered through the back door. When they entered the living room, a tiny Japanese woman gasped, and her eyes grew wide with fear; she drew her two children, who were sitting next to her, into her arms. Jon put his finger to his lips, and George spoke softly to the woman.

"Are you Mrs. Ito?"

The woman nodded and gathered her two children as close to her as possible.

"No harm will come to you or your children, Mrs. Ito. We are here to take you and your children and husband to the United States before the Russians or the Chinese Communists can capture and kill you. Do you understand?"

The woman nodded her head and sat rigidly stiff on the sofa with her children.

"Where are your winter coats?"

"In the closet next to the door."

"Do you have cold-weather clothing for you and your children?"

She nodded her head.

"Go get it; you'll need it. Your children will stay here; they'll be safe."

Ten minutes later, Mrs. Ito was back downstairs putting wool pants and shirts on her children. She had dressed upstairs in her warmest clothing. After the children were dressed, she went to the closet and returned with their heavy coats, scarves, hats, and gloves.

"Is this all you need?"

"*Hai*," Mrs. Ito said.

George noticed that she had also brought down a set of clothing for her husband, which she placed on the dining-room table.

Before the doctor reached his house, a Japanese Army vehicle with two Kwantung Army soldiers inside pulled up and parked on the gravel street. The soldiers stayed in the truck until the doctor's car pulled into the gravel driveway. It wasn't until then that Jon and George noticed a stack of luggage in a room off the main hallway.

"You're leaving tomorrow?"

"*Hai*."

Jon and Wong moved to positions where the doctor wouldn't see them when he entered the door. His guard opened the door and let the doctor enter, and then the guard entered and closed the door behind him. When the doctor saw his wife and a large man standing next to her, he froze. The guard noticed and attempted to pull his revolver. Jon clubbed him on the back of the neck with his pistol, as he didn't want the children to have to witness anyone being shot. Dr. Ito turned around when he heard the guard groan and fall to the floor. He stared at the pistol Jon was pointing at his head. With George standing guard, Jon tied up and gagged the guard.

"If you are going to kill me," Dr. Ito said in perfect English, "I would prefer it not be in front of my family."

"We're not here to kill you, Dr. Ito. We're here to get you and your family out of here and to the United States. Either you go willingly or we'll take you by force. If we have to take you by force, we'll leave your family here for the Russians to deal with. It's up to you," Jon said.

"What about my chauffeur and the soldiers outside?"

"The soldiers have been dealt with. We'll leave your chauffeur tied up in the house. Now, if you will cooperate, we'll leave right away. We have a long drive ahead of us."

"Captain Wong, have your wireless operator send the code informing headquarters we are on our way to the airfield."

Captain Wong's men filled the car with gas from several large cans of gasoline they had brought with them. The remaining cans were placed in the trunk. Everyone exited through the back door of the house and got into the staff car, which was already running.

Captain Wong climbed into the driver's seat, and Jon got into the front on the passenger's side. George had the doctor sit in the middle of the backseat; he asked the doctor and his wife to hold a child in each of their laps as he got into the back with them. Taking no chances, George held a gun to the doctor's ribs for the entire trip.

They drove through Harbin and turned north on a well-kept gravel road. Their destination was an airfield two hours north of Harbin. After the Japanese captured Harbin, the Chinese army had abandoned it. The Japanese chose not to use it because it was too far from Harbin. It had stayed abandoned until the OSS began to use it as a staging point to infiltrate and recover covert operatives in northern China. It had first been used by the Allies when Captain Wong was inserted from Russia.

When they reached the abandoned airfield, they found two Lancaster bombers waiting inside one of the large hangars. Both bombers had been refueled using the several hundred barrels of aviation fuel that had been smuggled in from Russia three years before. As the car's lights flashed across the taxiway, Jon scanned the area and noticed numerous Chinese troops with Thompson submachine guns standing behind sandbag bunkers.

"Those are Chinese freedom fighters," Captain Wong explained. "We have over a hundred protecting the airfield. Don't worry about any Japs; they're over three hundred miles away, getting ready to have their asses kicked by the Russian Army."

When the staff car pulled up to the hangar, the Ito's were escorted to one Lancaster while Jon and George went to the second. Before they boarded, Jon saw the flight crew helping the Ito children into cold-weather gear. Jon smiled. He felt sympathetic toward the wife and children, but he wished he had been ordered to kill the doctor.

CHAPTER 28

Calcutta, India

Agent Kelly Popper sat in the SOE classified briefing room, reading the first message from her two double agents in Singapore. After their fourth week back in Singapore, D'Arras and Ancelet had provided the names and locations of five Japanese agents who had infiltrated India, Burma, French Indochina, and southern China. The photographs of the three dead Cobra Team agents had convinced their Japanese handlers of their success and loyalty. As a result, the Japanese had released the women's children from the internment camp and allowed them to go live with relatives outside of Singapore. A great weight was lifted off the two women's hearts. Their husbands, however, remained in prison.

Once the decision had been made to send D'Arras and Ancelet back to Singapore as double agents, Jon, Miles, and Henri had met with a Hollywood theatrical-makeup artist, now an OSS agent. The makeup artist used his talents and makeup skills to make the trio look dead and bloody. Faking their deaths was a calculated risk. If the Japanese discovered the ruse, D'Arras and Ancelet would be shot or beheaded as American spies. Jon hoped it would work.

After the application of the theatrical makeup, the agents had been driven to three different locations, where Agent Popper used Anna's miniature Minolta cameras to take individual photographs of the three. Jon was photographed in an automobile, slumped over the wheel with one shot to the temple. Miles lay in an alley with three shots in his chest and another in his forehead. Henri was sprawled on a road where he had been jogging with a single gunshot to the forehead.

Jon didn't realize the true talent of the makeup artist until he saw himself in a mirror; it was very realistic. He shuddered at the thought of being dead. Until then, he had thought of himself as invincible, a force to be reckoned with. At that point he realized that he was as vulnerable as any soldier in the war. He bowed his head and said a silent prayer to Saint Christopher for protection.

The OSS makeup artist had explained his work in the United Kingdom before the Allied invasion of Normandy. He had made up a dozen OSS agents to look like wounded French civilians. The night before the Allied invasion of Normandy, in June 1944, the agents were dropped behind enemy lines. The agents knew the Germans wouldn't stop to help them, so they would sit next to an abandoned vehicle or in a bombed building next to a major road and count the number of German troops, tanks, and vehicles that passed as they went to the front. At night, they would move to a secure location where they stored their wireless radio and send reports to the OSS headquarters in London.

Agent Popper told everyone about the release of the families of D'Arras and Ancelet during dinner on the *Jacqueline*. Afterward, Jon led a discussion on what to do about the Japanese agents. The agents who had infiltrated Calcutta, Chittagong, and Rangoon worried Jon the most. The two who had gone to French Indochina and southern China could wait.

"Camille, are there any leads on the new Japanese agent in Calcutta?" Jon asked.

"No, but there has been a lot of sabotage on the docks and at several fuel-storage locations in the last two months; several military guards were found with their throats cut."

"Did anyone check with the CIC or OSS detachments?"

"I received information on several new sabotage attempts at the fuel docks from the CIC late this afternoon. Military guards were able to thwart the attempts, but the culprits got away. I'm going by the OSS detachment tomorrow morning to see if they have any new intelligence," Kelly replied.

"OK, but take Camille with you. I'll get the names of the Japanese agents in Rangoon and Chittagong to our intelligence units there. They may already be aware of the new talent in town."

"How do you want us to proceed with the agents here?" Camille asked.

"I'm thinking we need to work with the CIC to snatch them. Since Henri once lived in Rangoon, I'll send him and Miles to deal with the spy there."

"What about Chittagong?" Kelly asked.

"I don't think Captain Dubois would mind taking a trip back there. I know an OSS captain in Chittagong who will help. And Brunelle, our weapons expert here on the boat, is from Chittagong; he can contact his family members if we need them. With the help of Captain Butler, Captain Dubois should be able to find and eliminate the Japanese agent. Plus, there's a sleazy fishing-boat captain there that may be able to help. I'm pretty sure that his only loyalty is to himself. Captain Dubois should be able to get access to what he knows for a price," Jon stated.

Later in the evening, Jon spoke with Captain Dubois. The captain agreed to go to Chittagong once Jon received operational approval from G-2. Jon wrote the mission up and sent a message to G-2 detailing the three Japanese agents, their locations, and his plan to deal with them. In his last paragraph, he requested permission to implement his recommended actions.

A day later, Captain Dubois handed Jon a G-2 message authorizing his team to proceed with the three missions. A personal remark from the army chief of staff, General Marshall, was included: *While visiting with your father, I accidentally let it slip that you were married several months back. Your father says hello and congratulations on your marriage. He and your mother miss you.* Jon looked up from the message into Captain Dubois's face.

"Sorry, Jon," Captain Dubois said. "I had to inform General Marshall of your marriage."

"I didn't want my folks to know because they would worry twice as much. I guess they took it pretty well."

"I would recommend writing a letter telling them how and where you met and sending a photo of the two of you."

"Thanks; that's a good suggestion."

Jon hosted a meeting at the SOE detachment. In addition to all of Jon's and Captain Dubois's agents, OSS and CIC representatives attended. Kelly briefed the group on the information she received from her two double agents in Singapore, and Jon described his plans to deal with the three Japanese agents.

"Jon, why don't we send two of my female agents to Rangoon with Miles and Henri? The boys might not look so conspicuous if there are ladies on their arms," Captain Dubois said.

"An excellent suggestion, Captain. Kathleen, I think you and Camille should go with Miles and Henri to Rangoon. Don't forget that Brigitte's brother, Christopher Prefontaine, is in Rangoon. He's running a team of agents. George, Monique, and Brigitte can stay with Captain Dubois and head to Chittagong. Is that OK with you, Captain?" Jon asked.

Captain Dubois nodded his approval.

"I'll send Captain Butler a message to expect the *Jacqueline* in a couple of days. I'll secure passage for Miles, Henri, Kathleen, and Camille on the transport leaving for Rangoon at 0900 hours tomorrow."

Before the agents broke into separate groups to study and plan their missions, Jon drew Captain Dubois aside. Jon reminded the captain about his last visit to Chittagong and the fishing-boat owner and thug named Captain Aung. Jon told the captain he might want to start with Aung to get a lead on the Japanese agents that the notorious fishing-boat captain had smuggled into the city. He also warned him to be careful not to turn his back on the fellow.

"Aung is crafty and very good with a knife, Captain, so be careful. I would also appreciate it if you could look in on the owners of a certain café and make sure Aung isn't punishing the elderly couple for helping me during my last visit."

"I'll look in on them," Captain Dubois said.

After everyone left to pack for their trip, Jon and Kelly went into a separate briefing room. Kelly handed Jon a folder she had received from counterintelligence. Jon took his time reading the ten-page report.

Jon was surprised that the CIC had not run the Japanese agent to ground, until he realized that the experienced CIC agents had moved with the combat troops into Thailand and Indochina. Those left behind in Calcutta were green replacement agents who had filtered in from the States over the last three months. Jon decided he needed to select two CIC agents to work with him so they could gain some valuable experience. He immediately left to meet with the CIC detachment commander, Colonel Ronnie Ray.

CHAPTER 29

Chittagong, India

t took a day to refuel and prepare the *Jacqueline* for the voyage to Chittagong. Captain Dubois wired ahead and requested an OSS team to provide a discreet security detail for the boat. He didn't want any Japanese agents getting close to them. If anyone in Chittagong recognized his boat as the *Anne Marie*, he would say it was under new ownership and point to George.

When the *Jacqueline* docked in Chittagong two days later, a detail of six men waited for them at the dock. Captain Yul Butler, dressed in his best civilian attire and a large straw hat with a colorful hatband, stood there grinning. *So much for discretion*, Captain Dubois thought.

In 1943, Captain Yul Butler served as a civil engineer assigned to the Forty-Fifth Engineer General Services Regiment in northern Burma constructing the 271-mile-long Burma Road from Ledo, on the Indian-Burma border, into China. In May 1944, the Japanese captured Captain Butler during a raid and interred him in a prisoner-of-war camp in Thailand. He escaped from Hintok Camp after two months of captivity and made his way back to India.

Jon had interviewed Captain Butler in the hospital, during his recovery. He discovered Butler was one of a handful of black graduates of Ohio State University and that he had graduated with honors. The following day, Jon had gone to see Lieutenant Colonel Kenneth Taylor, the acting commander of OSS Detachment 101, and recommended he interview Butler and make him an agent. When Lieutenant Colonel Taylor met with

Butler, he took an instant liking to the jovial captain and asked Butler if he wanted to go home or join the OSS.

Butler chose the OSS and started his training in Calcutta. After two months, the OSS sent him to Ceylon, where he went through three months of Royal Marine commando training. There he excelled in hand-to-hand combat and arms training. When he returned to Calcutta, he looked like a new man. He had gained all of his weight back and now had a well-muscled and lean, hardened body. After several months of working with Kachin fighters in northern Burma, Butler was reassigned to Chittagong and given a detachment to command.

Captain Butler's success in Chittagong did not surprise Jon. He and his agents foiled a plot to blow up the base operation facility and fuel-storage depot at the Chittagong airfield. They also stopped an attempt to blow up the city administration building downtown. Twenty-five perpetrators were captured, tried by a military tribunal, and sentenced to death. Butler and his agents worked months to take down the Japanese agent and the group of dissident fighters who wanted to topple the current Indian government.

After the crew secured the *Jacqueline*'s mooring lines and put the gangway in place, Captain Butler walked up the walkway, stopped short of stepping on the boat, and saluted Captain Dubois.

Once aboard, Captain Dubois invited him into the lounge and introduced him to George, Monique, and Brigitte. After some small talk and getting to know everyone, Captain Dubois asked him if he had uncovered anything yet.

"Nothing yet, Captain, but Captain Aung is under surveillance, and I've talked to several retired British sailors who hang out near the docks. They all say they've seen him go out with his crew and come in with someone they've never seen before."

"I think we need to have a serious talk with Captain Aung some evening. If he won't talk, I can use the War Act and accuse him of treason. If we choose to, we can hold him indefinitely, and he knows it," Captain Dubois said.

Over the next two days, Captain Dubois, George, Brigitte, and Monique walked and shopped in downtown Chittagong, acting like wealthy visitors on holiday. During the day, the four dressed in colonial casual, the men wearing lightweight cream-colored slacks and expensive shirts and the women colorful, expensive sundresses with flamboyant, floppy hats. During the evening, all dressed to the nines in formal clothing. Each evening a Bentley from the Circuit House picked them up and took them to dinner.

At the Circuit House, the hotel manager, Alain Chandra, greeted them personally and escorted them to a private dining room off the hotel lounge. Alain commanded an OSS team working separately from Captain Butler's. A year ago, he had collaborated with Jon and Captain Dubois to take down a major Japanese spy ring in Chittagong. His team of agents were all low-level servers and workers at the area hotels and restaurants. They were inconspicuous but highly intelligent.

"We think we've discovered a new Japanese operative," Alain said. "He is working with a group of dissidents who want to overthrow British rule. I have one of my agents on the inside. He's telling me the operative, a Malayan man, is funding the dissidents and helping them plan the sabotage of a munitions train due in here on Sunday."

"How long has the agent been undercover?" Captain Dubois asked.

"Over eight months. He was undercover in the group before the Malayan arrived."

"Does your agent know the operative's habits? Where he lives? Where he eats or hangs out?"

"Yes, I have a detailed report of all his activities."

"We don't want to raid his residence and compromise your agent. So, we'll need to capture him when he's downtown or somewhere we can make it look like he made a serious mistake."

"I agree. A report and a photo of the operative are in this envelope. We also suspect there is a second operative. Someone who's been here a while."

"What do you know about the second operative?"

"No details, but I have photographed the Malayan talking to a new suspect in town. My agent photographed them while they were having coffee at the Chittagong Hotel. His photo is also included in the envelope."

"Thanks," Captain Dubois said. "We've got some work to do."

After landing in Rangoon, Miles, Henri, Kathleen, and Camille caught a taxi and checked into the Strand Hotel, a luxurious Victorian-style hotel in downtown Rangoon. Although its outer walls still retained the pockmarks from its strafing by Japanese fighters, the interior was luxurious. Before the Japanese captured the city, most of the fine furniture and Persian carpets had been removed and hidden. Miles, Henri, Camille, and Kathleen were given rooms where the luxurious furnishings had been moved back in. It was nicer than any hotel they had stayed in previously.

Henri detached himself from the group and met with Lieutenant Chris Prefontaine in a small maintenance shed next to the airport operations building. Chris was a scholar in high school and college. He worked part time at airports from the time he was fourteen, and he became a wizard with aircraft engines. A few months before the war broke out, his father was transferred, and the family moved from Singapore to Rangoon. When the Japanese invaded Rangoon, Chris and his family escaped to Chittagong.

Chris Prefontaine was recommended to the OSS by his sister, Brigitte, who joined the American OSS in 1942. At the time of his recruitment, he was completing his last year of school at the University of Chittagong. After joining the OSS, Chris recommended five of his closest friends to his OSS handler. They followed Prefontaine to Fort Frederick, Ceylon, and trained together. After graduating at the top of his class at Fort Frederick, Prefontaine, along with his five friends, infiltrated back into Rangoon and organized the local Burmese resistance against the Japanese.

Prefontaine's group had been monitoring the hotels and port facilities. Over the last three months, they had tracked three new visitors to the city. One of the men bore the name of one of the Japanese agents mentioned in the message from Anna D'Arras. The agent spent a lot of time with two other men and was now under surveillance. When Chris met with Henri, he told Henri that the Japanese agent had established a ring of Burmese operatives. Many of the people the Japanese agent had recruited were Indian freedom fighters who had fled into Burma from India, where they fought against British rule.

When Henri arrived at the Strand Hotel, Miles was waiting in the lobby. Henri followed Miles into the lounge, and they sat at a corner table where they could keep an eye on the bar's entrance and rear exit. Miles was not surprised to hear that the Japanese agent was forming a ring of operatives. In fact, he had rather expected it, because Rangoon was filled with dissident Indians and Burmese who wanted to end English rule. Plus, with Rangoon being the largest seaport west of Singapore, it would be impossible to keep up with everyone who entered the city. Henri showed Miles photographs of the Japanese agent and the two men with the agent.

Henri and Miles met Kathleen and Camille later in the evening and had dinner in a private dining room at the hotel. Henri explained what Christopher and his agents had discovered, showed Kathleen and Camille the photos, and laid out a plan. Henri did not want to take a chance and look for the Japanese agent during the day; he knew the Japanese had his and Miles's photographs. Instead, he decided to send the ladies to the restaurant the spies frequented. Since Camille and Kathleen had been part of the covert Allied team photographed in Chittagong the previous year, George encouraged them to change their looks. After dinner, both women cut their hair shorter and dyed it raven black.

The first day out, the women went shopping, going to no less than five shops, where they bought blouses, skirts, scarves, and several purses each. They each carried four bags of goods with them into the restaurant. When they sat down to order, they noticed the Japanese spy, Adira Trevena, talking with one of the unknown men Chris Prefontaine had photographed.

The two women sat near the front of the open-air restaurant next to the metal railing that separated the restaurant from the sidewalk. From there they could observe the entire restaurant. It was hard to keep their eyes off Trevena, but both managed to not look directly at the Japanese spy. The man sitting across from Trevena was much younger, taller, and leaner than Trevena. He was dressed in casual white slacks and a bright-colored shirt.

"Trevena's photo doesn't do him justice. He's a very handsome man, in a rugged, athletic way," Kathleen stated.

"And he's dressed in a very expensive business suit," reported Camille.

I could really like this guy, if he weren't a spy, Kathleen thought.

After Trevena's visitor left, Kathleen noticed Trevena scribbling on a piece of paper. When he got up, he walked toward the women's table, made eye contact with Kathleen as he passed, and dropped something on the floor next to her chair. It startled Kathleen when Trevena made eye contact. When he dropped the piece of paper in his hand, she noticed but didn't react. She waited several minutes before leaning over and picking it up; it was a note. After reading its message, Kathleen's face turned pale. She told Camille they needed to leave immediately.

CHAPTER 30

Rangoon, Burma

Adira Trevena was born in Singapore to a Spanish father and a Malayan mother. His father worked as an executive with the Royal Dutch Petroleum Company when the war broke out in the Dutch East Indies. The twenty-one-year-old Adira was a law student at Rechts Hogeschool when the Japanese invaded. In May 1942, a Kempeitai officer, or secret police officer, pulled Adira from a Japanese internment camp and coerced him into working as a covert operative for the Japanese. The lives of his parents and two younger sisters depended on his actions.

For two years Adira worked for the Japanese in Thailand and Burma, always under the supervision of a senior Japanese agent handler. When the Allies recaptured Rangoon, he was told to stay behind with his handler and wait for instructions. He and another young man from Singapore, who had also been coerced into being an operative, did as much as possible to undermine the sabotage missions assigned by their handler. Adira was ready to turn himself over to the Allies, but his intuition told him to hold off.

Today, he noticed a face he had seen in a photograph last September. Her hair was shorter and a different color, but he was certain it was the same beautiful Allied operative. She sat with another woman whose face looked familiar too. After his friend from Singapore left the restaurant, Adira hastily wrote a note and dropped it beside the woman's chair as he left. He hoped she or some other Allied agent would follow up and contact him.

Kathleen watched the folded piece of paper drop from Adira's hand as he walked past their table. She kept on talking to Camille but after a few minutes dropped her napkin to the floor. She leaned over, picked up the napkin along with the slip of paper, and opened the folded piece of paper in her lap. She did this so discreetly that Camille didn't even notice what she had done. It was a note, written in French, and the contents alarmed her.

"Camille, we need to leave right now!" Kathleen exclaimed.

"Why? What's wrong?"

"I'll tell you after we get to our room."

Kathleen and Camille left the café. Once back on the sidewalk, Kathleen kept a slow pace, stopping occasionally to gaze into a shop window, where she scanned the reflections in the glass, looking for a tail. Sensing something awry, Camille kept an eye on their surroundings as well; she became even more anxious when Kathleen refused to discuss their reason for leaving. After ten stops and two blocks, both determined that they weren't being followed. Nonetheless, they still took their time, walking and watching. It took them another thirty minutes to get to the hotel.

Once inside their room, Camille turned and looked Kathleen in the eye.

"What is so damn urgent, Kathleen?" she asked.

"Read this."

"Who is it from?"

"Trevena."

"Damn, we need to get with Miles and Henri right away," Camille said. She collected her purse. "Let's go."

Twenty minutes later, they were having coffee with Miles and Henri in a private dining room of the hotel's restaurant.

After Miles read the note, he passed it to Henri.

"Damn, we're compromised," Henri stated.

The fact that the Japanese agent had identified Kathleen was in itself a concern, but it was even more worrisome that this guy wanted to talk to their team leader.

"If this guy identified Kathleen, maybe his handler did too. What if it's a trap? How do we handle it?" Miles asked.

"From now on we'll travel in pairs only," Henri said.

"I think we should send Chris to make contact with Trevena," Camille stated.

"All right. Camille and I will drive out to the airport in the morning and talk with Chris and see if he will do it. If any of us are seen with Trevena, it might compromise him—that is, if this is on the level."

A day later, Chris entered a local restaurant where the spy usually ate. When he saw Trevena, he sat at the counter next to him and ordered lunch. He said nothing to Trevena, but as he got up to leave, he acted as if he had tripped and fell into him.

"Excuse me. Terribly sorry, ole boy."

Chris then bent down and picked a pen up off the floor.

"You dropped this when I bumped into you." Chris handed Trevena the pen and winked.

Trevena took the pen, said thanks, and went back to eating his meal. He couldn't chance opening the pen here. He knew there would be a response from the Allied agents inside.

The following day, Trevena knocked on the door of a hotel room that Miles and Kathleen had rented five blocks away from the Strand Hotel. Camille and Henri were monitoring the pair from the room next door, while Chris and six of his operatives were stationed inside the lobby and outside on the street to make sure no other Japanese agents approached. As Kathleen opened the door, Miles stood six feet behind her with a silenced nine-millimeter Beretta aimed at Trevena's heart.

"Do you speak English? Kathleen asked.

"Yes, but my French is better."

"French it is," Miles said. "Come in and put your hands on the wall and spread your feet."

"I didn't bring a weapon."

"I hope you won't be upset if we don't believe you," Miles said. Kathleen held her gun on Trevena while Miles frisked him.

"If the circumstances were reversed, I would be doing the same."

Over the next hour, Trevena told Miles and Kathleen how the Japanese had coerced him into being an operative. He wanted out but didn't know how to proceed. His main concern was his handler discovering him talking to Allied intelligence agents. If the handler found out, the Japs would kill him and his family as well.

Miles asked Trevena about the second agent in a photograph he handed him. Trevena told them that his situation was similar to Trevena's. After hearing Trevena out, Miles told the Jap operative he would have to check with his superiors. He also told Trevena to start eating at different restaurants during the week. Once he had an answer from his superiors, someone would contact Trevena. When Miles was finished talking, he and Kathleen left.

Lieutenant Prefontaine sent a message for Miles and Henri addressed to G-2, requesting instructions on how to handle the situation. The next day the lieutenant brought them the reply from G-2. It authorized Miles and Henri to work out a plan to get the two conscripted Japanese agents out of Rangoon and back to Calcutta. It also instructed them to find out where the agents grew up, where they went to school, the names of their parents and siblings, their occupations and whom they worked for, and their current location.

"Sounds like they want to do a background check on the two," Miles said.

"Accumulating data that can be verified," Henri stated.

"I bet they want to recruit them as double agents and send them back to Singapore or the Dutch East Indies to work for the OSS," Kathleen interjected.

"If that's true, the only way we're going to convince the Japanese handler these guys didn't desert is to fake their deaths," Camille said.

"And just how would you propose we do that?" Miles asked.

"Our Hollywood friend."

The weather in Calcutta wasn't cooperating, so it took Sergeant Dennis Vinklarek two days to reach Rangoon. The Hollywood makeup artist would now fake the deaths of Trevena and his friend, to convince their handler of their unfortunate demise.

Several evenings later, Trevena and his friend walked down a dark alley toward their rendezvous with their handler. When gunfire erupted behind them, they drew their weapons and turned to return fire; they were each gunned down by two shots to the torso. Across the street, their

Japanese handler sat in a restaurant, waiting to meet with them. When the gunfire erupted, he rose and walked across the street to the alley. He saw several dark-skinned men in native attire bending over the bodies of two men, searching for valuables. Two police officers arrived moments later, and one shone his large flashlight in the faces of the two men lying on the ground. The second officer put his fingers to each man's neck in turn to check for a pulse.

"They're both dead," the police officer said.

As soon as Prefontaine, dressed as a police officer, shone the flashlight into the faces of the men lying in the alley, the handler recognized his two agents. The two were lying in a pool of blood that was getting larger by the minute. As more people gathered at the entrance of the alley, the handler turned and walked away.

Two minutes later, Henri exited from a doorway in the alley.

"Did you see him?" Henri asked.

"Yes. I have a dozen agents trailing him," Prefontaine said.

Ambulance attendants placed the two bodies on stretchers and put them inside the ambulance. Once the ambulance had left the scene, Adira and his companion operative sat up in the back. Sergeant Vinklarek began removing the makeup from their faces and supplied them with a change of clothes. A mile down the street, the ambulance turned into a side alley and stopped. Adira and his friend exited from the passenger's side of the ambulance, walked ten feet, and got into the backseat of a black taxi. Camille sat in the driver's seat, with Kathleen in the passenger's seat next to her. Kathleen held a .32-caliber pistol in her right hand and aimed it at the pair.

Camille drove to the Rangoon airport and onto the airport tarmac and stopped next to a C-47 transport. All four left the taxi to board the transport, Kathleen holding her gun at her side, following behind the two Japanese agents. A member of the ground crew that was servicing the aircraft drove off in the sedan. Five minutes later, Chris Prefontaine pulled up beside the aircraft in a Rangoon police car and dropped off Miles and Henri.

Henri turned to Prefontaine after he and Miles got out of the car. "Good hunting,"

CHAPTER 31

Calcutta, India

"Colonel," Jon said, "If it's OK with you, I would like to use a couple of your agents to help track down the Japanese agents sabotaging our docks and fuel depots. Who would you recommend?"

"I have two agents, but both are inexperienced," Colonel Ray said. "They've been in the country for only six months, but both graduated near the top of their West Point class in 1943. You can use them if you like."

"I was hoping you could give me some of your more experienced men."

"I wish I could, but they're all in the field. Lieutenants Warren and Kasson are sharp agents, albeit with very little field experience."

"I'll need their service numbers and photos. Tell them to report to the SOE detachment tomorrow morning at 0800 hours."

"I'll have the desk sergeant give that information to you on your way out."

The following morning, First Lieutenant William Kasson and First Lieutenant William Warren reported to the SOE detachment's front desk. After viewing their photos, the first sergeant checked their service numbers against those on their ID cards before escorting them to the briefing room where Jon, Kelly, and several other SOE agents were discussing strategy on the Japanese agents.

"Sir, Lieutenants Kasson and Warren reporting as ordered," Lieutenant Kasson said. He and Lieutenant Warren came to attention and saluted.

Jon looked at the two counterintelligence agents and sighed. Both agents looked like model West Point graduates: burr haircuts, starched khaki uniforms, and shoes shined so well you could see your reflection. Both Kasson and Warren were slim, broad shouldered, and over six feet tall.

For crying out loud, these boys don't look like they're over eighteen years old, Jon thought.

"First, there will be no saluting inside or outside this detachment," Jon told them. "Second, no military uniforms; you'll wear civilian clothes only. Third, you will call us by our first names. We're agent operatives. Fourth, grow your hair longer so you won't stick out like GIs, and if you can, grow beards. Now, since the two of you have the same first name, what do you want us to call you?"

"Willie," they answered in unison.

Lieutenant Warren looked at Kasson for a second and nodded.

"You can call me Willie, sir, ah…I mean Jon," Lieutenant Kasson said.

"My friends call me Willie also," Lieutenant Warren said, "but my mom and my brothers call me by my middle name, Franklin."

"All right, Willie and Franklin, let's get to work. We're looking for one or more Jap agents who are sabotaging our docks and fuel-storage facilities. We know the name of one of the agents, who is of Malayan descent. I want you two to check all the hotels near the south-side docks. See if the guy is registered at any of them. There are at least a hundred. I also want you each to carry two guns, one in a shoulder holster and one at the small of your back or in an ankle holster. These guys are dangerous. If you run across their names in your search, I want you to return here immediately and report directly to me or to one of these five ladies. Do you have any questions?"

"Just one. We only have military uniforms," Lieutenant Warren said.

"Then I want you to go to Hassan's Clothiers on Noble Street. Tell him to fix you up with a couple of light-colored, casual suits like those the local businessmen wear and to put it on my account. You'll need them tailored for twin shoulder holsters and an ankle holster. You can pick up the holsters and your pistols at the base armory before you head downtown. Since you're both rather thin, I would suggest the nine-millimeter Beretta over the Colt .45 automatic. Tell him it's a rush job and you want them tomorrow at 1000 hours. After you pick up your suits tomorrow, you can start on the hotels. If you come across the Jap agents, do not, and I repeat, do not engage them. Instead, report immediately back here. Is that clear?"

"Yes, sir," the lieutenants said in unison.

"One other thing. Always stay together. Never break off from one another and go different ways; it will get you killed."

After Jon gave them the Japanese agent's name, Agents Kasson and Warren left. Jon turned toward Kelly and Camille. Camille and the others had landed late in the night, but Camille was insistent that she be part of the operation Jon was conducting.

"That advice applies to you too, Kelly. Never leave your partner's side. Always work as a pair."

"Sir, yes, sir," Kelly replied. She came to attention and saluted sharply. Then she and Camille burst out laughing.

"Oh, for crying out loud, everybody's a comedian these days," Jon said. He then turned and left the room.

By late afternoon on the following day, Agents Kasson and Warren had canvassed thirty hotels, shown the photos to thirty managers, and received thirty negative responses. At the thirty-first, their luck changed. The hotel clerk instantly recognized the two men in the photos and told Warren and Kasson that one of the men in the photos had walked out of the hotel with another man no more than five minutes before. Agent Warren handed the man five American dollars before he and Agent Kasson left the hotel.

When they got outside, Kasson wanted to go looking for the spies. Franklin, the calmer of the two, said, "No, we'll follow Jon's orders and return to the SOE detachment and report." Franklin prevailed.

After Najib Arshad and Saad Al-Buhary left their hotel, they walked to a small café on Mohan Chand Street. On the way, they passed two Caucasian men walking in the opposite direction. Najib noticed the slight bulges under their tailored linen sport coats. He immediately became tense.

"Saad, those two men..." Arshad said.

"I noticed, Najib. They're probably undercover navy cops patrolling the area for AWOL sailors. Did you see how young they were and how short their hair was? No cause for alarm. Keep walking and don't look back," Al-Buhary said calmly.

At the Night Owl Café, Najib sat down with Saad, his handler. Like his handler, Najib hated the British and therefore the Americans. The British, colonial rulers of their country for over a century, had pillaged Malaya's natural resources, becoming rich while the people of Malaya remained poor.

Najib had met Saad Al-Buhary a year after the Japanese invaded and defeated the British in Malaya. Saad had embraced the Japanese as Malaya's saviors and liberators and had become an agent and saboteur. He spent a year operating in India. When he returned to Malaya, the Japanese permitted him to recruit and train fellow Malayans. He and his best student, Najib, were then smuggled into Calcutta to disrupt and destroy Allied supply depots.

For five months they sabotaged convoys, storage depots, and the Calcutta docks where American ships unloaded vast amounts of war supplies. Saad told Najib every day that they lived in a target-rich environment with too few American and Indian police to catch them. Najib believed him.

Agents Kasson and Warren returned to the SOE detachment and reported what they had found on Saad Al-Buhary. Jon grilled them for ten minutes.

"Did you notice anyone on the street as you walked toward the hotel?" Jon asked.

"Yes, we passed several women and two men before we went into the hotel," Lieutenant Warren said.

"Can you describe the men?" Jon asked.

"One was my height with a large mole on the right side of his neck. The other man was shorter, maybe five foot five, with dark skin and a crooked nose, which I thought unusual," Lieutenant Kasson said.

"What was unusual about it?"

"It was curved to his right and had a red scar on the left side, as if it had recently healed."

"Any other distinguishing features you can recall?"

"The taller man had a gold tooth to the right of his two front teeth, as we came toward them," Lieutenant Warren said.

"That would be his left side," Jon said. "Do you think you could recognize them if you saw them again?"

"Yes," Lieutenant Kasson said. Lieutenant Warren nodded.

"Great job, guys. I'm proud of you. Now go through the photos here and see if you can find the two men. We'll put a plan together to watch the area around the south docks. Maybe we'll be able to apprehend these guys before they sabotage anything else."

CHAPTER 32

Chittagong, India

On their way to Chittagong, Captain Dubois sent a message to Captain Butler, instructing him to pull his men off shadowing Captain Jacob Aung. A day after docking in Chittagong, Brunelle, the ship's gunsmith and the sailor in charge of the armory, was given the responsibility of keeping an eye on Aung.

A lifelong resident of Chittagong, Brunelle went to his father's leather shop and asked for help. The next day, six of his father's closest friends, none of whom were Allied agents, began keeping tabs on Aung and whom he talked to. All of the watchers knew Aung and his reputation as a thug who worked for anyone with the money to pay him. Everyone in town who knew him suspected him of working with the Japanese.

Two evenings after the *Jacqueline* docked, Captain Aung left his favorite bar, Club Dhaka, on Strand Road. He crossed Strand Road and turned down a dirt path that took him by a large pond and past several large warehouses. As Aung stepped onto the wooden dock that led to his boat, Captain Dubois, hiding in the shadows, recognized Aung's short, stocky frame and pockmarked face. Before Aung reached his boat, Captain Dubois moved out of the shadows with a nine-millimeter pistol aimed at his chest.

"I was wondering when I would meet you, Captain Dubois."

"We need to talk, Aung. Let's walk to the *Jacqueline*, shall we? And be advised that there are a lot of men guarding me," Captain Dubois said.

"There are only six men guarding you, Captain. One of my men already informed me of the number of your guards and that you were waiting here. I have a dozen men in the vicinity, but don't worry. I'll be a good boy."

During the ten-minute walk to the *Jacqueline*, Captain Dubois concluded that Aung was not only dangerous but also extremely clever. No doubt he had recognized the *Jacqueline* as the yacht that had been in Chittagong a year ago. Once aboard, the captain offered Aung a drink, but he refused it.

"So what do you want from me, Captain?"

"Let's start with the names of the two men you smuggled into Chittagong several months ago and who paid you."

"Captain, I am an entrepreneur. I work for anyone who pays me money. I don't always ask their names. However, the information you seek will cost you five thousand American dollars."

"No loyalties, Aung? I should have expected as much. However, if the information is good, I'll pay what you ask."

"Oh, it's good, Captain. I can also provide the date, time, and location of my meeting with the next trawler. In fact, I'm scheduled to take three men to the trawler at the end of the week. That gives you six days to get your navy lined up to sink the Jap bastards. And you're right: I possess no loyalties except to myself, but I find the Japanese a disgustingly smug and arrogant people."

"Why are you giving up this information?"

"Isn't it obvious? For profit. Japan is losing the war and will not be able to move their spies into and out of this area much longer. Their sea-lanes are closing, thanks to your American submarines. In my opinion, Japan was doomed once they attacked Pearl Harbor. You Americans can build more ships, planes, tanks, and submarines than they can, and faster. It's just a matter of time before Japan is defeated."

"That doesn't justify your helping the Japs."

"I really didn't have a choice, Captain Dubois. I had to help them, or they would have killed my family. My loyalty was to my wife and children."

Captain Dubois was surprised by Aung's admission but wouldn't have put it past the man to lie.

"I can also tell you where a secret POW camp is located, Captain."

"What makes it secret?"

"Possibly the medical experiments being performed there on American and British captives."

"What do you know about it?"

"I overheard the captain of the trawler discussing something to do with germ warfare."

"Where is the camp located?"

"That will cost you another five thousand American dollars."

"Do you know how many prisoners?"

"The trawler captain mentioned sixty prisoners."

"All right, if that information turns out to be correct, I'll pay you another five grand. Half now, half once we confirm it. Now where is this secret camp located?"

"It's on an island off the west coast of Thailand. If you get out a map, I can show you."

Captain Dubois took Aung to the bridge, where he retrieved a nautical map of Thailand and laid it on the navigation table. Aung turned the map to orient it to true north and pointed at a small island, sixteen miles long and five miles wide, five hundred miles south of Rangoon in the Malacca Strait.

"It's called Ko Ta Ru Island. I heard the captain say that the camp is located on the south side of the island, just off a large half-moon bay. The captain of the trawler didn't know I spoke Malayan. I spoke to him only in French."

"Lucky for you."

"You can't put all your cards on the table at once, Captain. That's why I'm still alive."

"Again, lucky you."

"Actually, Captain, you're the lucky one. You can get two birds with one stone; three, if you count the trawler."

"All right, Aung, you write down the date, the time, and the coordinates where the trawler will meet you. I'll give you five thousand dollars up front and another twenty-five hundred after we sink the trawler. I'll give you the other twenty-five hundred for the POW camp once we confirm that the camp is there. Is that agreeable?"

"It's a deal, Captain."

Aung didn't bother to extend his hand; he already knew that Captain Dubois would not shake it because the captain thought of him as a pariah.

George, Brigitte, and Monique returned to the *Jacqueline* close to midnight. They told Captain Dubois about the information they had received from Captain Butler: Japanese agents were planning to sabotage an ammunition train at the end of the week before it arrived in Chittagong. Captain Dubois, in turn, told them about his conversation with Captain Aung.

"I bet that the Japanese agents are attempting to make a final statement before getting on that trawler," George said. "If I may make a suggestion, Captain, we need to send a message to Jon and ask him to get the ammunition train delayed."

"I was thinking that too. In the meantime, you three need to keep an eye out downtown. We know where one of the operatives is staying, but we don't want to do anything to alert him to our presence. So, just photograph everyone that the agent comes into contact with. We'll process the photos in the lab on the boat and give them to Captain Butler. I'll see that the navy takes care of the trawler, and Butler can deal with the freedom fighters."

That same night, Captain Dubois sent a coded message to G-2 at the Pentagon. When General Marshall read the urgent message the following morning, he sent a request to Admiral Louis Mountbatten, the supreme Allied commander of the South East Asia Command, for submarine support for their operation in Chittagong.

Six days later, the HMS *Storm* loitered submerged thirty miles southwest of Chittagong. An hour after Aung's fishing boat dropped off the three Japanese agents, the skipper of the HMS *Storm*, Commander Don Cowan, looked through the periscope and read off the final bearing of the boat.

"Fire when ready," Captain Cowan ordered.

A minute later, a single torpedo, launched by a blast of compressed air, left one of the *Storm's* twenty-one-inch bow tubes. A gyroscope held the torpedoes on course to the target, and a pressure device maintained a preset depth of eight feet. Sixty seconds after its launch, the five-hundred-pound torpedo struck the starboard side of the trawler, blowing it into two sections. It sank in under a minute.

CHAPTER 33

Calcutta, India

Agents Warren and Kasson searched for six hours through hundreds of photographs before Warren found a photo of the Japanese agent with the gold tooth. It took another hour to find the second operative.

"Good work. You're certain these are our guys?" Jon asked.

"Yes, sir," Agents Kasson and Warren said in unison.

"We'll meet with Agent Popper tomorrow morning and draw up a plan. I'll send three teams into the south end of town to look for the men."

The next morning, Jon sat in Colonel Ray's office, showing him the photographs of the two Japanese agents, Najib Arshad and Saad Al-Buhary.

"Two of my seasoned agents will be returning from the field in a few days. I can send them over if you still need them," Colonel Ray said.

"Great. I could use the extra help, Colonel. We've yet to identify the two spies' handler, but I'm having them tailed by several teams of our Indian agents. We may get some results later tonight or tomorrow. I want to nail these guys as quickly as possible, but I want their handler too."

"Good idea. Otherwise, he could prove to be a bigger danger. I don't want any of our men or women getting shot or killed."

Lunch was delivered to the SOE offices from the officers' club. While everyone else ate, Jon went over his plan with Agents Popper, Warren, and Kasson. Over the next four days, three teams of four Indian agents each watched and tailed the Japanese operatives day and night. Jon also decided he and Kelly and the two lieutenants would watch the dock for the next four nights. He decided to place his team near a cargo ship off-loading ammunition and 250-pound bombs destined for the Second Attack Squadron.

To stop the saboteurs, they would need to be invisible. They wore black pants, black shirts, and black knit caps. Before they left the detachment, they streaked their hands, necks, and faces with a greasy black cosmetic stick given to them by the Hollywood makeup artist, Sergeant Vinklarek.

"Nervous, Kasson?" Jon asked.

"Yes, sir, a little."

"Good. This is a dangerous business. Your nervousness will help you be more aware of your surroundings."

Jon preferred nervousness to excitement in new agents. Excitement might cause them to make foolish mistakes. Nervousness could save their lives.

Each agent carried a fighting knife, two silenced nine-millimeter Berettas, and another automatic pistol of his or her choosing. Jon had larger hands and preferred the Colt .45 semiautomatic. Warren and Kasson also chose the .45 semiautomatic as their backup. Agent Popper carried a .32-caliber automatic. Jon instructed everyone to aim for the midsection of the body and shoot only if certain of hitting the target.

"Make damn certain you don't shoot one of your team members or a navy guard, and don't shoot a bomb, for crying out loud. A stray bullet could ruin our whole night. Don't forget you are carrying subsonic bullets in your Berettas, so you'll need to pull back on the slide to eject the spent shell and insert a new one."

By 2200 hours, all four agents were in place. The 250-pound bombs and ammunition were stored on the opposite side of the warehouse, where Jon parked their car. The bombs and ammunition would be the saboteur's most likely target.

During the first two nights, nothing happened, but the third night Jon spotted someone moving between the stacked bombs twenty-five yards from the warehouse. Kasson and Warren squatted together near the south side of the warehouse and had the best view of the 250-pound bombs.

Jon signaled Kelly with his index finger, indicating one intruder, and moved from his position. Kelly followed twenty feet behind him. Kasson had noticed the intruder also, and when he saw Jon and Kelly move from their positions, he decided to move too; however, he didn't alert Warren and was gone before Warren could stop him. Kasson made his way north along the west side of the warehouse.

As Jon crept closer, he noticed the intruder stop and kneel. Jon, only four pallets away, chanced a peek down the row and saw the intruder place a canvas satchel between two bombs. The intruder's back was to Jon.

Jon crept as quietly as he could between the pallets of bombs. Deciding he wanted the spy alive, he knew he would need to rush the saboteur to capture him. When Jon was six feet away, the intruder heard him and turned. Before the intruder could bring his pistol to bear, Jon ran into him at full speed and knocked the gun out of his hand. With the intruder lying facedown on the concrete, Jon grasped him around the neck in a sleeper hold. After the intruder blacked out, Jon tied his hands and feet with strips of leather and placed a gag in his mouth.

Jon collected the canvas satchel charge and removed the pencil-fuse detonator. After clearing the area around him, he lifted the intruder onto his shoulder and carried him quietly back toward the warehouse.

Jon was thirty feet from the warehouse when he heard a loud pop. The bullet missed Jon, but a second bullet hit lower and caused splinters to fly from a wooden pallet and into his right arm. Jon turned and fired once before ducking behind another pallet of bombs and laying his captured intruder on the ground. He raised and leveled his gun in the direction of the shots and then fired once more.

When Kelly heard the first semisilenced report, she spun toward the sound, acquired a target, and fired. Keeping her head below the top of the pallets, she moved toward her target. When the second round of shots erupted, she saw Jon fire and crouch to the ground to ease the captured intruder off his shoulder. Jon heard Kelly coming up behind him and motioned that he was OK. He made his way north into the pallets of bombs, looking for the second intruder. He returned to Kelly several minutes later.

"Must be a second saboteur; he's gone now," Jon said.

"So is this one," Kelly said. She removed her finger from the neck of the saboteur and stood up.

"Crap, the other operative killed him so he wouldn't talk. He missed me by only inches. Let's get him inside the warehouse and see whom we've got."

Jon dragged the dead intruder into the warehouse and shone his flashlight on the man's face.

"Damn. It's neither one. Either we got the handler or there's a second team of Jap agents. Let's gather up Warren and Kasson and get out of here."

Jon went to collect the two young agents, but Warren was alone.

"Where the hell is Kasson?"

"I'm not sure. He left his position while I was looking the opposite direction. I didn't even get a chance to stop him."

"I'll go look for him," Kelly said.

She was back after five minutes.

"He's over there, approximately twenty yards; his throat's cut."

"For crying out loud!" Jon exclaimed. "I told you all to stay together!"

"I'm sorry, Jon. I was watching the area next to the ship. Before I realized it, Kasson slipped away. I didn't see where he went, and I wasn't about to make a move to find him, especially after I heard the shots."

"All right, you did the right thing. Let's notify the dock supervisor and navy guards and get an ambulance out here."

CHAPTER 34

Calcutta, India

The morning after Miles, Henri, Kathleen, and Camille returned from Rangoon, they completed their after-action reports and briefed Colonel MacKenzie on the two spies they had brought back with them. As the four agents walked out of the detachment to go to breakfast, Jon drove up in a staff car and let Kelly Popper out. Kelly stopped them and explained what had happened earlier on the docks. Kelly was visibly upset with the loss of Lieutenant Kasson and told them to go to breakfast without her, but they decided to stay and wait for Jon to return. Camille wondered how Jon was handling the loss.

After Jon and Lieutenant Warren dropped Kelly at the SOE detachment, they drove over to the OSS detachment to brief Colonel Ray.

"I'm sorry about Kasson, Colonel, but he disregarded orders and left his position," Jon said.

"I'm sorry too. If I'd known Kasson was a cowboy, I would have assigned someone else."

"What about the two agents who returned from the field. Are they available?"

"Not yet. One man's wife is having a baby, and the other experienced a relapse of malaria and is in the hospital. When they're available, they're yours."

"Thanks, Colonel. By the way, Lieutenant Warren demonstrates a good grasp of this business and does what he's told. He'll make a great agent."

"Thanks. I need men like him."

Jon left and returned to the SOE office. As he approached the door, Camille walked out to get a carafe of coffee from the officers' club, down the hallway. She walked up to Jon and gave him a hug and a kiss on his cheek.

"Glad to see you're OK, soldier. Sorry about Lieutenant Kasson," Camille said.

"How many times do I tell these new agents to stick together and never go off alone?"

"Dozens of times. It's not like you didn't warn Kasson, and it's not your fault he disobeyed orders."

"Yeah, but he was my responsibility, and I'm accountable for his actions."

"Not when he disobeys orders."

"I was in command, and he was my responsibility."

"You can't let it bother you. I need you focused," Colonel MacKenzie said.

"You hear from Captain Dubois yet?" Jon asked.

Colonel MacKenzie showed him the message from Captain Dubois.

"It states Captain Dubois's mission is a success. The HMS *Storm* sank the trawler with the three spies attempting to escape to Singapore," MacKenzie said.

"What about the train?"

"I made a call and delayed the ammunition train. Captain Butler's team of agents finished the job by rounding up most of the dissidents recruited by the spies."

"When will Captain Dubois return?"

"Captain Butler sent a message and informed us the *Jacqueline* left Chittagong yesterday. They should be back Sunday afternoon. I'll let you know as soon as the *Jacqueline* docks and Captain Dubois is ready to debrief."

"Thanks. Camille and I are tired of sleeping in a tent."

Later that day, Jon talked with one of the four-man Indian teams shadowing Najib Arshad and Saad Al-Buhary. They told Jon that the duo had stayed in their hotel rooms most of the time during the past three days and had gone to four different restaurants to eat. They made contact with no one.

"They probably did a dead drop at one of the restaurants. Did anyone on your team follow them inside?" Jon asked.

"No, we didn't want to expose ourselves. We stayed outside," the team leader said.

"All right, continue watching them, but try to get someone inside the restaurant next time."

After dismissing the team leader, Jon walked into Colonel MacKenzie's office.

"What do you make of the Japanese POW camp that Captain Dubois reported on?" Colonel MacKenzie asked.

"I looked through our files and checked with both the CIC and OSS. They don't have any intelligence on Ko Ta Ru Island. I guess we'll have to wait until Captain Dubois returns to get all the details, but it's a given that we will need to check it out. My only concern is that it's a trap to catch my team," Jon said.

"That's my concern too," Colonel MacKenzie concluded.

Three nights later, the *Jacqueline* docked in its hidden location. The next day, Captain Dubois, George, Brigitte, and Monique met with Jon at the OSS detachment. Colonel Kenneth Taylor, the recently promoted and new commanding officer of Detachment 101, listened as Captain Dubois debriefed the mission.

"The infamous captain Aung gave us information about a secret Japanese POW camp holding sixty or more American and British prisoners. According to Aung, the camp is located on a small island at the southern tip of Thailand, in the Malacca Strait. The island is called Ko Ta Ru," Captain Dubois stated.

"What makes it secret?" Jon asked.

"The possibility of biological-warfare experiments. Captain Aung told me he overheard the captain of the trawler discussing germ-warfare material with his first mate. I'm thinking the trawler dropped a supply shipment off at Ko Ta Ru before transporting the spies to Chittagong. He probably picked up chatter on germ warfare from the soldiers stationed there."

"And you trust Captain Aung on this?"

"Absolutely not, but we have to assume he is telling the truth and investigate."

"Do you want the OSS to handle this, or do you want your team to take it?" Colonel Taylor asked.

"We'll take it. We're getting pretty good at taking down POW camps. I'll submit the request to G-2 in Washington today."

"I think you may receive permission by the time you get back to the SOE detachment. Captain Dubois sent a message to the Pentagon before he left Chittagong. We received a message from the Pentagon shortly before you got here. It states that a G-2 colonel will arrive tomorrow."

"That's fast."

Jon was talking to Kathleen, Camille, and Kelly about the two Japanese agents Miles and Henri had brought back from Chittagong when he heard a soft knock on the door.

"I don't mean to interrupt, but how are you all doing?" Colonel Norm Hayward said.

"Norm, it's good to see you. I take it you didn't fly all the way from Washington this time," Jon stated.

"I was in New Delhi when I received a message to head here ASAP to see what you have on this secret POW camp."

"So, no new tasking for us?"

"G-2 gave me authorization to approve or disapprove your mission to the secret camp, but first let me say hello to these lovely ladies," Colonel Hayward said.

"Colonel, we need to finish our operation in Calcutta before we head east."

"I think I'll have our SOE asset in Malaya investigate the camp before sending you and George to the island. Can't Miles, Henri, and the girls handle what's going on here?"

"We sure can," Camille replied, before Jon could answer.

"Well, there you have it, Jon. Do you concur?"

"Yes, sir," Jon said, after getting the "you won't get any for a month if you say no" look from Camille.

"Great. Let's gather everyone up and go to the officers' club. You can buy everyone lunch. You still have your discretionary funds, don't you?"

"I do. In fact, I'm hosting a party for the officers tonight. I assume you'll join us?"

"After what Colonel Arvin told me about your parties, I wouldn't miss it."

General Marshall had sent Jon $100,000 in discretionary funds and ordered him to "spend it to boost troop morale." To date, Jon had followed the general's orders to the letter. Although Jon hadn't personally hosted a party in over six months, his two accomplices, Corporal Tommy Ray and Sergeant Ed Slater, had followed his instructions and spent the money he allotted them to host a Texas-style barbecue every month for the SOE, CIC, and OSS personnel. For morale purposes, his two friends had included all of the American, British, and Indian flying units and nurses at the base. The general's money was well spent, and troop morale soared.

The Texas-style barbecues Jon hosted had become known throughout the region. His barbecue chicken and brisket were the absolute best. No one could explain how Jon came up with the large amounts of booze and beef, and Jon wasn't about to tell.

Unknown to everyone, Jon's close friend Captain Marty Schottenstein was a supervisor of the US Army supply depot at the Calcutta docks. In 1938, Marty and Jon had graduated from the same high school in Columbus, Ohio. Marty managed to get anything Jon asked for, and Jon reciprocated by getting Marty copious amounts of vodka, gin, and single-malt scotch whiskey. No one knew Jon's source, and Marty never asked.

At Jon's last barbecue, three fliers from the Second Attack Squadron had ended up engaged to army nurses. All three men proposed at the same time, kneeling together in front of their girls and popping the question. One of the fliers was another of Jon's best friends, Tex Marin. Two months after the barbecue, Jon had ended up being the best man at his wedding.

"I'll grab the other folks," Jon said. "Might as well put the funds to good use."

When they returned to the SOE offices, Jon told the team that Miles and Henri would be taking over the Calcutta mission while he and George would be leaving on a top-secret mission. After Jon answered all of his team's questions on what had happened at the navy dock, Jon, George, and Colonel Hayward broke off and went to another briefing room to discuss the new mission.

"There's not a lot of information on the POW camp, Colonel," George said. "When Captain Dubois met with Captain Aung, Aung told him he picked up the Japanese agents from a fishing trawler in the ocean southwest of Chittagong. He was aboard the trawler for only ten minutes but overheard the trawler captain talking about a secret Japanese POW camp. He also heard the phrases *germ warfare* and *Ko Ta Ru Island.*"

"Jon, do you think it is a setup and a trap to catch your team?" Colonel Hayward asked.

"I can't say for certain. I believe the Japs are convinced of our death, since the two Japanese agents that Kelly Popper turned are still sending information to us. However, they may be setting traps for any Allied operatives trying to take their camps."

"Do we know if D'Arras and Ancelet are still alive?"

"Yes, confirmed by SOE agents in Singapore."

"And is the information they've sent us accurate?"

"So far, yes."

"You always trust your gut instinct. What is it saying to you now?"

"Caution."

"I was hoping you'd say that," Colonel Hayward said. "George, what's your take?"

"I think we need to go in and capture the camp, Colonel. If the Japs are experimenting with biological agents on our boys, we need to stop it."

"Then leave as soon as we hear back from our intelligence assets in the area," Colonel Hayward said. "If it's a trap, they'll sniff it out."

CHAPTER 35

Malacca Strait, Malaya

Their PBY flight path took them from Calcutta to Rangoon, where they refueled before heading south-southeast toward the Malacca Strait. They touched down on the nearly glass-smooth Indian Ocean and rendezvoused with the HMS *Storm* sixty miles northeast of Sabang Island.

"Good to have you back on board," Lieutenant Commander Mercer said.

"I hope we didn't spoil any of your plans, Commander," Jon said.

"Not at all. All we've done this trip is blow a trawler out of the water last week."

Mercer caught Jon raising his eyebrows at George. "More of that spy rubbish, huh? I thought it sounded like your gang."

"Some close friends of ours."

"Maybe the two blokes who are missing from your team today?"

"I hope you blew it to kingdom come," George said.

"Aye, we did indeed, sir."

Five minutes after they boarded, the submarine was moving on the surface at eighteen knots, aiming for Ko Ta Ru Island. Once Jon and George stowed their gear, they made their way to the galley, where Captain Cowan sat with a fresh pot of coffee and two mugs. Cowan was drinking hot tea.

"How are you, Captain?" Jon asked.

"I'm doing very well, Agent Preston. I take it we can thank you or one of your friends for the trawler we sank last week. Otherwise, it's been a pretty boring cruise. I didn't like these clandestine missions at first, but now I'm beginning to hear how important they are. I can't wait to get back to port to find out the latest scuttlebutt about secret missions and British agents. The speculation among the Royal Navy chaps can get quite humorous at times."

"You can tell your crew that the last time they picked us up they had a hand in destroying a significant Japanese research laboratory that was developing some very nasty weapons. It resulted in the saving of tens of thousands of military and civilian lives."

"Thanks. They need to know they are making a difference."

"How long before we get to our next rendezvous point?" George asked.

"Ten hours, give or take."

Before Jon could say anything else, the radar operator announced over the boat's intercom, "Aircraft five miles and closing, Captain."

"Clear the bridge and dive the boat," Captain Cowan ordered. "It's probably a Kawanishi flying boat on patrol. The Japs don't have any other aircraft this far south."

The COB grabbed the handset and announced, "Dive, dive, dive," and this was followed by three familiar blasts from the diving Klaxon. The two lookouts rushed through the bridge hatch into the conning tower. Lieutenant Commander Mercer, the last man through, closed the hatch with a loud bang and secured it.

"Hatch secure," Mercer called out. Jon felt the pressure change within seconds.

"Green board," the chief of the boat reported.

When Captain Cowan reached the conn, he announced, "Take it down to forty meters. Battle stations submerged." His order was followed by the bong, bong, bong of the Klaxon.

A minute later, Jon and George were thrown off their seats as a bomb exploded close to the submarine.

"Jesus, help us!" Jon exclaimed.

The sound of another explosion rang through the boat as a second bomb dropped harmlessly on the surface.

"Doc to the conn," Captain Cowan ordered over the interphone. "All stations report damage."

Over the next ten minutes, damage reports came in to the captain. Two men were injured in the forward torpedo room; one suffered a laceration on his leg and the other a broken arm. The XO had been tossed against an instrument panel and knocked unconscious. As Jon and George tried to exit the galley, they heard a sailor yell, "Make way," and two men passed the door, carrying the XO to his berth.

"How is he?" Jon asked as the doc walked by.

"Unconscious and a concussion for sure, but no laceration," Doc explained. "I'm leaving one of the radar operators to watch him and hold an ice pack on his noggin. I would be grateful if you two could relieve him in thirty minutes."

"No problem. George and I will handle it until you come back."

An hour passed before Captain Cowan came below. As he entered his berth, he saw his XO sitting up and holding an ice pack in his hand. A large red lump protruded from the side of his head.

"You OK, Larry?" Captain Cowan asked.

"Who...Who are you?" Mercer replied. He mimicked a bewildered look on his face.

"Don't screw with me. I know you too well, Larry."

A large smile crept across the XO's face as he winked at Jon.

"Had you fooled though, didn't I?"

"He pulls this crap all the time, Agent Preston. Thinks he's a regular Will Hay."

"Who?" Jon asked.

"British comedian," Mercer explained.

"It was rather funny, Captain," Jon replied.

"And I'll bet he rambled on about some big-breasted lass in Glasgow. He tells it to anyone who will listen."

"Quite a story though," Jon remarked.

"If you're here long enough, he'll get to the one about the twin sisters in Edinburgh. I'll send the doc back down as soon as he's through setting the broken arm in the torpedo room. I'll expect you back in the conn in two hours, Larry."

"Aye-aye, Captain," Mercer said. "He's not a bad guy, once you get to know him."

"How long have you two been together?" Jon asked.

"We grew up in the same neighborhood and went to the same schools. He was two years ahead of me. I broke his nose playing rugby; that's why his nose is a wee bit crooked."

Well within the Malacca Strait, the *Storm* surfaced after nightfall and resumed its eighteen-knot cruising speed. To watch for ships and keep track of their location in the strait, they relied on sonar, surface lookouts, and the occasional three sweeps of the radar. The last thing Captain Cowan wanted to encounter was a Japanese destroyer that might compromise their mission. Jon silently hoped the Japanese Navy would think they were just an Allied submarine on patrol in the Indian Ocean, once the plane called in its submarine-contact report.

Ten miles northwest of Ko Ta Ru Island, Jon felt the boat slow. In the control room, Captain Cowan watched the radar sweep three times and noticed a small return visible on the radar screen.

"Surface contact, Captain. Bearing 190 degrees, three kilometers," the radar operator said. "Doesn't appear to be a very big boat."

"Sonar contact, sir," the sonar operator stated. "Small craft."

"Slow to five knots," Captain Cowan ordered.

Captain Cowan picked up the intercom to the bridge. "XO, target at your one o'clock position. Get the raft ready to launch."

An hour later, Jon and George climbed aboard the forty-foot fishing boat piloted by Major Andy Larned.

As Jon entered the control cabin, he said, "This is getting to be a regular habit, Andy."

"Let's hope it's the last time we meet like this."

"Grab the rum and pour us a drink, mate," Marteen squawked.

"Hello, Marteen," Jon said. He reached to his left and stroked the bird's head.

CHAPTER 36

Ko Ta Ru Island, Thailand

Major Larned's boat was faster than it looked. It took a little less than an hour to get to the south side of Ko Ta Ru Island. After clearing the southwestern point, Larned turned the boat east, cruising four miles from the shore. When they reached a small cove on the southeastern tip, Larned dropped anchor twenty yards from a secluded beach. Jon, George, and the major rowed to shore in the six-man raft. They were greeted by the tall and muscular sergeant Grist.

"Good to see you again, Agent Preston. I don't think we'll be doing any flying off this island. It's too rocky and covered with forest," Grist stated.

"What did you find, Sergeant?" Major Larned asked.

"The Japanese POW camp is located in the middle of the half-moon bay, fifty yards in from the beach. There's a large rock formation and two caves there. The POWs are being housed in the larger cave on the east side of the camp, and the Japs are bivouacked in the cave to the west. There's also a fifteen-meter radio tower near the top of the hill."

"Have you come up with any ideas on how we might take the camp, Sergeant?" Jon asked.

"We can't take it head on, sir. Our best bet is for two commandos to rappel from the ridge above and throw satchel charges into the cave the Japs occupy. The rest of us can then storm the camp."

"George and I would like to reconnoiter the compound. How many Japs will we face?"

"There are a total of twenty Jap personnel, including the camp commandant. Two guards patrol the compound day and night, and two guards patrol the beach during the day and one at night. Two guards help the medical personnel, and there's a radio operator in the commandant's hut. There are also five medical personnel and four cooks."

"How many prisoners?" George asked.

"I'm not sure, sir. I couldn't see into the cave, but I did see them carrying four bodies to the beach yesterday evening. They put them in a small motorboat and drove around the west end of the island, into the strait. They returned without the bodies."

"How many men do you have, Andy?" Jon asked.

"The sergeant and me and four more who will be arriving later in the afternoon. All are commandos and very skilled soldiers. After they arrive, Sergeant Grist will show you the camp."

Commander Robert "Rock" Taulbe, Royal Navy, stood behind the bamboo bars that held him and his men inside the large cave. He was sick with anger because the Japanese had murdered four more of his men. Despite his constant complaints to the commandant, he was helpless. He knew that, later in the evening, four more men would be taken to the medical shack, and the criminals who called themselves physicians would extinguish their lives.

Taulbe and his crew had been captured six months earlier after a Japanese submarine put two torpedoes into their frigate. Thirty men had perished and gone down with the ship. The rest had been picked up by a Japanese destroyer escort and ended up in a POW camp in Singapore. A month later, all fifty survivors had been moved to Ko Ta Ru Island. Only twenty-eight men remained.

If he ever got out of here alive, he swore he would personally kill the monsters responsible for the deaths of so many of his men. However, today he would worry about the next four men who would be chosen to die in the name of Japanese research.

Jon, George, and Sergeant Grist entered the dense jungle and surveyed the Japanese compound from the east side. Jon's intuition told him something was wrong. He turned his binoculars toward the cliffs above. After a few minutes of scanning, he noticed a slight movement behind one of the large boulders perched precariously on a rock ledge. When he saw it again, he recognized it as a rifle barrel.

"Sniper, one o'clock high, behind the large rock," Jon said.

"If there's one, there's bound to be another," George whispered. "OK, got the first one."

"Second sniper one hundred feet to the right of number one," Sergeant Grist added.

"You think there's a third or fourth?" George asked.

"If there are, I bet they're near the beach," Jon said. "Sergeant, can you check the jungle around the beach and see if you can spot any other snipers?"

"See you back at the camp," Sergeant Grist whispered.

When Sergeant Grist returned, Jon was reviewing the attack plan with the marines and Major Larned.

"What did you find, Sergeant?" Jon asked.

"Two snipers on the beach, sir. It's as if they're expecting someone."

"My thoughts exactly."

"Either that or the Japs are putting snipers at all of their special camps now," George stated.

"All right, let's for caution's sake say we're expected. They probably have a frigate or a destroyer escort somewhere in the strait. I'm certain they'll want to catch us. We'll be the most vulnerable once the prisoners are freed."

"They might have forces positioned on the mainland, if it's a trap," Major Larned said.

"Andy, I want you to send a message to the *Storm*. Tell them we suspect a trap and ask them to patrol the waters south of the island. I'll need you to monitor the wireless and wait to see if they find and sink any Japanese ships. I'm sure Captain Cowan will be eager to engage them, if they're there," Jon said. He wrote the sub's radio frequency on a scrap of paper and handed it to the major.

"Do you think they spotted our boat this morning?" George asked.

"I'm assuming they did," Jon replied.

"They may have more soldiers up the mountain," Sergeant Grist added.

"Then we need to find out. Sergeant, can you and two of your marines scout the mountain?"

"Yes, sir. We'll leave straightaway."

"If you find any Japs, don't engage them; just slip back and let us know their location and strength. I'll decide then if we need to abort the mission."

"Andy, is there another place you can hide your boat?" Jon asked.

"There's a small island a mile east of us. I can be there in thirty minutes."

"All right, leave us one of the Paraset radios so we can contact you, and make sure you are well hidden. I suspect we'll be seeing several Japanese patrol boats in the morning."

CHAPTER 37

HMS *Storm*, Malacca Strait

Surprised to receive a message from Agent Preston, Captain Cowan read the brief message: "Suspect trap Stop MAYBE one or more JAP warships south of island STOP engage and destroy STOP PRESTON END."

Captain Cowan didn't waste any time. "Battle stations surface! Heading 180 degrees; all ahead full. Torpedo room, status?"

"Tubes one and three loaded, Captain; two and four will be loaded in ten minutes," the torpedo room replied.

The HMS *Storm* was cruising surfaced, ten miles due west of Ko Ta Ru Island. Seventy-five minutes later, the boat was twenty-five miles farther south. Captain Cowan ordered the boat submerged and dived to eighty meters. When they leveled off, the Captain picked up the phone. "Engine room. All engines stop." He placed the phone in its cradle. "Helmsman, put the boat on the bottom."

Captain Cowan maneuvered the submarine to a shallow portion of the strait, where it settled on the bottom in one hundred meters of water. They waited for over four hours, not even sure if there would be anything headed their way. The air in the *Storm* could last nearly twenty-four hours before turning stale. The worst part of their wait was having to remain absolutely quiet so Japanese sonar would not pick up any sounds.

"Sonar contact, Captain," the sonar operator stated. "Two different sets of screws. They're banging away with their sonar, Skipper, but at the speed they're running, their sonar will be useless."

"In a hurry to get in position before dawn, I suspect. Battle stations submerged," Captain Cowan ordered. "Helmsman, bring it off the floor. Heading 170 degrees, speed six knots. Take it to periscope depth. XO, you take the periscope."

Captain Cowan drove the boat on a south-southeast heading to be in a better position to come up with a tactical solution and sink the enemy warships. After ten minutes, he ordered an easterly heading of 110 degrees and slowed the boat to five knots.

"Sonar, any change in their speed?" Captain Cowan asked.

"None, Skipper."

"XO, you see anything yet?"

A full moon was high above, and the smoke from the two Japanese warships was clearly visible through the ten-power periscope.

"Two ships, Captain. Approximately twenty-seven hundred meters and closing. They appear to be destroyer escorts; the second is three hundred meters in trail."

The Captain waited another minute. "Distance?"

The wait seemed long, but the XO called, "Nineteen hundred meters, Skipper."

"Bearing on the lead ship?"

"First target twenty-six degrees to starboard; second target thirty degrees."

"Any evasive maneuvering?"

"No zigzag maneuvers at all, Skipper. They're coming right down the middle of the strait."

While the XO spoke, Captain Cowan monitored the chief of the boat, putting the distance and bearings into the *Storm's* torpedo data computer.

Captain Cowan started his stopwatch after the first bearing. "I want another bearing and distance in thirty seconds."

"Distance fifteen hundred meters. First target nineteen degrees and second twenty-four degrees. Down scope. Anytime, Skipper," Commander Mercer said.

Captain Cowan computed his firing solution and transmitted it to the torpedo room.

"Fire tubes one and two," Captain Cowan ordered.

The COB's palm pressed the firing plunger at eight-second intervals. The boat shuddered as the torpedoes burst from their forward tubes. The pressure change hit everyone's ears as the poppet valve released compressed air from the torpedo tubes back into the boat.

"Torpedo room, reload tubes one and two."

"Fish one and two in the water, running hot, straight, and normal, sir," the soundman reported.

"XO, bearing on the second ship," Captain Cowan requested.

After giving the skipper the bearing, the COB entered it into the TDC. It took fifteen seconds to provide the second solution.

"Fire tubes three and four and then reload." The COB pushed the big red button on the control panel, and the *Storm* shuddered again.

"Torpedo room, status on reloading one and two."

"Tube one reloaded, sir," the call from the torpedo room stated.

"Three and four in the water, sir. Running hot, straight, and normal," the soundman reported.

Four steam-driven torpedoes, twenty feet long and twenty inches in diameter, rushed beneath the dark waters of the Malacca Strait toward the two Japanese ships.

"Five seconds to first impact, Captain," the COB said.

"Up scope," Captain Cowan ordered.

The first torpedo hit aft of the forward deck gun; eight seconds later, the second hit amidships. The first destroyer escort went dead in the water. The second destroyer tried to evade, but both torpedoes hit in the midsection and broke the back of the ship.

"Both destroyers on fire and dead in the water, Captain," Commander Mercer stated. "They should go down in less than fifteen minutes, sir."

Shouts of joy could be heard throughout the boat as the *Storm*'s sailors reveled in their victory.

"Let anyone who wants have a look, Larry," Captain Cowan ordered.

At least a half-dozen enlisted sailors took turns watching the burning ships struggle to stay afloat.

"Raise the radar mast."

"Mast raised, Skipper," the radar operator reported.

"Radar, let's see what else is out there. Give me four sweeps."

"Four sweeps, sir. Radar is now in standby. No large contacts, Captain, but I count five small blips ten miles northeast of our position. Four more sweeps. I want to know their speed."

"Four sweeps, Captain."

The soundman paused to calculate the speed of the boats.

"Speed approximately twenty knots."

"What direction are they traveling?" Captain Cowan asked.

"The boats are headed to the southeast side of Ko Ta Ru Island, Skipper."

"Surface the boat. Battle stations surface. Heading zero-one-zero degrees; all ahead flank."

"What do you have in mind, Captain?" Lieutenant Commander Mercer asked.

"Those boys might be in a tight spot when those Jap boats get there; they'll need our help."

"What if those are torpedo boats, Captain?"

"If they were, I think they would be headed our way. So, I'm counting on it that they aren't." The captain picked up the intercom phone. "Torpedo room, what's your status?"

"Tubes one, three, and four reloaded, Captain. We're still working on number two."

The HMS *Storm* resurfaced and ran at flank speed to Ko Ta Ru Island. Two miles southeast of the island, the *Storm* submerged as the first light of morning began to show.

George sat on a rock with the radio headset over his ears. He finished writing down a message from the USS *Storm* on a small white pad as Sergeant Grist and the two marines returned to the camp. After searching the hills most of the night, they had found nothing.

"Message from the *Storm*," George said. "There are five small speedboats heading our way. They should be here in one hour, just after sunrise. The *Storm* sank two destroyer escorts headed our way. It's ten miles south of the island, heading this way."

"Did they say if they were going to engage those speedboats?" Jon asked.

"They didn't say. What do you think we should do?"

"I'm thinking you and Sergeant Grist should get to the high ground above the cave and take out those snipers. Right before dawn, rappel down and toss two satchel charges into that Jap cave and one on the radio shack. The rest of us will take on the Jap patrol boats."

"How do you intend on attacking?"

"We have the high ground and good cover in the rocks above the cove. After the satchel charges go off, the Japs in the boats will believe we are attacking the camp. They won't be expecting anyone at the cove. With only twenty yards of beach, it will be easy to toss grenades into the boats and then rake them with machine-gun fire."

"That's your plan? What if they land at the half-moon bay? Or what if they land at the cove before the satchel charges go off?"

"I'm betting they'll be cautious and land at the small cove after daybreak. When they hear the explosion, they'll be convinced we are attacking the camp with all of our forces. I can almost guarantee you they won't be expecting us at the cove."

"Sergeant Grist and I will get to the high ground. I'll make sure we toss the satchel charges at daybreak."

"Don't worry, Agent Preston. I'll take out the snipers above the camp," Sergeant Grist said. "I'll send Corporal Diebert to deal with the snipers on the beach."

Jon knew he was taking a risk by assuming the Japs would land the boats and unload troops at the small cove, but his intuition told him he was doing the right thing. He didn't understand his sixth sense, but he knew to act on it when it felt right.

On the cliffs above, Sergeant Grist was silent and deadly. The first sniper heard only the knife as it sliced through his neck. The second was asleep when Sergeant Grist pulled his knife across both of his jugular veins. George didn't waste any time. He tied his rappelling rope to a large rock directly above the camp and put on his rappelling harness. Sergeant Grist did the same.

As George and Sergeant Grist repelled down the rocks, Corporal Lee Diebert was taking out the first sniper on the beach. Neither sniper had changed positions, which made his work easier. After he dispatched the second sniper, he stayed hidden and watched the beach for Japanese boats.

Lieutenant Hitoshi Sugiyama stood in the lead boat with five other soldiers. He had received orders to proceed to Ko Ta Ru Island and prepare a trap for enemy agents who might be landing to capture the POW camp. With twenty soldiers he was confident he would defeat and capture any enemy agent who dared to attack the camp. He couldn't wait to parade them around the headquarters after he returned to Kuala Perlis.

Sugiyama planned to land his troops and hide them around the small cove on the southeast side of the island, the most likely place the enemy would attempt a landing. After his commander informed him one of the Kawanishi flying boats from the airfield at Kuala Perlis had engaged an enemy submarine in the Indian Ocean the day before, he suspected enemy agents might be landed from the submarine. His commander told him that two destroyer escorts were headed north to Ko Ta Ru Island to deal with any submarine or any surface ships that might be trying to infiltrate the agents. "If you are successful," his commander told him, "I will give you a field promotion to captain."

As his boat approached the cove, Lieutenant Sugiyama envisioned the three-star epaulet he would receive. When light began filtering through the clouds in the east, the lieutenant saw the beach. *Enough room for all five boats*, Lieutenant Sugiyama thought.

When they were thirty yards from the beach, Lieutenant Sugiyama and his men heard two loud explosions.

"They're attacking the camp," Lieutenant Sugiyama yelled.

Before he could exit his boat, Lieutenant Sugiyama heard a hard clunk on the floor of the boat. He thought that the boat had hit a rock as it settled on the beach, until he looked down and saw a grenade rolling around his feet. Before he could yell a warning, the grenade exploded. The soldiers who made it out of the other two boats were hit by concentrated fire from two submachine guns on the cliff above them. No one survived.

Wanting to avoid the gunfire on the beach, the last two boats slowed to a crawl and loitered a hundred yards from the beach. Within minutes of stopping, both exploded with such a force they disintegrated in a fiery mist. The *Storm* scored two hits.

After the satchel charges exploded in the cave where the Japanese guards were sleeping, George and Sergeant Grist rappelled to the ground and began firing at the perimeter guards. Corporal Diebert jumped up from his position and sprinted the thirty yards to the camp. As Diebert arrived, eight rapid shots rang out from the direction of the commandant's hut. Diebert saw George fall.

When Sergeant Grist disconnected from his rappelling rope, he turned to see an angry Japanese officer stop to insert a new eight-round clip into his Nambu Type 14 semiautomatic pistol and fire one shot before the pistol jammed. The shot missed Sergeant Grist by inches as he turned his Sten Mark III on the Japanese colonel and fired two short bursts. Both hit the colonel in the chest.

Sergeant Grist turned 180 degrees and saw a Japanese guard running toward him. He fired one burst, and the soldier fell. He turned in a full circle but found no other Japanese combatants. He then rushed to George, who was lying faceup on the sand. Hit twice in the leg and once in the shoulder, he was unconscious but alive. Corporal Diebert stood guard as Sergeant Grist pulled the medical kit from his belt, cut away George's pant legs, and placed a tourniquet above the two leg wounds. George was bleeding badly.

Grist took his knife and cut George's shirt away to reveal his shoulder wound. He opened two shaker envelopes of crystalline sulfanilamide, sprinkled them on the entry and exit wounds, and applied a sterile dressing. He completed the same routine on the two leg wounds. After applying two sterile dressings to George's leg, Grist snapped an ammonia capsule and placed it under George's nose. Several seconds later George snorted, shook his head, and opened his eyes.

"You're too damn ugly for this to be heaven, Grist," George said.

"You're a step away from heaven, mate. You've been shot three times, but I think you'll live," Grist responded. "I'm going to give you an ampoule of morphine, so lie still."

Sergeant Grist was placing one of George's ammunition bandoliers under his head when Jon approached and knelt to check on his friend. The other marines began checking on the Japanese in the cave and releasing the POWs. One of the prisoners walked over and knelt next to George.

In a heavy Scottish accent, the prisoner said, "Lieutenant Commander Bobby Johns, I'm a medical officer. Let me take a look."

Jon didn't say anything, but he nodded his head as he knelt next to George.

"Did you do this?" Commander Johns asked.

"No, Sergeant Grist did," Jon responded.

Johns turned to Sergeant Grist. "Damn good job, Sergeant. I'll tend to him and loosen the tourniquet every four minutes until the bleeding stops. We don't want the tissue in the lower leg to die. Leave the medical kit; he'll need more morphine later."

"Will he live?" Jon asked.

"He's lost a lot of blood. Does anyone have a field transfusion kit?" Commander Johns asked.

Major Larned knelt next to George. "I have one on my boat, Doc. I'll send Corporal Diebert to fetch it."

When Corporal Diebert returned, he handed the metal case to the doctor. "This is German!" Johns exclaimed.

"I picked it up in Tobruk," Major Larned said. "I thought it might come in handy someday."

In the early stages of the war, German doctors had developed the field blood-transfusion kit because of the inability to store blood in the field. The solution was a direct transfusion between two soldiers. A healthy soldier would lie next to a wounded soldier, and blood would be transferred through the transfusion set.

Commander Johns lifted George's dog tags. "His blood type is A Positive. I need a donor with the same blood type."

"I'm A Positive, Doc," Jon said.

After the doctor connected the rubber tubes to the unit, he slipped the needles at the ends of the tubes into Jon's and George's arms. Johns then connected the large syringe in the kit to the transfusion exchange unit and began pumping blood from Jon into George.

"So, what's the plan to get us out of here?" Commander Johns asked.

"Working on it," Jon said.

CHAPTER 38

Calcutta, India

The morning after the raid, George was taken aboard a Royal Navy frigate that arrived at sunrise. He underwent surgery to remove the bullet fragments and repair the damage. If not for the field blood transfusion, George would not have survived. After Major Larned transported George to the frigate, he began ferrying the POWs to the ship. The frigate had been dispatched to the island from Ceylon before the agents left Calcutta.

As the HMS *Storm* loitered under the Strait of Malacca to protect the frigate from unwanted visitors, Jon stayed with George on the frigate until he awakened in the recovery room. George, groggy from the anesthesia and pain medicine, looked at Jon though squinting eyes.

"I never got a chance to thank Sergeant Grist for saving my life."

"I thanked him for you."

"Help me sit up."

Jon gathered extra pillows from the small linen closet, eased George into a sitting position, and placed the pillows behind his back.

"It looks like the war might be over for me. I don't know what I'm going to do without you, Miles, and Henri to hang out with in the jungle," George said.

"The doc told me you will be transported to Calcutta once we make port in Rangoon. You'll recuperate there for eight to twelve weeks before they put you on a ship home," Jon said.

"Contact the OSS detachment. Tell Colonel Taylor I want to recover in Calcutta."

Six hours later, Major Larned ferried Jon to a US Navy PBY for transport back to Calcutta. When he landed at the RAF airfield in Alipore, a staff car was waiting to drive him to the *Jacqueline*. Camille and Captain Dubois met him at the bottom of the walkway. Camille grabbed him around the neck and kissed him for a good thirty seconds before releasing him.

"Sorry to hear about George," Captain Dubois said.

"The bullets damaged the clavicle and humerus. It's a good thing he was shot by a small-caliber pistol; otherwise he'd be dead. The Nambu Type 14 pistol round is smaller than our nine-millimeter Beretta cartridge. A larger caliber could have severed the femoral artery, and he would have bled to death. He'll be recuperating for three to five months," Jon said.

"The war may be over by then," Camille said.

"I sure hope so. What's happing here?"

"Let's get you a drink and a cigar, and we'll discuss it in the lounge," Captain Dubois said.

By the time they finished their second glass of champagne, Captain Dubois and Camille had completed updating Jon on the hunt still going on for the Japanese spies.

"They disappeared. No one has seen them since the day after you and George left. Even Miles and Henri are stumped. Maybe they left town," Camille stated.

"I don't believe they've left Calcutta. They're hiding in plain sight," Jon said.

"A gut feeling?" Captain Dubois asked.

"Yes, a gut feeling. Let's meet tomorrow at the SOE detachment and run through what we know. Maybe something we've overlooked will reach out and grab us."

Jon and Camille arrived at the detachment by 0700 hours the next morning. It took Jon an hour to read all the operational reports. After finishing, he leaned back in his chair, thinking.

"Hmm."

"I know that sound and look, mate," Miles said. "What are you thinking?"

"What if they simply changed their looks?"

"What do you mean?" Camille asked.

"Well, what if they carry war kits like ours? They could darken their skin and dress like ordinary Indians. To most they would look like locals."

"I don't know why I didn't think of that," Miles stated.

"We've focused on what they looked like when we first saw them. Let's look for them in some of the Indian neighborhoods, closer to downtown. They won't want to move too far from the wharves."

"I'll talk to Colonel Ray and see if we can get more CIC agents assigned to this," Captain Dubois said.

"Tell them to look for the taller man with the gold tooth. That will be one feature the operative can't hide."

By the end of the afternoon, Jon had briefed the CIC agents sent to him by Colonel Ray. With a team of twenty-eight agents, he could search more areas. It took five days before one of the CIC teams photographed two Indians together, one with a gold tooth.

"It looks like it could be them. Same eyes and noses. Those turbans and goatees make them hard to recognize. What do you think?" Camille asked.

"I think you're on to something. Let's give the guys a couple more days to observe them and see if they make contact with anyone," Jon said.

"What do you all think?" Jon passed the photographs to Miles and Henri.

"I agree, mate. We need to find their handler too," Miles said.

"What are you thinking, Henri?"

"I think one of us needs to check out their room."

"Would the one of us happen to be you?"

"Of course," Henri said. "I'll go out tomorrow morning with the CIC team taking the day watch at the boardinghouse. When the suspects leave, I'll have the manager open their door, or I'll pick the lock and get into their room."

"Watch out for booby traps and poisoned pins on the door handle."

"I'll take Agent Warren with me and give him some training on breaking and entering."

"Just be careful."

"Yes, Daddy," Henri replied. He and Miles broke out in laughter.

The following day, Henri and Franklin watched from a restaurant across the street as their subjects left the boardinghouse. They waited ten minutes before crossing the street. The room was on the second floor, near the fire escape.

"Good planning on their part," Henri said. "They have a quick exit with the fire escape.

At the door of room 215, Henri knelt down and inspected the door handle: no poison stick pens. He pulled his lockpick set out of his jacket pocket. "Don't ever go anywhere without this," he told Franklin.

Henri picked the lock in thirty seconds. He searched around the rim of the door before cracking it open, looking for anything that might serve as a trip wire. "They like to use monofilament line or nylon fishing line for their trip wire; it's easier to conceal."

After finding no trip wire, Henri slowly opened the door and searched the floor for monofilament line. After clearing the floor, he began looking through the room. He and Franklin searched for five minutes before Franklin found the Japanese version of the OSS war kit.

"Good job, kid; you found what we came for," Henri said. He photographed the kit with his miniature camera. "Put it back where you found it, and let's get out of here."

As Henri closed the door behind them, he heard the soft click of a door closing down the hallway.

"I think we've been made, kid. Let's get back across the street to the restaurant."

Twenty minutes after Henri and Franklin left the hotel, a short Asian man walked out of the hotel. Henri took several head-on and profile photographs with his MINOX subminiature camera and watched as two Indian CIC agents shadowed the suspect. Henri and Franklin waited another fifteen minutes before they left their position.

Once the film was developed, Henri showed Camille the photographs of the Asian suspect. Camille passed the photo to Jon.

"His features look Japanese, but the eyes are round. I've heard stories of Japanese spies having the tissue around their eyes surgically altered. Someone went to a lot of trouble to disguise him; this may be the handler. Nevertheless, I wouldn't expect them to be staying at the same hotel," Camille said.

"Neither would I, but if they're hiding in plain sight and aren't following the traditional spycraft rules, then all our current assumptions are useless. It's all we have to go on, so we'll run with it. Hell, we're making this art of spying stuff up as we go along. Let's get out there and take these people down," Jon said.

CHAPTER 39

Calcutta, India

Over the course of the next five days, CIC agents watched as the two Japanese spies changed hotels two times. They never saw the small Asian man again, but the team assumed he would be nearby, looking for Allied watchers.

When Jon walked into the SOE briefing room one morning, Colonel Ronnie Masek was there to greet him.

"I hadn't expected to see anyone from G-2 for another week or two," Jon said.

"G-2 dispatched me right after you got back from your last mission. I brought you another one," Colonel Masek replied.

"Where to this time, Colonel?"

"Hanoi."

"What's the mission?"

"First, we want you to find and eliminate the team of Japanese agents who killed two of our OSS assets in Hanoi. Second, we want you to liberate a POW camp thirty miles north of Hanoi where we suspect the Japanese are conducting more medical experiments on Allied prisoners. The camp is filled mostly with Australian and British soldiers captured at the fall of Singapore."

"What happened to the two OSS agents?"

"We air-dropped them into Hanoi ten weeks ago to investigate the POW camp. They teamed up with a group of local OSS agents. Someone on the local team must have let something slip, or else one of them is a double agent. Our agents were killed before they got a chance to investigate the camp."

"OK, let me go gather up Miles and Henri."

An hour later, Colonel Masek finished briefing Jon's team and Colonel MacKenzie on the status of the OSS in Hanoi and the location of the POW camp.

"The names of the two OSS agents I gave you are unknown to the other group of OSS agents in Hanoi. They will be your primary contacts. The POW camp is located thirty miles northwest of Hanoi. According to our native informants, there are at least two hundred prisoners." Masek then turned to Colonel MacKenzie. "Colonel, I know your team is conducting a major investigation here in Calcutta. Will you be OK with these three gone?

"We'll manage," Colonel MacKenzie said. "Jon, whom do you recommend I put in charge?"

Without any hesitation, Jon said, "Captain Dubois. With his Secret Service background and the missions we've been on together, he has the most experience. And I trust him. If he's not available, Agent Warren from Detachment 101 is my second choice."

"Warren's been in-country for only five months," Henri said.

"Yes, but he's been a quick study and excelled in everything we've taught him. His analytical mind and instinct are like mine, and he can think ahead and anticipate the Japanese agent's next move."

"I'll pass that along to Colonel Ray."

Jon walked into the briefing room where Captain Dubois and the four women agents were discussing the previous night's reconnaissance. From the look on Jon's face, Camille knew something was up.

"What's wrong?" Camille asked.

"We've got another mission."

Jon turned to Captain Dubois. "Richard, I've asked Colonel MacKenzie to put you in charge of the investigation. If you're not available, I want Lieutenant Warren in charge. We may be gone for several weeks."

"When do you leave?" Camille asked.

"Sunday. There's a lot of planning to do still."

"At least we have four days together. Should we kick Captain Dubois and the girls off the *Jacqueline* so we can have it to ourselves?"

"I think he would take offense to that."

"You're damn right I would. I'm not about to stay in a tent on base. Plus, the *Jacqueline* is my boat. And what about the other ladies? You don't want them in a tent with all those GIs around gawking when they hang their panties and bras out to dry, do you?" Captain Dubois asked.

"I don't know," Kathleen said. "I might enjoy having five thousand men around to choose from."

"And if we wanted some privacy, we could always bring one back to the boat," Monique said, giggling.

"Not on my boat!" Captain Dubois exclaimed. "You'll bring no man on the boat unless you're married to him."

"I guess we'll need to get married for a day or two," Brigitte said.

All the girls burst out laughing at the same time. Captain Dubois shook his head.

"All right, ladies, we've got work to do before you all run off half-cocked and get married."

"See what you started, Camille? I doubt you'll get any more work done today," Jon said.

Camille looked at the girls and burst out laughing again. The other ladies followed suit.

"Oh, for crying out loud, you all are cackling like chickens in a hen-house," Jon said.

This only caused the girls to laugh even harder. Jon and Captain Dubois couldn't stand it any longer and left the room. The laughing, joking, and speculation about what kind of GI they wanted continued for another thirty minutes. Jon liked it when they laughed. It helped release some of the stress they had been under for the last five weeks. When Captain Dubois walked back into the room, the girls were still snickering.

"All right, let's get down to business and figure out a way to catch these damn Japanese agents," Captain Dubois said.

Jon left the SOE building and went to the OSS detachment. He asked Colonel Kenneth Taylor to send a message to his two agents in Saigon. He wanted them to make contact with his friend René Clairoux. René owned a private detective agency with offices in Saigon and Hanoi. Jon had worked with René and his brother the previous year in Chittagong. If anyone could find the Japanese agents who had killed the two OSS agents, it would be René.

CHAPTER 40

Hanoi, French Indochina

At 0100 hours on Sunday morning, Jon, Miles, and Henri jumped from a dull black Lancaster bomber, five hundred feet above the ground. They landed in an open meadow ten miles west of Hanoi, near a village called Vinh Phuc. Greeting them were the two OSS agents and Colonel Võ Nguyên Giáp, the leader of the Vietnam Independence League, called the Viet Minh. The Viet Minh was trying to overthrow the French Vichy government, which was friendly to both Japan and Germany.

Following Germany's defeat of France in 1940, the French president appointed Field Marshal Henri Philippe Pétain as the premier of France. Field Marshal Pétain then organized the French government into an authoritarian-style government and collaborated with the Germans, but only after they agreed not to divide France among the Axis powers. To enforce French collaboration, Germany held two million French soldiers as prisoners in Germany. After the French Indochina government reorganized under Pétain, he ordered their military forces to actively engage the Allied forces.

Jon did not have any experience working with the Communist Viet Minh, but he knew they were friendly and helpful to the US Army. The more Jon talked to the Vietnamese colonel, the more he respected him. Giáp received his education in one of the most prestigious secondary schools in French Indochina, Lycée Albert Sarraut, where the local elite were educated. Later, he received a bachelor's degree in politics, economics, and law from the University of Hanoi. Afterward, he taught school in Hanoi and became a part-time journalist, writing for a revolutionary movement.

In 1930, the French arrested Giáp for sedition, and he spent thirteen months in prison. When he got out, he joined the Communist Party. When France outlawed Communism in 1931, Giáp fled to China and joined up with Ho Chi Minh. While he was in exile, the French colonial authorities arrested his parents, sister, and wife. After being interrogated and tortured, they were executed.

When Giáp returned to French Indochina in 1944, he helped organize the resistance against the Japanese occupation forces. Now he worked with the Allied forces to defeat the Japanese. Colonel Giáp was motivated in his mission to get rid of the Japanese as well as overthrow the Vichy government and end French colonial rule.

Under the cover of darkness, Giáp and the two OSS agents got the Allied trio into Hanoi, where they met up with René Clairoux. When the OSS request to find René went out, he was working in Hanoi. René readily accepted the offer to work with the OSS. He owed the American his and his brother's lives. When the trio walked into René's downtown office, however, he was astonished to see them.

"I heard the three of you had been killed by Japanese agents," René said.

"Can't believe everything you hear these days. How well do you know Hanoi?" Jon asked.

"As well as Saigon."

"Any leads on the Japanese agents we're looking for?"

"Yes, but it is best if we go elsewhere to discuss it. Japanese Kempeitai agents occasionally watch my office, and they're as bad as the German Gestapo. We need to leave before the Kempeitai watchers arrive. One of my men will take you through the backstreets. I will follow in fifteen minutes."

Jon, Miles, and Henri followed a young Vietnamese boy out of René's office through a door in the alley and moved through the darkness to a building six blocks away. René took a different route to the building and entered through the front door.

"I've never used this building before. I've been saving it for special use or an emergency. This seems to qualify as special use. You can stay here while you're in Hanoi, but we must be cautious when we meet, as there are a lot of Japanese informers here. My men are posted all around this area. If a Japanese patrol or the Kempeitai show up, I'll move you to another location."

Over the next two hours, René gave his assessment on the situation in Hanoi and detailed what he had found on the murders of the OSS agents.

"I received the information only yesterday afternoon. One of my informers overheard the two men discussing their work as OSS agents while secretly working for the Japanese. They were last seen in one of the lower-class brothels, boasting to each other about how they killed two Americans agents. I have the location where they live and the brothel where they usually drink until the early-morning hours."

"They're not afraid of the Kempeitai?" Jon asked.

"If any Kempeitai agents had overhead the two men, they would be lying in an alley with their throats cut. The Japanese don't take kindly to double agents shooting their mouths off. However, the Japs don't even bother to go into these vermin-infested ratholes."

"Is anyone watching the two men right now?" Henri asked.

"Yes, I have four three-man teams that watch them day and night. If there is any change in location or status, one of them brings me an update."

"Is there any way we could take these traitors tonight?" Miles asked.

"I don't see why not. The brothel they practically live at is only a mile from here. However, I cannot be seen with you, so one of my men will take you there after dark. The same man will deliver dinner to you. He is reliable and trustworthy."

"If we're successful tonight, we may not see you for a while. Will it be all right to use this place when we return in a week or so?" Jon asked.

"It shouldn't be a problem. The detective I've assigned to help you is called Joshua. It was good seeing you all. Go with God."

After midnight, the short, black-haired, and young Vietnamese boy named Joshua returned to get the trio. He wasn't quite the man Jon had expected for clandestine work. Joshua took them through alleys and shortcuts, staying off the main streets.

"The brothel is small, and the whores are ugly," Joshua said. "These guys spend a lot of time drinking beer. When they need to pee, they use the urinal in the alley."

"What are your orders, once you get us there?" Jon asked.

"To wait and report back to the boss on what happens."

"All right, but tell your other helpers to stay out of our lines of fire."

For his services, Jon handed Joshua a small bag of opium, one of the many he had procured from the SOE armory before leaving Calcutta. Jon paid all of his Asian contacts in opium. Colonel MacKenzie told him it was the only form of payment the Asians would accept. Paper money meant nothing to the average Vietnamese, but opium could be used to barter for anything. Jon asked the young man to stay and identify the two operatives.

Jon, Henri, and Joshua hid in the alley. Miles and the three watchers moved to the front of the building and monitored the front door. Joshua described the double agents to them as they settled into their hiding place.

"Both are stout and around five foot five in height, and both have very short hair and a tattoo of a dagger with a red snake coiled around it on their right arm. One man has a scar running from his right ear to his chin, and the other has a long scar on his left arm and walks with a noticeable limp. Their tattoos indicate they are assassins for hire. They won't be easy to kill," Joshua said.

"Then we'll take them one at a time, while they're taking a leak," Henri stated.

It wasn't long before the man with the limp and the long scar on his left arm exited the brothel and eased up to a bamboo trough next to the building. He was short but looked stout as an ox.

"Are you boys still out here? If I see you following us again, I'm going to kill you," the man with the limp said. His upper body swayed back and forth in front of the trough.

"Shame on you for picking on little boys," Henri said. He stepped out of the darkness behind the man and rammed his eleven-inch dagger into the stunned man's throat.

Henri held the man from behind until he died. He then dragged the body thirty feet down the alley and dropped it in a pool of filthy water out of sight of the rear door to the brothel.

"One down and one to go," Henri said.

Ten minutes later, the second agent exited the building, looking for his friend.

"Binh, where the hell are you, asshole? The girls are waiting. Are you throwing up again?" the man said. He bellied up to the bamboo trough.

"He's where you're going to be in ten seconds, asshole," Henri said. He then drove his dagger into the man's kidney.

When the knife entered his kidney, the man was stunned by the pain, and his head jerked up and back.

"Here's another scar for you, traitor!" Henri grabbed the man by the forehead and slit his throat.

When Henri turned around, he saw Jon staring at him.

"What?"

"I don't think I've ever seen you so angry."

"These two are French citizens. They betrayed France by becoming Japanese agents, and this is what they deserve for killing those OSS agents."

"He's right, mate," Miles said.

"What about the bodies? Shouldn't we hide them?" Jon asked.

"Hell, the pigs will eat them before the sun comes up. Leave them in the open for all to see," Henri said.

"OK, have it your way. Let's get the hell out of town and join up with Colonel Giáp."

CHAPTER 41

Vinh Lai POW Camp, French Indochina

The trio met up with Colonel Giáp and his Viet Minh freedom fighters four miles north of Hanoi. Colonel Giáp stood next to six sampans, waiting to take them up the Song Hong River to Vinh Mo. According to the colonel's two agents, most of the Japanese forces had pulled back into Hanoi to protect the city from an expected Allied attack, and no Japanese boats would be patrolling the river from Hanoi to the Vinh Lai POW camp.

The colonel explained that the prisoner-of-war camp was situated at the base of a small hill north of Vinh Lai Village and at the southern end of the huge S curve in the Song Hong River. A thick forest surrounded the camp to the north, east, and west. The south side of the camp faced the Song Hong River, where a sandy delta formed at the bend in the Song Hong as it turned north and the Song Da River branched off and turned south.

After ten hours on the river, the sampans stopped and let the soldiers and agents off four miles south of the POW camp. Colonel Giáp told the trio they would camp in the hills and trek to the camp the following day. Having been up for nearly forty-eight hours straight, the three agents were close to exhaustion. Thankful for the rest, Jon, Miles, and Henri lay down on a thick bed of grass and fell asleep within minutes.

The next morning, Colonel Giáp took the three agents into the forest to a grassy ridge overlooking the camp. After twenty minutes of scanning the compound, Jon counted only ten soldiers guarding what looked to be close to two hundred prisoners.

"It looks like two-thirds of the guard force has already withdrawn to Hanoi. I see only one officer and ten guards," Colonel Giáp said.

While Jon, Miles, and Colonel Giáp remained on the ridge, Henri took off down the hill thick with elephant grass to see how close he could get to the compound. On the far west side of the hill, he followed a dry creek bed to within thirty yards of the camp. He got close enough to see the only officer in the camp, a young lieutenant, yelling orders to the prisoners. Henri counted 205 prisoners doing morning calisthenics. He watched them for twenty minutes before retracing his steps up the creek and back to where Jon and Miles lay prone in the grass.

"Damn, I believe I could walk up to the gate and force the lot of them to surrender," Henri stated.

"I would chance it, but you've been a thorn in my side for so long, I don't know what I would do if I lost you," Jon said.

"Getting funny now, are we?"

"I think the kid's gone daffy from too little sleep, mate. Maybe we should let the boy get more rest," Miles said.

"Screw you both. How does the big field to the south of the camp look? Can we land a C-47 in there?"

"It's as smooth as a baby's bottom, but it may be muddy. When it rains, I bet the creek spills a lot of water over its banks and floods it. I'll need to walk it tonight to make sure it's dry," Henri said.

"I don't see a medical facility. Did you notice anything from the creek?"

"There's a fenced-off section on the west side, about an acre in size. Looks like there used to be a structure there. The posts are still in the ground. Other than that, I didn't see anything else. The other structures are made from bamboo with thatched roofs, and there's an open lean-to with five large cooking kettles under it. There's also a large garden in the middle of the compound. Since the prisoners don't look half-bad, I assume the Japs are letting them grow their own food."

"I noticed a guard with three prisoners heading toward the river to the east of the camp," Miles said. "The prisoners carried long poles, like they were going fishing."

"All right, what's your suggestion for taking the camp?"

"Let's take it tonight. We can move the colonel's troops through the dry creek bed and cut through the fence. This doesn't look difficult. We can easily take out the ten guards."

"That's exactly what worries me. We'll take turns watching the camp tonight. I'll take the first watch, beginning at 1800 hours. Now, let's go grab some breakfast."

Halfway through his four-hour watch, just before the sun set, Jon saw a Japanese version of a Willys jeep and a two-ton truck pull up to the compound. Two guards got out and lowered the tailgate. A guard from the camp hustled five prisoners from one of the huts and forced them into the back of the truck. The two guards got back into the truck, and the camp guard closed the tailgate. The jeep and the truck drove north.

Jon did not like what he saw. He surmised there must be a second facility to the north. It took him fifteen minutes to walk back to camp and tell the others. They would need to go north and find out what lay beyond the heavily forested hills.

The next morning, Colonel Giáp broke camp and used the tree line to mask their movement to the north. Two hours and five miles later, they came upon another compound. This one contained four large wooden buildings and five huge bamboo huts. A ten-foot-tall barbed-wire fence surrounded the compound, which Jon estimated to be three hundred feet square. Over three hundred prisoners milled around inside the fence, and he could see more inside the bamboo huts. Four guards walked the fence line outside the compound, and another two guards stood next to one of the wooden buildings. Off to the side of the building stood a forty-foot radio antenna. *That must be the commandant's office and quarters*, Jon thought.

The complications of Jon's mission doubled. They would need to hit both compounds at the same time to ensure success. Jon gave Miles and Henri the responsibility for the first compound. Jon and Colonel Giáp would take this one. The colonel assigned half of his men to go with Miles and Henri. Jon told his two agents they would attack both compounds at 0400 hours.

Jon didn't like splitting up his team. He knew they worked best as a cohesive unit. They knew each other well, how each reacted and how each handled himself in a crisis. Before Miles and Henri departed, Jon changed his mind. He decided they would take this compound first and drive the Japanese vehicles back to the other compound and surprise them during the day.

"Are you sure?" Miles asked.

"I'm sure," Jon said. "My gut is telling me something is not right. Maybe it's another trap. Maybe Japanese agents noticed the Lancaster take off from Alipore and notified their headquarters. Either way, something is wrong. I can feel it."

"If your gut feeling is that strong, maybe we should abort," Henri stated.

"We don't want to get too cocky for our own good. I'm not looking forward to telling Camille we lost her husband because he was too arrogant to abort," Miles said.

"All right, let's pull back into the forest and wait another day or two. I'll ask the colonel to send out some of his men to the nearby villages to see what they know. Hell, there may be a brigade of Japs hidden somewhere in the forest behind us. If there is, we'll bail. OK?"

"OK," Henri and Miles agreed.

CHAPTER 42

Vinh Lai POW Camp, French Indochina

For another three days, Jon's team and the Viet Minh freedom fighters monitored both camps. Nothing happened until the afternoon of the third day. That afternoon, a Kawasaki Ki-10 reconnaissance aircraft buzzed the northern compound, landed, and stopped one hundred feet from the front gate.

The biplane was used by the Japanese throughout Asia. The Ki-10s unequal wingspans was its trademark. The aircraft's all-metal frame was covered with fabric. The top wingspan extended three feet farther than the bottom wingspan. The bottom wings were fitted with ailerons on the trailing edge to allow up or down movement of the aircraft. Its armament consisted of two 7.7-millimeter machine guns synchronized to fire through the propeller. A liquid-cooled 850-horsepower Kawasaki Ha-9 V-engine powered the aircraft. Allied aviators called it a Perry.

Jon watched as an officer walked from the compound to the aircraft. The officer saluted the passenger of the biplane, and both walked to the commander's hut. Outside the hut, the officer pointed to the north, and Jon could see an animated conversation taking place. The occupant of the aircraft shook his head and quickly moved his arms out to his sides, as if indicating "No more." Then the officer saluted, and the visitor walked back to the aircraft. Five minutes later, the Perry was airborne and heading south in the direction of Hanoi.

"I would like to have heard that conversation," Colonel Giáp said.

"Me too," Jon said. "I got the impression the visitor didn't like something the officer was saying and cut him off."

"I suggest we wait another day or two to see if anything happens. Now let me tell you about the rumors I heard of the Japanese stealing our country's treasures. According to many of the villagers I've talked to, the Japanese have captured and extorted gold and silver from the people throughout this region. It is another reason why I wanted to come along. Since the Japanese invaded, my headquarters has determined that the Japanese have removed over twenty tons of gold and silver from my country, as well as barrels of diamonds, rubies, sapphires, and jade. Much of the gold is in cast statues of Buddha. One particular gold statue, removed from one of our most famous temples, was fifteen feet tall."

"That's a lot of loot. What are they doing with it?" Jon asked.

"My agents tell me most of it is being shipped to Japan. They've watched it being loaded on several different Japanese hospital ships, the ones with the green cross on the smokestacks."

"That's the first time I've heard of this. And, of course, our submarines will never sink a hospital ship. I'll mention this in my report when I get back to Calcutta."

The following day, Jon and Colonel Giáp observed a column of thirty-two heavy-duty trucks and twelve Type 1 Ho-Ha half-track armored personnel carriers driving in from the north. Jon was now glad he had followed his gut instinct and held off on his attack. This was obviously another trap to capture Allied agents. If he had attacked the two prisoner compounds three days before, they would have faced a sizable and heavily armed Japanese force.

"Looks like whoever that was in the biplane wanted those troops for something else," Henri said.

"I assume they are heading for Hanoi," Colonel Giáp remarked.

"Well, Colonel, what do you suggest we do now?" Jon asked.

"I have found the Japanese to be very clever at times. I would wait at least another day to see if another column of trucks goes through here. It's possible the Japanese are consolidating all of their forces around Hanoi."

"I agree," Jon said. "Colonel, I've been asked to look for an American B-24 bomber that went down east of here. Would you mind if I borrow a couple of your men and conduct a search? It should be no more than ten miles from here."

"I'll assign two men to go with you."

Twenty minutes later, as Jon gathered his backpack, two very young-looking Vietnamese men walked up to him. One carried an ancient flint-lock rifle and the other a machete.

"These are two of my best scouts. They are from a village twenty miles east of here. They know the territory well and are very good trackers and fighters," Colonel Giáp stated.

The three men walked close to six miles before the daylight gave way to a bronze haze and grayness. Before it got dark, they stopped and camped for the night. Despite their ability to speak French, the two Vietnamese men did not speak much. When they did, they spoke in Vietnamese. Jon offered the men some of the dried beef he carried. Out of respect for Jon, each took a small piece. Jon could tell from the looks on their faces that they didn't like it. Before the sun went behind a small hill, Jon pulled a string hammock out of his backpack, tied it between two trees, and eased into it. The two Vietnamese men slept on the ground.

The next morning they awoke before daylight. After eating, they started off on a northerly course. Two hours into their march, they came upon a large bamboo hut at the edge of the forest. Jon signaled the two men to stop. He conversed with them in French and told them to spread out before they approached the hut.

After waiting half an hour, Jon moved quietly through a copse of trees, eased up to the rear of the hut, stopped, and listened. When he didn't hear anything, he continued around the hut to a single door with a cloth flap hanging from the top of the frame. With his .45 semiautomatic in front of him, he slipped into the hut. Except for an occasional wooden bowl lying on the floor, the hut was empty.

Jon walked back outside and began walking around the hut. He walked back inside for several minutes and came back out.

"Something's not right here," Jon told the two men. "Would you two go inside and look around and come back out?"

The two men entered the hut and came back out two minutes later. When Jon asked them if they had noticed anything unusual, they both shook their heads. Jon squatted down and let his analytical mind work a while. After five minutes, he jumped up and stepped off the length and width of the structure. He went inside, measured it, and came back outside.

"It's longer on the outside than it is on the inside, by six feet at least," Jon stated.

All three went back into the hut. Jon then placed his hands against the far end wall. He ran his hands up and down the bamboo wall. He stopped, put his hand through a nearly invisible slit in the bamboo, and pulled. A door popped open, and Jon walked into a space the width of the hut and six feet deep. Inside the hidden space, Jon found four small bags of rice and several cooking pots and utensils. Before Jon could say anything, he heard a distinct clink and then voices.

"Don't talk," Jon whispered.

Jon move to the entrance of the structure and peered through the cloth curtain. He saw a dozen Japanese soldiers walking in a line toward the hut. *We're trapped*, Jon thought. He moved back to where the two men stood, ushered them into the hidden room, and closed the door.

"The Japs must be using this as an outpost for patrols. I bet they're looking for the B-24," Jon whispered.

"Are you good with the gun?" Jon asked.

"Very good," the man with the flintlock replied. "I can load it to shoot through two or more men."

"Load it for three," Jon said.

"I can kill very quickly with my machete," the other man stated. He was the larger of the two, with thick, strong arms.

"Good," Jon said.

Jon and the two Viet Minh men waited in silence. When the Japanese soldiers entered the hut, most sat on the floor talking, though several remained standing. Jon peered through the tightly placed bamboo. He was thankful for the poor lighting in the hut and prayed the Japanese didn't know about the hidden space.

Jon pointed to the young Viet Minh man with the flintlock, held up three fingers, and pointed toward the Japs. The man peered through a tiny slit in the bamboo and nodded. He looked again and put his gun up to the bamboo slit. Jon looked at the second man, who looked at him and nodded. When Jon looked through a small slit in the bamboo, he saw that all of the soldiers had removed their gear and weapons. Two men stood while the rest lay on the dirt floor. Jon nodded to the rifleman, who looked again, found two men facing each other, and fired.

Jon opened the hidden door and jumped out firing his two Colt .45 automatics. The big Viet Minh man leaped out behind Jon and began swinging his machete wildly. The rifleman came out last and began swinging his own machete. Out of the corner of his eye, Jon saw a head fly off one of the Japanese soldiers and then another.

The battle lasted a minute. Jon shot eight times, killing six soldiers. The rifleman killed three soldiers with one shot, two standing near the hidden room and one sitting at the far end of the hut. The big man killed five Japs. Only one Japanese soldier, an officer, remained alive. Jon wanted to take him prisoner, but before he could say anything, the large man with the machete took his head off.

Jon went through the officer's clothing and the leather map case. He took anything of intelligence value and placed it in his backpack. The two Viet Minh men searched all the soldiers and took anything of value. When Jon walked outside, he stared at the sight that greeted him. His two accomplices were placing the heads of the Japanese soldiers on bamboo stakes driven into the ground.

"Cut an ear off each one and take it with you. You can throw them away later," Jon said.

If another Japanese patrol finds these men, Jon thought, *they will be in for a shock. Nothing like instilling a little terror into the enemy mind.*

Once they were done, Jon and the two Viet Minh left the hut and continued their search for the B-24. They found it in a dense patch of jungle close to dusk. Jon entered the crumpled B-24, removed the Norden bombsight, and took one dog tag from each of the three bodies. While the Viet Minh set up camp, Jon buried the three dead airmen. They remained at the plane overnight and then started their trek back the next morning.

The moment Jon returned to camp, Mile and Henri filled him in on the Japanese truck column that had stopped at the two POW camps the previous day. They had loaded up all of the POWs and driven south. Afterward, Colonel Giáp sent a team of men north, to look for another Japanese camp. They found one, three miles north of the second compound, hidden in the thick forest. It was deserted.

"This was a major Japanese outpost. I guess we played this one right. Thank God for your sixth sense," Miles said.

Jon collected his radio, connected the battery, and sent a coded message to the SOE detachment in Calcutta, detailing the Japanese pullout. The message he received back was unexpected: "Japanese evacuating Hanoi STOP Return to Hanoi and secure the PRISONERS END."

CHAPTER 43

Calcutta, India

It was nearly midnight when Lieutenant Warren noticed the two Japanese agents returning to their hotel. Franklin, who was watching from the second story of a building across the street, put a walkie-talkie to his mouth and pushed the talk button.

"Chickens in the roost," Franklin said.

"Roger, we're moving into position," Captain Dubois responded.

"Team three moving," Camille said. She and Kathleen got out of a car a half mile to the north and began converging on the hotel.

As they walked along a street, Kathleen got the feeling something wasn't right, but she couldn't put her finger on anything specific. They walked another block when Kathleen put her hand on Camille's shoulder and whispered, "Stop."

"What?" Camille asked.

"I saw someone move in the alley behind us on the other side of the street."

"It could be anybody."

"And what if it's another spy?"

"OK, what do you think we should do?"

"Let's duck down this alley and hide and see if anyone follows us."

"For how long?"

"Long enough for whoever's in that alley to think we've gone this way and follow us."

The two agents hid in recessed doorways across from each other. Ten minutes later, a head looked around the corner of the building into the alley. Camille watched as the person entered the alley fifty feet away. She motioned to Kathleen, who nodded. When the person was fifteen feet away, Camille yelled, "Freeze and drop your weapon."

Before Camille could say another word, the intruder fired a pistol in her direction. Kathleen didn't waste another breath. As she eased her arm out of the doorway, Camille did the same. They fired their nine-millimeter pistols at the same time, both hitting the assailant in the chest.

Camille and Kathleen waited a good minute before they came out of their hiding places. Kathleen knelt next to the figure sprawled on the alley floor, put her finger to the assailant's neck, and searched for a pulse. When she lifted the dark knit cap, she noticed the assailant's long hair was put up in a bun on the back of her head.

"Oh my God, it's a woman!" Kathleen exclaimed.

"Crap, we've only been looking for men," Camille said.

"Let's get out of here; we're running late."

Captain Dubois, Monique, and Brigitte entered the hotel through a rear door opened by Sergeant Danny Grantham. Dubois ordered the SOE sergeant to stand watch at the bottom of the stairs. Danny didn't like staying behind in the lobby hallway, but he obeyed. Captain Dubois and the two women made their way to the third floor. As he turned the corner into the hallway, a shot rang out. Captain Dubois cried out and fell to the floor.

Brigitte and Monique didn't hesitate. They both jumped into the dimly lit hallway and fired at the gunman, who was running toward the fire escape. The gunman stumbled and fell. When he got up, he turned to face the women and raised his gun. Monique and Bridgette fired. One bullet hit him in the side of his chest, and the other hit him in the temple.

When Sergeant Grantham heard the gunfire, he turned to run up the stairs. A second gunman on the second-floor landing ten feet away shot him in the chest. The gunman then stepped over his body and ran out the back door. When he exited the door, he ran into Camille, knocking her down. The gunman, momentarily stunned, recovered and aimed his gun at Camille. Before he could pull the trigger, Kathleen shot him in the forehead.

As Kathleen knelt down to remove the assailant's knit cap, she heard a door open above her. As she aimed her pistol upward, Brigitte yelled down.

"Are you all OK?" Brigitte asked.

"Peachy," Kathleen responded.

"Go call for an ambulance. Captain Dubois has been shot."

When Camille and Kathleen entered through the back door, they saw Lieutenant Warren kneeling next to Sergeant Grantham.

"You call the ambulance. I'll help look after Grantham," Kathleen said.

Kathleen got down on both knees and checked the sergeant. Blood bubbled between his lips and out of his nostrils, and the pool of blood on the floor grew larger. She tore the sleeves off her blouse and used them as a compress to stop the bleeding from his chest. He was drowning in his own blood. Kathleen held his hand until he took his last breath.

Monique was the first to reach Captain Dubois. When she rolled him onto his back, she could see that he was bleeding badly from a wound in the side of his abdomen. When Brigitte rushed back to the captain's side, Monique was packing his wound with a large bandage from the first-aid kit she carried. By the time the ambulance attendants arrived with a stretcher, the captain was conscious.

"Help me up; it's just a scratch. I can walk to the ambulance," Captain Dubois complained.

"Sorry, sir, but walking would cause you to bleed more. We don't want you dying on us," the ambulance attendant said.

Despite his complaints, they lifted him onto the stretcher. Thirty minutes after the ambulance left the hotel, Captain Dubois was in surgery to repair the damage to the left side of his abdomen. The bullet that struck him ricocheted off a rib and away from his body, causing only minor damage.

When Franklin returned to the lobby, he called the duty officer at the SOE detachment and informed him that Sergeant Grantham had been killed. The duty officer called Colonel MacKenzie. Before Colonel MacKenzie had made it to the hotel, army ambulances had arrived and removed the bodies.

Camille was about to leave the hotel to go pick up her car when Colonel MacKenzie entered the hotel.

"Tell everyone to meet me in the lobby. I want a thorough briefing on what happened," Colonel MacKenzie ordered.

At least a half-dozen hotel visitors were now loitering in the lobby, and the manager was doing everything in his power to calm them. All were demanding their money back when Colonel MacKenzie shouted, "Everyone, return to your room, or I'll arrest you for interfering with my investigation."

Within minutes, all the guests had dispersed, and the lobby was empty except for Colonel MacKenzie and his agents.

It was 0400 hours before the colonel was satisfied with the verbal after-action report from each agent. The agents were extremely tired. The mission adrenaline had worn off hours before.

"I want a written report from each team on my desk by 0800," Colonel MacKenzie stated.

"Oh, for God's sake, Colonel," Kathleen responded.

"It's nearly sunrise, ladies and gentlemen, and you've got work to do. Let's move."

CHAPTER 44

Hanoi, French Indochina

The trip downriver took only six hours. It was well after midnight, but the city was alive with people celebrating on the streets. When Colonel Giáp and his men exited their boats, a large crowd gathered and began cheering. One of Colonel Giáp's spies walked up to him and saluted.

"Colonel, the Japanese are evacuating the city. They've moved all their forces to the docks and are bivouacked near the large Japanese-built wharf. They are waiting for a freighter to carry them to Singapore. It is arriving in the morning."

After the Japanese had evacuated the Vinh Lai camp, Jon didn't know what to think. Would the Japanese execute the prisoners in Hanoi as a way of saving face? Would they use them as a human shield to get onto the ships arriving in the morning and then take them to Singapore? The Oriental mind was a mystery to Jon. He worried about the heinous acts and cruelty of the Japanese and speculated that the prisoners would be executed, but until the transport arrived, he still had a chance to rescue them.

"Colonel Giáp," Jon said. "I would like to attempt a rescue before the Japs evacuate with our prisoners or, worse, execute them."

"The moment we landed, Agent Preston, I sent four men to find out their exact location. They should be back in a couple of hours. We'll find your people, and we'll help you free them. I am well aware of how the Japanese treat prisoners and that they regard them as less than human. Thousands of Vietnamese have died from disease, starvation, and execution while building the Japanese railroad in Thailand. Believe me: we know the pain of losing our people."

The two scouts returned and reported that the prisoners were camped a half mile from the main Japanese force and guarded by seven trucks with machine guns in their beds. According to the locals, several people handing the prisoners food and water as they passed were shot.

Six prisoners tried to escape, and four were shot in the back. Two wounded prisoners were placed on their knees and beheaded by a Japanese officer.

When the scouts told Jon seven Japanese trucks, with Type 92 heavy machine guns, were positioned in a half-moon formation on the south side of the prisoner camp, he concluded that the Japanese intended to slaughter the prisoners.

The Type 92 machine gun, air cooled and gas operated, was the most commonly used machine gun in the Japanese arsenal. The Americans had nicknamed it "the woodpecker" because of the distinctive stuttering sound it made when fired. The Type 92 fired a 7.7-millimeter round at a rate of four hundred rounds per minute. It was accurate out to a range of 875 yards. With its tripod, the Type 92 weighed 125 pounds and required several soldiers to carry and operate.

"Colonel, I think you know what the Japanese intend to do with those machine guns," Jon said.

"Yes, it's quite apparent."

Before Colonel Giáp gave the order to break camp and move the six miles south through town, he sent twenty of his best men with the American agents to deal with the Japanese trucks and machine guns. Outside the city, over five thousand Viet Minh soldiers moved in on the Japanese position. Colonel Giáp would attack the Japanese encampment with everything in his arsenal, striking the Japanese from the warehouses and buildings beside the docks, as well as from sampans on the river. He gave Jon until sunrise to rescue the prisoners, and then he would begin the attack.

If the American agents succeeded in rescuing the prisoners, he would position part of his troops between them and the Japanese. With an attack in progress, the Japanese would not be willing to expend resources to retake the prisoners.

By 0400 hours, Jon's team had moved to within one hundred feet of the camped prisoners and Japanese guards. Jon knew that Colonel Giáp had sent twenty of his best men because he wanted the Japanese machine guns. To give the Viet Minh time to dismantle and move the guns before dawn, Jon would need to take out all of the Japanese soldiers guarding the prisoners.

"Sergeant," Jon said to the leader of the Viet Minh soldiers, "I need you to send several men to take out the Japanese sentries. Knives only."

"I'll see to it personally, Cobra," the sergeant stated.

Surprised that the Viet Minh sergeant knew about the name the Burmese Kachin tribesmen had given him, Jon nearly laughed. The story of Jon stepping on the head of a king cobra and snapping its neck with a thrust of his boot must have traveled from tribe to tribe like wildfire. It was sheer coincidence the code name for his team, King Cobra, was so close to what the natives now called him. G-2 thought someone in Washington had leaked the name, but Jon knew better.

While the sergeant and four of his freedom fighters took care of the sentries, five Viet Minh accompanied Jon. He instructed Miles and Henri to take the four farthest machine-gun positions. There would likely be at least one Japanese soldier in each truck while another slept on the ground or in the cab. Jon instructed the freedom fighters to set grenade booby traps under the dead Japanese soldiers. Jon, Miles, and Henri, in the meantime, would place C-3 explosives under each truck and set timing fuses that would give Colonel Giáp's fighters enough time to remove the machine guns. Jon waited fifteen minutes for Miles and Henri to get in position before moving.

As Miles converged on the last truck in the half-moon, he stumbled over a Japanese soldier sleeping on the ground next to his truck. Henri clasped his hand over the soldier's mouth and thrust a knife into his neck. He then held his hand over the man's mouth until he went limp. Miles struggled to his feet and hurried to get beneath the open tailgate. Awakened by the noise, the soldier in the truck bed eased his head over the end of the tailgate to see about the commotion. Miles thrust his knife into the man's throat and yanked the blade sideways; the soldier stiffened for a second and went limp.

Henri and three Viet Minh stood guard while Miles eased into the back of the truck, moved the dead soldier away from the machine gun, and set a grenade booby trap under the soldier's body.

Over the next thirty minutes, Miles and Henri completed their task by neutralizing the remaining trucks' occupants.

When Jon and the Viet Minh soldiers approached their first truck, Jon walked into a sentry. Before the sentry could react, Jon drove his fist into the soldier's chest, below the solar plexus, driving the air out of his lungs. As the soldier gasped for breath, Jon hit him in the nose with the flat of his hand, driving the nasal bone into his brain. He left the soldier where he died and moved to the rear of the truck.

Jon eased up to the tailgate and tapped on the metal. When an awakened soldier eased his head over the tailgate, Jon thrust his double-edged knife into the bottom of his chin and straight up into his brain. Jon then eased into the back of the truck and killed a second sleeping soldier. Afterward, he rigged a grenade booby trap under both bodies.

At the second and third trucks, Jon let the Viet Minh soldiers do the work. They were as quiet and efficient at killing as he was.

The last truck proved difficult because its guard was sitting next to the cab, smoking a cigarette. Jon would have lure him to the tailgate to get a good shot.

During his mission to Harbin, Jon had learned several Japanese phrases from George. He used one of those phrases now. "Tetsudatte kuremasuka?" Jon whispered, which meant, "Can you help me?" When the Japanese soldier poked his head out of the truck and looked down, Jon shot him between the eyes with his silenced pistol. The somewhat-loud pop awakened a second soldier in the truck that Jon had not seen. When he rose up from the truck bed where he was sleeping, Jon threw his knife into the man's throat. The two Viet Minh looked at each other in amazement.

Outside the roped areas housing the Allied prisoners, the Viet Minh sergeant and his men eliminated all of the Japanese sentries. After all of the machine-gun positions were neutralized, the remaining Viet Minh eased into the compound and began ushering the prisoners up the main street to safety.

Ten men entered the trucks and, being careful not to disturb the booby traps, dismantled the machine guns and carried them away. From the far side of the compound, Jon, Miles, and Henri helped usher the prisoners northward. Before sunrise, all of the prisoners had been moved toward the safety of Colonel Giáp's camp, on the north side of Hanoi. Prisoners too weak to walk were carried by Viet Minh soldiers.

Once all of the prisoners had been moved out, Miles and Henri placed satchel charges between the gas tank and the frame of each of the trucks and rigged each one with a one-hour pencil fuse. Once the bodies in the trucks were found, Jon figured a Japanese officer would order the dead men in the trucks removed, but after the first grenade exploded, they would leave them alone until an explosives technician arrived.

At daybreak, Jon watched a Japanese truck with one officer and twenty men inside arrive at the camp. They were surprised to discover the prisoners gone and the soldiers guarding them dead. As predicted, the Japanese officer ordered the dead soldiers removed from the trucks. His soldiers climbed into two trucks, moved the bodies, and tripped the booby traps. Explosions ripped through the trucks, killing the soldiers in the trucks and several more on the ground. Before the explosives technicians arrived, the satchel charges exploded, killing a dozen more Japanese soldiers.

As soon as the satchel charges exploded, Colonel Giáp's soldiers began their attack on the main Japanese camp. Jon looked over his shoulder and saw black smoke rising into the morning sky two miles behind him. Most of the armed Japanese personnel carriers and light tanks were destroyed by bazooka fire in the first few minutes of the attack. The Japanese were caught unprepared.

The attack went on for two hours, and the outnumbered Japanese force was overwhelmed by the Viet Minh. When the battle ended, over six hundred Japanese soldiers lay dead. The Viet Minh soldiers had no mercy for the wounded Japanese.

When Jon entered the main Viet Minh camp on the north side of Hanoi, one of Colonel Giáp's soldiers met him and handed him his Paraset wireless radio. Jon sat down and sent a coded message to the SOE and OSS detachments in Calcutta: "PRISONERS SECURE STOP COBRA END."

At 0330 hours the next morning, ten C-47 transports and fifteen Republic P-43 Lancer fighters lifted off from the airport at Rangoon and headed for Hanoi. Thirty minutes after sunrise, they landed at the abandoned Japanese airfield on the outskirts of the city.

CHAPTER 45

Calcutta, India

Colonel MacKenzie gave his three agents a week off after they returned from Hanoi. Proud of his agents and especially of Jon, MacKenzie was over his ill feelings about the Yank. Preston had turned out to be a blessing, and his team's success was unmatched in any theater of war, British or American.

Knowing the war with Japan could be over within six months, MacKenzie felt uneasy. He worried about the massive reduction in British forces and what he would do afterward. No longer interested in law, he didn't want to give up the intelligence business. The excitement and joy of running SOE agents ran deep in his veins now, and the thought of returning to civilian life depressed him. He desperately wanted to remain in the intelligence business after the war, but despite the success of his unit, he didn't know any of the high-level intelligence directors at the SOE headquarters on Baker Street in London. He felt his chances of staying were slim.

MacKenzie decided he would talk to Jon. Maybe one of the colonels at G-2 or even General Marshall could help get an inquiry to the right person. After all, Jon had the ear of the US Army chief of staff.

After a rough start with his special-missions Yank agent, MacKenzie and Jon had become good friends. MacKenzie didn't want to take advantage of Jon's friendship and trust by coming right out and asking Jon if he could have General Marshall put in a good word for him at Whitehall or Baker Street. The English gentleman in MacKenzie wouldn't let him take advantage of Jon, but he could talk to him. Jon was wise beyond his years, and MacKenzie always walked away feeling better after they talked.

When Colonel Ronnie Masek had arrived in Calcutta with their mission to Hanoi, Jon had asked the colonel to carry a letter to General Marshall. Jon saw that the end of the war with Japan was coming and with it Communist expansion into the Asian countries decimated by war and vulnerable to new ideas that promised change. Jon, quite fond of Colonel MacKenzie, was not above asking the general for help when it seemed right.

Jon believed the Communists would easily take over China because Generalissimo Chiang Kai-shek had continually failed to engage the Japanese and develop experienced officers and armies. For this reason, Chiang Kai-shek's armies remained untested and unprepared to confront the battle-hardened Communist forces. Despite the information the State Department had given the president of the United States, Chiang didn't stand a chance against the Communists. This meant the United States, Britain, and France would be forced to deal with the Communists on two fronts: Europe and Asia.

Jon thought through the things needed to combat Communism: intelligence, intelligence, and intelligence. Intelligence would play a key role in the battle against Communism in postwar Europe and Asia and in the decades to come. Jon read the deciphered messages Stalin sent to the Russian embassies around the world and concluded that the Russians were preparing for massive intelligence gathering in the postwar era. Stalin already knew his enemies.

When Colonel Masek returned to Washington, he delivered the sealed envelope to General Marshall. The general didn't open it for three days, but when he did, he read in amazement what Jon had put together and recommended. The general was so impressed that he had photocopies made and sent to General Bill Donovan, the director of the American OSS, and to Rear Admiral Hugh Sinclair, the director of the British Secret Intelligence Service at Bletchley Park.

Jon foretold the need for human intelligence to combat Communism. Jon knew neither the United States nor the British armies thought highly of human-intelligence gathering and they relied on cryptanalytic intelligence.

He foretold that Britain would need to assign a director of intelligence for Asia, located in Calcutta, Singapore, or Hong Kong, to monitor the Chinese Communists. His recommendation to the SIS was to promote Colonel Michael MacKenzie to brigadier general and use his vast knowledge of Asia to lead the human-intelligence group. Jon also stated that it would be a shame to let his experience and expertise go to waste.

General Marshall sat in his overstuffed chair and contemplated what he had read. Jon was one of his most successful intelligence agents of the war. The wisdom of his proposal was ten years ahead of most of the senior military thinking in Washington. In fact, of the forty-four agents he and President Roosevelt had commissioned to do special missions, only two were still alive, and this made Jon special. If Jon thought this highly of his commander, then Colonel MacKenzie must be an extraordinary man and should be rewarded for his role in the joint American and British special-missions operation in Asia.

"Colonel Masek," General Marshall said, "I want you to prepare a citation to award Colonel MacKenzie the Distinguished Service Medal. Make sure it is well written. The Brits are sticklers for good grammar."

"Yes, sir. When would you like it?"

"In two weeks."

The Distinguished Service Medal was the highest award for noncombat duty in connection with military operations, and General Marshall knew it would put a kink in Winston Churchill's shorts when President Truman forwarded the citation and award to Whitehall. General Marshall knew Whitehall and British intelligence would be more skeptical than impressed; they would think the Yanks were meddling in their business. In the general's opinion, the Brits were too slow to pick up on good ideas. Everything the Brits did was driven by cost-effectiveness. The Brits, more dutifully than most, always wrestled with funding, whether they could afford it or not and despite the plethora of American aid. Sometimes he wished Washington would be so skeptical and prudent.

Jon stayed on the *Jacqueline* with Camille when he returned from Hanoi. After his second day of rest, he became restless, so Camille suggested he go to the office. Camille and the other female agents stayed busy trying to track down a female Japanese agent that they had received intelligence on from the OSS. After five days of searching, a proprietor at a female boarding house recognized the woman in the photo. When the proprietor was shown photos of the two male agents, she said she had not seen any men with the woman, but she had seen her with another female who was also Asian. Camille drove the proprietor to the SOE detachment and took her through several hundred photographs of suspected female agents. It took four hours before the proprietor identified a petite Asian woman with round eyes.

After lunch, Camille drove to Colonel Ray's office and gave him twenty copies of the photograph. Colonel Ray assured her he would put his CIC agents on it; in fact, he would assign Agent Warren as the lead. Later in the afternoon, Agent Warren stopped by the SOE detachment, seeking advice from Jon.

"Jon, I've never led a team this large before. How should I approach this?" Agent Warren asked.

"Do what we did last time, Franklin. After you find out where she's staying, tail her, learn her patterns and habits, see who she talks to, and photograph them. Set up tails on the people she spends the most time with. It's likely they're planning something big. Once you identify every aspect of all the individuals involved, come see me. I'll help you tag this woman and any other Jap agents."

"Colonel Ray gave me twenty agents, but ten just arrived in-country."

"Use the experienced Indian agents to tail her. If you don't have any Indian agents assigned to your team, ask the colonel for some. They blend in better. If you don't get any, get your war kit out, darken your skin, dye your hair black, and dress up like the natives. Don't be afraid to get creative, OK? And don't forget the ladies are part of the team and at your disposal, which gives you four more."

After four days of searching hotels and apartment buildings, Franklin and his team came up with a lead. A desk clerk in a downtown hotel identified the Asian woman; she roomed on the third floor.

Franklin implemented the tails using two Indian agents and two American agents made up to look like natives. On the second day, one of the American agents went missing. The Calcutta Police found him the next day in an alley with a bullet in the back of his skull. However, the Japanese agent didn't get away. The Indian agents found her the following day and tailed her from a downtown restaurant to a rundown hotel near the wharves.

Franklin was devastated. On his first mission, he had lost a man. Although the women agents tried, Franklin didn't want their consolation or pity. He was angry, and he was determined to get this Japanese agent before anyone else died. He met with Jon the day the police found the dead agent.

"What did you learn?" Jon asked.

"That regardless of how well you plan, how well you are trained, or how well you execute, people get killed."

"This is the most important lesson you can take out of this, Franklin, and don't ever forget it! No matter how good you are, how well you are trained, how well you plan, and how well you execute, people die. Now let's sit down and put together a plan to get this bitch!"

CHAPTER 46

Washington, DC

Station NEGAT, the code name for the US Navy's signals-monitoring and cryptographic-intelligence unit in Washington, DC, was responsible for working on Japanese military and diplomatic codes, as well as China's diplomatic codes. Anna Wang, one of two analysts working the China desk, completed translating a disturbing message intercepted from the headquarters of Mao Tse-tung's Chinese Communist Party (CCP). The CCP message, addressed to its representative in New Delhi, stated that an SOE intelligence team led by an American agent named Jonathan Preston had abducted a key Japanese physician involved in biological and chemical research. The SOE team violated Chinese sovereignty, and the CCP headquarters ordered the subject agent terminated as a warning to the American and British intelligence agencies.

This was not the first time and would not be the last time that American and British intelligence agents would violate China's sovereignty. The Americans wanted to capture physicians, microbiologists, and chemists involved in Unit-731 research. The most forward-thinking government officials and high-ranking US Army officers wanted to keep the biological- and chemical-warfare secrets out of the hands of the Russians and the Chinese Communists. They knew the Communists would be their next major military adversary. The fear that the Communists could weaponize biological and chemical agents drove the Americans to abduct as many Unit-731 assets and research materials as possible. Jonathan Preston was at the forefront of these covert operations.

Anna immediately took the message to her supervisor, who, in turn, put it in a locked pouch and gave it to an armed staff sergeant. The staff sergeant carried it to the army chief of staff's G-2 Directorate. It landed on the desk of Colonel John Renick, now in charge of cryptographic intelligence for all of Asia. When John eventually got around to reading the message, he immediately picked up his phone and requested a meeting with the chief of staff. Twenty minutes later, he entered General Marshall's office.

"What's so urgent, John?" General Marshall asked.

"Our boy in Calcutta," Colonel Renick said. He handed the message to the chief of staff.

"Crap, now the Chinese Communists want his head."

"What I don't understand, General, is why this information was communicated via diplomatic traffic. The Communists know we are monitoring and deciphering everything they send out."

"Colonel, I guess you need to know something we compartmentalized. We have an agent, a high-ranking Communist officer, deep within the CCP headquarters. He probably authorized the message to be transmitted via diplomatic traffic to give us a heads-up. I want the next G-2 colonel leaving for Calcutta to give Jon a heads-up as soon as he gets there."

"General, it might be too late by then. Shouldn't we send a message out immediately?" Colonel Renick asked.

"No need. Our source told us it takes weeks or months for the Chinese to put anything into place. I doubt they even have an agent in India. Plus, we believe the Russians have broken our code, and they might inform their Communist friends."

"Colonel Dixon is leaving tomorrow. I'll see he gets this information right away."

Lao Cheng-Gong was a general officer in the CCP army, not by choice but by opportunity. He was a minor Chinese warlord in northern China when the CCP came to power. When Mao Tse-tung approached Cheng-Gong and asked him to join forces with the CCP army, he jumped at the opportunity. The CCP promoted him to the rank of colonel and issued thousands of M1 rifles and Thompson submachine guns to his men, courtesy of the US lend-lease program. Because of his valor and success in attacking and fending off Japanese expansion in north-east China, Mao Tse-tung promoted him to major general. Now the general commanded all CCP military and diplomatic-communications organizations.

His sympathies lay with the Allies. Before joining forces with Mao, he was friends with a Baptist missionary in Baoding, a small city 150 miles south of Beijing. Five years before the war started, he secretly converted to Christianity. In 1942, the Baptist minister contacted General Lao through one of his sons. The missionary, now an agent with the American OSS, wanted to know if the general would work as an Allied double agent. Without hesitation, the general agreed, and over the last two years, he had provided classified intelligence to the Allies.

When General Lao received instructions from Chairman Mao to have the American agent, Jonathan Preston, killed, there was no way of contacting the missionary, and his son wouldn't visit him for another two weeks. The general wrote up the message executing Mao's orders and gave it to an underling lieutenant in his office. Because of the sensitivity and secrecy involved in the orders, the general normally checked the Diplomatic Pouch box at the bottom of the message form, which instructed the dispatcher to send a courier to carry the message by hand to the consular in New Delhi. Because the general didn't check the box, the lieutenant sent it via normal diplomatic traffic, a total breach of security. When the CCP internal security discovered the grave error, the lieutenant would be executed for not following instructions, but because it was imperative for the general to maintain his cover, this was the price of being a spy. He did feel sorry for the young lieutenant.

General Lao knew it would be only a matter of time before internal security discovered the error; they scrutinized every message sent out from the headquarters. However, internal security didn't review messages until after they were transmitted. After the lieutenant brought the handwritten message back to General Lao with confirmation it had been transmitted, Lao checked the Diplomatic Pouch box at the bottom of the message form and placed it on a stack of messages to be filed.

Ten days after its transmission, a colonel from internal security showed up at the general's office. Thirty minutes later, the underling lieutenant was taken from his desk, escorted outside, and shot in the back of the head. His body remained there for three days as a warning to not make mistakes.

Colonel Rick Dixon landed in Calcutta early in the morning. He went to the SOE detachment, where he slept on a cot in Colonel MacKenzie's office. The detachment's first sergeant woke him at 0645 hours, shortly before Colonel MacKenzie arrived.

When Colonel Dixon informed Colonel MacKenzie of the Chinese threat, MacKenzie was beside himself.

"For crying out loud, Rick, what do I need to do? Put a team together to protect my number-one team?" Colonel MacKenzie asked.

Colonel Dixon, sympathetic to the SOE commander, gave no response. However, he knew Jon would think of something.

When Jon, Miles, and Henri entered the detachment office, Colonel MacKenzie ushered them into the briefing room, where Colonel Dixon waited. The look on Colonel Dixon's face was grave.

"What's up, Colonel?" Jon asked. "You're not your happy self."

"Not good news, Jon. The Chinese Communists want you dead now."

"That's an interesting twist. I thought they were our allies?"

"Apparently, someone on Mao's staff lost face when you kidnapped Lieutenant General Ito out from under their noses. They somehow found out you were the team leader, and they want to make an example of you to deter Allied intelligence from doing it again."

"Colonel, I don't think we need to worry about the Chinese here in India. However, it might get complicated if we go back into CCP territory."

"Jon, they sent a message to their consular in New Delhi, tasking them with executing their wishes and assassinating you. They might use their resources in-country to carry out the task," Colonel MacKenzie stated.

"We're talking thugs, not trained assassins. What do you guys think?" Jon asked. He turned to Miles and Henri.

"As much as we travel in this area, I'd be worried about it. It wouldn't be difficult to track your activities back and forth to the *Jacqueline*. And it might put Captain Dubois and the ladies in danger," Miles said.

"Colonel, do you have an assignment that will take us out of here for a while?" Henri asked.

"Yes, and it takes you back into China, albeit not mainland China. You're going to the northeast coast of the island of Formosa."

"Another POW camp?" Jon asked.

"Yes," Colonel Renick responded.

CHAPTER 47

Calcutta, India

Asami Nakada spent the last three months getting to India. After she and her mother were notified of the deaths of her three younger sisters, Asami asked her commander to let her go to India to kill the American agents who killed her sisters.

"Asami," Colonel Uchito Tsukuda said, "the American agent called Cobra, the one you think killed your sisters, is dead, along with the two members of his team. Here is photographic proof." He tossed her the folder with the photographs.

Uchito Tsukuda, the new *shōshō*, or major general commander, of the IJA Intelligence Directorate in Hiroshima, was responsible for placing and running agents in Southeast Asia. The last commander had taken his own life after losing ten Japanese agents in two months. General Tsukuda's commanding general at the Imperial Japanese Army headquarters, Lieutenant General Kei Sato, promoted him to the position. General Sato was also one of Tsukuda's classmates at the Imperial Japanese Army Academy in Kyoto; they graduated together in 1924.

"Please, Uncle, I will only go after the female agents whom our French Indochinese cousins identified at the banquet in Calcutta," Asami pleaded. "I can't bear the pain of not doing anything."

General Uchito had always had a soft spot in his heart for Asami. Asami was the oldest of his sister's daughters, and he had spent more time with her. With the triplets it became more difficult. Asami became his favorite niece, and like her three sisters, she was brilliant and well trained.

Because Asami's father became an admiral in the Imperial Japanese Navy, Asami and her sisters attended private schools in Hiroshima. Her sisters graduated months before the Japanese Navy bombed Pearl Harbor. Asami graduated four years ahead of them. All four sisters scored off the charts in intelligence, and all four had trained in martial arts since the age of six. When war broke out, all became eligible for specialized training at the Rikugun Nakano Gakko School, a secret military school run by the IJA for training intelligence operatives.

Their training at Rikugun Nakano Gakko included eight of the eighteen ninjutsu disciplines: espionage, unarmed combat, throwing weapons, stick and staff, stealth and entering methods, sword techniques, tactics, and escape and concealment, as well as intelligence gathering, photography, bomb making, rifle and pistol marksmanship, and sabotage. Asami not only excelled and graduated at the top of her class but also stayed on as an instructor at the school. After her sisters died, she immediately went to see her uncle and asked to be put into the field.

"All right, Asami, I will put in the orders for you to go to India. But you must promise me you will be very careful. You are often too emotional and don't think before you act. Use your training to help control your impulsiveness. I could not bear to lose you too. Your mother will kill herself if you die. You are all she has now," General Tsukuda said.

Asami's father died during the Battle of the Coral Sea, when the Japanese carrier he commanded, *Shokaku*, was attacked by American dive bombers. Afterward, Uchito took his sister into his home in Hiroshima. When Uchito revealed to his sister that her triplet daughters were dead, she blamed him and would not speak to him. And now he was sending his favorite niece and his sister's only surviving daughter into *harm's way*.

It took Asami three months to get to Calcutta. She sailed in a small freighter from Hiroshima to Singapore. The freighter, small enough to hug the coast, successfully avoided the American submarines patrolling the East and South China Seas. From Singapore, she traveled via fishing trawler up the Malacca Strait and transferred to a smaller vessel that took her to Rangoon. From Rangoon, another fishing boat smuggled her into Calcutta. At each port, she waited as long as two weeks before the next leg of the journey started. Before she departed Japan, she cut her hair and dressed like a man; she didn't encounter any problems. Even if she had been harassed, she was trained to kill with her hands and fingers. She was as lethal as any agent Japan had sent into the field.

In Calcutta she worked as a cook in a Chinese restaurant. She spoke fluent English, so getting around Calcutta was easy. Her contact, from the Japanese consular in Calcutta, provided photos of all the American female agents they identified, including the ones from the hotel reception where her sisters had perished. She also received information from an informant about the Japanese agents who had vanished in the last two weeks. A team of American agents, made up of both men and women, had killed their agents in a shootout at a small hotel. The information was confirmed by multiple sources.

"Good," Asami said. "All the female Allied agents are still in Calcutta."

Asami was determined to exact her revenge, but before she tackled the men, whom she believed to still be alive, she would go after the women. Asami memorized the photos of the female agents. American men, she knew, were sensitive about and protective of their women. It was only then that she was reminded of one of her favorite quotes from Sun Tzu's *Art of War*: "So in war, the way is to avoid what is strong, and strike at what is weak."

Yes, Asami thought, *if the Allied intelligence organization has a weakness, it is their female agents. The men would die to protect them.* She would find the women and slowly and deliberately kill them, one at a time.

CHAPTER 48

Kinkaseki POW Camp, Formosa

M ajor Mark Ditzenberger bent over another prisoner in the small wooden hut he called his hospital. Smith was suffering from starvation and the vitamin deficiency called beriberi, as well as badly swollen testicles. Two days ago a Japanese guard had come into the hut and kicked Smith in the groin. The guard had then walked away laughing. Now Smith was dying, but not from starvation or beriberi. He had given up the will to live, and there was nothing Dr. Ditzenberger could do. But before Smith slipped into unconsciousness, he told the doctor a secret.

Corporal John David Smith was captured when Corregidor fell to the Japanese in 1942. Smith and two hundred other Allied prisoners were forced to work as slave labor, drilling and digging a network of caves on the rocky island. After one particular cave complex was completed, Smith and sixty other prisoners were chosen to unload thirty truckloads of brass chests and store them in the cave complex.

During the unloading process, one of the chests fell off the truck and spilled its contents of twenty bars of gold. One fell on Smith's foot and broke his ankle. Three days later, while he was still in the camp infirmary, Smith heard a loud explosion. He later discovered that after the gold was unloaded and stored in the cave complex, the prisoners who did the unloading and the Japanese engineers who designed the cave had been ordered deep into the cave complex to complete another project. While everyone was ninety feet underground, a Japanese intelligence officer ordered the cave entrance dynamited and sealed. After hearing about the atrocity, Corporal Smith realized he had been overlooked and swore he would survive to tell the story of his murdered comrades.

Dr. Ditzenberger was captured when Singapore fell to the Japanese in February 1942. Eighty thousand British soldiers were duped into surrendering to a vastly inferior force of thirty thousand Japanese invaders. Within six weeks, Ditzenberger and eight hundred British and Australian prisoners were loaded into the bottom hold of a cattle ship and transported to a labor camp. The hold of the ship still held manure from the previous voyage. It was so crowded that there was barely enough room for the men to lie down. They received one gallon of watery soup and one gallon of rice, twice a day, which they shared with twenty men. The ten-day voyage was hellish. Almost every day someone died of heatstroke or dehydration. There was no bathroom, and there were no pots to go in, so the men went on the floor of the hold and wallowed in their own feces and urine until arriving at their destination, a labor camp called Kinkaseki, on the island of Formosa.

Kinkaseki was located on a rocky hillside on the eastern side of the island. During the day, the prisoners labored in a copper mine a mile from the camp. At night, they were crammed into wooden huts and lay side by side on the hard bamboo floor. To get to the mine, they climbed five hundred feet up a rocky hill and then walked a mile downhill. They walked another mile into the mine before they got to the main tunnel, where they continued down another four hundred steps to get to their work areas.

Each prisoner worked with a mining tool called a chunkel and a two-handled basket. They scraped ore from the sides of the mine into their baskets and carried it to an ore cart. They labored all day in 110-degree heat with only a lunch break. At the end of the day, the teams that didn't make the daily quota of ore were beaten by the Korean guards.

Dr. Ditzenberger did what he could with the resources the Japanese gave him, which weren't much more than soap and water. There was no medicine, no equipment, and no surgical tools. When he did need to operate, the camp commandant issued him a two-edged razor blade along with a large needle and sewing thread. He performed several appendectomies with these crude tools, and the men surprisingly lived. Prisoners who came to see him often suffered from some form of nerve inflammation, which caused a loss of sensation in their hands, their feet, or both. The most common cause of the disease was beriberi. In addition, almost all of the men at Kinkaseki suffered from what Dr. Ditzenberger called explosive diarrhea, which caused tremendous weight loss, dehydration, and emaciation. Despite these illnesses, the men worked the mines every day. Those who died, Ditzenberger felt, were the lucky ones.

The other man Ditzenberger treated that day was covered in festering sores. The Japanese didn't waste their antibiotics on prisoners, so he wrapped lichen, which the guards let him pick off the rocks outside of the camp, around the man's sores. Miraculously, the sores vanished in a matter of days. Afterward, he used lichen on all sores, cuts, and beating wounds.

Jon, Miles, and Henri traveled for five days to reach Clark Field on the Philippine island of Luzon. From there, the USS *Coho* took them to within a mile of Formosa. After the sub surfaced, they made their way to shore in a six-man raft. They were met by a dozen British Commandos who had landed earlier in the night and a small Formosan man who was there to guide them to the labor camp. After Jon's team made it ashore, a navy LCM landed one hundred additional commandos. By the end of the week, a similar landing would occur at six other labor camps on the Formosan coast: Hieto, Keelung, Karenko, Muksaq, Takao, and Tomazato.

Once the additional marines were ashore, they wasted no time and started their 2,500-foot climb on a well-worn trail toward the village of Jinguashi, two miles inland. By dawn, the force arrived below the summit of a hill half a mile east of the village. As they hid and rested among the tropical mountainous red-cypress, ranta-fir, and dragon-spruce trees, everyone took time to eat. The commandos ate the traditional army field K-ration dinner, which consisted of a nonperishable, ready-to-eat meal of hard biscuits, dry sausages, hard candy, and chocolate bars. Jon, Miles, and Henri ate the smoked beef they brought from Calcutta and cooked rice prepared by the Filipino cook on the USS *Coho*.

As Jon relaxed under a red cypress tree, his thoughts drifted to when the war might end. Several months before, in February 1945, Major General Curtis LeMay had initiated B-29 bombing raids on Japan, dropping incendiary bombs on sixty-seven Japanese cities. For his raid on Tokyo, LeMay dispatched 334 Superfortresses, which, in a three-hour period, dropped over 1,600 tons of incendiary clusters and magnesium, napalm, and white-phosphorus bombs. Only 50 percent of Tokyo survived the firestorm. Nevertheless, despite the bombings of factories and cities, Jon knew the Japanese Army was still strong in Japan; he hoped an invasion of Japan could be avoided. *For now,* Jon thought, *I have a mission to complete.*

At sunrise, the trio and the 112 British Commandos walked down into a steep valley. They were invisible to the Japanese at the labor camp because they came with the sun at their backs. As the force passed through Jinguashi, the local inhabitants only stared at them. By 0900, the marines surrounded the Japanese camp in a half-moon from the north to the south. When everyone was in place, Jon stood up with a white cloth on a long stick, eased between two ranta firs, and walked twenty-five yards toward the camp's only gate; he was accompanied by a Japanese-speaking commando.

A Japanese guard noticed Jon walking his way waving the flag and summoned the camp commander. The commander and two additional guards met Jon outside the gate. When the interpreter informed the commandant that the war was over for him and his guards, the commandant snarled and cursed Jon. When Jon lowered the white flag to the ground, two snipers fired, taking out the guards standing on either side of the commandant.

"Tell him the next one will be between his eyes," Jon said.

Lieutenant Colonel Yoshikazu Endo came from a military family. His father served in the Japanese Navy during the war between the Russian Empire and the Japanese Empire in 1904. Yoshikazu chose the army over the navy when Japan declared war on the United States. As an infantry officer, he distinguished himself during the invasion of the Philippines and received rapid promotions culminating in the rank of major. After being wounded in 1943, he was sent back to Japan for seven months to convalesce. Once he recovered, he was promoted to lieutenant colonel, and he returned to service as the labor-camp commandant at Kinkaseki. In his opinion, it was a disgrace to his otherwise outstanding and distinguished service.

After the Allied interpreter gave Lieutenant Colonel Endo the ultimatum to surrender or die, he became infuriated with the offer of utter disgrace. With the speed and dexterity of a young athlete, he quickly drew his sword and swung the blade at Jon. Jon was prepared for this. He sidestepped the arc of the blade and moved inside the reach of Endo's arms, twisted the sword from his hand, and knocked the colonel down. Endo jumped to his feet and drew his pistol. As the colonel was about to fire, his sword, now in Jon's hand, sliced through the side of his neck, severing his head.

As soon as their commandant drew his sword, the Japanese soldiers inside the camp began firing on the Allied commandos, which were visible outside the camp. The British Commandos countered and opened fire on the exposed Japanese soldiers. The commando standing beside Jon was hit by two bullets and went down. With the bloodied sword in his right hand and a Colt .45 in his left, Jon charged the machine gun inside the open gate.

The first two rounds from Jon's pistol hit the Japanese soldier loading the strip-fed ammo into the tripod-mounted, 7.7-millimeter machine gun. His third round hit the third member of the machine-gun team, who was opening the wooden ammo boxes and removing the paper coverings from the ammo strips. The gunner, noticing the Allied soldier with his commandant's sword running toward him, turned his gun on Jon, but it jammed. The problem with the Type 92 machine gun was the factory-oiled thirty-round strips. The short strips limited the rate of fire, and the oil on the strips picked up dirt, which caused jams in the loading mechanism. Before the gunner could remove the jammed strip, Jon swung the sword, ripping through the side of the gunner's neck and severing his carotid artery.

Jon kicked the mortally wounded gunner to the side, cleared the jam, inserted a new ammo strip, gripped the drop-down spade handles, and began firing on the remaining Japanese soldiers.

When the fighting stopped, Miles and Henri ran to where Jon struggled to get up from the machine gun. He was rather wobbly, and blood was streaming down his face.

"Looks like you've been hit, mate," Miles said. "Let me take a look."

Jon turned toward Miles, took a step, looked at him strangely, and collapsed in his arms.

"Medic!" Henri yelled.

CHAPTER 49

Kinkaseki POW Camp, Formosa

After Henri helped Miles lay Jon on the ground, the commando medic poured part of his canteen of water on Jon's forehead to clean the blood from his wound.

"Looks like the bullet creased his head. It doesn't look too bad, but he probably has a concussion. I'll send the doc over when he's through with the more serious wounds. Keep his feet elevated until he comes to," the medic said.

Twenty minutes later, Jon opened his eyes and tried to sit up.

"Wha…What happened?" Jon asked.

"Easy, mate," Miles said. "You were struck by a bullet on your noggin. Better keep lying there."

"Screw that. Help me up, dammit."

Miles and Henri each grabbed Jon under an arm and lifted him to his feet. Jon stood with his hands on his knees until his head stopped spinning before easing to a standing position. They didn't let go of his arms.

"Status report," Jon stated.

"Camp secured, ten commandos wounded, two dead, and two hundred sixteen prisoners freed. All Japs died fighting," Henri stated.

"What about my interpreter?"

"Seriously wounded. One in the shoulder and one in the thigh."

"Will he live?"

"The doc thinks so."

"Take me to the wounded."

Miles and Henri walked beside Jon for forty steps to make sure he didn't fall. By the time they reached the makeshift field hospital, Jon was walking steady and seemed to have most of his strength back.

Jon stopped and knelt next to each wounded commando, shook his hand, and said, "Thank you." He took a little more time when he stopped next to his interpreter. The commando tried to speak, but Jon shook his head. "Don't talk, Sergeant. Just get well."

After talking to each wounded soldier, Jon moved to where Miles and Henri were talking with the senior Allied prisoner. A badly limping prisoner made his way to where Jon stood. He stopped and saluted.

"Excuse me, sir. Might I have a word?" the man said.

"How can I help you, soldier?"

"Lieutenant Lars Jorgensen, Royal Netherlands Navy, sir. I have some important information I need to get to naval intelligence."

"I'm with American intelligence. Can you tell me, Lieutenant?"

"Yes, sir," Lieutenant Jorgensen said. "Sir, several of us were brought here on a Japanese hospital ship, although it wasn't really a hospital ship."

"What do you mean it wasn't really a hospital ship?"

"It was the Dutch passenger liner *Op Ten Noort*, disguised to look like a Japanese hospital ship. Part of its superstructure had been altered, the hull had been painted white, and a green cross was painted on its funnel. When it left here, it wasn't carrying wounded Japanese soldiers."

"And how do you know it was a Dutch passenger ship?"

"In the early 1930s, my father was the captain of the *Op Ten Noort*. I used to travel with him and my mother on the ship. When I was old enough, I worked on the ship as a cabin steward. I would recognize the *Noort* anywhere, sir. Plus, it still carried its original life preservers."

"If it wasn't carrying wounded soldiers, what exactly was it carrying?"

"Gold bullion and precious gems, sir."

"And you know this how?"

After a coughing and wheezing fit, the lieutenant caught his breath and continued. "Sir, I was one of twenty prisoners tasked with loading gold bars into large bronze containers at a warehouse in Singapore. Afterward, we loaded the bronze containers onto the *Op Ten Noort*. It must have been close to ten thousand pounds of gold. While we were inside the ship's hold, one of the prisoners accidently released a rope holding a small chest being lowered into the hold. The chest fell and broke open, spilling the contents on the floor. It was filled with cut rubies."

"And they let you live after loading the ship?"

"Well, sir, after we finished loading the ship, the Japs lined us up on the dock and started shooting us in the backs of our heads, one at a time. I was saved when twelve US Navy attack planes began bombing and strafing the wharves and the cargo ships docked next to the *Op Ten Noort*. A bomb hit the warehouse next to the *Noort*, and the blast killed most of the guards. In the confusion, I ran and took cover next to a five-ton truck full of prisoners being readied to be boarded on the ship. While their guards hid behind crates and other vehicles on the dock, I slipped into the back of the truck. After the planes left, I boarded the *Noort* with the prisoners."

"That's one hell of a story, Lieutenant. I'm going to let you tell it again to Major Miles Murphy. He'll write down what you say and then have you sign it. Make sure you give him your full name, your service number, and the naval unit you were assigned to before being captured. And thanks for coming forward."

Before Jon could move away from the group, Dr. Mark Ditzenberger grabbed Jon by the arm. "If I may have a word also, sir. I overheard your conversation with the lieutenant. I have a similar story to add to his."

Thirty minutes later, the doctor finished his story about Corporal John Smith, the caves on Corregidor Island filled with hidden treasure, and the Allied prisoners and Japanese engineers sealed in the caves and left to die.

That afternoon, a flight of three American C-47s escorted by five US Navy fighters flew over the camp and dropped no fewer than thirty crates of food, clothing, and medical supplies for the starving, half-naked, and sick prisoners.

Toward evening, Miles rejoined Jon around a fire, where he sat enjoying a cup of freshly brewed coffee.

"Well, mate, how in God's good name did you survive this fiasco?" Miles asked. "I thought you were a goner for sure when all the firing started."

"I prayed very hard," Jon said.

As Jon was about to walk off, Henri came running up to him with several pieces of paper in his hand; the writing on them was all in Japanese.

"It's a good thing we got here when we did."

"Why is that?"

Henri held up the papers. "One of the Japanese interpreters says this is a message from the chief of staff of the Japanese Formosan Security Unit. It's instructions to begin killing all the Allied prisoners, two days from now. It states that the camp commanders are to eliminate the prisoners individually or in groups, by whatever means necessary, whether poisoning, drowning, decapitation, or burying them alive in caves. The intent was to not leave any traces of the prisoners being here."

"That would explain the reports from the commandos of explosives strategically placed in the tunnels of the mine," Jon said.

"Good Lord! We've got to notify headquarters and have them move up the timetable on the other camps," Miles exclaimed.

CHAPTER 50

Clark Airfield, Luzon Island, Philippines

Staff Sergeant Warren Hilderbrand, a G-2 agent, entered his commander's office, stopped in front of the commander's desk, and saluted crisply. "Staff Sergeant Hilderbrand reporting as ordered, sir."

"At ease, Sergeant," Colonel Sage said.

Hilderbrand noticed another officer sitting in the corner of the office. He was thin and tall, with a wide smile and perfect teeth. *He's young for a colonel*, thought Hilderbrand, *but then who isn't in this war?*

"Sergeant, let me introduce Colonel Ronnie Masek. He's with army intelligence. I would like you to spend some time with the colonel and tell him exactly what you told me about the Japanese hospital ship you photographed at Subic Bay in early August. You all can go into one of the briefing rooms, and my first sergeant will bring in coffee and something to eat."

"As long as it isn't K-rations, sir," Sergeant Hilderbrand said.

Colonel Sage smiled and said, "Not to worry, Sergeant. I placed the order myself. I hope you don't mind roast-beef sandwiches."

When they entered the briefing room, Colonel Masek spoke in a soft Texas drawl. "Relax, Sergeant. I'm not here to interrogate you. Just tell me about what you observed."

"I was stationed in Manila as part of the US Army Forces in the Far East in 1937, assigned to a training company. Our job was to train forty divisions of soldiers for the Philippine Commonwealth, collectively called the Philippine Divisions. The Philippine Divisions were to be used in case of a national emergency or for whatever duties they might be assigned by the Commonwealth. The plan was to build an active force of ten thousand and a reserve force of four hundred thousand over a ten-year period."

"How many did you actually train?"

"By mid-1941, the Philippine Divisions had close to seventy-five hundred officers and one hundred twenty thousand enlisted men, sir."

"How did you learn the Filipino language?"

"In 1938, I married a Filipino girl. Over the next three years, I learned to speak Filipino like a native; she taught me the Visayan and Tagalog dialects, as well as Spanish. I gained a lot of respect from the Filipino soldiers by learning their language. By the time the Japanese attacked in December 1941, the Philippine Army was trained but not well armed. Our officers told us the shipment of new arms General MacArthur was promised was rerouted to China as part of the lend-lease program."

"Everyone must have been pretty disappointed."

"More like demoralized, sir. We believed war was coming, and we were depending on those new arms."

"What kind of arms did the Filipinos have?"

"Mostly arms left over from World War I. Every man was issued a thirty-caliber M1917 Enfield rifle. Each infantry regiment possessed two .30-06-caliber M1917 Browning machine guns and six three-inch Stokes mortars and each infantry division eight seventy-five-millimeter M1897 guns. Some of the officers and platoon sergeants carried the .45-caliber M1921 Thompson submachine gun with the Type C drum cartridge. However, up to seventy percent of the ammunition was defective, probably because the cartridges were too old. Most had been manufactured in the 1920s."

"Where did the artillery school do its training, and how well were the artillery regiments trained?"

"The coastal artillery schools were at Fort Mills on Corregidor and Fort Wint on Grand Island. The field artillery training was conducted at Fort Dau. From what I observed, each unit fired only five rounds during their training."

"That's too bad. What happened to you after the Allied forces surrendered?"

"Well, sir, I was asked to lead a guerrilla group in the mountains north of Manila, northwest of Angel Lake. We operated in the jungle and constantly moved our camp location to avoid Japanese reconnaissance teams. In December 1943, a Filipino OSS officer made contact with me at our camp. He was ordered to contact and ask me to infiltrate Manila with him. Since my wife and her family and relatives lived just a mile outside of Manila, I decided to go."

"Is that where you learned about the gold?"

"Yes, sir. The captain and I were doing reconnaissance in a pirogue, which is a dugout canoe, in Manila Bay. We were dressed like fishermen. Our job was to photograph a Japanese vessel, a hospital ship. A large number of strange-looking bronze boxes were being unloaded from its cargo hold. After photographing the ship, we returned to the house the captain and I stayed in and developed the photographs. After the captain consulted a book with the profiles of Japanese vessels, we determined the ship was the passenger liner *Fuji Maru*. Its superstructure had been modified, and large green crosses had been painted on the funnel and hull. However, over the two days we observed it, we didn't see a single wounded patient being carried on or off the ship."

"What did you do after that?"

"The third day out, we decided to follow the trucks being loaded with the bronze boxes. We rode on motorized bicycles, so it was easy for us to blend in with the other bicycle traffic. We followed the trucks for ten miles into the mountains. When the trucks turned off the main road, we followed on foot and watched the Japs unload the bronze boxes and take them into a cave. The boxes must have been real heavy because it took four soldiers to move a single box. After they finished, they sealed the cave with a large blast of dynamite and put brush over the entrance to hide it. Three days later we returned to the cave with a dozen guerillas. It took us nearly a week to tunnel into the cave. Once inside, we followed the cave shaft over a hundred feet beneath the mountain and found two rows of bronze boxes extending at least a hundred feet on both sides of the cave. When we opened several of the boxes, we found they contained gold bars, each stamped with 75-*K* along with Japanese symbols."

"What did you do next?"

"The captain put the photographs of the ship and the gold bars along with his report in a waterproof satchel. We took pirogue back out the next night and met an American submarine. The captain told me the satchel was being sent to General MacArthur's headquarters in Australia."

"What did you do after the Japanese vacated Manila?"

"I was reassigned to the G-2 here in Manila, sir. That was when I met the captain's commander, Colonel Sage."

"Thank you, Sergeant; it's an intriguing story."

After Sergeant Hilderbrand left the briefing room, Colonel Sage entered and closed the door.

"So, what do you think of his story, Ronnie?"

"Almost unbelievable. Did Sergeant Hildebrand take you to the cave?"

"Yes, but the gold had vanished. According to what Sergeant Hilderbrand told me, I estimated close to thirty tons of gold was stored there."

"So, around thirty tons of Japanese gold has disappeared, and General Marshall didn't know anything about this until he received your report, which means General MacArthur has kept the information to himself."

"Hard to believe, isn't it?"

"Yes, very hard to believe."

CHAPTER 51

Washington, DC

General Bill Donovan, the director of the Office of Strategic Services or OSS, was driven from his office to the White House on Pennsylvania Avenue. After he exited the chauffeured automobile, he closed the door and walked casually up to the door; a guard with a Thompson submachine gun came to attention and saluted. Admitting only individuals authorized by the president, the guard consulted the clipboard hanging from a nail on the wall near the door. After confirming General Donovan's name on the official White House visitors' list, he saluted the general again and said, "You're clear to enter, General Donovan."

Donovan was immediately taken to the Oval Office by a Secret Service agent. When the Secret Service agent knocked, the president's chief of staff opened the door and showed General Donovan to a seat on the sofa to the right of where President Truman was still sitting at his desk, signing documents. The chief of staff then quietly exited through another door. When the president finished, he turned his leather chair toward the general.

"Bill, thank you for coming," President Truman said.

"It's good to see you again, Mr. President. What can I do for you?"

"General, I've been talking with several members of the Senate. I want a recommendation from them on how to counter the Soviet spy threat we will be facing once the war with Japan is over. As you are aware, the Russians are organizing a massive intelligence organization in Europe, Southeast Asia, South America, and the United States, and I am determined to counter their threat. Several key senators are recommending a new civilian-controlled organization responsible for intelligence gathering and covert activities outside the continental United States."

"Yes, sir, I am aware of what the senators are doing. In fact, several of them interviewed me and asked how it should be organized. They even wanted me to head up the organization—the Central Intelligence Group, I believe they called it. I refused their offer. I am concerned, however, with how you intend to deal with the Communist threat within the borders of the United States."

"They are recommending the FBI handle the domestic side. Is that what you are concerned with?"

"As you know, Mr. President, Director Hoover and I have never seen eye to eye; in fact, we strongly dislike each other. Hoover is too narrow-minded in his approach to intelligence gathering. He just doesn't think like a spy, which requires outside-of-the-box thinking. If he is given this responsibility, I predict the FBI will fail miserably."

"I tend to agree with you, but you know as well as I do that Hoover has dirt on most of the senators and congressmen on both the Senate and House committees looking into this. Plus, he's been lobbying to gain control of the entire domestic and international organization. I'll be lucky if I can keep him out of the international side of this new organization."

"If Hoover manages to get the foreign side, we'll be worse off than we were before Pearl Harbor, Mr. President."

The president nodded his head in agreement. He stood up and began pacing the office. "My biggest problem is the funding of such a large organization. Congress wants to limit the funding to two and a half million dollars per year. To be effective, I believe we need to budget at least a hundred million dollars over a five-year period. If we can't get the right funding, the new agency will be doomed from its very beginning, and I don't want to become the laughingstock of the Allied intelligence community."

Donovan knew how determined the president was to fight the Communist threat, but he was also fishing for information. *What he really wants is an off-the-books way of funding the new agency*, thought Donovan. Although Donovan didn't have the close relationship with President Truman that he'd had with President Roosevelt, he decided to take a chance with the president.

"Mr. President, what if I told you there is a way to fund the fight against Communism for the next twenty years without Congress knowing about it?"

"What do you mean?"

"Mr. President, only a handful of people know what I am about to tell you. Can I trust you to keep it to yourself? And I mean tell absolutely no one, sir, at least until you approve what I am offering."

"You have my word, General."

Over the next hour, General Donovan outlined the story of the buried Japanese gold in the Philippines, in Korea, and on the coast of China. Donovan went into detail about the ten hidden caves uncovered by his agents that held over fifty tons of gold bullion, ten tons of silver, and one hundred fifty-five-gallon drums of precious gems. The gold alone was worth $1.9 billion.

"Mr. President, this is what we've found so far, but I believe there are more caves and a hell of a lot more gold. We also believe the two brothers of the Japanese emperor are involved in the heist of this gold, all taken out of China, Malaya, the Dutch Indies, the Philippines, Burma, French Indochina, and Laos over the last four years."

"In my wildest dreams, I never would have imagined those countries could possess so much gold."

"They've accumulated it over several thousand years, Mr. President. A lot of it came from Buddhist temples. I even have a report of a ten-ton statue of Buddha being hauled off by the Japs. And the gold we've found doesn't include any the Japanese took out of China before Pearl Harbor, which I assume Japan has been using for the last ten years to build up their army and navy."

"Just what are you proposing?"

"I'm saying we keep the information about the Japanese removing plundered gold and precious gems from the Asian countries our little secret, much like what we've done with the Nazi gold. I propose we use the Nazi gold and the Japanese gold and gems to fund what Congress won't over the next ten to twenty years or however long it lasts."

"Bill, if our allies find out about this, they will want their gold back. Do you really think this can be kept secret?"

"I do, Mr. President, but I will need some very secret advice and covert help from some of the largest banking firms around the world."

"Well, you know most of the top domestic and international banking players, Bill. You have my authority to proceed, but I don't want to know anything more about it, and I don't want anything leaked to Congress, so chose your players carefully, General. Understood?"

"I'm an attorney, Mr. President. I understand the concept of deniability."

CHAPTER 52

Calcutta, India

Monique Basil and Brigitte Prefontaine, two of the four female OSS agents under the command of Captain Dubois, sat at the sidewalk café outside the Grand Hotel, chatting and acting like they were enjoying their meal. In reality, they were on assignment, looking for the one female and two male Japanese agents the SOE unit had discovered weeks before. After finishing a plate of *payasam*, a delicious, creamy rice-and-milk pudding with cashews and raisins, they asked their waiter for a refill of coffee.

"Brigitte, why don't we take a look in a few of the dress shops before we head back to Alipore? We have plenty of time."

"I don't see any reason not to. We can still do our reconnaissance."

Two minutes later, a small Asian man brought out two cups brimming with steaming coffee. He bowed after he set the cups on the table and walked away.

"Monique, what do you think of Lieutenant Warren?"

"He's kind of cute. Why? Are you interested in him? You are, aren't you?"

"Don't tell anyone, but he asked me to go out with him tonight."

"I think you two would make a…"

Monique suddenly began slurring her words and shaking her head. Brigitte, alarmed at Monique's behavior, tried to stand and move to her side, but her legs would not work. She could see Monique was having trouble breathing. The look of horror on Monique's face caught Brigitte by surprise.

"Oh God," Brigitte uttered. She slid from her chair onto the concrete sidewalk.

Several patrons at a nearby table screamed. By the time a waiter rushed to their aid, Monique and Brigitte's breathing had become erratic. When the manager saw the women lying on the sidewalk, he called for an ambulance, but before it arrived, both women were dead.

Colonel Kenneth Taylor, the OSS detachment commander, drove to the *Jacqueline* to give Captain Dubois the news. Although Captain Dubois was still recovering from his wound, he insisted that Colonel Taylor drive him to the base morgue to identify his two agents. When the sheets were pulled back and he looked at the young women, tears began streaming down his cheeks. He looked at Colonel Taylor and shook his head.

"I haven't lost any agents yet. Is it always this painful?" Colonel Taylor asked.

"Yes, always. Can you give me some additional assets to protect my other two female agents? I think whoever has done this will try to kill Camille and Kathleen next. I need to protect them."

"Where are they?"

"They're at the SOE detachment working with Lieutenant Warren. I need to let them know what happened before I head downtown."

"I'll send three agents over as soon as I return to my office. I'll drive you to the SOE. Are you sure you can manage this, Richard? It's been only two weeks since your surgery."

"Damn straight I can; it's my job."

Camille and Kathleen were devastated by the news. They cried and held each other and cried some more. Dubois asked them to return to the *Jacqueline* after they finished working and informed them Colonel Taylor was providing a protection detail to escort them to the yacht and to stay to guard them. Before he left the SOE detachment, Captain Dubois gave the two women explicit instructions.

"For your protection, do not go anywhere alone, and don't let anyone that you do not know serve you food or drink. Understand?"

"Yes, sir," they replied.

When Colonel Taylor returned to his office, he dispatched an automobile with two Indian OSS agents to pick up the captain. They would go everywhere with Captain Dubois and protect him.

By the time Captain Dubois reached the Grand Hotel, Counterintelligence Corps agents were on the scene conducting interviews. Captain Dubois personally interviewed the hotel manager and the waiter who served the two women.

The waiter explained that the women had asked for more coffee. When he returned to their table, one of the staff had already brought them two cups. A short time later, they started having breathing problems and fell out of their chairs onto the sidewalk. Before the ambulance arrived, both women were unconscious and had ceased breathing.

When Captain Dubois interviewed the remaining staff, he found that none of them had served his two agents the extra cups of coffee. Captain Dubois knew then that a formidable Japanese agent had targeted Brigitte and Monique.

A new player in town, Captain Dubois thought.

When Captain Dubois returned to the *Jacqueline*, Camille and Kathleen were already there, and Agent Popper had joined them. He ordered his agents to either stay on the boat or go only to the SOE detachment. In addition to the three OSS agents, Colonel Taylor assigned three teams of five Gurkha agents to guard the boat day and night; two would remain on the boat, and three would be on the ground.

All three women were close to Brigitte and Monique, but Kathleen had been the closest. She was enraged and wanted revenge. She was not going to let the deaths of her friends and colleagues go unpunished. After twenty minutes of ranting, she finally broke down and cried. Camille and Kelly cried with her. Too upset to eat, all three went to bed without supper.

The next morning, Captain Dubois woke the women and told them to be dressed and ready to leave for the base in one hour. When they arrived at the OSS detachment, Colonel Taylor, Colonel Ray, Colonel MacKenzie, Major Jim Ballangy, and Captain Bud Helms sat in the briefing room, discussing strategies and options on how to deal with the new threat to their teams.

"It's obvious a Japanese agent identified Brigitte and Monique as intelligence assets. Whoever did this followed them and waited for the right moment to strike. We have to assume the rest of Captain Dubois's team is also compromised," Colonel MacKenzie stated.

"After our last mission, we knew for certain there were at least three Japanese agents out there," Captain Dubois said. "However, I believe we have a new player in town. One who is clever and better trained than the saboteurs we've taken down thus far."

"What leads you to that conclusion, Captain?" Captain Helms asked.

"Our agents in Japan came across information on a secret ninja training school in Hiroshima; it's tied to Japanese intelligence. We don't have anything specific yet, but we've lost three agents trying to find out."

The conversation stopped when Lieutenant Colonel George Linka was brought into the room in a wheelchair.

"George, you shouldn't be out of the hospital. Just exactly what are you doing here?" Colonel Taylor asked.

"When I heard about Monique and Brigitte being poisoned and the meeting you were holding today, well, I had to come."

"Do you have some knowledge of what we might be facing?" Colonel Taylor asked.

"Yes, sir. When growing up in Japan, I took instruction in both jujitsu and Muay Thai. I was told by one of my masters that the art of ninjutsu was still being taught by several secret organizations in Japan. The symptoms Monica and Brigitte suffered are typical of puffer-fish poisoning. In feudal Japan it was used almost exclusively by ninjas. If you are going up against a ninja, you have a very serious problem."

"How do you propose we handle this situation?"

"Since we don't have our own ninja to advise us, we'll need to outsmart him. The only person I can think of who is qualified is Jon Preston."

"You're telling us that, between the nine of us, we aren't qualified to outthink this damn ninja?" Colonel MacKenzie asked.

"That's exactly what I'm saying, sir. The only person I know who comes close to thinking like a ninja is Jon. Ninjas are trained in unconventional methods. Nothing you or I have been taught can match their skills. We can't collectively think of all the ways a ninja can approach us. Our training is too linear and too conventional. That's why we need Jon."

"I see what you mean. Jon should be back in three days. In the meantime, we look for this assassin."

CHAPTER 53

Calcutta, India

After turning the Kinkaseki POW camp over to the commander of the British Commandos, Jon, Miles, and Henri made their way back to the coast, where they contacted a navy PBY circling high above the island. After it landed, they boarded and flew back to Clark Field in the Philippines. It took them another ten days to make it back to Calcutta.

When their C-47 landed in Alipore, a corporal with a staff car met them at the aircraft and drove them to the SOE detachment. Once they were inside, Colonel MacKenzie gave them the bad news about Brigitte and Monique. Jon, Miles, and Henri were stunned.

"We've waited for you all to return before we tackle this Japanese assassin," Colonel MacKenzie said.

"Why wait?" Jon asked.

"Because George believes we may be facing a Japanese assassin trained in the ninja arts. None of us here have the experience or the skills you have, Jon. You think differently than the rest of us, and you've taught that to Miles and Henri. George believes you all are the only agents who can outthink this assassin."

"I'm flattered, but I don't know much about ninjas."

"Then go talk to George and let him explain it."

Later in the day, Jon, Miles, and Henri entered the army hospital. After George's trip to the OSS detachment, he had started bleeding again. Now the doctors and nurses watched him closely to make sure he didn't leave the building without their authorization.

"Fine mess you got yourself into by getting out of bed, mate," Miles said.

"I had to, or they could have messed up and gotten someone else killed."

"Hell, George, you could have sent them a note marked Urgent!" Jon exclaimed.

"It wouldn't have had the same effect as going in person."

"So, how do we handle a ninja assassin?"

"We could send a note to the Japanese consular and tell them we aren't prepared to handle their assassin and we'd appreciate it if they could please wait a month or two," Henri said jokingly.

"Guys, ninja assassins are trained in eighteen of the ninjutsu arts. The closest any of us have had to this kind of training is you, Jon. You trained under the famous British Commando instructor, Colonel William Fairbairn, for nearly four years before you entered the army. You're the only person in India who comes close to having the skills to tackle this. And you are the only one who thinks the way they think: nonlinear, unconventional, outside the box."

"George, I've heard that most ninjas train from childhood. I've only trained for four years," Jon said. "Are you sure there is no one in British or American intelligence with ninja training?"

"I'm quite certain. We only have you. You were trained in hand-to-hand combat, knife fighting, shooting, strategy, assassination, sabotage, explosives, intelligence gathering, and bomb making. The only skills you haven't been taught are stick fighting, Japanese throwing weapons, and the alchemy of poisons. Your greatest weapon, however, is your mind, and I would bet most ninjas don't possess as good a mind as you do."

"All right, if you think I'm good enough, I guess I'm nominated. Now, let's put our collective heads together and see what we can come up with. Maybe we can outthink this damn assassin."

Asami Nakada was satisfied with her actions after the deaths of the two female Allied agents. The fact that she could transform herself from a woman to a man and back was one of the keys to her success. Her master had reminded her before she left Tokyo that ninja warfare was based on not being seen. Asami assured herself that she would not be seen, but her actions would be known. Her next move would involve attacking the other two women at the yacht on which they lived.

Asami chose a moonless night to approach the boat moored in the secluded basin. She would have preferred a busy yacht basin because the activity at the basin would distract the guards. Regardless, she knew she would succeed.

She approached the yacht from the east, through a dry creek bed. When it ended at the river, she moved north a hundred yards, through thick brush and trees, to where the boat was moored. She was sixty feet from the boat when she heard a faint tinkling sound emanating from the boat. An instant later she heard a loud pop, which was followed by a flare bursting overhead, bathing everything in light.

"Not tonight, ninja," Jon yelled. He and the two Gurkha guards sprayed Thompson fire in the direction of the assailant.

Shocked, Asami had to roll away from the barrage of bullets several times to avoid being hit. She retreated and ran back up the dry creek bed, only to see the outlines of several soldiers with submachine guns against their shoulders, ready to fire. She moved away from the creek and retreated into the darkness, where she would be safe.

Jon had guessed correctly. The Japanese ninja went for the ladies on the boat. To create a warning mechanism, the Gurkha guards had suggested using a thin monofilament fishing line and glass chimes. The Gurkhas strung the line low to the ground in the brush in straight lines leading away from the boat. When the assassin moved across the monofilament line, the line was tugged, and a chime attached to the yacht sounded. The Gurkhas had set up a different-sounding chime for each of four fields of fire in order to zero in on the assassin.

Jon knew from his studies that the Japanese looked upon their enemies as inferior in intellect. He figured the Japanese operative would be supremely confident in his success. When he yelled at the assailant and fired his weapon into the brush, he was rubbing the ninja's nose in it.

Camille and Captain Dubois ran out on the forward deck after Jon fired the Thompson.

"Jon, what the hell is going on?" Captain Dubois asked.

"Sorry, Captain. I set a trap for the assassin. He tripped one of the wires we set."

"Do you think you hit him?" Camille asked.

"No. But I think he knows we're onto him. There's nothing like a little failure to stir up negative emotions in an enemy."

Captain Dubois shook his head and led Camille into the pilothouse, where they walked down the stairs to their respective cabins.

At her boardinghouse, Asami sat contemplating her defeat. She had not only been expected but was nearly killed by a trap the Allied agents had set. Whoever had yelled at her had planned on her moving on the *Jacqueline* next. How was it possible, and how did they know where she would strike next? The Allied intelligence agents weren't supposed to be that smart, and they certainly did not have her training in ninjutsu. She concluded it was blind luck and seethed at the thought of failing.

Next time, she swore to herself, *they won't know what hit them.*

The next morning at breakfast, Jon addressed the group on the boat.

"I apologize for not informing you of my plans to protect the boat. I didn't want to alarm anyone in case I was just being paranoid."

"Well, I'm damn glad you did, but next time give me a heads-up," Captain Dubois stated.

"Are we keeping secrets now?" Camille asked.

"I'm sorry. I didn't want you to worry about a possible attack and lose sleep."

"In case you've forgotten, Mister, I'm a trained agent too," Camille stated. She said it with a definite hint of anger in her voice.

"I promise it won't happen again. Everyone will be fully informed."

Three mornings later, Asami waited in an abandoned warehouse that the women's car passed everyday on its way to the American base. From her position she was able to observe the women leave the boat and enter their vehicle. She lost sight of the car for a minute as it drove through a narrow lane in the woods prior to reaching the warehouse. As it came around a curve, an explosion on the right side of the vehicle tore into the metal frame and flipped it onto its top.

The gas tank should have erupted, and the car should be in flames, Asami thought. As she waited for the gas tank to explode, a lone figure crawled out of the driver-side window and slowly stood up. He wore a steel helmet and what looked to be several flak vests, one worn correctly and another covering his crotch. Several more were wrapped securely around his arms and legs.

"Not today, ninja," Jon yelled. He pulled his Thompson from the car and began spraying the abandoned warehouse with .45-caliber fire.

CHAPTER 54

Calcutta, India

As Asami ducked the bullets striking the building less than a foot above her head, she thought, *Who is this American, and how does he know I'm a ninja?* More concerned with her life than answering her own question, she crouched as low to the floor as possible and scampered through the building and out a broken door on the opposite side. Asami was disciplined enough not to panic, and she made her way along a small inlet leading to a fishing dock. She slowed as she came upon three fishing boats and the nearly naked workers moving supplies onto them. Five blocks from the warehouse, she disappeared into a crowd of workers heading north toward downtown Calcutta.

When Miles and Henri drove up in a Willys jeep, Jon was bent over, dusting himself off.

"I guess you called this one right, mate," Miles said. "Your sixth sense is something else."

"I can't explain it, but I'm glad I have it."

When Jon, Miles, and Henri reached the SOE detachment, Jon's ears were still ringing, and despite the flak vests and helmet, he was bruised from head to toe. Still, he couldn't help but feel good because he had outwitted the Japanese assassin again. How long his luck would hold, he didn't know. He decided he needed to go to the mission to see Father Doherty.

Colonel MacKenzie wouldn't let Jon go alone and made sure two Gurkha guards accompanied him everywhere. As Jon parked the staff car, Father Ed Doherty was standing in the door of the chapel, speaking to one of the nuns assigned to the mission. When he saw Jon, he excused the nun and walked over to where Jon stood. Father Doherty clasped his shoulders firmly and hugged him.

"Jon, it's good to see you. What brings you here?"

"I need to confess, and I need some heavy-duty prayers for protection."

"Let's go into the chapel." He ushered Jon through the door and toward the confessional.

After confession they sat in the priest's office and drank coffee. Jon took his time explaining his situation and dilemma.

"God has given you an exceptional gift, and from what you've told me, you are using it wisely and effectively. I do not doubt God will be with you throughout this war and you will prevail over this assassin. As for the others, it's up to God. He has not given me insight into them. You just do your best and listen to what your gift is telling you."

At the *Jacqueline*, Captain Dubois was backing the yacht out of its berth. Once the *Jacqueline* cleared the dock, he steered right rudder and turned the boat until it faced the river. He then moved the throttles to one-quarter forward power and moved the yacht toward the river.

Two days earlier, Jon had convinced him to move the *Jacqueline* to the yacht basin at Fort William. He hoped the vast amount of open space at the basin would deter the assassin's return. Of course, the clear field of fire could be an advantage to the assassin. After the bomb exploded beneath the car, it didn't take too much to convince Captain Dubois that Jon was clairvoyant, and he went with Jon's suggestion to move to Fort William.

After his meeting with Father Doherty, Jon returned to the SOE detachment and found Colonel MacKenzie pacing near the first sergeant's desk. As soon as Jon came through the door, the colonel ushered him into the briefing room, where Miles and Henri sat going through a stack of photographs. He picked up a photo from the desk and handed it to Jon.

"Whom does this remind you of?" Colonel MacKenzie asked.

Jon took the photo and stared at it for fifteen seconds. He stood for another minute with a faraway gaze and then looked at the colonel.

"It looks like one of the Nakada sisters. Where did you dig this photo up?"

"It was taken yesterday by one of our agents here in Calcutta."

"You're making this up, right?"

"No, he's not, mate," Miles stated. "I personally talked to the agent who took the photo. He was following up on another character when this woman sat down with him in a restaurant."

"You think this is the ninja assassin we're looking for?"

"I certainly do, mate. If there's another Nakada sister in Japanese intelligence, she would want revenge. She thinks the three of us are dead, and now she's coming after the ladies involved in her sisters' deaths."

"I see your point, and it would better explain the deaths of Brigitte and Monique. She's hitting us where she thinks we're vulnerable. She knows we'll do anything to protect our female agents, even to the point of making a major blunder."

"I know that look. What are you thinking?" Henri asked.

"I'm wondering if I didn't already make a blunder by moving the *Jacqueline*."

"Why would you think that? We've outmaneuvered her two times, and now she's beginning to doubt her abilities," Henri said.

"She's desperate for a win, which may be an advantage for us."

"So what do we do? Give her a win?" Colonel MacKenzie asked.

"That's precisely what we'll do—or sort of," Jon stated.

For the next three days, Asami did reconnaissance, looking for habits, routines, and any mistakes the Allied agents might make. She discovered two additional Allied agents; both were men. One was obvious. He was young, tall, lean, light-skinned, and blond. *American*, Asami thought. The other was older and darker and sported a heavy beard. *European. Most likely French.*

But both, Asami noticed, had probing eyes, eyes that watched without the head turning, eyes that drank in everything. She knew immediately these agents would be dangerous, until she noticed the younger one walk off for three minutes. When he returned to where the older agent stood, she overheard him admonishing the young, blond-haired American.

"Dammit, kid, don't ever walk away alone again. You want to get yourself killed? You stay close to me, or I'll put your ass behind a desk," Henri stated.

"Sorry, sir. I saw something in the store that I've been meaning to pick up," Lieutenant Warren said.

"Kid, you're too impulsive. If you don't stop and think about what you're doing, you're going to make a serious mistake. And mistakes will get you killed."

Yes, they will, Asami thought.

Asami followed the two agents for three blocks. When the blond kid made the same mistake again, she thought, *I got you.*

Asami made her way across the street, moved a block ahead of the two men, and entered a candy store. She moved about the store and discovered it didn't have a rear exit. She left and walked on, looking for a store the Americans might enter. *All Americans smoke cigarettes*, Asami thought. At the first tobacco shop she entered, she noticed the back door to the alley was wide open. While she browsed the different brands of cigarettes and cigars, she anxiously touched the slender stiletto up her right sleeve to make sure it was still there.

Asami watched as the two Americans approached the shop. The blond stopped at the store window while the other walked on. The blond called to his friend, "Hey, I'm out of cigarettes. I'm going to duck in here and get a pack."

"Just hurry, kid. I'm hungry and want lunch."

When the blond American stepped up to the counter and asked for a pack of Lucky Strikes, Asami noticed he paid little attention to her, standing ten feet away. *Stupid American.*

Asami moved toward the Allied agent with the thin stiletto in her right hand, but before she could strike, the blond American turned and struck her arm with an exceptionally hard blow. Asami dropped the knife and, without thinking, kicked with her left foot, knocking the American agent off-balance. As she exited the back door of the shop, a loud pop resonated from a silenced weapon.

By the time Henri made it out the door, Asami had disappeared around the corner of a building thirty feet from the store. Henri turned to reenter the store and saw Franklin limp out the door, trying to shake off the pain. When Franklin bent over to rub his leg, he noticed a trail of blood leading toward the street.

"It looks like you hit her," Warren said. He bent down and touched a spot of blood with his finger.

"Maybe it will put her out of action for a while. You all right, kid?"

"A little shaken."

"Well, you did real well. In fact, you were exceptional."

Henri walked back into the store and picked up the stiletto meant to kill Franklin.

"Here, kid, keep this as a souvenir."

CHAPTER 55

Calcutta, India

Asami ran four blocks before stopping to tear a length of cloth from the bottom of her blouse. She tied the cloth around her left forearm. Although the bullet had only clipped her forearm, it bled heavily. Instead of returning to her boardinghouse, she moved into the northern part of the city to a hotel room she had rented in case of an emergency. She would make it back to her regular room and retrieve her clothes and weapons later.

The loss of blood made Asami light-headed, so she decided to lie down and rest for a few minutes. When she woke, it was 0100 hours, and she was hungry. There was no food in the apartment, and it was too late to go to a restaurant. Although she had learned to ignore pain, tonight her arm was throbbing and hurting. Asami's self-confidence and focus were in ruins. Three times she had failed to get her prey, and each time it appeared as if the Allied intelligence agents were reading her thoughts and knew her intentions.

Depressed by her failure, Asami thought of Akemi, Akiko, and Akira, lying dead in unmarked graves. *After Japan wins the war*, she thought, *I will find where they are buried and return them to Japan.* As she lay there, the worst thing that could happen to an assassin happened: doubt began filling her thoughts.

Jon was not happy that the assassin escaped. He wanted to post more men downtown, but more men would have been too obvious. He concluded that the ninja would notice the extra agents and would shy away.

"You're getting slow, Henri," Jon said.

"I slipped on something on the sidewalk. Otherwise, she would be dead. I'll get her next time."

"There may not be a next time. She may disappear and take time off for her wound to heal."

"I'm sorry I messed up," Warren said. "I thought I had her, but she was so damn quick, and her kick was extremely powerful for such a small woman. I underestimated her."

"She knows where to kick for maximum effect. If she had stayed any longer, you might be dead. She knows half a dozen ways to kill you with just her fingers. You are damn lucky to be alive."

Henri then turned to Jon. "Do you think she'll leave Calcutta?"

"No, I don't. If she is the sister of the triplets, she's out for blood. I do think she will disappear for a while and let her wound heal, but this is good for us. She'll be distressed by her third failure, and doubt will impede her ability to think clearly, at least for a while."

"I agree," George said. He entered the room on crutches. "Ninjas are trained in strategy and tactics, and when she strikes next, it will be something totally unexpected."

"Such as?" Henri asked.

"I took the liberty of drawing up a list of ways she could come at us. I hope this will be useful."

Henri took the list of over thirty different methods and tactics that ninjas used in assassinations.

"Is this all?"

"No, but it's a start to what you need to be thinking about."

After Jon read through the list, he said, "Humph. Quite a list. I especially like the poisoned blow dart, but I think she may try something more conventional."

"Like what?" Henri asked.

"I think she might try to take the remaining ladies head on. We've foiled her attempts three times now, and I believe she's extremely frustrated. She is probably used to killing on her first try. I think she'll take a risk and make a mistake. When she does, we'll take her."

"Jon, was this last gig your idea?" George asked.

"Yes."

"And now what? You want to expose the ladies so this assassin can hit them head on and have a chance to succeed?"

"Something like that. But this time I'll be the one taking the risk."

"Like hell you are," Camille said. She stood glaring at Jon from the doorway. "What makes you think you can kill this bitch? She's a damn chameleon. We won't know if she'll be dressed as a woman or a man."

Jon saw the fear in Camille's eyes, so he stood silent for a few seconds, wanting to choose his words carefully.

"After three attempts she still hasn't gotten to us. We've all thought long and hard on the ways she would approach us, and we've outwitted her every step of the way. We took measures to be forewarned at the boat. We assumed she might try to hit us on the way to work, so we pulled that armored embassy car out of storage. We came up with locations and places where she could take us downtown, and we were prepared when she struck. She's beginning to doubt her ability to carry out her assignment, and that will be her downfall. In fact, I'm beginning to think this may be her first mission as an assassin."

"Well, I don't like it one bit."

"None of us like it, but we can't just walk away from this. It's what we do."

"I still don't like it," Camille said. She turned and walked away.

After supper, Jon walked Camille out on the aft deck of the *Jacqueline*. There was a half-moon, and Jon took her hand and kissed her fingers one at a time. He held her for a few moments and then kissed her neck and nibbled at her ear.

"If you think this is going to change my mind, you're wrong."

Jon didn't stop. He kept kissing her on her neck and lips. His hand unbuttoned the top two buttons of her blouse, and he kissed her breasts. Camille moaned softly and arched her head back.

"But it will get me in bed. Let's go to our cabin."

CHAPTER 56

Calcutta, India

The three agents, Jon, Miles, and Henri, sat in silence as Colonel Rick Dixon anxiously paced the briefing room. Colonel MacKenzie, who stood in the far corner, looked even more stressed and worried. Dixon had arrived late the previous night and looked tired from his trip.

"Gentlemen, I hate to take you away from your current investigation, but I need to send you all to the Philippine Islands, specifically Luzon. We've received reports from Filipino guerillas that the Japanese are digging large tunnels in the Santa Maria Mountains, north of Manila. We need to determine what these sites are for."

"You suspect this may be one of the sites where the Japanese are burying the gold they plundered from the Asian countries, don't you?" Jon asked.

"Yes, we do. And we need confirmation on what they are doing, along with photos. We want a quick 'get in, get documentation, and get out' mission. It will be a very dangerous mission, gentlemen."

"As are all our missions, sir," Miles stated.

"Yes, but it will be all the more dangerous for you because the Japanese Fourteenth Army is battling the US Sixth Army under the command of General Walter Krueger. You may have to make it through the Japanese forces in the mountains and avoid our air forces dropping bombs on anything Japanese. If the Japanese catch you, it will mean your death."

"When do we leave?" Henri asked.

"Tomorrow morning. One of our special modified B-24 bombers will fly you to Myitkyina, Burma, refuel, and then move on to Guilin, China, where you will spend the night. The next morning, you'll take off and proceed to a recently constructed air base at Saint Fabian, on the coast of the Lingayen Gulf of Luzon, óne hundred thirty miles northwest of Manila."

"Won't that put us over Japanese-held territory?" Miles asked.

"Yes, but you will have an escort of two P-47 Thunderbolt fighters from Myitkyina to Guilin. At Guilin, you'll be escorted halfway to the Philippines by four P-51 Mustangs from the Chinese Nationalist Air Force. At the halfway point, you'll be met by four P-61 Black Widow fighters, which will escort you to the air base at Saint Fabian. We have air superiority throughout most of Southeast Asia, so there shouldn't be a problem."

"I wish George was available to go with us, but he's still on crutches," Jon stated.

"Actually, he was declared medically fit early this morning. George left for Saint Fabian four hours ago. He'll meet you at army-intelligence field headquarters in Saint Fabian. He'll have maps and a team of Filipino guerillas to guide you to the area where the Japs are tunneling. Any questions?"

Miles said, "I guess we'd better head to the armory and fetch our gear, mates."

"One other thing. I would like you all to wear the new reversible leopard camo fatigues I brought with me from Washington. They've been modified for your type of fieldwork. There are more and larger pockets on the pants and extra pockets for Thompson clips on both the pants and the shirt. The outer shell is more greenish, while the inside of the reversible is brownish. It will provide better concealment in the jungle and forests."

"They've also been tailored and sized for each of you," Colonel MacKenzie said. "They're in my office."

"Concerned for our safety, Colonel?" Jon asked.

"Yes, plus General Marshall says we can't afford to lose you and your team," Colonel Dixon replied.

When the trio landed at Saint Fabian three days later, George, still limping from his wound, greeted them at the airfield and led them to a G-2 headquarters tent. George showed the trio the best route to the Japanese tunnels, avoiding the US Sixth Army's thrusts and the Army Air Forces' targets.

"The locale we're headed for is the village of Kayapa, which is halfway between Baguio and Bambang. When you get close to Kayapa, you'll be met by several Igorot tribesmen. The Igorot are the local mountain people and are intimately familiar with the terrain and the jungle in this region. Many of their people were conscripted by the Japanese to help build the tunnels. They are worried about what the Japanese will do to them when the tunnels are completed. The tunnels are being built where a creek intersects with the Santa Cruz River. From the information we have received, each tunnel runs over one hundred meters into the mountain," George said.

"Do the Igorot know what is being stored or buried there?" Jon asked.

"No, but they reported there are heavy brass-colored trunks in the beds of the trucks. It takes four men to move a trunk, so I suspect gold bars."

"How are they delivered to Kayapa?" asked Miles.

"The tribesmen reported that forty truckloads of the trunks have arrived each day for the last fifteen days. I estimate around two thousand tons of gold."

"For crying out loud," Jon said. "That's over four million pounds, worth, what…two billion dollars?"

"Kind of makes you wonder what this war is all about, doesn't it?" Henri chimed.

"I believe Japan is more worried about surviving the war financially at this point," Jon stated.

Entering their briefing room, Colonel Sage said, "You're not far off the mark."

"What's that in your hand?" Jon asked, motioning to a paper in the colonel's hand.

"An intercept from Imperial Army headquarters in Tokyo, stating that no prisoners are to be left alive after burying the honey."

"They're calling it honey?" Miles asked.

"Well, just think about it. Gold is kind of honey colored in the bullion form; it doesn't have a luster to it until it's polished," Jon stated.

"Then let's go find the honey, honey," Henri said. He mimicked a kiss to Jon before cracking a huge smile.

Jon blew a kiss back and laughed. Colonel Sage shook his head and said, "Let's stay focused. This is serious stuff."

"What do we do when we get there, Colonel?" Miles asked.

"Get photos of the trucks, the brass trunks, the gold, and anything else of importance," Colonel Sage answered.

"That may be difficult at night," Jon said.

"Your cameras are loaded with a special low-light film. We stole the design from the Germans. The light from the full moon should be sufficient. Also, take compass bearings from at least three distinguishing landmarks so we can recover whatever is in the caves after the war is over."

"I'd like to be around when that happens," Jon said.

"More than likely, you will be part of the recovery team, if the chief of staff has his way. He's working with the president and a close group of advisers to begin a recovery right after the Japanese surrender."

"What about the Allied prisoners? The Japanese are going to kill them."

"Your orders are to discover what is being buried and get out. I have arranged for half a dozen fighters to cover your ass when you lead the prisoners out, but there aren't any additional troops to help you."

"I understand, sir. Thank you."

"What do you think they will do with the gold, once it's recovered?" Miles asked.

"Good question, Miles, but I'm afraid I don't have an answer."

"Classified?" Jon asked.

"Yes. Plus, I'm not at a high enough pay grade to know."

"I should have guessed that, Colonel, and if you were at a high enough pay grade, they wouldn't let you tell us."

"No, I don't imagine they would."

"George has transportation arranged. You all will be taking a Paraset wireless radio, but no unnecessary contact with us. The Japanese have direction-finding equipment and could possible track your location. Another thing. The fighters, which are P-61 night fighters, will be available only early in the morning. I've made arrangements with the squadron commander for them to be refueled when they return to base at 0400 hours and have bombloads put on. They can be airborne by 0600."

"Is that in the orders for our tasking?" Jon asked.

"Not in the tasking orders, but the chief of staff included a private note in the attaché pouch delivered to me yesterday. He said you would attempt a rescue despite orders and asked me to assist in any way I can."

"I guess he knows me pretty well by now."

"When do we leave?" Henri asked.

"At daybreak. We don't want to chance you being shot at by our own troops."

"Yeah, let's avoid that," Jon said. "One other thing. I want George to stay behind."

"Can't do that," Colonel Sage said. "You need George to interpret for any documents or any Japanese prisoners you capture."

"He's still limping from his gunshot wound, and he'll slow us down."

"I'll keep up," George said. "If not, you can send me back with one of the Igorot guides."

Jon didn't say anything, but the look on his face told everyone that he was concerned about George. If George did begin to lag behind, Jon would have the Igorot tribesmen rig a sling and carry him. He knew he would need George on this mission.

CHAPTER 57

Kayapa, Philippines

They drove two army jeeps three hours northeast to Baguio, where the US Sixth Army had its forward operating headquarters. Fierce fighting was already in progress two miles away. The concussion of two dozen American artillery pieces a hundred yards away vibrated throughout their bodies.

"I wouldn't want to be on the receiving end of those guns," Henri stated.

"Those are one-hundred-fifty-five-millimeter howitzer cannons," George said. "They can fire six-inch shells with fourteen pounds of explosives over sixteen thousand yards—fourteen thousand meters to you Brits."

"Ouch, that's a lot of bang," Miles said.

They left Baguio by foot and traveled ten hours through dense jungle and mountain terrain to a village with no name on Binga Lake, halfway to their destination. At the village they met up with ten Igorot tribesmen and continued another ten hours to a mountain overlooking the Santa Cruz River, two miles southwest of Kayapa. Surprisingly, George kept pace and never tired or complained.

"There are a dozen Igorot villages within a ten-mile radius of Kayapa. Relatives of most of these men," George said.

"Any more warrior tribesmen?" Jon asked.

"Over a hundred if we need them."

"We'll need them. Send four of the Igorot out to fetch them. I want them here by 2000 hours."

Jon and George pointed their binoculars farther up the mountain and observed the two caves.

"Not very big entrances to those tunnels; tall enough for a man to stand and wide enough for four. Should be easy enough for them to blow and conceal when they finish," George said.

"My main concern is the prisoners they are using as slave labor," Jon said.

"I hope you know what you are doing."

"Have I ever failed you?"

"Not once."

"How many prisoners and natives do the Japs have working here?"

"The tribesmen said close to one hundred of each."

"We can't let those people be killed or, worse, entombed alive inside that mountain."

"How do you want to do this?" Henri asked.

"I'm thinking we free the prisoners at night while they're resting. There look to be only thirty guards, so there are probably another ten sleeping during the day. We can take out the night guards and move the prisoners across the river, but we're going to need air support to keep the Japs at bay, once they discover they are gone."

"What about our reconnaissance of the site?" George asked.

"Henri and I will do what we can from nightfall until 0300 hours. The rest of you will locate where the prisoners are kept and get into position. When Henri and I return, we'll move on the guards."

"What if you and Henri are discovered?"

"Not an option here, so don't even think it."

"Yeah, but what if?"

"Then use your best judgment. You'll have the ten Filipino guerillas, the ten tribesmen, however many more tribesmen show up by 2000 hours, and the element of surprise. They won't be expecting us because they still think this location is a secret."

"All right, we'll do our job. You all get back in one piece."

Jon and Henri moved down the mountain, keeping to the shadows and out of the sunlight. Jon stopped and pointed.

"We need to move farther south to cross the river. There's a staging area for the trucks we need to go around."

"Looks like a primitive road below us that turns southeast," Henri stated.

"I'm guessing it's the road from Aritao. The Japanese completed a road from San Jose to Aritao three months ago to route the trucks coming from Manila. The Japanese must have suspected US forces would land at the beaches on the Lingayen Gulf."

"Did George mention if any more truck convoys are on the way to Kayapa?" Henri asked.

"Two, but they are traveling only at night. With our P-61 night fighters and the full moon, it's doubtful they will make it. Let's rest for a couple of hours. Once it's dark, we'll cross the Santa Cruz into enemy territory before the moon rises above the mountains."

By 2200 hours, the team had crossed the river and made its way up a mountain behind the Japanese encampment. Two Igorot tribesmen left the group to find where the prisoners were being held. Over a hundred additional Igorot tribesmen arrived just before they broke camp.

As they approached within a hundred yards of the far eastern cave, Jon noticed four heavy-duty trucks parked on the road, fifty yards below the tunnel. He watched the trucks for over ten minutes to make sure no one was around. He motioned for Henri to follow.

They moved within ten yards of the Type 94, six-wheeled trucks and hid among a dense group of *Aglaia* trees and mountain shrubs. Jon crawled up to the back of one of the trucks and climbed into the bed. There were twenty-four brass trunks inside, yet to be unloaded.

Jon quietly undid the latches of one of the trunks. Inside were two eighteen-by-five-by-four-inch bars weighing what he judged to be over 150 pounds as he lifted one end of a bar. He pulled his knife out of its scabbard, peeled off a thin, four-inch slice of the metal, and stuck it in one of his pockets. From another pocket, he pulled out his miniature Minolta camera, and he took photos of the trunks and the bars. He then closed and latched the lid and eased out of the truck bed.

"I think they're gold bars, but it's hard to tell in the moonlight. Hopefully the sample I got will be enough to prove the gold's existence."

They moved away from the vehicles and back up the mountain toward the prisoner encampment. On the way, they encountered a Japanese guard taking a leak in a stand of shrubs. His rifle was leaning against a large tree.

Jon motioned to Henri to take the guard out. Henri drew his knife and moved quickly and silently. Within seconds he was behind the guard, grabbing his head and pulling it backward before slashing his throat. Henri held the guard a few seconds before lowering him to the ground.

Jon and Henri continued up the hill until an Igorot tribesmen moved out of the shadows, stopped them, and motioned for them to follow. He led them another two hundred feet up the mountain and turned south on a well-worn trail. Jon caught a glimpse of three dead Japanese soldiers lying on the path.

After another fifty yards, the tribesman stopped and squatted. Jon and Henri followed suit. George eased from behind a large tree and squatted next to them.

"We've killed all the guards at the prisoner keep," George said. "There are two soldiers in a tent where the radio is kept. We'll need to take them out and destroy the radio before we move the prisoners. Also, there's a larger encampment of Japanese one hundred yards farther up the mountain. I estimate a hundred soldiers, but half of them are probably drivers."

"Anyone made contact with the prisoners?" Jon asked.

"Two tribesmen infiltrated the group of natives, and Miles has made contact with one of the Allied prisoners. They are ready when we are."

"Did you contact HQ and confirm our air support?" Henri asked.

"Yes, they're still on. They just landed to refuel and load bombs."

"Good job. Now I suggest we take the radio and remaining soldiers out and get the prisoners across the river before daylight."

The two radio operators were bent over the radio console, listening on headphones, when Miles and Henri walked up behind them and cut their throats. It took Miles two minutes to find and remove the radio crystal and destroy the radio equipment. Henri rifled through the small desk the radio sat on, found the Japanese codebook, and put it in his breast pocket. A small safe sat below the desk with its door open. Miles grabbed everything inside the safe and stuffed it in a small tote he carried.

They exited the tent and motioned to Jon. Jon gave a hand signal, and the ten Filipino soldiers entered the prisoner keep and began moving the prisoners downhill toward the river. In case the Japanese up the hill were alerted, the one hundred extra Igorot tribesmen took up positions between the fleeing prisoners and the Japanese. All carried the M1903 Springfield, a .30-06-caliber bolt-action service rifle that the US Army had used for close to forty years.

An hour later, they had all the Allied and native prisoners safely on the west side of the Santa Cruz River. Jon thanked the tribesmen for their help and released the majority to get their friends and family members away from the area. The ten Filipinos and ten original Igorot tribesmen would stay with Jon's team and escort the Allied prisoners back to Baguio.

The Igorot tribesmen fashioned sling carriers out of bamboo and vines to carry the dozen or so prisoners unable to walk. It was dawn before the Igorot tribesmen took the lead and began moving the prisoners west toward Binga Lake.

Jon's team and the ten Filipino soldiers were about to follow when they heard a ruckus at the river below them. Jon moved to get a view and saw close to fifty Japanese soldiers hurrying across the shallow river, along with three teams carrying Type 92 "woodpecker" heavy machine guns.

"Form a defensive line behind this ridge of rocks," Jon ordered. "I want three sharpshooters on those machine-gun teams, now. The rest of you wait until they are within forty yards."

"You three," Jon said to Miles, Henri, and George, "get your grenades out. We're going to flank them. Miles, you and Henri go west. George and I will go east. We want to catch them at a forty-five-degree angle so we won't be shooting each other, so don't go too far downhill. Wait until they are within twenty meters before you lob those things and then fall back while they are still confused. We'll meet a hundred yards farther up the trail."

"Aye-aye, boss," Henri stated.

"One other thing. If you all get killed, I'm going to kick your asses all the way back to Calcutta."

"Don't worry about us, boss," Miles said. Then he and Henri slipped away.

As Jon and George moved to the enemy's right flank, they heard the familiar crack of M1 Garand rifle fire. *Lord, let their aim be accurate*, Jon prayed.

The sharpshooters were accurate but were receiving heavy fire from the Japanese. Unnoticed by the enemy, Jon and George stopped behind several large boulders and a clump of shrubs.

"Let them have it," George said.

Both tossed a grenade into the midst of twenty or more Japanese soldiers. The explosions were tremendous, much more than two grenades should have made. It was then that Jon heard a twin-engine aircraft screaming overhead. Thirty seconds later, another aircraft swooped in and dropped another bomb on the group of Japanese soldiers.

As some of the smoke and dust cleared, Jon saw the Japanese in full retreat. As two P-61s strafed the retreating soldiers, two more P-61s dropped bombs on the group of forty trucks parked close to the edge of the forest. A direct hit on one of the trucks hurled debris three hundred feet in all directions.

On the southern side of the mountain, Miles and Henri hit the ground as debris began raining down from above. Both heard a loud thud as something landed directly between them. When Miles raised his head out of the dirt, he noticed a large rectangular shape sticking out of the dirt. Henri reached for it and pulled his hand away. It was still hot from the blast.

"Crap, would you look at that?" Miles said. "I believe we've been delivered a bar of gold."

Henri kicked the bar from the ground and said, "Make that half a bar."

CHAPTER 58

Washington, DC

Colonel Norm Hayward entered the outer room of General Marshall's spacious office. He had been summoned, but no reason had been given. As he entered the office, a senator from Texas was walking out of the general's private office saying, "Thank y'all, General."

"You can go on in, Colonel Hayward," Linda Dixon said. Linda was the general's private secretary.

General Marshall was still standing when the colonel entered.

"Thanks for coming, Norm. How are Brenda and the kids?"

General Marshall had been to Norm and Brenda's home on many occasions over the last four years. Norm's children loved the gentle giant, and on almost every visit, the general would get down on the floor and wrestle with the two young boys. Each time, General Marshall would teach the boys that real soldiers, men who were heroes, never quit and never gave up. "Your dad never quits. He's a hero," General Marshall would tell them.

Every time either of them wrestled the general, he would pin one of the boy's arms behind his back. Each time the general would ask if he wanted to give up.

"If you give up and want to quit, say uncle," General Marshall would say. "I'll release your arm."

"Never in a million years," the child said. Only then would the general release his arm.

"They're all doing very well, General."

"Norm, I want you to draft a message to the SOE, CIC, and OSS commanders in Calcutta. I want Captain Dubois to bring Agent Preston and his wife back to the United States when he sails the *Jacqueline* back to Washington at the end of September."

"Anything else, sir?"

"We received word, through the Red Cross, that Camille's and Kathleen's parents died in a Japanese internment camp near Singapore. Make sure Captain Dubois breaks the news to them personally and expresses my deepest sympathy. Also, if Kathleen Lauren wants to immigrate to the United States, cut orders for her to sail on the yacht as well. This office will arrange everything with immigration for both women."

"Do you know something I don't, General?"

"If everything goes according to our plan, the war should be over in a month. I don't want any Japanese or Chinese hit team killing our favorite agent or his wife."

"Sir, are you saying we won't be invading the Japanese mainland?"

"No, I didn't say we wouldn't invade Japan. In fact, forget you ever heard that last statement of mine."

"Yes, sir. Will that be all, General?"

"How is the award coming for Colonel MacKenzie?"

"The president signed the citation last week and sent it along with a personal letter to both the prime minister and to King George, as well as the Defense Ministry."

"Did we break protocol by sending it directly to the king?"

"No, sir."

"I hope we didn't pour it on too thick."

"No, sir. The citation was succinct and to the point. Although it wasn't our main intent, it is quite possibly good enough to qualify Colonel MacKenzie for a knighthood."

"Hell, if that won't frost Churchill's ass, nothing will," General Marshall said.

"One other thing, Norm. I want you to write separate Medal of Honor citations for Agents Preston, Murphy, and Morreau; they've gone far above the call of duty it takes to be awarded one. Make sure it's scrubbed of classified data. Use general terms and the number of covert missions each went on and how each risked his life to rescue over a thousand Allied POWs. Mark the recommendations and the citations 'Top Secret Eyes Only,' for the president. I'll approve the requests and deliver them to the president. I'm sure he will want to award Preston his in a private White House ceremony. It's unfortunate the specifics of his missions will remain a secret for the next fifty years. I would like him to get the public credit he deserves. The president will ask General Eisenhower to award Murphy's and Morreau's. I don't know what we would have done without Preston and his team in the CBI theater."

"I'll see to it, sir. Is there anything else?"

"Yes, cut orders promoting Preston and Linka to full colonel. And award Linka the Distinguished Service Cross. It's still the second-highest medal we can award, isn't it? I can't seem to keep up with all the new awards Congress comes up with."

"Yes, sir, it's still the second-highest award. Anything else, General?"

"Yes, tell Colonel Arvin I want to be briefed on everything we have on the Japanese gold that Preston and his team uncovered. Make sure he invites General Donovan. I'd bet a hundred to one odds he knows a lot more than we do."

CHAPTER 59

Tinian Island, Pacific Ocean

Colonel Paul Tibbets keyed his interphone. "Copilot, contact the tower and get us taxi clearance."

Captain Robert Lewis depressed the toggle switch on his UHF radio. "Tower, Dimples Eight-Two is ready to taxi."

"Roger, Eight-Two, you're clear to taxi. Runway Alpha 27 is the active runway," the tower controller said.

Tibbets pushed up the throttles on the huge B-29 bomber and slowly taxied to the east end of Runway Alpha. *Alpha* was the designation of the first of five runways on Tinian. *Two-Seven* indicated the compass direction of takeoff: 270 degrees. After completing his before-takeoff check, Tibbets asked the crew to respond when ready for takeoff. All eleven crew members toggled their interphone switches and gave the "Ready for takeoff" response to their aircraft commander.

The B-29 was powered by four Wright 23A Duplex-Cyclone turbo-supercharged radial engines, each capable of creating 2,200 horsepower. The aircraft's length was ninety-nine feet, and its wingspan stretched one hundred and forty-one feet. The B-29's effective combat range was thirty-two hundred miles. It carried ten .50-caliber Browning machine guns (BMGs) in remote turrets and two .50-caliber BMGs in its tail. The B-29 could carry up to twenty thousand pounds of ordnance, but for this special mission, the *Enola Gay*'s bomb bays had been modified to carry a single ten-thousand-pound atomic bomb.

"Tower, Dimples Eight-Two is ready for takeoff," Colonel Tibbets reported.

"Dimples Eight-Two, you are cleared for takeoff on Runway Alpha 27; wind is 285 degrees at ten knots; altimeter setting is 29.92."

At 0245 hours on September 6, 1945, Tibbets pushed the four throttles on the B-29 Superfortress forward and steered the aircraft straight down the runway centerline. After two-thirds of the runway rolled past, the lumbering giant had still not reached its takeoff speed. The copilot anxiously watched the airspeed indicator and waited for his aircraft commander to rotate the aircraft, but Tibbets held the aircraft on the ground, coaxing as much speed as possible out of the heavily loaded B-29. Just before the aircraft entered the overrun, at the end of the runway, Tibbets pulled back on the yoke and eased the bomber into the air.

Once airborne, the anxious Captain Lewis looked over to his pilot and said, "Damn, Colonel, I thought we were going to crash."

Tibbets kept his eyes focused on his instruments and called, "Gear up; flaps five degrees."

Captain Lewis pulled up on the lever that retracted the gear and reset the flaps as they began a slow climb to nine thousand feet. The navigator, Captain Theodore Van Kirk, gave the pilot an initial heading of 358 degrees magnetic and an ETA to Iwo Jima of 0545 hours. The *Enola Gay*, named after Colonel Tibbets's mother, was on its way to bomb Japan.

As Tibbets nursed the B-29 to altitude, he reflected back on what it had taken to get his aircraft and crew to this point. It began on September 1, 1944, when General Hap Arnold chose him to command the bomb group that would drop a single special bomb on Japan. Initially, he was told nothing about the bomb. After six months he was told it would be a fission or atomic weapon and it could quite possibly end the war. Its energy release was unknown, but scientists estimated it at somewhere between that of twelve and twenty thousand tons of TNT. Tibbets did a quick estimate in his head and concluded it would take two thousand B-29s carrying twenty thousand pounds of bombs each to match what he would be dropping today.

In twelve months, Tibbets had put together an organization consisting of 225 officers and 1,540 enlisted men. They included pilots, navigators, bombardiers, flight engineers, radiomen, gunners, crew chiefs, logistics men, maintenance men, security personnel, meteorologists, clerks, and cooks. Within eight months Tibbets had trained his fifteen B-29 crews to drop a ten-thousand-pound bomb within a three-hundred-foot radius from thirty-one thousand feet. Those who couldn't hack the program, he replaced. Those who became security risks, he sent to Alaska, where they would have no contact with anyone until the war was over. In the end, his fifteen crews were honed into some of the best B-29 flight crews the Army Air Forces ever trained. At the end of June 1945, Tibbets moved his organization to the Pacific island of Tinian.

The choice of which crew would fly the first atomic mission came down to just two crews: Captain Lewis's and Captain Eatherly's. Captain Lewis's crew won out in the end. Lewis, whose ego was as big as Texas, where he grew up, was the best damn pilot in the unit and was extremely cool under fire. Lewis knew that Tibbets was aware of this. Lewis figured from the beginning that he would fly the mission as the aircraft commander.

What Lewis didn't know was that the chief of the Air Corps, General Hap Arnold, had selected Paul Tibbets to fly as the aircraft commander, relegating Lewis to copilot. The morning of the flight, Lewis discovered that Tibbets had ordered the name of his aircraft painted over and replaced with *Enola Gay*. Although furious, Lewis protested only mildly to Tibbets, because he didn't want to be bumped from the historic mission.

At the final mission briefing, Tibbets informed the three crews flying the mission that the *Enola Gay* would be dropping an atomic bomb. All crew members and passengers were issued welding goggles to put on prior to the explosion. The two aircraft flying alongside the *Enola Gay* were to be used as observation platforms. They would record the event on film and drop monitoring canisters to record the radiation, blast, and wind direction. They would take off minutes after the *Enola Gay* and would travel different courses to Iwo Jima, where the three aircraft would rendezvous and fly in formation to their target.

Two additional aircraft were already airborne. Their mission was to observe the weather at the primary target, Hiroshima, and the secondary target, Nagasaki. If there was cloud cover over Hiroshima, they would proceed to Nagasaki. If both targets were covered by clouds, they would abort the mission and return to Tinian.

When the crew arrived at the *Enola Gay*, it was surrounded by floodlights and close to a hundred people. Army film crews began filming when the first crew member stepped out of the crew bus. Several crew members had microphones shoved into their faces and were asked what they thought about being famous; most of the crew was overwhelmed. Finally, at 0220 hours, a group photo was taken, and Tibbets released the crew to begin their preflight checks.

Two minutes after the *Enola Gay* took off, the second aircraft, *Great Artist*, rolled down the runway. Aircraft Number 91 followed two minutes later. It would be six hours before their arrival over Hiroshima.

CHAPTER 60

Hiroshima, Japan

I n an uncomfortable silence, Tibbets flew the aircraft without the use of the autopilot. At 0300 hours, the nuclear specialist, navy captain Deak Parsons, informed Tibbets that he and his assistant, navy lieutenant Morris Jeppson, were heading to the bomb bay to begin arming the weapon. Thirty minutes later, Parsons and Jeppson climbed out of the bomb bay. The only thing left to do before the weapon was operational was for Parsons to replace four green dummy electrical fuses with four red functional fuses. The red fuses would be installed an hour out from the target, and until then the bomb would be unable to detonate—theoretically.

Theoretical information was all that the nuclear scientists could give Tibbets, because they had never tested a uranium bomb. The weapon they had detonated at Alamogordo, New Mexico, had been a plutonium bomb. It worked without a hitch. However, the uranium bomb was an unknown, and many of the scientists were betting that it would be a dud, which was one of the reasons for not warning the Japanese or providing a demonstration for the world to see. If the United States dropped a dud bomb after telling the world the atomic bomb would end the war, the United States and its scientists would become the laughingstock of the world, and Japan would never surrender.

When the *Enola Gay* arrived over Iwo Jima, the darkened sky to the west had already turned a pale gray. Flying at 195 knots, the two observation aircraft joined the *Enola Gay*, and the formation headed northwest toward Japan.

A hundred miles southwest of Hiroshima, Captain Kata Kumao took off from Shimonoseki Air Base, ferrying a senior officer to the Japanese Second Army headquarters in Hiroshima. Captain Kumao, a flight instructor for student pilots learning to fly kamikaze aircraft, was irritated. His commanding officer had turned down his fourth request to transfer to a fighter unit. He was told that he was too valuable to the war effort. However, his commander did tell him that they would both fly a kamikaze mission, once Allied ships arrived off the coast of Japan. Today, he was flying a lieutenant colonel to an important meeting in Hiroshima to go over Japan's communications plans in preparation for the imminent Allied invasion.

In Hiroshima, Dr. Iwa Yasuza prepared for surgery at the Shima Surgical Hospital. The doctor planned to complete his half day of surgery before departing for his wife's surprise birthday party, to be hosted by his three daughters. He stood scrubbing his hands when he heard the air-raid siren. When one of his nurses came running up to him, he told her, "Relax. The Americans have never bombed Hiroshima, and it won't happen today."

What Dr. Yasuza didn't know was that Hiroshima and five other targets for the atomic bomb had been intentionally spared from American bombings so a comprehensive damage assessment could be made of the effects of the nuclear explosion.

On board the *Enola Gay*, the radar operator, Lieutenant Jacob Beser, monitored Japanese fighter and ground-defense frequencies. Two hundred miles out from their target, Beser caught a Japanese radar sweep and then another that locked onto his aircraft.

"The enemy knows we're here, Colonel," Beser reported over interphone.

"All right, crew, heads up and keep a lookout for enemy fighters," Tibbets ordered.

Lieutenant Jeppson, sitting in the cockpit jump seat, tapped Colonel Tibbets on the shoulder and motioned with his head that he was going back to arm the bomb. Jeppson entered the bomb bay carrying the red electrical fuses. He pulled off his heavy gloves to unscrew the green fuses, and within seconds the minus-twenty-degree-Celsius temperature began numbing his fingers, making it difficult to feel if the red fuses he inserted were securely in place. To warm his fingers, he put his gloves back on. It took donning and removing his gloves several times before he determined that all four fuses were properly secured.

When Jeppson returned to the cockpit and nodded to the aircraft commander, Tibbets toggled his interphone and said, "Folks, we are now carrying the world's first fully armed atomic weapon."

If any of the crewmen were awestruck, they didn't acknowledge it or say anything. Most concerned themselves with doing their jobs and not making mistakes. Their lives depended on it.

At 0710 hours, the weather-reconnaissance aircraft, *Strait Flush*, reached Hiroshima and found a large opening in the overcast sky. When they reached Nagasaki, cloud conditions were similar. The *Strait Flush* transmitted a coded message: "CLOUD COVER 3/10. RECOMMEND PRIMARY TARGET." With history only an hour away, the navigator of the *Enola Gay* gave a course correction to the bombing initial point (IP), where they would start their bombing run on Hiroshima.

At 0730 hours, Captain Kumao touched down in his two-seat trainer at the airport three miles southeast of downtown Hiroshima. He taxied and stopped the aircraft in front of the flight-operations building. After his passenger was picked up by a staff car, Captain Kumao went into the base operations and walked into the small restaurant attached to the building. He ordered a breakfast of rice, stewed vegetables, and soup.

Exactly on time, the *Enola Gay* reached the IP at 0812 hours, at an altitude of thirty-one thousand, on a heading of 264 degrees.

"IP," Captain Van Kirk called out on his UHF radio.

Flying a mile in trail, the *Great Artiste's* bombardier heard the IP call, opened the bomb-bay doors, and released a five-foot-long canister on a parachute. It contained blast and radiation detection devices. The *Great Artiste* then executed a 155-degree descending turn to the right. The Number 91 aircraft made a 90-degree turn and got in position to take photographs and motion pictures of the detonation.

The bombardier of the *Enola Gay*, Major Thomas Ferebee, sat at his Norden bombsight. His eyes moved back and forth from the bombsight to the photographs of the aiming point, the T-shaped Aioi Bridge on the Ota River. As Ferebee made his final adjustment to the aircraft's course, he turned on the bombing tone signal; it was a low-pitched buzz sent through the interphone and UHF radio systems to signal fifteen seconds prior to the bomb dropping. Everyone in the three aircraft put on their welding goggles.

At 0815 hours and 17 seconds, the *Enola Gay*'s bomb doors opened, and the atomic bomb was released to begin the six-mile drop toward the city of Hiroshima.

"Bomb away," Ferebee called over UHF.

Over ten thousand pounds lighter, the *Enola Gay* pitched upward more than a hundred feet; Colonel Tibbets then executed a hard diving right turn to a heading of zero-six-zero degrees.

After rolling out on heading and leveling off at twenty-nine thousand feet, Tibbets and his copilot donned their welding goggles.

When the 28-inch-diameter and 128-inch-long Mk-1 atomic combat weapon, code name Little Boy, fell from the aircraft, electrical connectors pulled loose from the bomb, activating the fusing system. Fifteen seconds later, the radar altimeter activated, and a barometric-pressure gauge began measuring altitude. At 1,900 feet, the firing switches closed and ignited four bags of slotted-tube cordite, sending a uranium projectile into 140 pounds of U-235, seven feet away. The impact resulted in a nuclear chain reaction, and the atomic bomb detonated directly above the Shima Surgical Hospital.

In the first millisecond after detonation, a fireball hundreds of feet wide erupted; the temperature at the core of the explosion reached fifty million degrees centigrade. Fifty thousand people and the buildings they occupied were instantly incinerated, and sixty thousand of the one hundred thousand buildings in Hiroshima were destroyed. Thirty thousand people received serious injuries when the heat of the explosion fused clothing to their skin, imprinting the pattern of the clothing on their bodies after it burned away.

At twenty-nine thousand feet, the inside of the *Enola Gay* was bathed in a bright blue light created a few milliseconds after the explosion. From his tail-gunner position, Sergeant Bob Carson became engrossed by the fireball, which was moving at thirty yards per second from the epicenter, consuming everything within a two-mile radius. A mile-wide column of superheated gas formed a mushroom cloud over the city. Ten minutes after the detonation, the massive cloud reached over thirty thousand feet. Far below, fires were spreading throughout the city.

Milliseconds after the detonation, a shock wave traveling at the speed of sound moved toward the *Enola Gay*. When the wave hit the aircraft, it tossed it several hundred feet upward and then down, jolting it left and right. It was like being in the middle of the up- and downdrafts in a thunderstorm.

After a second shock wave hit the aircraft, the radio operator transmitted a coded message given to him by Colonel Tibbets: "MISSION A SUCCESS STOP AIRCRAFT AND CREW OK STOP RETURNING TO BASE ETA 1500 END."

At the Hiroshima airfield, the stunned captain Kumao came running out of the partly demolished operations building. He sprinted toward his aircraft, only to find it bent and twisted like a child's toy. Despite the damage, he managed to start the aircraft and began taxiing it to the active runway.

In his peripheral vision, Captain Kumao saw movement. When he looked left, he saw a group of survivors moving onto the airfield. They looked like raw, burned meat, their clothing burned off and their bodies blackened by the effects of flash burns caused by the radiant heat from the initial explosion.

Despite the condition of his aircraft, Captain Kumao somehow managed to get airborne. He leveled off at 1,500 feet and flew around the southern side of the city. What he saw was the utter destruction of Hiroshima. *We have lost the war,* Kumao thought.

CHAPTER 61

Calcutta, India

Asami Nakada spent the next four days in seclusion, letting her arm heal and trying to rid herself of the depression that had set upon her. When she ventured out, she wore a long-sleeve blouse to cover the healing wound. She also left a message at one of her dead drops. The following day, an undercover contact left her a message and a key. Her clothing and firearms were at a house the contact rented and stocked with food in an upper-class residential area west of the Hugely River. After she moved into the house, she spent most of her time planning how she would kill the last two female operatives, the ones responsible for her sisters' deaths. But first, she would do some reconnaissance.

After midnight, Asami went back to the abandoned warehouse close to where she planted the bomb. She entered the woods to the south and moved in the direction of the dry creek. When the dry creek ended at the channel, she slipped into the water and swam toward the dock.

The boat was missing. She cursed herself for not asking her consular contact to do the legwork for her. After she made it back to the warehouse, she changed into dry clothes and went back to her house.

The next day she left a message at a different dead drop and went to a nearby restaurant to eat. She was having trouble getting her mind focused on her mission. It would wander aimlessly. Today, her thoughts took her back to when she was a child playing with her three sisters in a park two blocks from their home. Her mother was sitting on blanket, calling them to come to lunch. The picnics with her mother were some of the best times of her childhood. Her father, gone most of the time, was a career navy man, "on the fast track to flag rank," she heard her mother say to a neighbor.

When she did see her father, she had a wonderful time. In the summer, he would take the girls kite flying or to the zoo or boating. In the winter, they would ice-skate, and occasionally they would drive into the mountains and go cross-country skiing. It was one of her father's favorite sports. He had been raised in the village of Joetsu, near the coast, northwest of Tokyo. He was a tremendous athlete in his teens and a member of Japan's Nordic ski team that participated at the FIS Nordic World Ski Championships in 1925 at Johannisbad, Czechoslovakia. He didn't win any medals, but he placed sixth in the Nordic combined competition. When the team returned to Japan, he was a national hero. That same year he graduated from the Imperial Japanese Naval Academy.

Asami tried to remove these thoughts from her mind but found it nearly impossible. So for the next three days, she meditated, breaking only to eat and sleep. At the end of three days, she felt refreshed and could finally focus on her mission. She would need several days to plan her next assault on the female agents.

Her consular contact left a note at a drop informing her where the *Jacqueline* could be found. In the afternoon she changed buses several times and got off at the Government House on Clive Street. She walked south for a quarter of a mile before turning west on Strand Street to the northern boundary of Fort William, called Eden Park. Strand Street ran the width of the park before curving ninety degrees at the river and continuing north, parallel to the Hooghly River.

Asami made three separate trips on buses up and down Chowringhee Road to view Fort William. Built in 1701 and named after King William III, the fort was two miles in length, north to south, and a mile in its east-to-west width at its widest point. It was built in the shape of an irregular octagon and enclosed two hundred acres of downtown Calcutta. The eastern bank of the Hooghly River made up its western boundary.

The fort was a garrison for ten thousand British troops and their families, and it now also held close to twelve thousand refugees from across the British Empire's Asian colonies. Asami decided to pay the fort a visit. She felt that she could hide among the vast number of refugees and not be noticed. She climbed over a ten-foot earthen embankment that bordered Clive Street and walked across the soccer field currently occupied by five thousand refugees. She moved to within two hundred feet of the yacht basin, as close as she dared to go. Then, as abruptly as she slipped into the fort, she left and walked to the end of Clive Street. There she left the sidewalk and walked down the steep slope to the river.

From the edge of the shore, she saw the *Jacqueline* one hundred yards to the south, its aft deck facing north. It would be easy to approach the yacht from the soccer field. The park was mostly an open grass area with large cypress trees surrounding the soccer field. She could easily pitch a small tent and wait for the women to leave the boat or walk out on deck before taking them out with a rifle. However, this strategy would put her in danger, especially if one of the refugees or roving guards noticed her with a rifle, and even if she dared a shot and killed one or both women, she would still need to escape. She decided the risk in the park was too great. She was not on a suicide mission.

Asami was about to leave when she noticed a four-foot concrete culvert hidden behind some thick shrubs, twenty yards outside the boundary of Fort William. When she pushed aside the shrubs and squatted next to the culvert, she decided it was an ideal location for what she was planning.

CHAPTER 62

Calcutta, India

Captain Dubois eased the 126-foot *Jacqueline* into the outside berth of the ten-slotted boat basin at Fort William. Despite the yacht basin's secure location on the northwestern edge of the Fort William army base, Dubois felt ill at ease with the refugees only fifty yards away. To reduce his fear, he maintained the Gurkha guard presence for protection. Prior to moving the yacht, he had called on the commander of Fort William and asked for an increase in guards at the soccer field and Eden Park. The commanding general turned him down, because his resources were already strained to the limit with the refugee presence.

The Fort William yacht basin was not the most ideal place to berth the 126-foot yacht, because it was built to hold only a total of ten power and sailing yachts up to forty feet in length. However, the outside deck on the end of the dock stretched ninety feet along the river and held ten docking cleats, enough to secure the *Jacqueline*'s four mooring lines. Dubois maneuvered the yacht into position, facing the bow downriver. After the crew deployed the yacht's dock fenders, the heavy-duty cushions that hung over the side of the *Jacqueline* and absorbed the contact force between the boat and the dock, Captain Dubois shut down the engines.

As Captain Dubois scanned the boats in their berths, he doubted the average army officer at Fort William could afford a twelve-foot sailboat, much less a forty-footer. He decided that the boats in the berths belonged to officers that came from wealthy families or to members of the royal family.

Jon didn't seem to mind the presence of the five-thousand-plus refugees so close to the yacht. He told the captain not to worry because the refugees were loyal British subjects and would sound an alarm if they noticed an Asian carrying a rifle, or anyone else for that matter. Plus, the fort's commander placed at least twenty British guards in and around the park day and night, not to mention the ten Gurkha guards on board and surrounding the *Jacqueline*.

That afternoon, Jon and his team began focusing on where the assassin might strike next. Now that the armored car was out of commission, Jon worried about the women being driven from the yacht to Alipore and back. He left the SOE detachment during lunch and drove to the American consulate offices. He asked permission to borrow the remaining armored consular car. The old 1905 Packard did not have a steel-reinforced floorboard, but it did contain bulletproof glass and steel-reinforced doors, top, and front and rear panels. Jon decided he could live without the reinforced floorboard and accepted the risk. The chances of another bomb attack, he thought, were slim. Colonel MacKenzie wasn't so sure and, deciding the Packard alone wasn't enough protection, ordered two additional escort vehicles. When someone needed to go somewhere, one escort car would proceed ahead of the Packard while one followed behind. In each vehicle there were two armed British marines and a driver.

Jon also scouted the area around the park and yacht basin, trying to determine where he would strike from. He ruled out a sniper shooting from the opposite side of the river after visiting the far banks. The wind along the river was too variable this time of year. After a week of searching around Fort William, he worried even more about the women's safety, but he was determined to continue his search for the perfect spot a sniper would use.

A night later, Jon and Camille were driving south on Government Place East, returning to Fort William from a dinner date. At the end of the block, Jon turned right onto Lawrence Road, drove two hundred feet, and crossed Government Place West onto Auckland Road, passing between the Legislative Council Chambers and the Calcutta Cricket Grounds at Eden Gardens. He drove another three hundred feet before turning south on Strand Road, which would take them to Fort William.

As they drove past the George Memorial and turned left on Kingsway, Jon caught a glimpse of a person darting behind a group of small rhododendron trees that grew adjacent to the Hooghly River. He continued another fifty feet, turned right, and drove through the Calcutta Gate of Fort William, parking at the yacht basin. Jon paused before getting out of the vehicle.

"Something wrong?" Camille asked.

Not wanting to alarm her, Jon said, "No, just thinking."

He then turned in his seat, touched his hand to her face, and gently kissed her.

"I like your line of thinking," Camille said. "Come on, handsome, let's go to bed."

As they walked onto the Jacqueline, Jon felt a familiar tingling on the back of his neck. He would have to check into what he had seen, but not tonight.

After driving the ladies to the SOE detachment the next morning, Jon took the car back to the yacht basin. He then set out on foot, walking along the river toward the George Memorial, a hundred yards away.

As he approached the group of rhododendron trees he had driven by the night before, he had to climb the riverbank to avoid a thicket of thorny shrubs. Skirting the shrubs, he noticed a large but well-hidden concrete drainage pipe that emptied groundwater runoff into the Hooghly River. He climbed back down the riverbank, eased through the thorny shrubs, and discovered a small shoe print in the sand near the pipe. Curious, he knelt next to the pipe, and then stood up and looked south over the top of the pipe. After a few seconds, he dropped back down and looked into the opening of the large pipe.

It was too dark to see very far, but it was just large enough for him to walk into while bent over. After ten minutes inside the pipe, Jon exited and made his way back to the *Jacqueline*, where he changed clothes before heading to the SOE detachment.

Asami watched as the old Packard and army escort vehicles entered and exited Fort William. She had already decided against another bomb because it would needlessly expose her and take too much time to position.

She needed stealth. Asami left and placed a note at a dead drop for her consular contact. She hoped the consular office would have what she needed. Two days went by before she found a message left for her at the house. Later that evening, Asami made her way back to the end of Clive Street and the drainage pipe. Inside the pipe she found a waterproof black canvas bag with a sniper rifle, scope, and ten rounds of ammunition. She spent the next hour inspecting and cleaning the weapon.

The Arisaka Type 97 sniper rifle fired a 6.5-millimeter reduced-charge cartridge, which improved its accuracy, limited the sound, and camouflaged the muzzle flash. The rifle was a manually operated bolt-action rifle. The rifle's magazine held five rounds, more than enough for her purpose. The barrel length of the Type 97 was thirty-one inches with an overall length of fifty inches; it weighed close to nine pounds.

Asami had trained for several hundred hours firing the Type 97 rifle at the Rikugun Nakano Gakko School in Tokyo and had spent another thousand hours teaching students how to take it apart, clean it, and fire it, at the advanced training facility in Hiroshima. She was the best marksman at the school and could hit a four-inch target twenty-five out of twenty-five shots, from three hundred meters away.

At Fort William, the soccer field's lights were left on until 2100 hours each night. At the request of the *Jacqueline*'s captain, the commanding general allowed one-third of the lights to remain on all night. Due to the large number of refugees, Captain Dubois had increased the size of the Gurkha force from ten to fifteen, but despite the larger force, he still felt something was wrong. In an attempt to ease his mind, he ordered all the exterior lights on the boat extinguished, but for some reason Dubois still felt uneasy—until he realized the *Jacqueline* was also vulnerable from the water and posted three of the ten Gurkha guards, whom he had gotten from Colonel MacKenzie, to watch only the river.

Asami waited in the brush behind the drainage pipe. When she noticed someone walking out onto the fantail deck, she raised the rifle to her shoulder and set the long wooden fore-end of the rifle on the top of concrete pipe. With one-third of the soccer-field lights on, she had ample light to use the rifle's 2.5-power telescopic sight. When she looked through the scope, she saw two figures on the fantail, but they had their backs to her. When they turned toward her, she brought the scope into focus. One was an armed guard with a Thompson submachine gun, and the other was probably the boat's captain, because he wore the same type of billed hat her father used to wear and what looked to be a white navy uniform. She brought the rifle back down and waited until 0100 hours before she packed the rifle in its watertight bag, put it inside the pipe, and left.

She went back two more nights but failed to find her targets. She went back again on Saturday night in hopes of finding the crew having dinner on the fantail. The weather was cooperating, but her targets weren't. She panned her scope several times across the windows and caught a glimpse of a group of people sitting in the dining room just off the aft deck, but the windows were too high to identify anyone or to get a good shot.

Asami decided to go back on Sunday night. Just when she was about to give up hope, she noticed two people walk onto the fantail. Asami slowly brought the rifle into position and looked through the scope. After she brought the scope into focus, she gasped and froze. It was the face of one of the male Allied agents who was supposed to be dead—the one who had killed one of her sisters. She pulled the rifle back toward her and ducked behind the pipe. As she closed her eyes, her mind began to seethe with anger, and her hands began to tremble. If she took the shot now, she knew she would more than likely miss her target. *Meditate*, she thought.

It took close to ten minutes for Asami to focus her mind and slow her heart rate down, but when she did, she was more composed than she had been in her entire life. She stood back up and looked through the scope again. The agent was embracing the woman with him and kissing her. *Maybe this is his girlfriend—or, better yet, his wife*, Asami thought.

She turned and squatted down behind the pipe, thinking about what she should do. As she slowed her breathing and calmed her mind even more, the Sun Tzu saying came back to her again: "So in war, the way is to avoid what is strong, and strike at what is weak."

Whoever this woman was, she was obviously someone that the agent cared for. When Asami stood back up and looked through the scope, she was able to see the woman's face; it was one of the two remaining female agents she was looking for. Now she knew what she would do. She steadied her body, braced the rifle on top of the pipe, took a deep breath and let it out slowly, took careful aim, and squeezed the trigger.

Author's Notes

appreciate your purchase of this World War Two thriller. I would also be grateful if you would take the time to post a review of my book on Amazon.com. It's the best way to provide me with feedback.

Steve Doherty

Author Biography

Steve Doherty is a retired United States Air Force officer and business owner. He grew up in the small community of Muldoon, Texas. He obtained an undergraduate degree from Texas State University, a master's degree from Chapman University and completed post-graduate work at The Ohio State University. While in the Air Force Steve flew the KC-135A, T-29C and T-43A aircraft. He currently lives in New Albany, Ohio.

Other Books by Steve Doherty

"Steve Doherty's Operation King Cobra is a World War II thriller in the vein of Where Eagles Dare and The Guns of Navarone. Action, history, espionage, romance—it's all there. Recommended." — Robert Gandt, Author

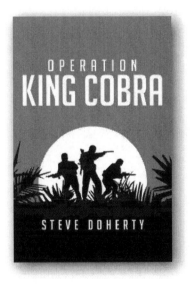

Available at:
http://www.steve-doherty-books.com
http://www.amazon.com
http://www.barnesandnoble.com/
https://www.tatepublishing.com/

Made in the USA
Charleston, SC
28 October 2015